Praise for *La Vie en Bleu* . . .

Other Books by Jody Klaire . . .

The Above and Beyond Series

Book 1: *The Empath*
Book 2: *Blind Trust*
Book 3: *The Empath*
Book 4: *Hindsight*

La Vie en Bleu

Jody KLAIRE

La Vie en Bleu

BInk

Bedazzled Ink Publishing • Fairfield, California

978-1-939562-98-2 paperback
978-1-939562-99-9 ebook

Cover Design
by

DESIGNS

Bink Books
a division of
Bedazzled Ink Publishing, LLC
Fairfield, California
http://www.bedazzledink.com

For,
Em—because it's fun to make you smile.
And,
For everyone who believes in love.

Acknowledgments

La Vie en Bleu has given me the chance to show my love for a country very close to my heart. I wanted to fill it full of light, laughter, and love. Behind every book there's a network of people that have helped me, inspired me, and cheered me on throughout the journey.

First of all I would like to thank you, the reader. Whether you have followed my writing so far or are joining me for the first time. Welcome aboard. I hope that you love your time with Pippa and her friends.

To those on social media who have supported me and continue to do so, thank you. It's wonderful to know there are so many lovely people out there. A big thanks goes to Georgia Beers and Gerri Hill for the welcome and guidance. Thank you ladies!

To my fellow Cloudies and Bedazzled Ink family, you inspire me, drive me to improve, and cheer me. It's a pleasure to write alongside you. Special thanks to John Taylor and Katherine Hetzel, your friendship and camaraderie make a big difference, so thank you. Ann McMan, thank you once again for a wonderful cover and the patience and hard work you put in to each creation. Once again, it's sublime.

To the GCLS Writing Academy, you worked incredibly hard and it was heart warming to know how much passion and drive you put in to deliver the course. I learned a lot, laughed a lot, and Saturdays were great fun.

My fellow students. You're all inspiring and every one deserved their graduation certificate. I look forward to seeing your stories take flight.

Liz McMullen. You are as cool as pie. Hard work, patience, hospitality, and a pleasure to know. Thank you for your support.

Sandra Moran, you know I think you rock. You helped me to bring France to life and your time, energy, and friendship mean a great deal. Thank you.

MC Henrichon and Pauline Reibell: Alors, Je vous remercie

de votre patience avec ma tentative du français. Merci de partager votre langue qui m'inspire. Que ce soit en France ou au Canada, votre accueil signifie beaucoup pour moi. J'espère avoir montré mon amour pour la France et que cela vous fait sourire et rire. Merci!

To Casey and Claudia at Bedazzled Ink. Thank you for having the faith to let me try romance. Thank you for the patience and gentle guidance to help me make it a book that makes me smile. It's always a pleasure working with you, a joy to learn from you and what is romance without dangling participles? Thank you both very much.

To all at the CNB parish, those friends close, whether neighbour or far away, you bring light, love, laughter, and I feel honoured just to be counted one of you. Thank you especially to Moira Spence, Jayne Shaw, Mike Komor, and Sue Beverley (and Mr B) for guidance, for sharing, for making such a difference in my journey. Thank you.

To my betas: Sarah Green, Mel and Glenda, Moira and Ian and the Team Truth girls: Karen Kormelink, Gena Ratcliff, and Dani Dixon. Thank you for working with me, for your love, support, and all the time you put in. Overworked but loved dearly! Thank you, my friends.

To Debi Alper for your continued support and red pen when I need it. I love learning from you, so thank you for sharing your knowledge and time.

Brie Burkeman, when I thought of a city to place Pippa in, your words and guidance drew me to London. When I write, I count on the wisdom you shared. You make me strive to grow, to believe, and to work hard. Your patience helped me lay many solid foundations and I hope that this book gives you a lot of laughter. Thank you very much.

To my family both near and in the next room. There is nothing like being amongst good company and being reminded that the best family trees are full of nuts.

Uncle Terry—thank you for sharing your love of language, I hope you chuckle along at my humour.

Mum, for your help with grammar . . . well actually, your help with pretty much everything. Writing this book reminds me how blessed I am to have a mum like you.

Little Fergus and friends. Okay, so you can't read but you play a starring role in my heart and my day. Thank you.

To Em. What do I say? Other than the fact that you would rock a cherry red helmet and sunblock? The most ardent, most dedicated, and most patient of my supporters. Knowing how much you love this book makes it all the more worthwhile. Home isn't home without you.

To THS, a lamp for my feet and a light for my path. You are in all things. You are love, you are light. Thank you for Pippa's story and for blessing me with your love.

Jody Klaire
August 2015

*"My command is this: love each other as
I have loved you."*
—John 15:12 [NIV]

"To love oneself is the beginning of a lifelong romance."
—Oscar Wilde, *An Ideal Husband*

Chapter One

THE HOT SUMMER air caressed my skin, leaving beads of sweat to trickle down between my shoulder blades. Other people would complain at such an onslaught but just to stand in the fierce heat reminded me of her. If only for a fleeting moment, a secret, unthinking moment, I could close my eyes and feel the touch of her. Warm fingertips, light, teasing, trailing their way up my bare back, her soft laughter in my ear. The sound that had seeped into every breath I had taken since. She was the thudding of my heart, the wriggle in my stomach, the hammering of the pulse in my ear.

Her soft, knowing lips brushed across my exposed neck. I leaned to the side, baring all to her, even if she only existed in my memory now. Sweet, nipping kisses, the feel of her arms as they slid around my waist. Her mouth moving over my neck, my chin, my cheek, searching, demanding—

"Pippa?"

I snapped my eyes open and rubbed my tingling skin, wanting to scratch the very sordid thought from me. "Yes, sweetheart?" Blowing the guilt, the moment away, I turned to Doug and smiled. Why did it still make me so sick to the stomach?

"You didn't answer my question," he said, concern, trust, and love in his eyes. What had I done to deserve him? "Do you want to help me set up the new centre?"

My conscience screamed no. No, I didn't want to go anywhere near that country. It was easier to forget this far away, easier to believe it was only a dream.

"Of course." I smiled to cover my desperation. "I know how important it is to you."

"I was thinking that you could show me 'round." His smile was so different from mine, so encouraging, sweet. "You never really talked about your time there."

"There isn't much to talk about."

He gave me an ever patient look and took a deep breath. "You

were there for a year . . . You lived in the city as a Frenchie . . .
Aren't you aching to get back?"

Aching yes, but to return, to risk seeing her, no. What if she
still lived there? My heart thudded. It was a nightmare. What if
she remembered? What if she didn't? How was I going to get
out of this? When Doug got something in his mind . . . This was
impossible.

"I'll check with Rebecca, okay, check if I can get the time off?"
I said.

Not a chance if Rebecca knew what was good for her.

"Promise?" He gazed at me with those gentle blue-grey eyes,
so much like a puppy dog.

"Course." More lies, more guilt. So long ago and yet that
madness still haunted my life.

Doug planted a gentle kiss on my still-tingling lips. My
stomach tightened up until I felt sick with guilt. I watched his
retreating back. What would he think of me if he knew, if he knew
just what a coward I really was?

I stared out at the weak spring sunshine in a quiet corner of the
world. A small Yorkshire hamlet. Miles upon miles of green, cut
into fields by armies of wide-crowned trees. Hedges that buzzed
with the scents and sounds of spring. Quaint cottages dotted along
winding lanes. His house, a converted Tudor mansion, gated off
from the sleepy village beyond. His family home. It would be our
family home one day, at least when I . . . we . . . found the time to
put down roots.

I picked up my keys from the sideboard and wheeled my
suitcase to the car. In a few traffic-riddled hours, I would be back
in a place I knew. London, the city of rain, grey, and congestion
charges. The best place to block out the noise. The only place I
seemed to have half a chance of forgetting her in.

THE M25 HAD thrown its worst at me. The entire motorway
had been backed up. It was nearly the end of the working day
when I squeezed into the last space in the cramped NCP car park. I
sprinted through the deluge, risking life and limb dashing in front
of a bus, and ducked into the three-storey office.

"Hi, Pip!" the squeaky-voiced receptionist chimed at me as
I shook off the rain from my jacket. I never understood how

Yorkshire could be sunny and London in the middle of a monsoon. Whatever happened to the grim North?

"Hey, you seen the boss?" I mumbled, attempting a smile.

"Lucky for you, she's been on a course all day." The receptionist, whose name I could never remember, tapped her nose. "As long as the cat's away . . ."

"You're a Godsend."

I couldn't afford the time off and there was no way I could afford it unpaid. Making a note to send the receptionist—Mary, no, Janet . . . no . . . well, whatever her name was—some chocolates or flowers, I hurried into the lift. Only three floors but it would have been quicker to scale the outside with my tights like Spiderman.

I stared up at the numbers which seemed to slow down. I hated confined spaces. Why did they make lifts look like something from a tin factory? At least this one didn't have a mirror. Those were just weird. Who wanted to gawp at their own reflection while dangling from a cheese string? Come on, come on. If it didn't hurry up I'd start thinking about the film *Speed* again. No, not good. Hurry up, hurry the—

The doors dinged open and I toddled down the corridor. Plush was one way of putting the decor. Lots of glass, strange blobs in primary colours that I assumed was art, and closed-off wooden boxes for meeting rooms. No one was around. Thankfully most of them were already on their way home. I wobbled as I turned the corner to an open plan space. Great. One of my shoes had decided to rub a hole in my heel. Doug had offered for me to have tailor-made swish things but I was not going to become some rich, doormat woman who needed her husband for everything. Oh no, if I was marrying Doug, I was staying me.

"I hate to tell you this but unless they work on California time up in Yorkshire, you're way late." Rebecca, my best friend, stood outside my sugar-lump-of-a-cubicle with her arms folded.

"What did you do to your hair?"

Rebecca grinned. "You like?" She turned around on the spot for me.

"You look like a hedgehog had a nasty accident with bleach." I shook my head. I had never understood Rebecca's fashion sense, even in college. I doubted I ever would. "Why did they shave only one side?" I decided, and not for the first time, never to use the same hairdresser.

"It's cool, fuddy duddy." She pointed to her feet. "And you didn't see the shoes."

"How could I with the beacon on your head?" Sighing, I looked down. Some sort of loafer shoe, a crocodile skin pattern on them. Hideous beyond words. "Nice, my dad has a pair, I think." At least he had in the seventies.

"Who chewed your cheese?"

Ignoring the man's shirt, man's trousers, and her penchant for silver *everywhere*, I attempted my best smile. It was good to see her. "No one. Traffic. The M25 is backed up—"

"If you think that will buy you a pardon . . ." Rebecca smiled. "It will. The boss has been out, you're in the clear. I stuck a meeting in your planner."

I dumped my sodden jacket on the back of the chair, then winced as it creaked. Someone had stolen mine again. "How is everything?"

"You mean how was my hot date on the weekend or how do I feel about the un-British sunshine we've been enjoying?"

There were times when I wondered where my social skills had disappeared to. I was terrified of getting lost in Doug and Pippa but he had to take priority, didn't he? Sighing, I wondered where had Pippa, the friend, disappeared to? Try again.

"Yes," I said, turning to look at her. "How was your weekend?"

Rebecca raised her unruly eyebrows at me. "You serious?" She took a chair and wheeled it over.

"Why not. Did this one steal your heart?"

Rebecca laughed. She had an annoyingly cocky laugh that had always driven me insane. "No, but she was hot. I mean, you should have seen her legs." She whistled like a heckling builder. "And let me tell you—"

I held up my hand. Wonderful, I'd chipped my nail polish. "Why do you do that?"

Rebecca frowned. "Do what?"

"Act like you're an ass." I didn't get her, I never would. "Why don't you ever stay around?"

We'd had this conversation so many times that she almost mimed my question. "Some women don't want forever, roses and all that crap."

The soft laughter in my ear, teasing fingers tickling over my rib cage—

"Pip?"

"What?" The panic caught in my throat. Had I been thinking about . . . I couldn't . . . I was tired, just tired.

"Where did you go?" Rebecca wiggled her eyebrows. "And you got a place for me in there?"

"I was thinking about Doug," I lied. "So no."

Rebecca narrowed her eyes, and I could tell that she didn't buy my excuses but after all these years, I hoped she'd given up trying. I knew she knew I was hiding something. It was better I headed her off before she started probing. "He wants me at his new centre opening next month."

"The one in France?" Rebecca leaned back, with a bored expression as her gaze drifted over to the new mail courier. "Why?"

"To support him." I tapped her hand as a sly smile drifted across her lips. Letch. "I've never been to one before. I guess I owe it to him."

"You owe him shit." Rebecca crossed her leg over her knee, her sleeve of tattoos showing.

I did not want to get into this argument again. "Either way, I said yes but . . ." I sighed. "I really don't want to go back to France."

"You said yes but you don't want to go?" Rebecca laughed that cocky laugh again. "Now that isn't in the little wife of the year book, is it?"

"When did the hot date tell you she was married . . . to a man?"

Rebecca opened and closed her mouth. "I hate that you know me so well."

"That makes two of us." Why did we put up with each other and what were those socks. Neon yellow socks. "So, I need you to find a reason for me not to go."

"Wow, where is he opening it, a prison?"

I didn't care, but I did, far too much. Anywhere in France was too near, too risky. How much did I say? It wasn't like Rebecca just couldn't ask Doug herself.

"Marseille." I tried to keep my voice level, my tone neutral but my heart burst into a sprint in response. Even thinking about it made my hands shake.

"Where you lived in college?" She narrowed her eyes, leaning in. "But they don't even have one in Paris yet, right?"

There was no need for me to even shake my head, she seemed to read my eyes.

"Oh, that's just wonderful." She wheezed out her breath, rapping her ring heavy knuckles on the desk. "Can't he leave one part of you without his stamp on it?"

The anger in her voice surprised me. "What do you mean?" She'd always liked Doug, he'd always liked her. Where had this come from?

"Pip, I love the guy but . . . at this rate there will be nothing of *you* left."

"There's plenty of me. I'm successful in work . . ." I motioned to the office. We both looked at my cramped cubicle, the computer which looked older than me, and the mountain of admin in my inbox. Hmmm, not quite the winning argument I was going for. "I have you . . ."

"Smooth talker."

Thankfully, she seemed appeased. Rebecca went back to shooting bedroom eyes at the flirty vixen of a courier. She wasn't even attractive.

"I think you should tell him not to open it there." Her eyes met mine for a moment. "We both know something happened there that changed you."

"Nothing happened there." Oh, but it did. Too much. Everything happened there. No, no, it didn't. It was just stupid, foolish . . . those lips—

"See." Rebecca folded her arms. "You never did that before you went there."

"How would you know?" I scowled at the courier. What did she want, a photograph? "You were too busy trying to seduce every woman you could find."

A dreamy smile crossed her face. "Yeah, those were good days."

"Not for the poor soul who slept in the bedroom next to you."

"Hey." She held her hands up. "I put up with you and, 'so good' Doug." She made huffy-breathing noises in imitation and I couldn't suppress the snorted laughter.

"I hate that you heard that."

"Whatever." She wagged her finger. "Serious, Pip, you need to veto the centre." She leaned on the desk, but not before flashing a flirty wink at the courier. "What did happen, you never said."

"Nothing." I switched on my computer which groaned and wheezed into life. The thing sounded like my grandfather who smoked forty a day. "You heard anything about the job yet?"

"No." Rebecca shook her head and polished her disgusting crocodile shoes. Where did she shop? "Why are you avoiding the question?"

The monitor flickered on like it had a raging hangover. Even the computer had more of a life than me. "I thought you would know if you got the promotion by now. Didn't she say you were guaranteed it?"

"Yes and no." Rebecca folded her arms. Were there more tattoos? How much ink did she want to be covered in? "Why won't you tell me?"

Looking through the stack of papers that all said "urgent" on top, I tried to mentally calculate how late I was going to be stuck at my desk. "Did you sign off those invoices I got to you on Friday?"

Rebecca waved a hand. "Of course I did." She rapped her knuckles on the desk again. I swore my computer winced, its screen flickering. "You are not getting away with avoidance."

"Only if you tell me what happened between you and Miss Evans."

"Bitch."

"Me or her?"

"Both of you." Rebecca got to her feet. "I hate how well you know me."

"So you keep telling me."

She pecked me on the cheek and swaggered off towards her office. She even walked like a cocky idiot. "Get working. I guess it's me sticking dinner on?"

Dinner, oh I was so hungry. "I forgot lunch."

"Bottom drawer."

I opened the drawer, pulled out a plastic tub, and yanked it open. Tuna and mayonnaise sandwiches never looked so good. "I love you!"

Rebecca winked at me before shutting herself in her office. We'd joined the company together when they were recruiting in our final year of technical college. They'd offered two doe-eyed idiots a mediocre wage and a chance to live in the city of London. Naturally, we had both signed up on the spot. A decade later, I was no closer to my dream of being a master carpenter and Rebecca was about as close to her dream of being an architect. In short, we were wonderful underachievers.

The only thing that seemed to redeem me was Doug. I'd met him when our brilliantly drab firm held a gala for the white-pearled smiles of the rich and elite. Doug had made a beeline for me which I still believe was down to my red cocktail gown. It had a halter neck to make anyone drool. Generally Rebecca, but then she drooled over anything in a dress.

Doug was a master at fairy tale romance. He was great and lovely. Still, even though I'd promised to be his wife, I was ever so slightly reluctant to leave my pokey flat and live in a palace with him. Most women would have thrown themselves into it with gusto. He was the ultimate gentleman. Dirty blonde hair and blue eyes, chiselled chin and broad shoulders. He looked good in everything, whether it was a tailor-made suit or a scruffy pair of jeans. In short, he was prince charming. I just liked him better when I wasn't living with him.

Besides, I loved girls' night with Rebecca. I loved vegging out in front of endless DVD box sets in my pyjamas. If I moved out, Rebecca would never make the extortionate rent. This was always my case for holding off nuptials when Doug probed. Probably best he didn't know that my father actually owned the building and we paid next to nothing. I loved Doug to pieces . . . I just loved space too. There was nothing wrong with that, nothing at all.

"Pip?"

I opened my eyes and looked at the caretaker. Someone had switched off the lights. "Why is it dark?"

"It's gone ten," he said. "I got to kick you out."

Looking down at my watch, I sighed. The urgent invoices were all still neatly labelled in my inbox and my computer was still on the log-in screen. Ah.

"Right . . . sorry . . ." I turned my computer off and stumbled to my feet, sending the chair clattering as I yanked my coat from it. "Home."

"You work too hard, Pip," the caretaker said. "They don't appreciate you."

I smiled at him and wandered down the corridor to the lift. Had Rebecca seen me sleeping? Had I been dribbling? I took out my phone to text Rebecca and smiled as I realised the date.

I'd met her on a rainy night just like this, although the summer was in full swing in France, the heat sizzling off the sun-baked streets—

Ding.

"Crap." I dashed between the closing doors of the lift and out into the deluge.

Where had I parked the car? After texting a quick message to Rebecca beneath my jacket, I dashed across to the car park and spotted my little banged-up baby at the back. Doug had offered to buy me a brand new shiny thing with some green badge and heated seats.

Where was the fun in that?

So, I couldn't see through my windscreen for twenty minutes in the winter and had to hang out the window like a mutt to get air in summer. My car, Winston, had character.

As I squelched into the seat and yanked the creaky door shut, I smiled. Character, I liked character.

Chapter Two

THE WEEK PASSED by in a blur of me trying desperately to claw back some hours at the end of the month. We worked on a "flexible working scheme" which meant that I could accrue hours or diminish my working day. It was a lot like a credit card and I spent most of the latter half of my months making up for the deficit I'd created at the beginning. Ten years and I still hadn't learned.

Friday night finally came and I was sprawled out on the second-hand squishy sofa as Rebecca set up. We were about to start our DVD fest complete with crisps, pop, and pyjamas when a knock sounded at the door. An unmistakable knock, the Doug tap.

"What is he doing here tonight?" Rebecca threw the controls to the side in a huff. "It's our night."

"I don't know why he's here." If I was honest, I was as disgruntled as she was. He never intruded on girls' night, ever.

"Tell him he sucks."

"Tell him yourself." I opened the door to his best charming grin. He knew he was trespassing. Cute or not, he was invading.

"Before Rebecca throws knives at me, I have a very good reason." He held up a massive box of chocolates.

"He brings chocolate," I called out to her. "Big, Swiss chocolate."

"He's got five minutes."

I opened up the door wider, making a show of snatching the prize from his hands. "Speak fast, Fletcher."

"See, here's the thing . . ." He walked to the centre of the open-plan space to address us both. The man should have been a politician. "I have this wacky idea that I think you girls are going to love."

I handed the chocolate box over to Rebecca who examined it like it was a diamond.

"Expensive . . . hazelnut . . . creamy . . . acceptable." She nodded at him and ripped open the box. "Continue."

Doug grinned. "I want to bring you both dinner."

"You brought chocolate," Rebecca mumbled through her munching. "Same diff."

"This is better. I brought someone around . . . someone who was in a meeting with me today."

Doug was so excited that I felt a warm glow of affection for the numbskull. He was the sweetest man sometimes.

"Judy?" Rebecca's face had drained of all colour as she uttered the name. Our boss, Judy Evans was not a woman with whom I envisaged having a fun dinner. Rebecca's reaction however made me cock my head. What was the deal there?

"Yeah," he said, ploughing on completely ignorant. "I was saying how I wanted to take you to the centre opening in France and—"

"Sweetheart," I whispered. "I'm not sure if Rebecca is feeling all that well."

We both looked at her. She sat there frozen, her mouth open, chocolate stopped half way.

"She's just outside . . ." Panic filled his eyes. "I thought a bit of social time with you guys would soften her up. I—"

"It's okay," Rebecca managed. "I just need a minute to . . . I just need a second." She dashed off towards her bedroom and I went over to Doug.

"You did a sweet thing," I told him. "You weren't to know."

"So she isn't okay?" Bless him, he looked so confused.

"Let's not leave Miss Evans out in the hallway, hmm?"

"Right." He shook himself out of his daze. "Yes . . ."

He hurried to the door, and the middle-aged, power-suited beauty sashayed into the apartment, literally, she walked like she was prancing down a catwalk. She also looked like she was on a mission. The woman terrified me at the best of times.

"Miss Evans," I said, extending my hand. "Nice to see you . . . again." Didn't I see her most days? What kind of hello was that?

"I hope that you don't mind." She shrugged.

Tight skirt, fitted blouse, fitted jacket, all in charcoal matching her auburn hair. Miss Evans was the kind of woman used to getting what she wanted, when she wanted it.

"I saw Doug and he was insistent that I came."

No doubt he had been. Doug had a habit of getting what he wanted a lot too. "Well, come in . . . take a seat." I pointed to the sofa. She didn't really look like the kind of woman who graced second-hand cast-offs. Ah well. "You in the mood for any food in particular?" Had she liked Chinese or Italian better? "Doug is paying."

Doug nodded. He looked so pleased with himself. It was cute.

"I don't mind." Her eyes scanned the apartment and I tried to hide my smile. It was going to be an interesting evening.

"Rebecca will be out in a second. She's . . ." Think woman, think. "Changing." Of course she was. Phew.

Doug opened his mouth. "I thought she was—"

"Changing."

He caught the warning glint I shot him and went to the kitchen. "I'll pull out the menus."

"So, Miss Evans, I hope that Doug was gentle in the meeting?"

I watched her soak in every detail of the apartment. Her eyes lingered on the discarded pair of crocodile shoes. A smile danced across her lips. If I didn't know any better, I would think *she* was pursuing Rebecca. Now that was a turn around.

"You have him impeccably trained." She pulled her eyes back to me. "It's good to know that my favourite worker has a handle on the client."

Her tone was playful enough that Doug laughed. Poor thing didn't realise that the woman was deadly serious. Doug was only using my company because . . . well . . . I was working for them. It was probably the only reason why my poor-excuse-for-a-performance was tolerated. I was a terrible administrator. I couldn't organise myself let alone an entire sales team.

"If you hadn't been so . . . er . . . giving, letting me attend that dinner, Doug and I wouldn't be where we are." If Rebecca's ashen face was anything to go by, Miss Evans was more giving than I'd realised.

Do not laugh. Do not laugh at your own joke, Saunders.

"Yes, Pip is right." Rebecca's voice held her usual cocky confidence as she strutted into the room. I didn't miss the lingering glance of appreciation Miss Evans gave her. Oh boy, it was like hunting season.

"Italian good?" Rebecca asked us before flashing a confident smile at Miss Evans. "Do you want that?"

Miss Evans smiled, her lips pursed. "*Si.*"

Doug didn't seem to understand why Miss Evans stared at Rebecca for so long and looked to me for some explanation.

I went to him, kissed him on his full lips, and took the menu from his hand. "I'll tell you later."

"So, I didn't blow it?"

"Not sure yet," I said, thankful I didn't have to be hunted by anyone. "But if the awkward silences continue, you may get to sleep over tonight."

Before the promise sunk in, I took the menu and broke up the staring match. "Italian," I said as though speaking to toddlers. "Maybe we could narrow it down?"

"Spinach tagliatelle," Rebecca said.

"Pasta e fagioli," Miss Evans shot back as though it were a competition.

Calm down, woman, it's food not quiz night.

"You get that, Doug?" I said loudly enough to snap them out of it. "You want something to drink?"

"Red," they said at the same time, then laughed.

Wow, I needed a whistle.

Rebecca mouthed, "Save me," as Doug drew Miss Evans's attention by hurrying to her with a bottle and some glasses.

"You want to give her the tour?" he asked Rebecca as he filled up their glasses and turned to Miss Evans. "Rebecca has a great view of the . . . er . . . canal."

"She does? Now isn't that nice," Miss Evans crooned.

No, not really. It was beyond the fence and some stingy nettles that made me itch just looking at them. Okay, so it was my dad's responsibility to maintain the place but he liked to hire people we didn't really want to let loose on anything. Cheap didn't always mean a bargain. Alas, it was only us and two flats below so no one complained. Probably because our two elderly neighbours were just happy to pay half rent.

Rebecca put her hand on the back of her neck and smiled. I narrowed my eyes at Doug.

"Oh . . . it's, well . . . I . . . You want to see?" Rebecca looked like she wanted to climb out of the window.

"Why not?"

Rebecca and Miss Evans headed off for the grand tour. It would take all of seconds. Our place consisted of a living room, a tiny excuse for a kitchen, a bathroom, and our bedrooms. Rebecca always said it looked like the apartment in *Friends*. I reminded her that they could fit our place in the kitchen and that they had an awesome window. It held views of New York and Central Park, ours held a view of the street outside. If we were really lucky, misty rain permitting, we could make out the top of the street which held a row of second hand and charity shops. I watched Rebecca head straight for her room, getting her bottom pinched for good measure.

I spun around to glower at Doug. "Now why are you trying to get rid of them?"

He slid his arm around my waist. "If Rebecca is busy entertaining and boring Evans with stories . . ." His kiss was confident. "I get to keep you."

"You get to keep me anyway." I enjoyed letting his lips linger over mine. So familiar, so safe. "That's what the ring is all about."

"Then come with me," he said, leaning in and sliding his hand around to my back.

I tapped him on the nose. "I think they deliver."

Doug smiled. His lips brushed over mine. He didn't give up easily. "Not the Italian. Come with me, Pippa." He kissed me, gentle, unhurried. "Come with me to France."

Ice cold guilt shot up my back. I pulled away and grabbed the menu from the counter. "If we don't call them, no one will eat tonight."

"What does that matter?" He tried to pull me back. "I can just cook breakfast instead."

My sweat trickled down from my armpits. My stomach churned. France? Oh no, not France. "But my boss is our guest."

Doug went to speak but I stomped over to Rebecca's room and slammed open the door. "Need your help."

Rebecca looked like she wanted to hurl herself at me. Miss Evans looked like she may fire lasers from her eyes, and I wanted to bolt before *I* climbed out of the window.

"You're coming with me to pick up dinner," I said to Rebecca. "Doug can catch up with business while we're out."

"Sure." Rebecca tried to read me but I grabbed her hand.

"Doug, set the table."

"But—"

"Set the table."

I was barking orders at him now? When did that happen?

Doug was polite enough not to argue but I could see the flicker of something in his eyes. Hurt? Irritation? Shock?

"Okay, I get why I'm freaked but what is going on with you?" Rebecca asked as we hurried down the staircase like bank robbers fleeing the scene.

"I'm hungry."

"And I'm straight."

I sighed. "You need some time to gather your thoughts." Not even a good lie. "Looked like she may pull out a rifle and mount you on her wall."

"I wouldn't put it past her." Rebecca shoved her hands in her pockets as we power walked down the street. "And you look like I feel. Who poked your pickles?"

"Where do you get those sayings from?" She drove me crazy. "That doesn't even make sense." The wind whipped up and I shivered, then looked down. Wonderful, I was still in my pyjamas.

Unfazed by my nightwear, Rebecca nodded. "You understood the context and stop avoiding the question."

Oh balls, I'd forgotten my—

Rebecca beeped her car. "You were ready to bolt, thought it would be more efficient with keys." She pulled a long coat out of her boot. "And pink bears are not cool in public."

"I love you, you know that."

"Then tell me what rocked your river."

"Rocked my—" I sighed, pulling on the coat. It didn't hide my fluffy slippers but it would have to do. "You talk so much crap. How do so many women fall for it?"

I climbed in the passenger side as Rebecca started the engine. "They don't know me like you do."

I lay my head back into the heated seats as the car purred through the city. Rebecca's company car was a better option than Winston in the rain. Still, Winston had his own tape deck. How many people still had tape decks, huh?

As creatures of habit, we only ever went to one Italian, Gino's. There was no better place. It was about three miles from our flat, like I had any clue about distance. Basically with lights, rain, and traffic, it could take us at least twenty minutes to drive there. It would be far easier and quicker to actually walk but then my fluffy slippers would get wet. That was my excuse and I was sticking to it.

"Did Doug say something?" Rebecca asked as I turned off the radio. I hated the radio. I hated the nattering between songs.

"He asked me if I would go to France with him," I mumbled, digging for something resembling music in her glove compartment.

Rebecca sucked in her breath. "Does he not get the message about it yet?"

"Evidently not." I held up a CD, raising my eyebrows. The Spice Girls?

"Hey, they were cool." She took it off me and shoved it in the player. A moment later I was hollering "Wannabe," like I had a clue what it meant.

We stopped at a traffic light, still bouncing about inside as rain started to sprinkle onto the windows. "Fancy a drink while we wait?"

"Er . . . I have this baby to control and we have guests." Rebecca rested her head on the wheel with a groan as "Two Become One" wafted out at us. "Surprise guests."

"Doug sabotaged girls' night." I sounded more irritated than I felt. Was I really angry with him? What had he done wrong other than be sweet? Okay, he wanted his own way so there was an ulterior motive but still, he was a sweet brat.

"She tried to seduce me." The red light turned to green and Rebecca pulled off. "I said no."

I did a double take and squinted to see if Rebecca was playing with me.

"Last weekend when you were at Doug's." Rebecca turned and laughed at my expression. "I was so freaked out . . . so embarrassed, I didn't even tell you."

The city lights twinkled in the raindrops, misting up the windscreen. There was nothing quite like a rainy London night. Rebecca could have named all the buildings but to me they looked like a mass of brick jutting up into the night. Buildings were her thing.

"You turned her down?"

"Yeah . . . her come on was cringe-worthy . . . I mean, I'm not fussy but she's . . . she's—"

"A bitch?"

Rebecca nodded, overtaking a bus that seemed intent on blocking the whole road. "That too." She sighed. "Never once in ten years did she act anything other than professionally towards me. I don't get it."

"So why now?" I didn't understand the shift myself. To all intents and purposes, she resembled a piranha in a foot spa to me. "She's a beautiful woman . . ."

"And was married to the director, Pip." Rebecca bit her lip. "What do I do?" She tapped the wheel, her eyes on the Mercedes in front. "I haven't felt this trapped since . . . well . . . since college."

Seeing her cocky aura shatter was enough to terrify me. Rebecca had been all set to head off to university and start her degree but her father had found out about her sexuality and booted her out, cutting her off from her funding and her dream. Horrid man.

"I wanted to tell you but you've been . . . well . . ."

"Distant?" I was a crappy friend, a really crappy friend.

"Yeah." Rebecca knocked off the CD as we both scanned for a parking space. "Anyway, she told me that no wasn't acceptable."

"Over there." I pointed to a free space, with a celebratory grin. It was akin to finding the right pair of shoes on discount and in the right size. Go, Saunders. "It looks like she meant it."

"She was still married, Pip." Rebecca's voice wobbled. "I like the director."

"When has a ring stopped you?"

The rain blasted me in the face as we got out and hurried into the warm ambience of an Italian villa. At least it was on the inside. Outside it was sandwiched between a barbers and a DVD rental store.

"I don't touch women who are, or have been, married. I would never knowingly do that. It just feels wrong."

For once, I believed her words. It wasn't something I had noticed but when had I bothered to look? Why did she suffer my company?

"Last thing I needed was for her to show up tonight."

I patted her hand as we took a seat at the bar. Giovanni, Gino's son, hurried over to us. "Orders, ladies?"

Covering up the pink showing under the coat, I smiled. "Take away if you don't mind. We have guests."

He smiled, his brow shiny. He whipped out a handkerchief to mop it. "Wonderful, usual for you two?"

We nodded.

"Extras?"

I counted the orders on my fingers. "Pasta e fagoli and . . ." Crap, I'd forgotten to ask what Doug wanted. "Hold on . . ." I looked for my mobile. Crap, it was on the table. "You got yours?"

Rebecca shook her head. "You can't remember his favourite?"

"Yeah, any dish that involves as many types of meat on it as possible." I sounded irritated again. I hoped Rebecca didn't notice.

"Meatballs with spaghetti, thanks," she answered for me. It was as good a shot as any.

Giovanni smiled and hurried off while I tried to study the beer mat with fascination.

"I spilled," Rebecca said, her voice low. "Your turn."

"It's nothing." Her eyes seemed to burn into my cheek until I looked at her. "It's nothing . . ."

"Tell me." She leaned on the bar. "Or I will get you hammered and drag it out of you."

"Do you want me to tell Doug to make her leave?" I wasn't sure how I could make good on that promise as I had no phone but maybe Giovanni would let me use his. He'd once given me extra breadsticks. Maybe he'd be charmed by my fluffy attire.

"She said I give in or she will tell the director that I came onto her." The sound of defeat ebbed from her and I leaned my head against her shoulder.

"That sucks." Miss Evans was indeed a bitch.

"Yeah."

I nudged her shoulder. "I like your hair." She looked at me and raised her eyebrows. "I mean it, it's growing on me."

"Liar, but thanks." She prodded me in the ribs. "Now, spill it."

Fear, guilt, tension, and that flash of excitement shot through my stomach and once again I broke out in a sweat. My neck itched and burned. The secret had been buried for so long that to speak a word, to actually say the words out loud, felt like unleashing a slumbering beast. Two sides to every story, maybe, only one side of mine led to the other and I couldn't even think about it without getting nauseous.

"Could it be worse than my sad tale?"

Little did she know. "Yes."

"Good." She motioned to the bartender. "Double whiskey for my dear friend and a lemonade for me."

"It won't work."

Nudging the glass towards me, Rebecca batted her eyelids. "It's to calm your nerves." She smiled a cocky smile. I needed to tell her at least some of it. I couldn't just daydream my way through every single day. I was going to get married, at some point. I needed help, support, therapy.

Rebecca took my hand. "I'm on your side what—"

"I fell in love with another woman."

Rebecca slipped off her stool. I grabbed her to stop her clattering to the ground.

She retook her seat and stared wide-eyed at me.

"Well . . . say something."

"In France?" Her brow wrinkled up her nose, her voice squeaky. "Like a female woman?"

Now she was just being daft. "Yes, I fell in love with another woman." Didn't those words sound freeing and terrifying all at once? This was how people who had committed crimes felt in confession, I was sure. "In fact, I had a yearlong affair with her."

"You're . . . but you're not . . . I mean . . . you love Doug."

"Of course I love Doug." What the relevance was in that I didn't know. "It was years before him."

"Like . . . a love affair . . . I mean . . . like . . ."

For someone so keyed up on seduction, she looked more shocked than I had expected. "It was a long time ago."

"Oh shit." She put her head in her hands. "This woman still lives there?"

My whiskey arrived.

Rebecca downed it.

"Oh shit . . . Oh, this is bad."

I stared back at her. Great support. "You're not making me feel better here."

Rebecca signalled to the bartender again. "Pip, he is totally set on you." She bit her lip. "It'll break his heart."

"Why does he need to know?" I frowned at her and folded my arms. "I haven't cheated on him."

"But the woman still lives in Marseille?" The second time she'd asked the same question.

Another whiskey arrived.

She downed that too.

"Yes, but it's a big city."

Holding up her fingers to order another, Rebecca looked at me as though I would grow tentacles at any moment. "So . . . are you saying that you are . . . I mean . . . is that why?"

"For a gay woman, you're a terrible confidante." The third double arrived. I placed my fingers over the glass. "I love Doug. I am marrying Doug."

"And the woman, I mean, she must have been some woman." The way she hung on the word "some" was reminiscent of a teenage boy. Shocked hadn't made her less smutty it seemed.

Giovanni hurried over with our order and I pulled Rebecca away from the double before she grabbed for it.

There were women, then there was *her*.

"I think I . . ." I wasn't sure how I could explain all that had happened as we headed out into the downpour. What words could adequately describe *her*? "I mean . . . I don't know . . ." How to pinpoint why she had overwhelmed my senses. "You see . . ." How to justify how one woman had untied every knot in my heart and shred every resistance I'd had. "She was French."

Rebecca took the bags as I got in the driver's side. "That's it? You land that on me and put it down to the woman's nationality?" She shook her head as I pulled off. "There's a load of people living in France and you weren't ban—"

I shoved a bread roll in her mouth. "You're so crass."

"How did you keep that secret?" Rebecca chomped on the roll. "I mean, how did I not get any vibes from you?"

I turned right, the rain got heavier. "There are no vibes to find. I don't feel anything for any other woman, I promise." That was the truth. I'd never felt even an inkling towards anyone else, full stop. I'd been oddly surprised I was actually attracted to Doug. He wasn't *her* but he was nice. I liked nice. Nice didn't make my brain dribble out of my ears.

"You sure?"

"Trust me . . ."

Rebecca and I had watched countless romantic films and I'd even read a couple of the steamy novels she so enjoyed. I wasn't revolted and I wasn't overawed. Perhaps I was not that kind of woman. My relationship with Doug was steady and comfortable.

"I love Doug, there is no question about that. I'm marrying him. That is all that matters."

"You're right not to tell him." I was glad she agreed with that. "He'll think I've been getting it on with you too."

"It would be like kissing my arm."

Rebecca frowned. "Hey, I'll have you know that I can kiss better than any French chick."

Not her, not those long languid kisses that permeated my dreams. Not the sweet promising caress or the hot heavy demand—

"It's red." Rebecca flicked my ear, snapping me to the present.

"Red, right." I stopped the car.

"You have that look again." She frowned. "You're thinking about her, aren't you?"

"No, I'm thinking about Doug."

"I'm not sure I believe you." I was glad she was eating her way through the rolls, hopefully it would soak up the two doubles. With Miss Evans around, she needed her wits about her.

"He's on a promise." I flashed her a dazzling smile, the light turning to green. "It's only fair as he was trying to help."

"Right."

I shoved another roll in her mouth. "Stop looking at me like that."

"I can't help it. You just told me that you had a sordid affair with another woman." She laughed around her roll. "I mean, you, the upstanding moral compass."

"Maybe I was experimenting." I pulled into a spot close to our flat. "That's what they call it, right?"

Rebecca shook her bread roll at me. "Oh no . . . experimenting is a night, a few too many drinks . . . it's not twelve *months*." She chomped another piece as we got out of the car and I took the bags as she locked it. "Experimenting is not getting in a cold sweat at the mention of the country."

"Fine." Rebecca took a bag as we entered the lift. "Whatever it was, it's in the past. I would really prefer it if Doug and I didn't bump into her. Me *not* going to Marseille guarantees that." It also guaranteed that I never had to face what had happened. Oh, that rolled my stomach.

"Hey, you got no annual leave . . . none . . . I told you that I've got your back."

"You also got my whiskey." I opened the door and we stood in the entrance hall. Hmm . . . so the lift was working as well as always.

We stared up at the steps. I took a deep breath only to realise that Rebecca had done the same. "After you?"

"I can't believe you had a lesbian affair and it wasn't with me," she whispered at me as we huffed our way up the three flights. "That's mean, Pip."

"Like kissing my arm," I muttered as Rebecca let us into the flat. I smiled at Doug who, after a few glasses of wine, was entertaining Miss Evans with golf stories. "Besides, I love you too much to have you slobbering on me."

"Maybe I should have tried a French accent?" Rebecca placed the bags on the counter and put two bread rolls above her upper lip.

"Get stuffed." I shoved one of them in her mouth. Rebecca, Doug, and Miss Evans all looked a little tipsy. Lucky them.

"Either way, mission no annual leave is commencing." Rebecca grinned, her pale cheeks rosy. "I love that you have skeletons."

"I hate that I told you."

"I hate that you *didn't* for so long."

I gave her a quick peck on her cheek and dished out the food. I put half of mine onto Doug's plate, knowing he would only steal it if I didn't.

"It felt good to release it."

I sounded so sure of that fact but why was my voice wobbling and why were my hands trembling?

"It's not easy to deal with sometimes . . . especially when you don't want to feel something," Rebecca said.

Nodding, I picked up the plates. It wasn't the full story but it would have to do for now. "I'm sorry she's hunting you like an animal."

"I'm sorry you're a floozy."

Snorting with laughter, I nudged into Doug who looked up at me with a hunger in his eyes. Oh brother.

"Now look what you've done," I whispered at Rebecca as she passed.

"Maybe he should grow a moustache?"

"I hate you."

Rebecca grinned at me and handed Miss Evans her plate. "I know."

Chapter Three

DOUG SHIFTED IN his sleep as I tried to wrestle back some of the covers. No doubt, by the rumbling snores, I would have little in the way of peace. Giving up on a bad job, I got out of bed and crept into the kitchen. Rebecca was raiding the fridge.

"You sleepwalking or consciously hoarding?"

"Awake," Rebecca mumbled. "You should be with the foghorn."

"I can hear him through my earplugs."

"That's what happens when they win a tournament. You're lucky he isn't tied to a lamppost naked."

Rebecca pulled out the box of pizza from the fridge and wandered to the sofa. She had a t-shirt and boxers on. A pair of boxers I knew only too well. "I take it, your bed mate is snoring too?"

"Didn't bring her home."

I pulled out the jam and buttered some bread. "That bad, huh?"

Rebecca sighed, her eyes staring into nothing.

"Miss Evans again?"

In the month since our little share-fest, Miss Evans had been relentless. Warning Rebecca that she was playing with fire was not an option.

"I want to tell her it has to stop."

"But she has you where she wants you." The woman did too. She'd gotten Rebecca nice and inebriated, leapt on her, and had taken pictures. Now, there was no escape route.

Rebecca groaned. "I hate it."

"I know."

I sat beside her and munched on my bread and jam. "Doug is set on me going with him to Marseille." I took another bite. "He is obsessed with the place."

"I told him you'd go if he opened it in Paris," Rebecca offered. "He didn't bite."

"Maybe I should tell him that something awful happened there and I can't face going back." I shuddered. Too close to the truth. I couldn't do that.

"You think the woman will remember?"

Would she? Had it been as unforgettable for her? Had her heart been as totally etched with that time as mine was? "I doubt it."

"If Doug is anything to go by, she'll be clambering over the seats to get to you." Rebecca smiled. "Maybe I could track her down and distract her?"

"Don't you dare." The venom in my voice shocked me.

"You just don't want to go back there because you're scared." She looked at me. "Not about him finding out . . ." She frowned. "You're worried that *she* will."

"Don't be ridiculous."

"I'm not." She sat up straighter, pizza forgotten. "Pip, you are worried how you'll react."

"It's a big city." I held my hands up. I couldn't cope with this. We'd get to why I left and then I'd be a jibbering idiot. "She's probably not even living there anymore. She probably went home to her parents." At least I hoped so. It was bad enough I had deserted her without thinking of her being alone.

Rebecca laid her head back on the sofa. "Will you stay in mine tonight?" She nodded to her room. "He's gonna be roaring like a lion until well past midday."

"Thought you'd never ask." I pulled her to her feet and put the pizza box back in the fridge.

"Why did you never look at me like that?" Her words were so quiet, I wondered if I'd imagined them.

"I promise you that I have never looked at any other woman . . . like that." I linked my arm with hers. "Trying to explain it makes it even more irrational." She opened her bedroom door. "I mean, it was just her as a person . . . the whole package . . ."

"What did she look like?" Rebecca pulled back the bedcovers and patted the pillow down. "And don't just say French."

"Well, that's what she looked like. Tall-ish . . . olive skin, long brown hair . . . I guess, sinewy?"

I cuddled up to Rebecca as she wrapped an arm around me. "What about her job? What did she do?"

"At the time, she was training to be in the gendarmerie but she worked back home, helping her dad in his stonemason's business too." Just talking about her made my pulse quicken with joy.

"She could philosophise and discuss any topic with a passion that invigorated everyone around her."

"You're right," Rebecca said. "She does sound French. I wonder what they feed them over there."

"Food is a passion for them, I swear." I smiled, the memory of lively debates on everything from cooking preparation to ingredient choice. "In her case a salade niçoise was her favourite."

"She ever take you to an Italian?"

"Yes." I was not getting sucked into Rebecca's trap though. "I can't remember what we had."

"Liar."

Her voice was heavy with sleep. I was thankful that probing me had helped still her restless mind. I had no idea how she coped with being forced to "entertain" Miss Evans.

It made me glad that I was off the market. Doug was all I wanted. It made things an awful lot simpler that way. *She* was more than likely married and happy to some model-esque wife who was perfect in every way. She wouldn't even spare a thought for me, would she?

THE RAIN HAD decided it would camp out in London for the spring as the month wore on. Rebecca had been at Miss Evans beck and call which meant Doug had happily muscled in. He'd been so constant that I was starting to wonder if he had actually moved in. I wasn't overawed with finding his socks in my pile of laundry. When he told me he had to go away for a business trip, I was guilty of feeling just a tad bit relieved.

"I'll be gone a few days at most," Doug told me as he held me tightly. "I want to get some things sorted for the centre and I'll be back." He smiled. "Or you could come visit?"

"I'm busy, sweetheart." I would be so for as long as I could delay. Space, space and quiet. Space, quiet, and control of the TV. "Last thing I want is to be going back there."

A frown wrinkled his forehead. "What?"

"A year was long enough in that place." I hated lying, but the closer his centre opening got, the more the panic seemed to warp my thinking. "Now, if you offered me Paris or maybe Toulon . . ."

"I thought you loved it there?"

"I love the memory of it." At least that wasn't a lie. "But I don't want to revisit the past." Again honesty, I was on a roll. "I'd rather make new memories with you."

He squeezed me tightly, his kiss more possessive than usual. Did he want to shove me in his suitcase or what? "We will. I love you, Pippa."

Clinging to the hope that he had gotten the hint at last, I returned his kiss in kind. "I love you too, sweetheart."

An hour later I was in my cubicle thumping away at my sticky keyboard. Rebecca summoned me into her office.

"You okay there?" I asked as I shut the door behind me.

"No." She had puffy eyes and her nose was streaming. Did she have a cold? "Judy."

I hurried around to her. "What happened?"

"She wants more."

That did not sound good. "How do you feel about that?"

"You sound like a shrink."

"You're avoiding the question."

She rested her head on my chest as I perched on the arm. I hoped it would hold me or we'd end up sprawled in a heap. "I'm heavier than you, quit worrying."

I kissed the top of her head and held her close. "What do you want to do?"

"Nothing." Rebecca sighed. "She was married to the director. I don't care what she wants." She nuzzled in closer. "I can't do it."

"Wow, you sound so noble." I wanted to squeeze the pain out of her. "Why couldn't you have been like this all along?"

"Where would be the fun in that?"

"You might get a woman that deserves you instead of the rubbish you pick up."

Rebecca chuckled. "Oh they do deserve me . . . A cocky idiot like me is what you get for straying."

There were times I wanted to knock sense into her. Why couldn't she see what a wonderful woman she was? "So what did you say?"

"That I didn't want to know." She gripped hold of my shirt, squeezing it between her hands. "I told her we had to stop talking."

"You did the right thing." I was so impressed by her strength that I felt a new wave of affection for her. "How 'bout we forget work and go watch some DVD's—"

"She fired me."

"What?"

Rebecca pointed to the box on the desk. I'd walked straight past and not even noticed. Good thing I'd never wanted to be a detective.

"But they can't do that!" My heart thudded and my stomach churned up with the injustice of it. That couldn't happen, there were laws. There were . . . well . . . laws.

"She did."

Security knocked on the door. I clung to Rebecca. No, no, that wasn't fair.

"Miss Whitely?"

Rebecca got up and picked up the box off her desk.

I seethed with thudding anger as I watched her walk out of her office. No, this was wrong.

"Wait." The lovely security guards, who I often skived off work to chat to, stopped and let Rebecca turn around. "Just wait there a moment . . . please?"

Not waiting for a reply, I marched down the corridor and burst into the meeting room.

The director, Miss Evans, the board, all looked up at me.

"Something wrong?" the director asked.

I took a deep breath. "Yes."

Expectant eyes waited for me to say something else. It was wrong, Rebecca . . . It was wrong. "Your ex-wife is unprofessional." Bad start, I would never make a good lawyer.

"Excuse me?" The director was a nice guy. I really did not want to rip his heart to shreds. Everyone knew he still loved the wench.

"Miss Evans. She fired someone without grounds for dismissal." Was that even a term?

"Miss Saunders, please explain yourself."

Miss Evans sat there with a smug grin on her face. I was never one to open my mouth about anything. I never rocked the boat. Here I was about to destroy the poor bloke's heart. What did I do?

"She blackmailed Rebecca." Nice start, numpty. "Now she's fired her."

"You fired Miss Whitely?" The director frowned. "Why?"

Miss Evans did not look so confident now. "She made inappropriate suggestions—"

"You're lying!"

The director looked as shocked at my outburst as I was. My knees felt like they were about to buckle and I could see my own hand wobbling as I ran it through my hair. "She came to our flat. Doug can vouch for that."

"I simply—"

"She told Rebecca that if she didn't . . ." I wasn't brave enough to actually say the words so instead motioned with my hands and nodded to signify that it was in *that* way. "Then she would get her fired."

"Judy?" The director seemed less than surprised at her. An element of boredom seeped through. Ah, so she'd always been a floozy. "Miss Whitely was a perfectly good sales rep."

"Was?" I scowled. "You can't do this to her."

"I think you have said enough, Miss Saunders," the director said. His voice was gentle but enough to tell me that the matter was closed. "We will talk about this at a more appropriate time."

They were going to sweep it all under the carpet. Miss Evans looked quietly smug at his words.

"No."

"No?" The director looked over his glasses at me.

"No. I will not talk about this at an appropriate time." No way. I wanted to throttle the vicious bitch. "I'm done. I quit."

Miss Evans and the board looked unmoved.

"And I will be making sure that Doug knows about the way you treat your employees."

Boy, didn't that change the mood. "Now, Miss Saunders—"

"Forget it." I stomped towards the door. "Consider Fletcher Enterprises an ex-client." I slammed the meeting room door closed with a satisfying thud and turned to see Rebecca, the security guards, and a gaggle of staff all staring wide-eyed at me.

"I was saying . . ." I took Rebecca by the elbow and led her towards my cubicle to pick up my bag, my coat, and my little ornament of a hug Doug had bought me. "We need to go watch DVDs."

"I think I may fight Doug and propose," Rebecca mumbled as we headed into the lift. "I don't think I've ever seen anything as awesome."

My hands were still shaking as I gripped hold of my ornament. "I can't believe I just quit."

Rebecca adjusted her hold on her box of things and shook her head. "*I* can't believe you just quit."

Rebecca followed me out to Winston. I guessed the company car was a moot point now. Aptly enough, it was still raining so our riding off into the sunset was more a sodden squelch to the car park. Elizabeth Bennett never had to deal with this crap.

"We're jobless," Rebecca said, stowing her stuff in the back seat. "What do we do now?"

"I would say call my mum but I doubt even she could fix this," I said as we got in.

Rebecca squeezed my knee. "DVDs it is then."

Winston spluttered into life and Rebecca's teary words rose above the squeaky brakes. "I love you. You know that, right?"

"I'll remind you of that when we are scrabbling for pennies to eat."

Rebecca laughed. "Thankfully you have a rich fiancé."

Ah, Doug. I really hoped he would become a hero, Mr. Darcy style, and make good on my threat. I really hoped that he could support us until Rebecca and I found new jobs. He'd always offered and now it seemed like we couldn't refuse.

"At least he'll get his wish, huh?"

Rebecca nodded. "Yeah. Don't think we have an excuse not to go to France now."

"We?"

She squeezed my knee again. "Like I said, I have your back." She smiled at me. "Besides, maybe some French R and R is just what we need."

Chapter Four

IF I HAD expected Doug to be disappointed in my rash decision to leave or disturbed by the fact I had told the company he would ditch them, I would have been completely wrong. Doug was not only impressed by my sudden insanity, he was beyond delighted. "I'm so glad you finally came to your senses," and, "that dump was below you," were two of his encouraging remarks. One, however, shocked me into silence.

He had been dressing for work while I lounged in bed, wondering what I was going to do with my day, when he turned and smiled. "At least now you won't have to quit when we're married."

Not quite one hundred percent awake, I mumbled, "Quit what?"

"That place," he said, planting a kiss on my lips. "Last thing you want to be doing is working." He smiled. "There'll be so many kids to look after you won't have time."

Not sure if I'd fallen into some kind of dream, I frowned. "Are we buying an orphanage?"

He laughed. "No, our kids." He fixed his tie, planted one more kiss on my lips, and strolled out of the room. "That's a job in itself."

Over our brunch, I'd told Rebecca what I thought I'd heard. I had convinced myself that she would tell me I was crazy and Doug had not turned into a caveman before my eyes. Instead she offered me a pitying smile.

"Come on, Pip," she said. "The guy comes from a big family. He was bound to want a rugby team."

"But he doesn't have to squeeze them out of him, does he?"

Rebecca chuckled between crunching on her cornflakes. "You telling me you don't want some fantasy with a zillion sprogs scampering around . . . Pip . . . Pip . . . you okay?"

I cradled my head in my hands. I felt a sudden wish to dig an escape tunnel. Raising children was something that grown-ups did, people with real jobs and . . . well . . . I wasn't mature enough for that. I mean, maybe in ten years or . . . well . . . just when I was older.

"Pip, you look like you're going to pass out on me."

"It's nothing . . . I . . . It's nothing."

Rebecca rubbed my back in soothing circles. "Hey, you'll find another job. We'll find something else."

"Doug was serious. He really meant what he said."

She handed me some orange juice. "Hey, he's a guy. They like all their ducks in a row."

"I can't be one of those bored housewives." Days of golf clubs and school runs and the WI. The nausea rolled in my stomach.

"There are worse things." Rebecca furrowed her eyebrows at me. "It's not all that bad."

Sure that she must think I was losing the plot completely, I tried to calm my breathing. Why did the sudden realisation make me want to run? What was so wrong with kids and marriage? Why did I feel like I'd been given a life sentence?

"It's not like you have to get married tomorrow, Pip."

Deep breaths. Slow . . . deep . . . focus on the tension leaving the body. "Right, you're right."

She leaned in closer. "You don't have to get married *at all* if you don't want to either."

Slow . . . deep—"What?"

"You don't *have* to marry Doug." She crunched more cereal. "There's no law."

"I promised." That sounded like a pathetic reason to walk down the aisle. "I mean, I love him . . . I want that." Why did that sound like a question instead of a statement? "He's great, isn't he?"

"Right." Rebecca smiled. "Prince charming and all that."

"Yes, he's handsome, rich, sweet . . . he loves me." Slow . . . deep . . . calm . . . Maybe it was just nerves? All women had nerves, right?

"Doug is the best." She drained her bowl of the remaining dregs. "You want a cheer or something?" she asked as I stared at her.

"You think he'd let you live with us?"

Rebecca's eyebrows shot upwards. "Pip, I think even Doug may draw the line at that." She leaned her head against mine. "Growing up sucks sometimes."

I thought of losing my space, my time with Rebecca. Pyjama days replaced with day care. Was it too early to start drinking?

My phone buzzed with an incoming call and Rebecca answered while I tried not to bang my head against the table. Why was I panicking now? I'd been engaged to Doug for over two years and I'd coped just fine. Maybe it was resigning my job. Maybe I'd dreamed the whole thing?

"Pip, Doug wants to talk on speaker."

I wondered why she was announcing it over the sound of my own raspy breathing. Did other women hyperventilate at the thought of marriage? "Okay."

"Hey, babe . . . you dressed yet?" He chuckled.

I didn't. I wasn't dressed.

Was he going to turn into one of those men who ordered me around? Would he become a tyrant?

"I'll dress when I want to," I snapped. Stick that. Yeah, I could be a slob if I wanted to be.

"Pip." Rebecca prodded me in the shoulder.

"What was that?" Doug was in the car. He still didn't seem to understand that when you were on speaker phone, it was better to have the windows *up.*

"Nothing." I shrugged at Rebecca's frown. "Everything okay?"

Was he calling to check if I had dressed or was he concerned about me? Maybe he thought I'd become one of those neurotic women who used a whistle to snap their kids into line. Oh crap, a rugby team. I couldn't imagine one baby let alone a whole team—

"Pip," Rebecca prodded again. "Doug asked if you are free this afternoon."

"Are we?" I wasn't about to ditch my friends for him. Oh no, Rebecca needed a place on the grounds. I would need help with the mob of children. How did he expect me to cope with all those—?

"Pip!"

"Right." I shook the thoughts away. "Don't think we have anything pressing."

"Great." Doug sounded elated. "You want to pack a case, ladies?"

Rebecca grinned. "Somewhere warm?"

"This is a workman's holiday." He sounded almost singsong. The kind of tone he always used when he thought he was doing something wonderful. "You'll need some working clothes but yeah, the summer is looking good at your destination."

"We're on it." Rebecca hung up and dragged me off the chair. "Get in your room and pack."

"So he just snaps his fingers and you jump?"

Rebecca burst into laughter. She clutched her side, howling until the laughter became silent. Her eyes screwed up, her mouth open.

"It's not funny."

She bent over at the waist and leaned against the doorjamb to my room, the tears dripping off the end of her nose.

"It's not!"

She was gasping for air and I felt myself chuckle in response. I wanted to be angry but the chuckles grew louder. Her eyes squinted up completely and I broke into sobbing laughter with her.

"Pip, don't do that to me," she managed, wiping tears from her eyes. "I needed that."

"You think I'm being crazy, don't you?"

"I *know* you're being crazy. Now, get yourself in there and pack."

Grumbling, I did as told. I'd never been great at packing. Rebecca rolled everything up into neat piles, everything colour co-ordinated.

After changing, I looked at my wardrobe. What to take? What was a workman's holiday? Stumped, I pulled everything out and crammed it into the case as it was.

"If I become a robot, I'm blaming you," I muttered her way as she unpacked my attempt and redid the whole thing. "I can't raise people without you to help. I can't even pack my own suitcase."

"You won't have to raise them alone. That's what Doug is for." She zipped closed the case with practiced ease. "It's not like I'll be far away."

"But I can't sneak into your room when he snores."

"Pip," Rebecca said, squeezing my shoulders. "You'll have kids' rooms to go hide in."

The whole thing sounded terrible. Maybe I could delay the wedding for at least ten or so years. I'd be ready then.

"Good thing he doesn't know about *La femme Française, non*?"

Having managed to go a whole two weeks without one thought about my time in France, I ended up hugging myself for support. If Doug found out that I had wandered over lines, he would never believe I hadn't done the same with Rebecca. The sole reason he was so trusting with her was the fact he believed me to be one hundred percent straight. Which of course was about as true as Rebecca's fashion sense. I doubted discovering my little secret would help convince him that I was not running around cavorting with every woman in London.

Doug had a weird perception that all lesbians were Casanovas. I doubted they were all like Rebecca, she just had an air about her. It was called eau-de-cocky. She swaggered, women swooned, and I rolled my eyes.

"Pip, I'm just kidding." Rebecca rubbed my arm. "You'll love having your own house and the Fletcher brood."

Not sure why her reassurances weren't helping, I feigned a smile. "I guess so."

The Doug tap sounded and I jumped away from her like I'd been shot at.

He walked in, grinning, followed by the chauffeur. "Ready to get some sun, ladies?"

"Let's go, Saunders!" Rebecca lugged my case into the living room, her glance at me suspicious. I shrugged. I was acting guilty, of what I didn't know.

The chauffeur took mine and Rebecca's two cases and hurried out. She always packed the British way, which meant for every single weather event she could think of. Another British strength, the ability to pull out a raincoat like a gunslinger. I had the visual of Rebecca at high noon and chuckled. Doug was watching me as if he expected excitement. Rebecca was staring at me as though she wanted an explanation and I . . . I really didn't want to go.

"Come on, Pip." Rebecca strode out of the door, leaving me with no option. I couldn't just stay there.

Doug flashed a dashing smile my way and I felt myself relax. He was amazing, why was I worrying? He looked toned and handsome in his tailored suit. The tie had been discarded and the buttons popped open, making him look a lot like a film star.

"You ready, babe?"

Taking a deep breath, I smiled. "Why not?" Being Mrs. Doug Fletcher wouldn't be so bad, right?

Chapter Five

DOUG HAD THOUGHT it amusing to blindfold me for the last hour of our journey. He felt it would spoil his surprise if I looked out at the beautiful scenery. The lack of complaint from me must have made Rebecca suspicious as both of us knew how much I hated not being able to see. In my stress-addled brain, I thought that if I couldn't *see* France then technically I wasn't in France. It was clutching at crushed lemons, as Rebecca would say, but it was my delusion, so I wasn't going to argue with it.

"Pip," Doug whispered into my ear. He had sounded more and more like a naughty schoolboy the longer we drove. "We're just pulling up now."

"Funny," I said. "I don't remember us being in a plane."

Rebecca chuckled in the back of the car at my pathetic joke but Doug let out his sigh. It was the one he always used when he missed my point completely. He had never gotten my sense of humour.

"Baby," he said. "You're an odd one."

The first time I'd heard that line, I'd been offended. Since I'd heard it countless times over the years all it did was make me picture Rebecca in my head. It was one of her best impressions of Doug. Another laugh fell from my lips, which must have made Doug think it was caused by him as he squeezed my knee. Sometimes I wondered if he understood me at all.

Before I could ask him, the car slowed to a stop and my heart decided to pound its way into my throat.

"I'll get the door." Rebecca's voice bounced with excitement, which in turn, made my stomach wriggle. Okay, so she was the equivalent of an over-enthusiastic three year old with *everything* but still.

"Pip," Doug said, helping me from the car. "Time to see your project for the next few months."

If it was a nursery, I was running. The warmth on my skin

made my muscles relax and I could smell . . . well . . . countryside. Freshly mowed grass, some kind of flower, and fresh clean air.

"Don't look so worried," he said, taking my blindfold off. "It'll be ours then. We can start a life here."

Vivid green, deep blue, rich reds, the colours flooded into my eyes. France had always been such a vibrant palette of colours in my memory but I'd put that down to the rose-tinted viewpoint I'd had. But no, France was vibrant, the trees looked abundant with health as if I'd stepped from a greyed-out print right into a Renoir.

A little stone bridge rolled over a gently trickling brook. An old farmhouse set in a vista. I stared for a moment at its blue door, paint peeling, grubby windows in the top panel. A little light hung over the centre, cocked to the side and smashed. It was framed by some kind of plant, maybe ivy, which had embraced the walls with splashes of pink and white. It was unloved but something about that door seemed to stir me.

France. I was in France once more. I turned to drink it all in as the hillside swept down to fields full of crops, interjected with swathes of lavender. The spire of a church peeked over a copse of trees in the distance. We had to be in the South with the Benedictine look of it. Sunshine felt like medicine here, like rays of health bathing my skin until it tingled. France did something to my soul. I could feel my heart thumping with joy at our re-acquaintance. I'd dreamed of it, yearned for it and now the dusty soil baked beneath my trainers and the endless blue sky welcomed me.

The down side was that it almost looked like her hometown.

She'd taken me to visit quite a few times in that year. Ajoux-Sur-Rhône, a quiet, quaint village nestled along the mighty Ardèche. Strong sweeping curves, rugged, untameable. She loved it there, working on her—

"Pip, I take it you like?"

I jolted myself out of my thoughts. Where was I? I needed to stop daydreaming. Focus, Saunders. "I love." I walked to him and showed my enthusiasm with a kiss.

Rebecca cleared her throat. "So, what's the job, Dougie?"

He frowned. He hated it when she called him that. "You always wanted to be an architect. I can't give you a degree but I'm hiring you to project manage the renovations." He smiled at me. "Meet your head carpenter."

"What?" The both of us stared at him. Was he serious?

"Well, you both were something before you joined that place." He added venom to "that," which I knew was more to show he was on our side than anything else. "If you do a great job. Who's to stop you there?"

I wasn't sure which one of us wanted to kiss him most.

"Could you be any more perfect?" Rebecca was close to it, I was sure. If she could have wowed him by batting her eyelids and looking up at him shyly for effect, she would have.

Doug folded his arms with his delight shining in his eyes. "Keep talking, keep talking."

I kissed him again, this time with every single inch of joy I felt.

I think I shocked him by the wide-eyed look he gave me. "Wow, Pip. If I'd known this was all it would take to woo you, I'd have found you more wrecks to fix."

At last, he was finally getting me.

"Berne and her father will be along later."

I tripped over a divot in the grass and nearly ended up in the front wall.

Rebecca caught me, a flash of suspicion in her eyes. "Berne?"

"Yup," Doug said with a chuckle. "If we're in France then who else would I have to be the main contractor."

Berne . . . How did he know her name? Had I talked about her *that* much? Oh brother, please tell me I didn't talk in my sleep.

"I knew you loved it when you were in Marseille and you said that the woman you knew lived in Ajoux-Sur-Rhône."

"I did?" I squeaked. Had I been drunk? I must have been drunk. I *never* mentioned her name. To mention her name was to . . . well . . . it sounded so good, so smooth, so—

"Yeah." Doug was completely ignorant to me gripping onto Rebecca's arm like it would save me. "When we first met. You were telling me how you would have loved to have worked with her on a project."

Ah. Had I been merry that night. Our first date and nerves had gotten me into a gibbering mess. Doug, thankfully, had not noticed quite how drunk I'd been. Rebecca had nursed me through that weekend.

"Really?" Rebecca raised her eyebrows. "So this Berne will be working with us?"

"And her father," Doug said. "After all, they are the local artisans."

Rebecca caught me before I passed out on the spot. Oh crap, we were in Ajoux-Sur-Rhône, oh crap, oh crap. My heart beat so fast that I was sure that it showed through my rib cage.

"She okay?" Doug caught on that I was looking less than glowing.

"Heat," Rebecca mumbled, gripping hold of me. "You want to get us inside in the cool?"

"Right." Doug hurried to the door, unlocked it, and let us in the almost derelict open-plan cottage. "Have some water, Pip."

I took the offered bottle and used it to focus on something other than . . . well . . . Slow sips, cool liquid, Evian was so smooth, Berne was smooth too . . . oh no . . .

"So talk us through what you want," Rebecca said, leading Doug away to give me time to think. Thank God for her. Thank God she knew me.

Sipping at my Evian, I focused on the surroundings. There would be a lot of repair work needed to the stone. The rafters and floors were rotted through. Where I sat, on the damp remains of a stair, I could see black charred marks. It explained why the place had been open plan and why there was so much water. I hoped no one had been inside when the place went up in flames.

Curious, I got to my feet and wandered through to the left. It had been some kind of entertainment room, the remains of a billiard table in the centre. There was even a melted TV still mounted on the wall. The blaze had ripped right through the place so I was careful to watch my footing. It had been over a decade since I'd done anything more than DIY at the flat. However nice it was that Doug trusted me, I would need someone with a lot of experience to help. And Berne and her father had it in abundance. Berne was ten years older than me and well, she'd always been the voice of experience and wisdom and . . . just breathtaking.

Balls.

"Bonjour?"

Uh oh.

My skin tingled with just the sound of her voice. My heart

pounded. I froze to the spot. Oh, how even a hello pulsed energy through me. I was in trouble.

"*'Allo?*"

She'd seen me. I tensed. Her heavy boots clomped on the hollow floors. I couldn't pretend I was deaf. I couldn't exactly throw myself out of the window and run either. For a start, that wasn't polite and if anything, I was polite. A deserter, a coward but a polite one.

"Madame?"

Her hand touched my arm. I started with the reality of it. She was here, she was touching me. I needed to lie down.

"I'm sorry," I managed, sounding like I was hyperventilating. "I didn't hear you."

Do not turn around, woman, stay staring at the mess. Where was Rebecca? Where was Doug?

"It is a tragedy, *non?*" Berne's voice gave a hint that she had recognised mine. Her questioning tone almost adding, "Is that you?"

I couldn't do this. I couldn't cope. It was too raw, too real, *she* was too real.

"What happened here?" My voice was shaking. I tried to keep my tones clipped, unrecognisable. Why, I didn't know. She would soon see me. What would she think? Would she still think I was beautiful? Would she be?

"A rich man from the city bought it." I remembered enough to know that to her, the city meant Marseille. "He had the place gutted, but he spent no time here."

Berne speaking English, her dropped H's and her smooth tones. It was always a tone or two higher when she spoke a foreign tongue. In French it was deeper, richer . . . melodic, enchanting, the way she caressed each vowel was so—

"Ah, so you've reacquainted!" Doug strode into the room with a clomp. "What do you think, Pip? Can you fix her up?"

Fix anything? The effort of standing felt like I had run around the South of France, twice.

"Pippa?"

My skin did a rippled Mexican wave when she whispered my name. Uh oh. How did I get out of this? What was the proper conduct? How did one greet a woman, who was the love of my life, a woman I'd abandoned, in the presence of my soon to be husband? I couldn't just stand and stare at the devastation.

Move, woman . . . you need to move. "How did you find the place?" I sounded unnaturally cheery as though I were either about to pull out a gun or dissolve into maniacal laughter.

"I was looking, the guy said he was done with the place." Doug walked to me and placed his hands on my waist. "Thought there was no place you'd rather have a holiday home than where Berne was."

Silence.

Thick heavy silence.

Berne was taking it all in. I could feel her watching me. I knew her well enough to know she was taking in every detail. Doug's words would confuse her no doubt. I wasn't meant to care anymore. I left after all. Why would I want a holiday home in her hometown? Who did that, ever?

"So," Rebecca said, clapping her hands. "You guys fancy some sunshine discussion?"

I heard the sound of footsteps behind me as I riveted my gaze to the charred table.

"You want to help me grab some rocks to arrange for it, Berne?" Rebecca asked, always the hostess. "It's a pleasure to meet you at last by the way."

"It is nice to meet you also—"

"Rebecca."

The, "ah," in Berne's response made me smile. I'd talked of Rebecca a lot during my time here. Berne had always wanted to meet her. I think to determine if there was anything going on between us. It was one of the reasons why I hadn't told Doug about the true nature of my relationship with Berne. He'd think the same thing. That, and I was a chicken.

Doug left my side to join the introductions. "I'm Doug Fletcher. We spoke on the phone."

"*Oui.*" Berne's tone was icy at best. "I did not know that you knew of me."

His confident laugh showed just how much of a clue he *didn't* have. "Course. Pip talked so fondly of you that I've been itching to find an excuse to meet you."

Now I knew *that* was a lie. If I'd mumbled anything about her, it had been on that first date and at no time since. I couldn't. I'd loved her so much that it physically hurt.

"She did?" Berne sounded shocked.

I closed my eyes. What must she think of me?

"So, let's head outside and talk shop, yeah?" Rebecca saved the day once again. I owed her chocolate for a month.

I heard the three of them leave, walked to the billiard table, and resisted the urge to curl up on top of it until it all went away. It had taken me two years of living in a daze just to not wake up with her on my mind. Banishing her from every conscious thought, I had slowly, surely begun to crawl from the emptiness being without her was. I still wasn't over it. I doubted I ever would be.

"Pip, you doing okay there?" Rebecca walked in and stood by my side. "Berne senior has just showed up so I thought I'd come check on you."

"I'm just great." I sounded more like I'd been impaled on something sharp.

"Pip, you said that you wanted to marry Doug."

"I do." That sounded like a question.

"By the look on her face and the deer-in-headlights reaction you're sporting, something tells me there's unfinished business."

That was putting it mildly. "I'd better get out there before she says too much."

The fear of facing Berne paled in comparison to the fear she would tell Doug the truth. I couldn't face that conversation. I couldn't face having to explain to them both why I was so pathetic. The shame of it made me sick for a start.

With Rebecca trudging beside me, I stepped out into the sunlight and promptly wanted to get in the car and speed off.

"Won't work," Rebecca whispered, holding my elbow. "Doug's got the keys."

"I hate that you know me so well."

"I know."

Berne appeared from around the back of that little beat-up van her father had when I was here. It had been ancient then. It made Winston look like a spring chicken.

Berne however looked even more spellbinding than she had when I had known her. I had to stop for a moment at the sight of her. Tall, olive-skinned with shoulder-length brown hair that she always tied back when working but never enough to stop a strand on each side from falling into her hazel eyes. The sun just seemed to dance across her skin. I couldn't explain it but Mediterranean blood seemed to make her blessed by sun.

"You were right," Rebecca said, forcing me to move. "She *is* French."

I could only nod, feeling as though I were being led to the gallows.

"In fact, she's gorgeous . . . I mean look at those arms."

The prompt did not help. Berne had spent her life lifting stone and spent her summers on the Ardèche kayaking. Needless to say, the term buff should have her as the description in the dictionary.

"Not to mention her as—"

"You're not helping!" I glared at Rebecca.

She chuckled. "I don't think I've ever seen you this flustered. There is a woman beneath the lady after all."

"It's not funny." Now I sounded like I was begging. "I can't do this . . ."

"Hey." Rebecca rubbed soothing circles on my back. "You'll do great. It's just the shock of seeing her, that's all."

"Right." I could work with that. "A shock."

"Besides, Doug is rich and handsome."

I nodded, puppet-like. "Rich and handsome."

"And a man," Rebecca added with a sly smile. "Important for you being *straight* and all."

"Quite." I turned to walk the rest of the way, ignoring the teasing in Rebecca's voice.

"Really, *really* straight. Not staring at those lips, nuh, uh."

Was I?

Balls.

I was trying to read what Berne was saying, that was all. I took a deep breath. I had absolutely no feelings for her what-so-ever, nope. Not one.

TORTURE WAS A strong word to use but it was the only one that could describe our little business meeting. Doug and Berne's father made hard work of communicating through Doug's terrible French and Berne's father's broken English.

Rebecca could speak the language as fluently as I could but

acted ignorant, enjoying Doug's attempts, while I stared straight down at the floor, trying to avoid Berne's gaze.

My heart happily pounded away as if I was swimming lengths in the pool, my brain joining in the torment by replaying every clandestine memory it could find.

I knew there was talk of me working closely with my old friend, as Doug kept calling her. I knew the plan was that Rebecca would project manage. I was sure that Monsieur Chamonix was quite confident that we could have the project finished by Christmas and from Rebecca's laughter I knew she thought that was crazy talk.

Snippets, moments of the afternoon flittered by but what was noticeable by its absence, was Berne's voice. Like me, she had not uttered a word.

As the sun started its evening descent, Doug made the suggestion to leave us alone while he, Rebecca, and Monsieur Chamonix headed to see a problem section. Neither of us could really refuse. What possible reason could there be for two old chums, as Rebecca was calling us, not to catch up?

"Don't do anything I wouldn't do," Rebecca left hanging in the air as the three of them abandoned us.

Traitor. That's what she was. A traitor.

"Pippa?"

I closed my eyes, wondering if I tried really hard like in *The Wizard of Oz*, I'd wake up in Kansas or even better, somewhere they didn't have rattlesnakes.

"Pippa, you cannot bury your head. I am right here." The purring sound of her dropped h's made my stomach gurgle. I rubbed it.

"Must be hungry." I didn't believe my own words for a minute.

"That is because you did not eat."

The feel of her hand on my arm sent a shivery ripple up my skin.

"Doug," I said, clearing my throat. "Doug is always hungry."

Oh nice one, Saunders. Start off by shoving your fiancé in her face. Bravo, you numbskull.

"He seems like a nice man." Her tone didn't seem to agree with her.

"Wonderful. And rich and handsome." That was what Rebecca said, right? Rich, handsome, wonderful, yes.

"He cares for you deeply."

I nodded and slid my left hand in my pocket as though I'd committed a crime.

"Pippa, he said you talk of me?"

Well done, Doug, tell her that why don't you. What kind of a thing was that to say anyway? "Yes, well . . . Why not?"

She grunted and I tensed for it. I couldn't even look at her. I just kept my gaze on the bridge as if it could save me.

"Perhaps because we were lovers, *non?*" She teased out the word lovers in a way that made me want to run to the car, smash the windows, and crawl inside. I couldn't do this, she was too Berne . . . too her . . . too . . . French.

"He doesn't know." I shrugged, feeling her gaze on my face. Was she looking at my lips? "He can't. I can't . . ."

"You wish to marry him yet you conceal your deepest truths?"

That made me glare at her. I was face to face with the beauty I had spent a decade trying to erase from my mind. She'd aged to perfection—the sun had highlighted her hair in touches only nature could pull off. Her hazel eyes deep and as big as ever and those—

"He doesn't need to know everything," I squeaked, stepping backwards. Desperation pounded in my neck. Could you have a neck attack? "I . . . he . . ."

"You run away from me," she said, her hand on my elbow, those eyes searching. "I wake to find you gone. No trace . . . nothing." The hurt flashed across those gorgeous eyes. "You turn up now, here, with *him*. You think I stay quiet?"

"No." My heart felt so constricted by her pain that tears filled my eyes. "I didn't know anything about it, I swear." Touching her hand, I felt the familiar calluses from her work, knowing how hard those hands worked, how strong. "I would never have done that to you."

"Yet you wish me to remain some sordid secret?" Berne stepped away. "You wish to play pretend, very well." She looked at the house. "I would not want Vivienne thinking that I would be unfaithful to her anyway."

Didn't that one land like a prize punch? "Vivienne?" I knew that I'd disliked that name all along. What kind of a person was called such a name, huh?

"*Oui*, my lover." Again, that longer than necessary emphasis which gave me another shudder. "We have been together many years."

Ouch again. It didn't matter that I deserved it.

"Yes, well. You were always too good for me," I snapped.

My words sounded so angry that I almost took them back but I heard Rebecca's voice. I turned from Berne and stomped towards the doorway.

"Do we have a place to stay or do you expect us to live in a ruin?" My tone was even icier to Doug who seemed not to notice.

"Sure, I hired the place down the road. Rebecca's got one all to herself for once."

"Maybe she doesn't want that?"

Poor Doug twigged that I was beyond PMS and held up his hands. "Now, Pip, Rebecca isn't that far away—"

"Her place have two rooms?"

Now Rebecca was staring at me along with Berne who cast a suspicious glance in her direction.

"Does it?"

Doug nodded. Poor man must have wondered if I was crazy. "Yes . . . but—"

"Then you can find me there."

Doug sucked in his chin. He wanted his own way. "Now, Pip—"

"Key." I was sure that if he didn't hand it over, I may drop to the floor and kick and scream. Toddlers had it pegged, there was nothing like a good temper tantrum.

I'd never even had a heated word with Doug before but why not start now. I could be one of those neurotic wives that had him followed and changed his diet on a whim.

He handed it over and I didn't miss the look of "help me" shot Rebecca's way. Rebecca shot him one back that said, "Don't look at me, she's a lunatic."

Berne studied the whole situation, sussing out where the lay of the land was, who Rebecca was, and reading my every emotion like I'd been written just for her. How did she do that? It was unfair. Spectacularly unfair.

"I will help her to unpack. I am delighted to catch up with my old *friend, non?*" Berne could barely keep the sarcasm out of her voice. "You can drive."

She threw the keys at me and I caught them dumbstruck. I

knew I wasn't the only one staring at her. Doug sprang to life first
and piled my things into her van like he'd get on the next plane to
England. Wow, this was going well.

ONCE MY THINGS were in the Chamonix van, I drove us in
awkward silence. The roads were so tight that I wanted to breathe
in as we squeezed through lanes. To the left, up the hill, was a
huge ruined Benedictine abbey. We'd had picnics in the grass
expanses between the old buildings dotted around. To our right,
the hill sloped down. The village plonked in a smooth plateau.
The sun beat down through the windscreen as I slowed the van to
look. Every single inch of the square was etched in my memory.
The cragged steps of the houses, shutters painted green or blue,
the flowerbeds spewing vibrant reds, yellows, and whites.

I swore it was even the same group of elderly men playing
boules on a patch of muddy stone. France in the summer, how I
loved it. I could almost hear the clink of coffee cups. The scent
of rich *café* mixed with freshly baked bread. Humming chatter of
locals, their accents so different from the North. The relaxed soul-
soothing beauty of a small country square centred around a tree
that had white blossoms during the summer months.

Berne's parents lived on the edge of the square in a large stone
house with green shuttered windows. Monsieur Chamonix's
furniture and masonry shop sat to the side of it, hand-painted
letters on the peeling wooden sign. The furniture and sculptures
were Berne's. It was why I'd been sent to study under her by a
friend of my father. She could work any surface, any material with
ease, but stone was her forte.

The cottage Doug had rented for Rebecca was straight over the
crossroads towards the gite holiday park. I knew it the second I
saw the key. It was where my father's friend had stayed and why
he'd known of Berne in the first place.

My father had been supportive. More so because he'd wanted
his youngest daughter to explore her love of language other than
wood. He had a view that after that year, I would have endured all
the culture I could stand and come home. I would then have been
ready to marry a doctor, or even better a man with an estate, and
live some weird Jane Austen parody.

Unfortunately, I'd returned back from France a gibbering wreck who'd spent the first two years secretly spending my money on counsellors. Then, Rebecca's father had found out about her and we'd headed off to London.

Again, my father had been gracious. He'd bought our house so we could rent a flat in it cheaper. He did love Doug. That was my soul redeeming feature. I'd bagged the rich man and so to my father all was well.

I didn't quite feel that way. What I felt was akin to a kept woman. I had gone from parental allowance to a pathetic excuse for a job and would probably have a credit card and allowance from Doug. My older sister was happy living like it. She completed the collection with two kids, a dog, and a Land Rover. I'd never wanted that and yet, here I was on the very same path.

Only, I was in a dinky van with a woman who had meant freedom once. Now, she just reminded me of how empty everything seemed to have become.

The little cottage was in a row of holiday conversions. Ample parking space, two floors, a nice veranda on which to enjoy the spectacular views and shutters painted in different colours. What was France without painted shutters?

I shut off the engine and stared out over the steering wheel.

"Answer me some questions, *s'il te plaît*."

Sighing, I rolled my head to look at her. "I'll try."

"Why did you leave?" Her eyes tracked over the painted front door.

"I got scared."

We both knew that. Why was she bothering to ask?

"Who is Rebecca, a lover?"

"Oh goodness no." Berne smiled at the force of my denial. "She's my best friend in all the world, like I told you."

She held my gaze. "Do you love him?"

"I'm marrying him."

"That is not what I asked."

I picked at the steering wheel, which was faded from the years of sunshine baking it. "I know."

Her smile crinkled the corners of her eyes. That seemed to satisfy some train of thought and she squeezed my knee. "Let me help you unpack and we will start again . . . as new friends."

Those words hurt even more than her confession about

Vivienne but that's what I wanted, wasn't it? The fact she was talking to me was enough after all I'd done.

"Friends it is."

THE AFTERNOON WAS a mix of joy and angst as Berne helped me to unpack in silence. Doug, it seemed, had been preparing and had brought a million essentials. I swore the man had packed half of England. Some of it would have to go to his bachelor pad up the road. I had no intention of turning on the whisking machine thingy, let alone deciphering what I needed to whisk in it. The more stuff we unpacked the more Berne found it funny. She'd only been with me a year and she knew I couldn't cook a sandwich let alone anything else. I was no baker and certainly no Mary Berry.

It scared me just how easy it was for Berne and I to fall into a comfortable peace. It was almost as though I had never left and our lives were not separate. It had always felt so effortless with her. We made the perfect team. Working side by side, it felt . . . it felt . . . a *relief* to be next to her.

Balls.

The thought dawned on me as we unloaded the last of the boxes and panic raced around my body. There was no way I could do this. No way I could be around her for any extended period of time and not feel, not want—

"It will take some adjusting," Berne whispered, her strong hand on my elbow. "We will find a way. Do not worry."

Did I even want to adjust?

I shook my head free of the thought. Doug, I was marrying Doug. He was going to be my husband. We were going to make a rugby team. The sudden nausea of that made me drop the box I'd been carrying.

"You over think this, *oui?*" she said, picking up the box and heading to a pantry-like cupboard. "One thing at a time. We are taking boxes up the stairs, cleaning the kitchen, nothing more."

Out she came with a mop and bucket and proceeded to fill it with soapy water. It was something she had done as routine. Her mother had drilled it into her that a clean kitchen floor was essential. I'd missed that little quirk.

"Then why does it feel like . . . ?" I clamped my hands over my mouth. How dare I even think such a thing?

"Because we once did it before." Berne's smile twinkled through her eyes. "As I recall, it took a long time, *non?*"

The fact that one, she knew what I was thinking and two, she had brought up our moving-in day made heat, embarrassment, and a very unwelcome tingle burst through my system. My brain turned to mush with the memory. I was in awe, still, of my own reckless behaviour. Whatever had come over me, I didn't know.

"I see that you do not forget so easily," she said. "*Mais,* I am sure you have many more memories with him."

I snorted. "Are you joking?" Closing my eyes at my own emphatic confession, I tried to ignore Berne's soft chuckle. Something told me that she was enjoying the torment she was inflicting. "I mean, of course. Why wouldn't we?"

Berne looked as convinced as I felt, a strange "uh oh" sounded in my head as everything around us seemed to take a breath. Her eyes fixed on mine. I was too close to her. Had I moved or did she? Either way we were getting closer. Each breath harder to take, each beat heavier and louder. Her full, moist lips—

"Pip?"

In my haste to put as much distance between us as possible, I clattered over the mop bucket. The soap suds gushed all over the floor. I felt my feet slip and flung my hands out to stop myself.

I couldn't.

I smashed nose first into the pantry door.

"Pip?" Rebecca's voice grew more urgent and I heard her barge in through the doorway as if she were riding to the rescue. "Pip, what—?"

"This is why I don't do housework." I reached up to touch my nose only for Rebecca to bat my hand away.

"Ice compress," she muttered.

"I have it here." Berne's voice. Such a wonderful sound.

The cooling vapours of freeze-dried peas made my throbbing nose calm, if only a little. I looked up at her trying not to show I was in pain. "Id it brogen?"

"*Pardon?*"

"She said is it broken," Rebecca translated. "Should hear her when she gets a cold."

I loved Berne's gentle smile. She looked as though she wanted nothing more than to ask Rebecca to fill her in on every gap she'd missed. I wanted to tell her every detail but then I'd have to explain why . . . no, no, bad idea.

"*Imb* fine," I managed, reaching for the pantry door to pull myself up but it was remarkably difficult bearing pea compress. "*Jub neeb* to get up."

They hoisted me to my feet and carried me to a leather and delightfully squishy sofa.

"*Doub?*"

"Monsieur Chamonix has taken him to the local old pub, I think, something about football?"

Berne beamed. "Marseille play Lyon tonight. It will be fierce."

"*Doub won hab* a clue."

Berne raised her eyebrows and Rebecca stepped in. "Doug isn't a sport kind of guy unless you count golf, which I don't."

"It is more a hobby than a professional sport you feel?"

Rebecca nodded. "Sport should make you exert and sweat, and you shouldn't have people carrying your equipment for you."

I looked at Berne who perched on the edge of the kitchen table as Rebecca sat next to me. "I prefer more active sports also." Ever the diplomat, the woman should have been running the country by now.

"You want to stay, eat?" Rebecca asked, getting to her feet as though she had mischief on her mind.

"*Imb* sure Berne *wan* to go *homb*."

Berne raised her eyebrows once more.

"She said make yourself at home."

I scowled at Rebecca but she was too busy luring Berne into the kitchen where the two of them cleaned up my mess. "So you're a stonemason by trade?"

"*Oui.* I was going to join the gendarmerie *mais* I decided that I prefer it here." Berne took the mop bucket that Rebecca had refilled and started to sweep across the floor.

"You live here permanently?" Rebecca moved around the incoming mop and washed the ingredients in the sink.

"Here and the city," Berne said.

Rebecca looked at me.

"She *meanb Marbsay.*"

"Ah, so you still live there too? Do you do the same thing there?"

Berne picked up the used bucket and emptied it outside. Sounds of sloshing water gushing into a drain mixed with Rebecca's chop chopping on the board.

"No, I go there to see Vivienne."

My nose seemed to hurt more at the sound of *her* name. It was a dumb name, like Virginia, I mean . . . come on, who called their kid Virginia?

"I take it she's not just an old chum?" Rebecca flashed me a wicked grin. I wanted to curl up into a ball and cry.

"*Non*," Berne whispered.

"You been with her long?" Rebecca seemed to read the look on my face and frowned. I got up and wandered towards the bedrooms.

I didn't want to know how long they had been together or how wonderful life was for them. Just hearing her say that she had even looked at someone else felt like my insides were being ripped out through my stomach. No, better to pretend that she wasn't invading my thoughts with her gorgeous smile or her laugh, or . . .

Oh, get a grip. Focus, decor, rooms. Inspect the rooms like mother.

The bedrooms were everything that could be expected from a holiday rental, neat, airy, and without personality. My nose had calmed enough for me to regain some sense of smell and I breathed in slowly, trying to clear the foggy pain.

I sneezed, nearly knocking myself backwards.

Holiday places all had a summery, musty smell that seemed to linger. I stood, wondering what it was. I discounted frozen pea. The linen was fresh, the sheets no doubt were crisp, yet every place I'd been abroad smelled like . . . well . . . adventure.

"Rebecca is asking if you would like to have bacon in your omelette?"

Rebecca knew full well that I *always* had bacon in my omelette and was checking on me. So much for decor. I couldn't give a crap where I was as anywhere Berne happened to be in was perfect. "You were set on the gendarmerie. Why did you really come back?"

Berne smiled. "*Mon papa*, he had a stroke. My brother was

already doing so well in the force that it seemed only right that I come back to help."

I stared at her with the news. I couldn't imagine how much she'd been through. She adored her father, as had I.

"It is okay," she said with her trademark effortless shrug. "He is a little slower, a little bossier, *mais* . . . he has good health."

What must he think of me? I was sure that he must have known Berne and I were much more than friends. "Does he recognise me, I mean today?"

"*Oui*. You are hard to forget."

I made the mistake of meeting her eyes. Love or lust or whatever went on between us was meant to fade over time, was meant to be smothered by my abandonment. Instead the space between us seemed to me as though it may shimmer and pulse with the force of my own feeling. Oh, I was in trouble, real trouble. Leaving was supposed to stop this, was supposed to drive these feelings away.

"Ladies." Rebecca cleared her throat, frowning at me once more. "You ready to eat or what?"

"Yes." I snapped my eyes away from Berne. "Yes . . . starving."

The soft chuckle from Berne as I walked by told me that she understood exactly how I felt. Earlier, I wondered how we'd get through the project together without me losing myself but right now, I would be happy just to get through dinner.

Chapter Six

I WAS ARTFUL in avoiding any interrogation from Rebecca by feigning tiredness that night. I awoke to the sound of a cockerel crowing and fumbled around searching for my alarm and smacking it for snooze. Berne had been ever present in my dreams throughout the night leaving me wanting nothing more than to escape into my head a little longer.

We'd met when I had been sent by my father to study with her in Marseille. She was working on a major renovation in the city and I could learn from her, get great experience, and get first-hand knowledge of France and its language.

Well, they did say that the best way to learn French was to fall in love with a French person.

How lost I had felt in those first few days of talks and greetings. My father's friend had taken me around and showed me little places he knew of. There had been no sign of this mysterious Berne Chamonix who I was meant to work alongside. Then came a hand-written note in her swirling letters, simply her address and she signed it "B" at the bottom—

Cock-er-doodle-doo!

I blinked open one eye, that wasn't five minutes. No fair. I hit the button again. Berne swam before my eyes. She played the piano in the heat of the summer storms, the windows wide open, her slow, taunting melodies lured me in. That's how I'd discovered her, running from the rain, from the lightning—

Cock-er-doodle-doo!

What? No, no, that wasn't enough time. I slammed the button on the clock once more. That sound, an aching call. So smooth and haunting, calling me closer, closer . . . her skin glistened with the rain, her hair wild, she turned—

Cock-er-doodle-doo!

I was going to hurl the stupid thing across the room. I groaned and opened my eyes. The scent of fresh bread, warm summer smells filled my nostrils.

And, ow, ow, ow, did my nose feel like a foreign object. The cockerel alarm continued to taunt me with its cheery cries. Who was that happy about morning anyhow?

I glared at my clock. The alarm wasn't even on. It was eight o'clock.

"I don't work anymore," I told it. "I'm a bum."

The cry sounded again and I rubbed my eyes, wincing as the skin pulled making my nose ache. Had I set my phone alarm? Would I do that? The only time I bothered looking through the hundreds of odd apps littering the screen was for two things: the alarm, which I took an age to find, and a cute little lemming game that I was slightly addicted to. Had I bothered to go through all that and if so, why? What was so important that I needed to be up in the early hours?

Cock-er-doodle-doo!

"Will you give it a break?"

Where had I put my phone anyway? Was it in my trousers? Wait, had I been wearing trousers or shorts? I scrambled out of the sheets, getting my big toe stuck in the corner. I wrenched it free and stared at the clean floor. I swear I'd left them where I always did. Had I been drinking?

Cock-er-doodle-doo!

"Where are you?"

"You need something?"

I waved at Rebecca, distracted by my hunt. Were they under the bed? Maybe I'd kicked them under there. I looked at the wardrobe, then shook my head. Fat chance.

"Pip, you okay there?"

I dropped to my hands and knees and flung an arm underneath the iron-cast bed. Nope. I glanced up at Rebecca. "My alarm keeps going off. I can't find my phone."

Rebecca pointed to the nightstand. My phone happily sat there as though amused by my predicament.

"Right," I muttered, heading to it and sweeping my hand across the screen. "I must have set it."

Cock-er-doodle-doo!

What? The thing didn't even sound like it was making a noise. I flicked the screen with irritation and took a picture of my toes.

Rebecca pulled the phone from my hand and led me over to the window. "You should be in a funny farm, you know that?"

A preening cockerel strutted across the yard, looking very pleased with himself. "Please don't tell me he's going to do that every morning?"

Rebecca nodded. "I'll ask about ear plugs." She smiled at me. "Your nose looks less purple."

"It feels mashed up like one of those old boxers."

"Well, sting like a butterfly and float like a bee." Rebecca thumbed to the doorway. "You want breakfast before we head to work?"

Oh, yes. I wasn't a bum was I? No, I was employed by my own fiancé, working on a house he wanted for us with a woman who so far exceeded any description adequate enough.

I wanted to go back to bed until it all went away. Would anyone notice?

Rebecca grabbed hold of me as I was in mid-stride and pushed me toward the breakfast table. As always with her cooking, my stomach betrayed my attempt not to be moved. It sounded like a pack of dogs had decided to make a rap record.

"I got freshly made French bread," she said. "And . . . chocolate spread."

The rap turned to a chorus. "Why didn't *we* get married again?"

Rebecca guffawed. There was no other way to describe it. Her unruly eyebrows shot up so high that she looked like a model with a facelift. "Did you seriously just say that?"

"I can joke." I sat down at the table, a little wobbled by my words myself.

"Pip, you make it clear any way you can that you are little miss straight." Rebecca flashed a cocky smile, wiggling her eyebrows. I fought the urge to throw my bread at her. She was crass. "Maybe you're mellowing in the light of the French sun, huh?"

"I'm glad you find my plight amusing." I was really glad that she was. That she didn't hate me for, one, not telling her and two, being so duplicitous about my past.

"You deserve to get teased," she said. "But it's only because I know it's all in the past and you adore your hunk-in-boots."

"Hunk-in-boots?" I spread the chocolate over my bread, took a bite, and licked the corners of my mouth, delicious fatty goodness. "Where do you get these sayings?"

"Stop avoiding the question."

I crunched through the bread and the smooth sugary bliss

oozed into my mouth, the chocolaty delight smothering my lips. Oh yes, I loved food. "I'm not," I mumbled around my groaning. "You didn't ask anything."

Thankfully Doug waltzed through the doorway at that point. He was an annoyingly cheery morning person, one who spoke loudly and made a racket. If he was up, everybody else had to be.

As he slumped down on the seat next to me and planted a kiss on my lips, I found myself really looking at him. He was broad shouldered and toned, more from time spent in the gym than any actual activity. His wide chin sported reddish-brown stubble and his hair was neat, cropped, respectable. Every inch of him was the product of his upbringing. Born with a silver spoon in his mouth, he embodied everything an upper-class man should be.

He was always respectable, always polite, always well-mannered. He did what was expected of him and demanded that those around him did the same. His grey-blue eyes, so piercingly clear, made him difficult to resist. And after eight years, he felt like an appendage. I was scatty, disorganised and, as he called it, untamed. It made me wonder just what he saw in me.

I would say he needed committing but there you go.

"I was thinking that you could start working with Monsieur Chamonix after the locals I hired have removed all that's left in there." He smiled, a patient smile. "I did tell them I wanted it done *by the time* we arrived but you know foreigners—"

"Which is exactly what we are, Dougie," Rebecca said, smattering her bread in yummy chocolate. She loved it as much as I did. Sometimes we'd appreciate its wonder in silence together. There was nothing like chocolate. The one thing that united women across the world in all generations.

Doug crossed his legs and popped the end of my roll into his mouth as I watched on forlorn. "I can't help that they can't even speak English now, can I?"

Rebecca looked at me and passed me the end of her roll. "We are in France."

"Who doesn't speak English these days?" He laughed as though that settled the matter and squeezed my knee. "Your mother will be popping in on the weekend. Maybe time for a little shopping?"

I shoved the roll in my mouth.

Rebecca blinked a couple of times. "Her mother?"

"Of course, who else would help her pick out a dress?" He seemed delighted at this turn of conversation. "What better way to break in the house, hmm?" His mobile beeped and he held up a finger as though checking for wind direction. "Right, yes . . . no, no, no . . . no you need to change that." He put his hand over the mouthpiece. "I have to take this. Dinner?"

I nodded, chewing on my roll. He planted a kiss on my cheek, tutted at the chocolate on my lips, and strolled out of the door.

"Your mother."

Swallowing was far harder now. "My mother."

"A dress." Rebecca reached across the table and patted my hand.

"A dress."

I stared down at my hands. "He doesn't mean a nice summer gown for a ball, does he?"

She shook her head.

I shook mine.

We stared down at the tub of chocolate.

"You want a spoon?" Rebecca asked.

I nodded.

She fetched two and handed me one. "You think he really wants us to fix up the house?"

I plunged my spoon into the tub, hung it upside down, and clamped the chocolate against my tongue. "Think he'd notice if we ran?"

"Me, not so much," Rebecca said around her own mouthful. "You, well . . . I'm not sure if he'd stick a collar on you."

"You think he would?" There was something in my voice that did not sound anything like joy or excitement. "He is going to make me join a country club or something, isn't he?"

"Not if you don't say 'I do.'"

How could I not say those words? I'd promised to. It wasn't polite to break promises. "What do I do?"

"In your situation, if I wasn't running under cover of darkness, I would do what any self-respecting gay woman would."

The mark of how very straight I was. I didn't even know there were standards. "And what is that?"

Rebecca grinned. "Play with power tools."

"Can I play with a hammer and saw instead?" Me and anything pneumatic was a bad idea.

"If you're picturing cutting up frilly wedding dresses then that's just fine."

We both shuddered at the W word. It was good to know that she felt as jarred by Doug's sudden announcement that nuptials were looming. What I couldn't shake was if I really was terrified at the prospect of marrying him or whether I was confused by Berne being near. That's all it was, yes, the shock was making me jittery.

Just shock.

Not Berne.

Nope.

Balls.

I needed more chocolate.

Chapter Seven

WE GOT TO the site only to find that the local men that Doug hired had all but stripped the place already. I had been expecting a slow, leisurely pace that with a little dragging out, could give Rebecca and I time to come to terms with all the grown-up stuff. At this rate, I'd be married and pregnant by the end of the month.

In a word, *merde.*

"Berne, Pip, you want to come over here a minute." Rebecca had her work clothes on, complete with a checked shirt and white vest.

I hadn't missed Berne smile at the fashion statement. Berne had her work jeans on, which wrapped snug against her powerful legs. Still, they weren't so powerful that you could mistake she was a slender, gorgeous walking work of—

"Pip, quit drooling and focus."

I heard my own gasp and my neck itched with the ensuing blush. "I hate you."

Berne laughed as we huddled around Rebecca's little gas stove. "And you, Bebe."

Rebecca frowned. "Did you just call her baby?"

Berne laughed again as I felt myself blush, again.

"*Non.* It is my nickname. Here, in France, you take the first part of your name and répété?" She smiled. "It can be your *prénom* or your . . ." She made the delightful humming sound when thinking. I leaned on my fist, enjoying it. Goodness she enchanted me.

"Surname?" Rebecca asked, prodding me.

Right, focus. Yes, where were we?

"*Oui. Par example,* my brother is Erique and so it would not work . . ."

I wondered how Erique was. I'd only met him once. He was as charming as she was.

" . . . *Alors* they call him Cha-cha."

"That sounds kinda camp," Rebecca said.

I poked her in the back. She shrugged.

"There is nothing camp about Erique Chamonix, believe me," I said. "He has enough charisma to make even you take notice."

Berne smiled at my defence of her brother or maybe it was Rebecca's look of mild disgust.

"Well, funny things do happen to go on in this country. Your sexuality seems void here, right?" Rebecca folded her ink-covered arms across her bust. I decided to ignore one tattoo that I hadn't noticed of a rather . . . well . . . curvaceous woman. She was an anchor away from joining the Navy.

"So, why are we huddled, *Ree-Ree?*" I said, sticking my tongue out for good measure.

"I have a plan." Her eyes lit up as she formulated my name into the mould. Hear it came. I folded my arms, waiting for it. Yup, cue adolescent mirth.

"*PeePee!*" She gripped her stomach as she howled like the adolescent teenage boy she was inside.

I knew her far too well. "It's Pep-pee actually."

Berne nodded in firm agreement.

"Like the cartoon skunk?" Off she howled again.

I sighed at Berne. "You can't take her anywhere," I said in French. "If there's anything remotely gross or any innuendo, she is your girl."

At the sound of my rusty French, Berne beamed. "Very good," she whispered back. "You still remember much."

"I had a good teacher."

The twinkle in her eyes pretty much rooted me to the spot. I was aware that the builders were casting glances at us. Quite possibly, leaning towards her as I was, may suggest to some that I was about to throw myself into her arms. They were strong arms. I had no doubt she'd be able to catch me. In fact once, she'd carried me down a set of stairs. And was it me or was I close enough to just reach out and—

"So, plan, focus on the plan, ladies." Rebecca recovered from her hysterics and cleared her throat.

"You speak French too?" Berne was very impressed. In fact, I could almost see her deciding that she liked Rebecca. A twinkle filled her eyes in such a way that I had only seen when she looked at her family or her beloved best friend, Babs.

"A-level . . . and my tenses suck but I try." Rebecca looked very much as if she was coming to the same conclusion about Berne. What a regular love-fest.

"So are you going to get on with it or swap numbers?" Ooh, didn't that sound less like the joke I'd intended and more . . . well . . . jealous.

"Cool it, *bride to be*," Rebecca said, eyeing me like I'd sprout tentacles. "I worked out a way to lengthen things out for you. You want to get married next week?"

She waved her thumb at the efficient team buzzing in and out of the building. Some were grinning at Berne like they were in love. I didn't blame them.

Rebecca prodded me, again. Oh right, wedding. "You have?" I knew there was a reason I loved her. "Don't stall, out with it!"

I made a point not to look at Berne whose eyes seemed to burn my cheek. Yes, I wasn't a willing bride. It was nerves. That was all.

"Okay. Now every planning permission and plan has been passed. Our boy is hot on his legal bows." Rebecca nodded as though she were leading the troops in battle. "The way to counter his plans is to drag out stabilising the foundations of the place."

It sounded like a logical step to me but what did I know? Solid foundations sounded a good idea.

"Now, 'cause there's that little river trickling away near you, it stands to reason that in the winter, that could rise." Rebecca leaned in, hovering over the gas stove.

Berne nodded. A grave look in her eyes. "*Oui*. It almost reaches the top of the bank."

We all looked at the area in question. That was a pathetic attempt at flooding. "Seriously?"

"*Oui*. This is not far enough downstream to hold much water. Besides, it is only really a stream." She flashed a smile at me. "It is not like the Ardèche, *non*?"

Images of giggling while Berne navigated us in a kayak down the rapids burst into my mind. I hadn't laughed like that before. I wasn't sure if I had since. "*Doug* doesn't know that though, does he?"

Rebecca chuckled a mischievous chuckle. "Are you seriously considering lying to your future husband, Miss Saunders?"

"You want me to have a rugby team?" I nodded at her as she

paled even more than the milk bottle she normally was. "You want me to talk about baby clothes?"

I thought she was going to dive onto her knees and beg me not to for the frown on her face. "The river rises really high, Berne, really, *really* high."

"I cannot say this." Berne's brow crinkled in disgust. She was always someone who felt truth was paramount. "He is paying good money. It would not be fair."

Rebecca turned to her and I wasn't sure if she was going to rugby tackle her. "He wants Pippa to shop for wedding dresses this weekend."

Berne looked at Rebecca who nodded gravely. She looked at me and I did the very same. She rubbed her hand over the back of her neck, something I knew she did when anxious. "It will take a conversation with my father."

Rebecca smiled, punching her on the bicep. "I knew you'd get it."

OVER THE NEXT few days, we worked on breaking the news to Doug. Monsieur Chamonix had been as onside as Berne. I had no idea exactly what she had told him but I was glad of his support.

In normal circumstances, Rebecca had told us all that the basement, which would act as Doug's den, would need to be tanked. She had droned on in great detail about the intricacies but in short it was like making the outside of the basement like the inside of a bath, i.e. waterproof.

I wasn't comfortable with making Doug spend unnecessary money or messing around with the beautiful river. So Rebecca came up with some ingenious solution that involved some kind of sandbag type system that would soak up any water then dry back out. Being mischievous seemed to become her.

Doug had offered to move in the heavy equipment to speed up the process but Berne and her father had told him that they would need a gentle approach. Monsieur Chamonix had even compared the stone to a woman's curves, saying that it needed caressing not bulldozing. Now, I knew were the Chamonix children got their charm. Even Rebecca blushed.

Doug went along with the advice but I could see him fuming at the delay behind polite smiles. He was not a patient man in business, and come to think of it, I wasn't sure why he'd been so with me.

With our cunning plan in action, we started to dig down the eight feet we would need in order to fulfil our flood-proofing. At least it was a great plan until half way through the Friday afternoon when it started to rain.

"Tell me again why we thought this was a good idea," I mumbled as my back protested at the constant digging.

I was out of shape to say the very least. My gym membership had concluded sometime in my mid-twenties. Apparently years without any exercise could possibly make you unfit. Who knew?

"You needed time to build your energy before you start breeding." Rebecca had forgone her builder's attire for shorts and t-shirt.

She hadn't begun inking up her legs yet, thank goodness. I was starting to wonder if she would start playing football for all the tattoos. Either that or join a gang.

"Right," I said and glanced at Berne.

She was far fitter and stronger than the pair of us and seemed as unflappable as ever. I wondered if her skin even knew what sweat was . . . prompting me to get a very vivid reminder of just when she did. Oh boy.

"Staring again." Rebecca threw dirt in my direction. "You know, if you marry *her* already, we can stop digging."

The thought of such a thing made me giggle and not just a soft one. Nope, a teenage girl giggle that made me want to hide my head in the muck.

Berne looked up in response and raised an eyebrow.

"Cut it out." I shoved the spade into the mud. "It's not as if she would want that anyway."

"Want me to ask her?"

Yes. Wait, no, no . . . marrying Doug. Doug, nice manly Doug with fluff on his chin and a milk bottle for a chest. Doug. "What are you going to do this weekend?" I asked, to try and throw her off. "You know, while I'm with mother." I knew the last word was through gritted teeth.

"Berne is heading back to Marseille for a few days," Rebecca said, cocking her head at me. "Thought I'd tag along."

The spade narrowly missed my foot as I rammed it into the dirt. "Really?"

Uh oh, that tone sounded unnaturally high pitched.

"You're shopping for wedding dresses, Pip. Give her a break."

"Whose side are you on?"

The sky opened up with rain as though it understood exactly how I felt. Marseille meant Vivi-vixen time. Stupid name.

"Traitor."

Rebecca held up her hands, her spade clattering into her knee. "I'm on yours, as always." She sighed and held my gaze. "You know, if you talked to her—"

"Marrying Doug." I slammed the spade into the dirt again. Berne turned and looked. "Happy, wonderful fabulous Doug."

So she was going back to Marseille and the old crow waiting for her. I mean, what did she see in the rich old cradle-snatcher anyway? In my mind, Vivienne was old, ugly, and needed dental work. Wait, no . . . she didn't even *have* her own teeth. Yeah.

"Do I need to hide the sharp objects?" Rebecca did look genuinely concerned. Berne looked slightly amused and I was sick and tired of digging.

"No." I saw Doug pull up and threw the spade into the dirt. Fine. If Berne wanted to run off to some old letch then what did I care?

I stomped up to Doug, launched myself into his arms, and put every ounce of confusion and irritation into it. Rebecca was right, I was unhinged. Maybe it was hormones. What was wrong with me?

"Hey, babe." He gripped hold of my waist. "You miss me, huh?"

"Yes." I buried my head in his shoulder. The familiar smell, the scent of his presence. Aftershave. Strong. It made my nose twitch. "You were away too long."

He pulled me to arms-length and then sighed at the dirt on his shoulder. "Pippa, look at this shirt. It was clean on today."

Way to fizzle the moment. "It's just a stupid piece of cloth."

I could feel Berne and Rebecca watching me while Doug put his hands on his hips. "It's handmade and tailored. You know how expensive it is."

Part of me wanted to grip a handful of mud and smother it over his shirt in protest. Of course, that would be the height of bad manners and I was polite. Mud fights were something other people did. Fun people.

The sudden sorrow of that made me burst into tears and I was certain that I may need to be committed for my own safety.

Doug didn't seem to notice, he was too busy walking over to Monsieur Chamonix.

"Shush now. What makes you feel so lost?" Berne's voice beside me made me cry even harder. Her hand on my back made me shudder.

"You are going to Marseille, he is worried about his shirt, and I'm fed up of digging."

The rain, which had started as drizzle, grew heavier.

"I need to see Vivienne. It is our weekend."

Short of saying, "I don't care. Why aren't you pining for me?" there was not a lot I could say to that. I turned away from her and from Doug and trudged up the stone bridge.

"Pepe, where are you going?" Berne, not Doug, Berne was the one following me. Her voice, not his, hers called out to me. She wasn't even supposed to care and she was the one who came after me. There was something very skewed about that. "You must let these things out or they will drive you crazy."

"*You* drive me crazy," was what I wanted to say. Instead I kept walking, Berne catching up.

"What did he do that was so bad?" I could hear that she didn't even want to utter his name. It didn't make me feel better, it just made the tears flow faster. "You looked pleased to see him."

How could I tell her that the only reason I'd thrown myself at him was the desperation to rid her from my thoughts? "I got mud on his shirt."

"I can think of nothing better."

"That's because *you* love me." I clamped my hand over my mouth but the words hung there between us, in our breathing as we started down the hill towards the town.

"*Oui*," Berne whispered. "This will always be true."

I didn't know if that made the aching more prominent or if it made it more bearable. My heart did a happy dance just to confirm it. She still loved me.

"He doesn't understand me." I ran my hands through my mud-soaked hair and sighed. "He doesn't even notice who I am."

"Sometimes we do not see the value in what we assume will forever be ours."

I glared at her. "*You* did."

"Look where it got me." Her voice was filled with defeat. She stared out at the misty rain clouds.

"You think I don't love you?" Anger mixed with confusion and jealousy. "You think I want you to go sauntering off to the city to be with *her*?"

Berne blinked a few times as she took in what I had said. "You love me still?"

"Of course I do!" I put my hands on my hips. I clung on to stop from closing the gap between us. "You think these tears were for him?"

Oh, that sounded cold. That sounded terrible. I was a terrible person.

"Now I am not certain." Berne's eyes searched mine. Her rain-soaked hair dripped water down her strong cheek bones. "You left . . . Pepe . . . I do not understand."

"It doesn't matter." I closed my eyes for a moment. I couldn't do this. There was no choice in the matter. I couldn't explain and I couldn't argue. It was done. I was marrying Doug. I had to. Still, I wanted her to know one thing. "I love you. I hate that you are with someone else and I hate that I left you." I sighed. "I'm so sorry I did that to you. I'm sorry I never called . . . I'm . . . sorry."

I wished I could tell her why. She'd make it all okay, she always did but I couldn't risk it.

Berne's lips slid into a smile. "That is something I have longed to hear. Thank you." She looked up the road the way we'd walked. "What do you wish to do?"

"What I want and what I have to do are two different things. I promised to marry him. He's not you but I haven't wasted eight years of his time not to go through with it."

Wow, wonderful reason to get married. Well done, Saunders.

Berne stood closer. "I meant about the fact we stand in the street . . . we walk far from the house."

To any British person, her proximity was within the massive personal space zone. A place that only people who you really wanted to be there could stand. It felt intimate and made my body fizz with excitement. She was standing there, all nonchalant, mud-soaked and beyond tempting.

"Oh," was about the only thing I could squeeze out.

Her laughter and the twinkle in her eyes undid me. I hurled

myself at her and wrapped my arms around her. I'd never wanted to hug anyone so much before. Okay, so I wanted more, I *needed* more but it would have to do now.

"I make a promise to Vivienne also. It is not a ceremony but I am loyal to her." Berne held me tight. The rain dribbled over us. "*Alors* I do not like that you are with him, I hate this. *Je t'aime tout les temps*." She took my hand and led me up a very familiar side street. "You have not seen my mother in some time. You come, clean, eat."

"What do we do?" I clung to her hand like she could hold me steady in the storm of my own making. "Tell me how to do this?"

"We will do it as we always did." She guided me towards the door. "Together."

Chapter Eight

IF DOUG AND Rebecca had wondered where I'd spent the evening, they said nothing the next day. I was silent at breakfast as Rebecca packed her overnight bag and told me all about her confidence that the foundations would be dug out soon.

All I could think of was the meal in the Chamonix house and how much Madame Chamonix had welcomed me like a long lost child. Although it appeared she was not as close to Berne as her father because they didn't work together, Madame Chamonix doted on Berne and it was returned with fervour.

When I'd sat through lunch with my mother and Doug, I had answered as I was meant to, neither of them noticing that my mind was elsewhere. Berne and I had sat with her parents, chatting about the wonder of the food, the fact that the winds along the Ardèche were unseasonably strong this year, and Marseille's narrow victory over Monsieur Chamonix's belovèd Lyon.

As my mother dragged me onto the plane and we landed in Paris, she was so busy looking at all the designer options that I doubted she noticed my mental absence. Berne had walked me home, her hand strong, holding mine. She had told me of how she planned to take over her father's business, perhaps expand it in times when there were less local jobs into making stone sculptures.

I tried on dress after dress as though I wanted to wear it. Smiling at the right times was easy, I seemed trained to do so. Behind those smiles I replayed one moment over and over.

"You should head inside. You will get cold again."

I couldn't let go of her hand, I couldn't let go of her. "Thank you for taking me home tonight." I felt over the calluses on her palm. "Seeing them, catching up . . . it was perfect."

"Oui, it was."

Her eyes glimmered in the moonlight with unshed tears. In my foolish intention to wipe them away, my thumb traced over her smooth skin.

"Why do you always make me want to sing?"

She nuzzled into my palm and kissed it. "Because around me, you let the truth free, non?"

I brushed her hair out of her eyes and stepped forward. "And what is that truth?" For some reason, my heart had squashed all logic and was driving me onwards.

Berne leaned her forehead to mine. "That you are more than what you appear. That you are another woman inside that shell."

She brushed her lips over mine. Hovered. Waiting. Waiting for me to answer. Electricity rippled up and down my arms as I looked up into soft, gentle, patient eyes. Her eyes.

Uh oh.

"Why can only you see that?"

I wrapped my arms around her shoulders and sank into a kiss. Every pore thudded with the contact, with the relief, with the elation. Her mouth swept circles around my every sense. Her kiss seemed to reach through the mist I had found myself wandering in, pulsing like a light up ahead. Blindly, I followed, my lips desperately searching. Thirsty, parched emotions flooded with the building moment.

I had to breathe. I didn't want to let go. I needed to breathe.

We broke away. Breathy, ragged kisses, wanting, searching for more. Warmth, soft strong shoulders, her hair glossy and thick between my fingers. I placed my forehead to hers. It felt so real, so needed that I whimpered. I needed her so much.

"Bon nuit, *Pepe."*

I pulled her back to me at the sound of her name for me, managing to whisper words between kisses. "Dors Bien, Bebe."

Her response was to pull me closer. She dragged me under once more. Her hands running up and down my back, soothing the aches from the work. Soothing the ache in my heart. "I must go now." She pulled me back and held me at arms' length as her chest rose and fell. "You must be bright for your mother."

She made no attempt to leave. I made no attempt to let her go. Our kisses had confirmed everything to us both. How could we pull this off when just kissing her felt so good?

"I hate mornings."

A movement upstairs finally drew us apart. A sultry smile touched her lips. "You did not hate them so much with me."

Mean, mean and sly. "That's because waking up with you was a reason to greet every day with joy."

Berne's eyes darkened. She moved forward but the sound of Rebecca calling out stopped her.

"Bon nuit." *She shot it at me as though she hated having to say it at all.*

She spun on her heels and strode away. I stood helplessly watching. Unsure that she would ever be that close again. I took in every moment, the rugged rocky roadway under her feet, the way she moved, the way her hair bounced along behind her. I leaned against the wall, wishing I had the courage to follow but knowing that, for her sake, I couldn't. It had to stop. I had to let go, somehow. How did you let go of the love of your life?

"Phillipa, are you listening to me?"

I nodded to my mother, smiling to cover my lapse in concentration. Could heartbreak be an ongoing thing? It had been long enough that I should have been over it by now.

"Do you want these or in the other style?"

Looking down at the shoes, I blinked back Berne's soft smile. If I was marrying her, which ones would I have chosen? I pointed to a pair on the side. I liked how her eyes travelled over my legs when I wore heels. I liked knowing how I held her undivided attention. "Those."

My mother picked up the others, unflattering, boring. "She'll take those," she said to the shop assistant in French.

If that wasn't a reality check, what was? I *wasn't* marrying Berne. She would be drooling over some other woman in Marseille by now.

I was marrying Doug. Somehow I doubted if either he or my mother really cared who lay beneath the polite manners and well-choreographed responses. It didn't matter what I wanted, what I needed. Berne needed me to stay away from her. She was better off without a coward like me.

Besides, I would cease to be myself as soon as I walked down the aisle. I'd cease to be anything but Mrs. Doug Fletcher, the mother of his children.

Yippee for me.

PARIS IN THE springtime.

Technically it was early summer and the city felt alive with an energy I couldn't explain. The weather was warm and the cafés poured out onto the ancient streets. There was nothing like people watching the Parisians. You see, they were so very different to the rest of France. They were the capital's dwellers and they carried themselves with extra confidence. Men sat cross-legged in shirts with jumpers tied around their shoulders. Others in polo-necked jumpers, jeans, and suede jackets. They just looked like culture. Of course, the younger generation looked like they did back home, texting, giggling, or wandering around in packs and yelling to one another.

I'd consoled myself during the afternoon, watching young couples wander to and fro as I stood diligently being fitted for this and that. It reminded me of when I'd visited with Berne. One young boy strolled along with utter confidence. He threw his empty pop bottle in the air as he tried to act nonchalant for the girl beside him. She gazed up at him, attempting to look bored but I could see her nerves from where I stood. An odd ritual that I was sure happened the world over for the young and in love.

I'd followed Berne down the same street towards the Eiffel tower. She'd been animated, dazzling me with the history of the city and making me laugh at her impressions. I knew I'd carried the same adoring look, attempting to cover it with some kind of coolness.

Young love in Paris, what a perfect way to start the summer.

I had lived in that memory during the evening until Doug and my father flew up to meet us for dinner. The very chic restaurant was exactly what most women would be awed by. The cuisine was perfect, the maître d' was everything you could wish him to be and Doug looked every inch a prince.

I felt as though I were watching the whole thing on a screen. Someone else's life that I'd stumbled into. How had that happened?

I'd kissed her. She'd kissed me back.

"So how is the little project coming along?" my mother asked when Doug went to the men's room. She had an odd smile on her face that made me wonder if she'd drunk a bottle of red by herself.

"I'm certainly feeling it in my back."

She and my father laughed as he patted her hand. Had they *both* been drinking?

"How far along?" Her eyes twinkled.

"Not long, it's going to be closer to Christmas than I would like."

My father clasped his hands together. "How wonderful. Such a gift for the new year."

Quite taken aback that they were so pleased with my professional life, I found myself quite flushed. They'd never really taken an interest in my work before.

"When will we get pictures?" The tone in my mother's voice made me smile. She really was interested, wow.

"I'm thinking of creating a study, you know at each stage of development, so that I can document it." I picked at the napkin. "It'll be good to have when we go for more later on."

"You sound so calm about it all," my father said. "How wonderful that you feel so confident."

"Well, I've got great support and I'm not alone. So it's perfect and perfect timing really after leaving *that* place."

My mother "mmm'd" in agreement. "They never appreciated you, I told your father . . ." She nodded to him. "Didn't I? I said, 'They don't know what a gem they have.'"

"She did," my father confirmed.

Wow, I'd never seen this side of them before.

"And bagging a catch like Doug," she said, making my father nod in hearty agreement. "Wonderful man—"

"Wonderful," my father added.

"And to think in college we were worried." She laughed.

I didn't. How had I made her worry in college? I'd had the best marks in the year for a start.

"Hanging around with those girls who were *less* than reputable."

"You mean Rebecca?" I had never been one for a million friends. Women tended to find me hard to figure out, so most of my social group was male.

"Yes, well, the less we say about her the better."

"Now, Daphne," my father said. "Rebecca is a wonderful young woman."

"Oh, you would say that after she fixed your car." My mother looked over her thick-rimmed glasses at me. "Hopefully now, you'll move in more acceptable circles."

Are you kidding me? was the first thought, followed by a sudden nausea that my mother felt such a thing about Rebecca. "She *is* acceptable."

"With all those tattoos? And that hair . . ." My mother clapped her hands in a dramatic show of disgust. "No wonder she can't get a man."

"She doesn't want one," I hissed through my teeth.

"What is she going to do when you're busy, hmm?" my mother asked. "What then? She can't just tag along everywhere."

"Why not?" I knew that was borderline teenager but I felt like someone had thrown the ice bucket down my back. "A ring doesn't mean a lobotomy."

At least I hoped it didn't. What if that's what Doug would order? I shook that thought free. Not good.

"You hardly want her *influencing* the little one." My mother beamed at my stomach.

I looked down to try and see what she was gawking at.

"Little what?"

Had I dropped something?

My father laughed. "You were the same, Daphne . . . grumpy and in a daze." He beamed at her, patting her hand as though she were a pet pooch. "Such a torrid time."

My mother leaned into him. "Sent you out to buy onions at three in the morning . . ." She turned to me. "You'll need to take a good look at those toes because if Doug is anything to go by you'll be twice the size I was."

The penny finally dropped.

My stomach seemed to drop into the abyss with it.

Oh shit.

"Everything okay?" Doug sat next to me.

I stared ahead, my mother's mouth moving yet I couldn't hear her words.

"Pippa, you okay?"

Oh shit.

They thought I was . . .

Oh shit . . .

Nausea swished around in my stomach. All that perfect French food cried out in panic and readied arms to make a break for it.

"She'll get like that." My mother was in my face now, her hand on my head. "We should get her back to the hotel, rest up."

Why, why would they think such a thing?

Was I?

Oh no . . . no, no, no . . . no . . .

I wasn't . . . was I?

In panic I started cycling through my memory. When was the last onslaught from period purgatory?

Was it two . . . ?

Wait . . .

Had I had it that month?

The new car smell made me realise we must be in the car. My father was chatting to Doug happily in the front about stocks and shares. My mother rubbed my arm.

Had I had my period?

I needed to call Rebecca . . .

She'd know . . . She was good with these things.

Why didn't I write the stupid things down like she'd told me to?

"Slow breaths," my mother said. "I'll get you some ginger tea when we get back. Was a lifesaver for me."

I'd kissed Berne.

I could be having Doug's child.

He wanted to get married.

I wanted to go back to London, to Winston, and beg for my old job back. I also wanted to take Winston, drive to Marseille, and beg Berne to take me back.

Uh oh. That was *really* not good.

My chest tensed up so tight it was painful to breathe.

"Calm," my mother urged. "It'll pass over."

My shoulders decided I wasn't getting enough air and joined in, moving forward and back in support. The food continued its little revolution inside, charging to and fro with wild abandon.

"Come on now. We're at the hotel." My mother guided me out of the car, Doug's hand was on my back. The sweet reception girl waved hello.

"Hold onto me now." My mother cooed like she had when I was a small child. The lift slid into motion.

"You know what it is yet?" my father asked.

"Bound to be a boy first time, don't you think?" Doug said. "I mean, I'd love a girl too but be good to have an heir to hold the name steady."

"Best way," my father said. "We did the same."

My own heartbeat thumped in my ears. Why had they turned into something from *Pride and Prejudice*? An heir? Doug wasn't the king of England.

Unable to hurl a tirade of abuse, I let my mother lead me from the lift and hurried into our penthouse rooms. It was less like a usual hotel suite and more like a large apartment.

I staggered up the steps, into the bedroom, and shut the door behind me.

"Be fine . . ." I managed. "Bathroom."

I could hear them all laughing in delight, more baby talk ensuing. I scrambled for my mobile and dialled Rebecca.

Ring, ring . . . ring, ring.

I could visualise the awful ringtone in my ears. Why she thought that TV theme tune was cool, I couldn't fathom. The show had finished well over a decade ago.

Ring, ring . . . ring, ring.

"Pick up!"

Where was she? I slumped down onto the bed. The realisation buckled my legs.

She was in Marseille.

With Berne.

Berne and Viper-Vivienne, the creepy, toothless, old bat.

Ring, ring . . . ring, ring.

"I need you . . . Pick up the phone." I held my forehead with my palm, hoping it would calm the pounding behind my eyes.

"Pip?"

Relief washed over me, then tears. "You sober enough to be trusted?"

"Pip, it's ten o'clock and I had a glass with dinner."

Oh, so the bat cooked. Bet she *was* like Mary Berry—focus!

"When was my last red mark?"

"Are you seriously—?"

"Please." I sounded like I was appealing for help on a desert island. I was half ready to unfold my clothes in the shape of letters and flag a passing helicopter.

"Last week," Rebecca said. "Yeah, you ate us out of Carte Dor, remember?"

"So I'm *not* pregnant?"

Rebecca sucked in her breath. "Not since last Tuesday. What is going on?"

Relief flooded through every pore I had. Oh thank you, thank you, thank you. "Doug said I was."

"He what?" The anger in her voice made me smile, ever my hero. "What did he do . . . ? When—?"

"Wait." I knew what her next question was. "We haven't . . . not since . . ."

I didn't remember when I'd last let Doug stay over. I'd been in flux since I'd left work.

"Why did he tell my parents?"

"He *told* your parents?" I could hear her explaining to someone, the muffled tones as she covered the mouthpiece.

Berne's voice in the background made me sigh in relief then tense that she wasn't alone. Another voice, a sultry voice. My stomach revolted at the sound of the toothless cradle-snatcher's soft tones.

I dived for the bathroom. "I need to go."

"Wait . . . Pip . . . I'm here . . . talk to me."

I shook my head, stupid because she couldn't see me, but it made me feel better.

"It's Pip," Rebecca said to someone in the background. "Doug told her parents she was pregnant."

"She is?" Berne's voice sounded like she wanted to strangle someone.

"Who is Pip *encore?*" The third voice. *Her* voice. "She is your girlfriend, Rebecca?"

"Er . . . yeah. She's . . . er . . . my girlfriend."

Way to sound convincing Rebecca.

"No, she's not pregnant. He's wrong. He's also an idiot."

It had to be *her* if Rebecca was lying. Oh that hurt. My heart skipped several beats in response as if it wanted to stop then and there.

Vivienne didn't sound old, she sounded like she probably looked, gorgeous.

"I have to go."

I disconnected the call and turned the phone off. I hadn't even bothered to switch on the lights in my haste to slam out reality.

I rolled off the bed and walked to the un-shuttered window.

Paris carried on below, the lights of the city a stream of reds and whites. Summer in the air and the smell of possibility, of dust, and fragrant sweetness. Sounds of mopeds and distant life buzzed on. I'd always adored France, adored the history, adored the people and the flow of life.

Berne had brought me here that summer weekend. We'd travelled up on the TGV train and stayed near to the Champs D'Élysées. Berne had shown me the city, every quiet forgotten corner that hid from the tourists' eyes. A little café which made the best pizza that I've ever tasted.

The owner was from Portugal. His laugh had filled the small place. His wife bounced their baby boy on her lap as she chatted with another woman. Berne's hand in mine beneath the silvery-shined table. Her whispered purrs in my ear as she challenged me to order. I'd been so terrified to speak the language, so worried I'd get it wrong.

A stroll along the moonlit Seine. Her gentle hum as the tourist boats swished by. Water lapped against the wall below us. I was due to go home for a week after our time there. I hadn't wanted to go back, to leave but she wrapped me in her arms.

"We're only a moon away, *non*?"

I looked up now, tonight, at the same full-beaming face high in the clear night sky. We couldn't have been the first to use her quiet smile as a messenger while two hearts beat apart.

Somewhere out there, I kept the comfort that Berne was gazing up in wonder too.

THE MOON SHONE in glorious wonder over the Mediterranean. It was still tonight, the heat building as it always did this time of year. Marseille was an eclectic city, one Berne both loved and loathed. In her heart, she was as much part of the Ardèche as the rocks themselves. City life had never been for her but it had been too lonely in Ajoux-Sur-Rhône. She had great friends in the city and it was where Vivienne lived but it was nothing without Pippa.

"You are quiet tonight."

Berne turned and smiled at Vivienne, taking the offered glass of champagne. "It is a beautiful night, there is nothing like a full moon."

Vivienne placed a kiss on her neck and Berne relaxed into it but her thoughts strayed far from the lips she could feel to the lips she desired.

"This has much to do with your new colleague?" Vivienne smiled and touched the back of her hand to Berne's cheek. "I know you too well. I know when you worry."

Sighing, Berne turned back to the room. Rebecca had left not long after the phone call to drive back to Ajoux-Sur-Rhône. It had taken every ounce of self-control for her not to go too. If Rebecca was worried, then no doubt she had good cause.

"This man who her girlfriend marries, he is a bad man?"

Was he? Was there any sign that Doug had done anything but adore Pippa?

"*Non*, he is just. He does not always think before he acts."

Vivienne chuckled and held out a hand. "What lover ever does?"

Berne knew what the gesture was, where Vivienne was going with the look in her eyes. It had always been enough, enough to make her feel something. Not a fiery burning need like she'd known before. No, not a soul-soothing relief, not even close to the emotion she had once felt and yet it had been sufficient.

That was before she had kissed Pippa again. What was meant to be a moment of memory and nothing more had reignited every flame she'd spent so long fighting to extinguish.

Foolish to think that any caress of Pippa's could be resigned to a single second. It was so foolish to have given in. They had been in each other's presence a week and already they had come undone. Already they had betrayed the people who loved and trusted them. Never before had Berne lied to Vivienne but to speak the truth about Pippa was madness. She would never allow her to work alongside Pippa. Regardless of their arrangement, Vivienne expected faithfulness and Berne just wasn't the kind to be anything but.

Yet, she'd kissed her. She'd already been unfaithful. Why did it feel as though being here was the crime?

All that deceit seemed to be worthwhile, for the sound of those words, "I love you," echoed in every thudding of her heart.

Pippa still loved her.

"You must not fret so." Vivienne's voice grew more insistent. "She will only break Rebecca's heart anyway, *non*?"

"What do you mean?" The instinct to leap to Pippa's defence only barely restrained, Berne tried to cover her frown as though she were contemplating Vivienne's words.

"If she loved her so much, she would leave this man. She would not play games."

"Like we do not?" A hint of bitterness seeped in. Years of frustration, heartbreak, and molten pain fuelled her grumpy mood.

"Neither of us is married, Berne." The bored tone irritated her further as Vivienne sipped on her champagne. "What games are there?"

A dramatic sigh made Berne's stomach clench. She hated it when Vivienne did this. What did she know? "The ones where you hide me from your life like a lover hiding from a spouse."

Having never complained of the situation before, it seemed so hypocritical for her to do so now. Still, the knowledge that she was nothing more than a sordid secret sparked a sudden need to get away, to run, to be free of the chains.

To run to Pippa. She loved her. So why weren't they together? Why had she left? Why had they wasted so many years?

"You know why, Berne. I cannot do my job if my private life is questioned." Vivienne narrowed her eyes. "And, I don't like people thinking I'm like your new *friend* or the one you insist on keeping close."

"What are they?" Berne's anger bristled. "What makes them so bad?"

"I need men to find me attractive, you know that." Vivienne rolled her eyes. "They need to think they can capture my heart." A slow smile played across her lips. "But they are not the one I wish to seduce, *non*?"

Berne's mobile buzzed in her pocket. She yanked it out and read the text.

"It is Rebecca. She has managed to talk to her. She is okay."

How true that was she didn't know but it wasn't her concern anymore. Pippa was not hers to worry over. The pain made it hard to swallow. Pippa wasn't hers but she still loved her.

"You wish to waste the evening thinking of some stranger?" Vivienne's voice oozed with impatience. She'd never needed to wait for anything. With her looks, her status, everything fell into her lap with a simple smile. Berne, much to her own disgust, had been much the same.

How could she not have been flattered that this actress wanted her? It beat brooding over Pippa, it dulled the ache.

It was only to be a brief affair but that had stretched out into nine long years and she was still at Vivienne's beck and call. She was still no closer to being treated as someone Vivienne truly loved and respected.

But then, Vivienne didn't know her like Pippa did. There was only one person who came close to it. Someone she really needed. "I should go and see Babs."

Not waiting to look at Vivienne, she hurried out of the door and strode away. The claustrophobic secrecy squeezed at her chest.

As she rounded the corner from the apartment, she fought to suck in the hot humid air. She pulled her mobile from her pocket and dialled Rebecca.

"Berne?"

"*Oui.* She is okay, really?"

Rebecca sighed. "Yeah, I mean. She's freaked. Which she needs to get over by the morning or she's gonna face some uncomfortable questions."

Barmy summer heat, moon glow overhead, Berne made quick work of the journey to Babs's place. Hopefully her old friend would be alone. It was wishful thinking but maybe she was. "Why would they question her?"

"Because . . ." Rebecca sighed. "Look, I know that whatever happened between you was epic but she's supposed to be marrying prince charming."

Berne heard the sound of clanging and Rebecca huffing.

"I mean, he's like *the* dream for her parents. He's rich, he's handsome and they want her breeding future heirs."

"That is her dream too?"

"No," Rebecca said. "You and I both know that Pippa's dream would be to own some kind of wood-crafting business and eat chocolate."

Again more clanging. What was that noise?

"Thing is, she'll do what her parents want and what Doug wants . . . and regret it every single day."

"Why?" Berne stared up at Babs's window. She was in, the light was on, the main light. Maybe she was alone?

"Manners, politeness . . . social expectation. Her brother is a colonel in the army, her sister is married to some barrister. Pip wouldn't dare rock that image."

"That does not sound like the woman I know." Berne had no doubt that she knew the real, indefinable, raw passion that was Pippa. Her laughter, her wish to dance under the moonlight like they did in the movies simply to feel the romance of it.

"Probably because you bothered to fall in love with who she really is."

Rebecca clanged something again and swore under her breath.

"What is happening with you?"

Rebecca grunted. "Stupid car broke down."

"Where are you?"

"Haven't the foggiest. I got off the motorway or whatever you guys call it and I'm somewhere between there and Ajoux."

Guest or no guest, Berne decided that she would have to break up the interlude. Babs would love the adventure of it anyway. "Stay with the car. We will come get you."

"Look, that's lovely but I'm sure you and Vivienne want some peace and quiet—"

"I am not with Vivienne . . . I leave . . . I . . . *alors* . . . My friend, Babs, we will be there soon."

Rebecca chuckled and a car door closed. A second later the lock sounded. "I'm more than happy to get off the spooky country road then."

She disconnected and took the steps to Babs's apartment two at a time. Anything but wander around staring up at the moon.

She hammered on the door. Perhaps it was too late for such noise but she didn't care. She felt like she was breaking free. It felt good. *Vive la liberté.*

"What the—?" Babs face broke into a grin and she hurled herself into Berne's arms. "You are too long away from me!"

Berne offered the double-kissed greeting, walked in, and grabbed Babs's keys. "You fancy rescuing someone?"

"She worth my time?"

Berne smiled. "Let's just say that she is a friend of someone who you may wish to see again."

Babs picked up her door keys without even casting a glance at the mess behind her. She was much like Pippa in that sense, organised chaos. "Renee?"

Berne shook her head, searching for the little Clio.

"Stephanie?"

"We need to get to Ajoux-Sur-Rhône," Berne said, opening the door to the little red car. They'd had some great adventures in her.

"Emilie?"

Berne got in the passenger side and handed the keys to Babs. "*Non.*"

"I cannot think who." Babs started the car and screeched out of the parking space. "I have not seen you this happy in years—" She slammed on the brakes. "*Non?*"

"Keep driving."

Berne couldn't hide her smile even when the driver behind them held down his horn for nearly a minute.

After hurling expletives out of her window, Babs roared the car into life, whipping in and out of the traffic like always. "Could it be . . . ? Pepe returns?" She scowled and wagged her finger. "I am still angry with her."

"I know." Berne squeezed Babs's knee. "And you will forgive her as quickly as I did."

"So she is back for you?"

Swallowing back the answer, Berne concentrated on the city whipping past.

"Bebe?"

"She is marrying someone . . . a man . . . I am working on their house." Berne shrugged as Babs swung the car through a gap in the traffic and tootled up the road, leaving the city. "*Mais* . . . she told me that she loves me still."

"She does?" Babs honked the horn for good measure. "She does not love him?"

Berne shook her head. No, she knew that, she could see it in Pippa's desperation. She was fond of him but she didn't look at him the same way.

Babs's black hair whipped behind her as she rolled the window down. "Then we need to bring her home, Bebe."

"I cannot do that." She wanted to. It would be heaven to wake up in Pippa's arms again. "There is Vivienne—"

"*Merde* to that. She is not Pippa." Babs honked the horn again. "We'll get her back."

Trying not to get carried away with Babs's enthusiasm, Berne attempted to turn the talk to more mundane things.

She hadn't seen Babs in months. If she was honest, Babs and Vivienne had hated each other at first sight and so it had been difficult for nine years. Not that it stopped them meeting when Babs was home. It was harder to pretend she wasn't in the city when Vivienne wanted to see her that was all.

Nine long years of faking it.

She shook her head as the city roads became narrow country lanes. Garish lights faded and the blissful quiet of the country made her rest her head back. Babs was a busy woman. Head of her own business, an internationally renowned business. Not bad for a five-foot-nothing dynamo. Berne smiled. Pippa had dubbed her the Flying Frenchwoman. She was right and it was good to know that energy hadn't faded.

Babs hurtled around a bend and Berne spotted a car at the side of the road. "There."

"*Non* . . . I would not have guessed." Berne tutted at Babs's sarcasm as they pulled over.

They both got out of the car but Berne took out her mobile. Rebecca was in a foreign country, alone on a road. It was best to warn her. "I will call."

"Please tell me that's you closing in on the car," Rebecca said.

Tempted to tease, Berne waved into the wing mirror. "*Oui.* You can come out. We do not bite."

"Speak for yourself," Babs shouted from behind her.

The door opened and Rebecca got out into the moonlight, her bright hair evident even in this light. She was everything that Pippa had described, and every bit as loyal as Berne had always imagined.

She was, well, English. Pale, with reddish-blonde hair, at least under the dye. She was stockier than Pippa, more swagger in her walk. The tattoos and the fashion made her a walking statement of, "I don't care," yet under it, Berne could tell she was sensitive.

Rebecca also had a real maternal side to her too. Berne had watched her mothering Pippa, affectionate and gentle in her chastising. She knew that her friend was struggling and she was trying to help her.

Berne wanted to ask her why, why had Pippa left. Why had

she run if she still loved her like she did? Only pride stopped her. If Pippa wished her to know, she would open up in her own time. She hoped.

Berne turned to look at Babs and smiled at the glint in her eyes. Rebecca was everything Babs made impassioned vocal arguments against. She hated tattoos, she hated odd hair colours, she hated cocky arrogance, and she often left women when their fashion sense irritated her.

Pippa had said Rebecca didn't date short women. She didn't date women who embraced fashion as art. According to Pippa, Rebecca felt they were false, shallow, and unintelligent.

Berne smiled at that. She and Pippa had made a bet, which one would crack first. Which heartbreaker would win the battle of France versus England?

"Hi." Rebecca smiled, motioning to the car. "Thanks for coming to my rescue."

"*Pas de problème.* This is my friend, Barbara Henri." Berne didn't miss the appreciative glance that Babs gave Rebecca. "Or as Pippa named her . . . Babs."

"Er . . . *Bonjour*—I mean *soir . . . bonsoir.*" Rebecca wiped her hands on her jeans and held one out. "I'm Rebecca. Pippa calls me a lot of things but none of them are repeatable."

Babs's hearty laugh made Rebecca jolt but then Babs laugh did that to most people. "Then our girl has not changed, *non.*" She gripped hold of Rebecca's hand, yanked her forward, and placed two kisses on her cheeks.

Poor Rebecca looked shell shocked.

"Let's head to the village. It is better to stay there. Maman will wish to feed us tomorrow." Berne doubted that they could fix the car in the dark. It wasn't going anywhere.

"You sound like Pip now," Rebecca said as they climbed into the Clio. "She is always thinking of her next meal." Rebecca met Berne's eyes as Babs slammed the car into motion. "Which she didn't do before coming here."

"Food is more than just to sate the appetite, *non?*" It was good to know that she'd made an impact on Pippa's life, on her passions. It had been a joy to show her France. Watching her experience it and fall in love with it stirred something inside her. She hadn't meant to fall in love.

The eighteen year old who had wandered into her flat during a summer storm had stunned her. Drenched from head to toe, she had a dreamy look in her eyes, as if she understood the feeling in the music.

Eighteen and way too young for her. Berne was ten years older, she was training to be a gendarme. She'd waited until then to help out her father but had found herself in the city more and more.

Pippa had wanted to learn everything she could about France, about working with wood and stone, about the language. It had been hard to ignore the lingering looks, the feelings etched across her gentle, soft features. Pippa didn't even realise she was doing it half the time.

It just made her all the more pleasurable to be around. She cared, really cared, about the mundane to the profound. She wanted to know how Berne felt, what she was thinking. Pippa reached her in a way that no one had ever come close to. And, she had been eighteen.

Berne had been given a gentle warning from her father when he met Pippa that Berne was to do her job, tutor the girl, and make sure she had a wonderful time.

That was it.

Yet, her parents had been delighted when Pippa wriggled her way in to Berne's heart. She'd never seen them as happy for her. Of course, they had to keep it away from the friend of Pippa's family.

He had given them a huge contract that had given the family much needed money. It had taken seven years to complete the Gite village but it had secured her parents retirement years. Pippa had always been mindful of the risk their relationship could have. Berne often wondered if that was the reason why Pippa had left.

They hurtled over the humpback bridge at the bottom of the village, jolting her back to the car. Babs whooped and Berne laughed at the tickle in her stomach.

"Dumb question but one, is this car stolen?" Rebecca asked and Berne turned to her. "And two, where are the seat belts?"

"Relax, my little English lightbulb," Babs purred. "You are in safe hands with me."

Berne noticed a slight blush creep over Rebecca's cheeks or was that just her eyes in the dim light?

"She thinks she is amusing," Berne offered in case Babs had caused offence.

Rebecca winked. "Only if you slow down, my little French lunatic."

Babs roared with laughter once more and Berne relaxed back into the seat as Rebecca grinned her way. Berne smiled to herself as she looked from Babs to Rebecca and out of the window.

The competition was on. Interesting . . . very, very interesting.

Chapter Nine

SUNLIGHT STREAMED THROUGH the open windows and roused me into consciousness. I had fallen asleep to the sound of lovers giggling in the street below and woken to the buzzing rumble of a city on its way to lunch.

Staring up at the white ceiling, I let myself doze to the beeps and roaring engines. It felt to me as though Paris was almost a country of its own in some respects. There was no doubting that this was France, yet Paris embodied a unique spirit all of its own.

A tapping on my door swept my thoughts from the vibrant world below to the mess of a life I had found myself in. For the first time in years I seemed to wake up to the fact that I was living someone else's life. This wasn't me, this place I'd ended up wasn't me. Not that it was a bad place but nevertheless it wasn't where I felt happy.

Groaning, I put my hands over my face with the admission. I wasn't happy. What did I do about that?

"Phillipa Grace Saunders, you open this door right now!"

Uh oh, my mother was in a rip. What a way to start the morning. I glanced at the window and thought about scaling down the side of the hotel. Anything was better than dealing with hurricane Daphne Saunders.

Another thundering knock made me roll out of bed and I yanked open the door, sending my mother sprawling. She'd obviously been listening at the lock.

Oops.

"Is there something wrong?" I thought about helping her up but she was faster than a sprinter on an Olympic track, leaping to her feet like a starter pistol had fired.

"You lock yourself away like goldilocks, give us all a scare, and you ask me if something is wrong?"

"It was Rapunzel," I said, attempting to help her to straighten out her clothes.

"What?" She batted my hands away.

"Rapunzel was the one in the tow—Oh, never mind. Is Doug around?"

My mother shook her head. "No. Your father has gone with him to the new centre. You're lucky that he is so patient with you."

The relief of not having to face him made my mother's words take until I'd half dressed to sink in.

"What?" I asked, yanking up my too tight dress. Had the stupid thing shrunk overnight?

"He's gone to the—"

"Not that, why am *I* lucky?" And why wouldn't the dress budge?

"You have so many faults, darling. You know that. Most women without as many would be lucky to bag a man like him."

I blinked a few times as I stared at her. Wow, it was good to know how much she thought of me. "And what faults are they?"

"I'm your mother. It's my job to be honest—"

"What faults?" I yanked up my dress and closed my eyes at the ripping sound.

Wonderful. Just wonderful.

"Now look what you've done." My mother tutted as she hovered. "Can't even dress yourself."

I threw the dress onto the floor. "Then I'll just wear something that *I* want to wear." I stomped into the apartment-like space of the main room, greeting the maid who was lurking, to my overnight bag. I pulled out my comfortable cargo shorts and a shirt. My favourite shirt.

"We are in Paris," my mother said. "Have some decorum, girl."

"It's a French rugby top. I'll fit in just fine." It was silly to feel such defiance lifting me but so good. "And I'm not pregnant."

My mother frowned. "Pardon?"

"I'm *not* pregnant. I know that you wanted another grandchild but I'm not."

If I'd expected her to mourn, I was quite taken aback by her sly grin. "Atta girl."

"Excuse me?" I looked at the maid who raised her eyebrows and went into the bedroom. At least *she* could escape.

"Sometimes you need wiles to keep them honest. Good way to hurry his commitment too."

Never before had I actually smacked my palm to my head but that moment was the first. When did I wake up in the dark ages?

I strode to the window to check what kind of vehicles there were down below. No, that was definitely a brand new Merc pulling in. We hadn't gone into a time warp.

"What are you doing?" My mother peered over my shoulder. "Has he come back?"

"No, I'm looking for horse and carts."

My mother put her hand to my forehead. "Maybe you're coming down with something?"

I wriggled free and picked up my bag. "Is Doug coming back here tonight?"

My mother nodded. "He has booked the opera."

"Good," I said. "You've always loved the opera."

I needed to get away. I needed to think without distractions, without anyone influencing me. I needed to remember who I was again and understand what *I* wanted.

"Tell Doug that I am going offline for a few days. I'll give him a call when I'm ready to talk."

"Phillipa—"

"I will call him then. Have fun." I hurried out of the door and power walked to the lift.

In the reception, the sweet lady behind the counter bid me a cheery good morning. I smiled back then skidded to a stop on the shiny marble floor.

The woman raised a bored Parisian eyebrow at me.

"Can I ask you a question?" I said in French.

"You already did, Madame." Her lips twitched in a smile.

I cocked my head. Rebecca smiled like that quite often. "It's a personal question."

Again that smile. "Madame?"

"Do I look happy to you?" What a stupid thing to come out with. I needed a straightjacket not a wedding ring. "I mean, do I look like I should be with Doug?"

"Madame, I—"

"I'm asking you as a person not a service provider."

She looked into my eyes with deep brown ones. Every bit Parisian elegance but no doubt there was Spanish or Italian in her genes. "Honestly?"

"Please."

"*Non.*"

And cold water seemed to drench me from head to toe. "Will you tell me why?"

She wagged her finger in the air. "Madame, the fact that you ask *me* of all the people here should tell you something, *n'est pas?*"

Should it? I looked around at the other staff members.

"What do you mean?" She looked perfectly reliable and helpful. She was friendly. "You're the receptionist."

"*Oui*, Madame."

The third time she'd smiled at me in that knowing way. When did Rebecca use that smile? Why did it make me think of—?

I looked at the porters, the maids, the staff buzzing around, and back to her.

"You're gay, aren't you?"

Her smile turned to a charming grin.

Uh oh.

"Is this your way of telling me that you think *I'm* gay?" Okay, so I was in love with Berne but that had never registered as anything other than, well, I was in love with Berne.

"Madame, if my girlfriend was not the security guard, I would happily speak of it to you all day."

The laughter burst out from my lips before I could hold it in. She was beyond charming and now I knew why I'd liked her. She was like Rebecca, being gay had nothing to do with it but being a cheeky charmer did.

"In that case, I'd better not ask too many questions." I smiled at the rather intimidating security guard watching us like a hawk. "She's a lot taller than me."

The receptionist laughed. "Pay no attention to it. She is nothing but a big bear."

Leaving her with a smile, I headed out into the busy Parisian afternoon. I dodged the line of Spanish students yabbering on about seeing the Eiffel Tower and over to Doug's driver.

He was one of two men I'd seen who Doug used on business trips or left to babysit me when he thought I'd get lost in a foreign city. It was sweet and irritating all at once. I still wasn't sure if I liked the fact he was attentive or annoyed that he thought I couldn't cope.

I could cope.

I was adept and in contr—

"Careful, Madame." The driver caught me as I tripped over my own foot.

"Thanks. You fancy dropping me at the station?"

He smiled. "I can take you anywhere, Madame. There is no need for the train."

And that way Doug could keep tabs on me. "No, thank you. I've got some girlie things to do . . . you know . . . wedding and all that . . . Can't have you spilling the beans now, can I?"

Poor guy lost me at spilling beans, but nevertheless nodded and beamed. "Whatever you wish."

THE TGV WAS one of my favourite ways to see the country. France was so beautiful and so vibrant that each moment was like gazing at living art. No wonder the renaissance artists had found inspiration here. France was sunshine to the creative mind, easing the depth of imagination from the soul and basking it with light.

Each region, each department in the country was different in personality, in accent, and yet unmistakably French. Berne was much like that, unique in every single sense but there was no doubt that her blood ran blue.

La vie en bleu, life in the blue of France. It had been an education for me. The sing-song sound of *l'accent du midi*, made my schoolgirl French useless. Factor in the multitude of cultures crammed into the packed Côte d'Azur during the heat of summer and it was a nightmare. Berne had given me a basic overview of stereotypes. I could never tell if she was teasing or not but I took her word for it.

The city of Nice and the Niçois had a Latin outlook and temperament, a zest for the good life. She made them sound Italian in a way. Personally, I'd assumed all French people were like this, and if I was honest, I still did.

People from Monaco, the Monégasques often were more refined. A bit like my upbringing I guessed—posh and liked dressing up. I wondered if they had the same odd traditions and rituals as the Brits did.

The people of Marseille were very proud of their city. A little more rough and ready than the rest of the region and massive fans of football. Marseille was a base for Berne because it had more of a community. At least this is what she told me. I never ventured anywhere that constituted rainbow flagged.

And yes, that was exactly as it sounded. I, at eighteen, was slightly homophobic. Laughable as I fell in love with a woman but it was true. Lesbians, or at least what I thought constituted a lesbian, terrified me. They still did in many ways. I knew Rebecca and so I understood how she saw the world but some of her *acquaintances* had scared the living French fries out of me.

One woman seemed so intent on staring at me, without blinking, and competing with everything I said that I was sure she wanted to attack me. Rebecca had later said that she'd found me charming. I couldn't really say I returned the sentiment.

Rebecca, Berne, and her best friend Babs were different to me. They had passed through my odd little fear barrier and were people. In Berne's case, I was also slightly biased. She found it amusing.

Instead she'd shown me the south of France from a point of view I could understand. We'd explored art galleries, museums, little villages off the beaten track. She'd kayaked me down the Ardèche, taken me cycling in the Alpes d'Huez. We'd tried dishes like bouillabaisse, which I'd hated, and Niçois salade, which I adored. I had never been a drinker and so wine wasn't a great idea but there had been a wine-tasting day. I still couldn't remember much of it.

France. Berne. Both were ingrained in my consciousness. It meant excitement to me, it meant freedom and adventure, it meant love.

Before I'd succumbed to her effortless charisma, Berne had given me tasks to help me learn her language. One had been to catch the TGV from Marseille to Perpignan and get passengers on the train to teach me "La Marseillaise."

Berne had sat a few seats behind me, which I hadn't known at the time, and had watched the chaos unfold. By the time I'd gotten to Perpignan, the packed train was in full voice.

I'd gotten three marriage proposals and had learned every word. Turning around at the station and seeing the smile on her face had been a moment etched in my memory ever since.

In that moment, I had understood that I'd felt more than friendship. I'd never been more scared in my life. The building torrent of feeling was not something I'd ever experienced before.

Berne against the sunshine through the window, the scent of the dusty station outside. Berne lounging in the seat, a proud smile on her face and hunger in her eyes. It was the first time I'd caught her looking at me like it. My heart had hammered in response. My feet had lost the ability to move.

Berne.

My mobile vibrated in my pocket. I pulled it out and looked down at the caller ID. "Hey, did you get back to Ajoux okay?"

"Yeah," Rebecca answered. She was crunching crisps. The sound made me hungry. "Weirdest thing is, I got a call from your mother."

I hadn't eaten when I'd gotten up and my stomach rumbled. I ran my hand over it to try and quell its protest. Why didn't I pick something up on the way? I could never concentrate when I was hungry.

"You listening or what?"

"Hmm?" The man across from me had some kind of roll. It looked yummy. Ham, was there ham in there?

"Pip!"

"Right, yes . . . my mother."

"Yeah, your mother," Rebecca mumbled between crunches. "She said you went AWOL on her."

Maybe I should go see if there was a buffet cart. Did the TGV have one? I swore I'd brought lunch when Bern—

"Pip, focus!" Rebecca sighed in the background.

My stomach rumbled louder. I was starving now.

"Pepe, where are you?"

Berne's voice brought my stomach to attention. In fact, my whole body did an about turn.

"On the train." I had no idea why I'd whispered like I was in a library.

"Where are you going on the train?" Berne whispered back.

Her response made me chuckle. It was official, I was a loony. "*Je ne sais pas.*"

"You do not know?" Berne tutted. "I do not think that is true."

My first thought to flee the stifling baby talk in Paris had driven me to the train. I'd intended to get on the train and go somewhere quiet to think. Looking down at my ticket, I felt the embarrassment wriggle up through my stomach until it heated my cheeks.

"If I tell you, it won't be a secret."

"This is true," Berne said. "*Mais*, if you tell me, I will keep your secret and your maman will not need to send out a search party, *oui?*"

"I'm an adult. I can get on a train if I want to." Yes, because that was so mature. Thirty-one going on eight. "I told her I needed a few days to think."

"Then, let me meet you at the station and escort you to this place of thought, *S'il te plaît.*"

"I'm not going to Marseille," I said. The fact Vivi-vixen was strutting her sultry voice in the same city coated it with a "no go" sign.

"But you go to Lyon, *non?*"

I looked down at my ticket. Hmmm . . . maybe. "No?"

Berne laughed, her voice filled my ears and made me feel like I'd ended up in some bad country song. Why was everything about her so close to need? Why did she do this to me?

"Let me get you to your sanctuary. I will ask for no more."

"Liar."

Berne laughed again. "Then I will feed you first, *oui.*"

Oh low blow. My stomach rumbled. It was hopeless. She was like breathing. "I'll be at the station in half an hour."

"*Merci.* I have someone who will bring a smile to your face."

I doubted it. The last thing I wanted to do was to face anyone. "Rebecca is more likely to give me stomach ache."

"But this is not her." Berne's dropped H's made my stomach growl again. I knew how it felt. "This is someone who misses you much."

A smile split across my face, making the man opposite grip his baguette like I would launch myself at him. "Babs?"

"Who else?"

My intended solitude forgotten, I lay my head back against the chair. Babs was one of the most electric people I'd ever met. She was thrumming with energy, laughter, and an erratic spirit that exhausted and exhilarated anyone who came within feet of her.

"Keep her away from Rebecca. Poor girl won't know what's hit her."

Berne chuckled once more and my mood was lifted. It was official. She had some kind of superpower that made my brain dribble out of my ears. "It is too late for that, *mais* I think your friend has some wiles of her own. It will be an interesting battle."

I looked out at the scenery and remembered a very old bet Berne and I had once made. I smiled. It would be more than interesting, it would be epic.

"SHE GOT ON the train to Lyon?" Babs's lips curled into a smile as she swung Clio around a bend and Berne tried to suppress the jolt of electricity in her stomach. It didn't mean anything that Pippa had run towards her and not London.

"I can't believe she ditched her mother and ran," Rebecca said through gritted teeth, her knuckles white on the seat. "I have never seen her so much as breathe out of place round the old bat before!"

"Her mother is strict?" Berne rubbed her hand over her tense stomach muscles as they whizzed along the road towards an old guy on a bike. It had shown courage for Pippa to walk away but what did that mean? Was she following her heart once more?

"Yes and no," Rebecca said. "Think it's the fact that Pippa never felt good enough, never quite fit the box her mother wanted."

"I cannot imagine Pepe feeling such doubt." Babs yanked the steering wheel to avoid the cyclist, throwing Rebecca into the door. "She is sure of her heart and soul."

"She was sure enough to leave." Berne shrugged off Babs's look. It was foolish for such a betrayal to ache after all these years. Pippa had her reasons back then, she had apologised. Why then, did it still hurt?

"You know, I'm gonna be grilling her about that." Rebecca nodded as Berne turned around to look at her. "It's not like Pip to duck out on anyone without at least explaining."

"Like she has with her mother?"

Rebecca sighed. "You got me there. Something is shifting inside her cold shell if she's breaking free." She offered a gentle smile and let go of her seat long enough to squeeze Berne's shoulder. "Maybe you hit her deep down."

"Perhaps." Berne braced herself as Babs overtook a tractor on a bend. "*Mais*, it is not my place to find out these things."

"It's always your place, Bebe," Babs said. "I married you, remember?"

"You what?"

Both Berne and Babs turned to look at a stunned Rebecca.

"You . . . what?"

"Not officially," Berne said, grabbing the wheel and steering the car onto the right side of the road as Babs adjusted her bobble. "Babs decided that we would be so during a day at the beach."

"What did you do to her?" Rebecca shut her eyes as Babs leaned forward to dig out a hairbrush. "Doug had to blackmail her into getting engag—wait."

Babs took control of the wheel as Berne tried to read the frown on Rebecca's face. "There is a problem?"

"Oh great llamas in pyjamas!"

Berne looked at Babs for help only for her to shrug.

"Did you give her a ring?"

Even the thought made Berne grin from ear to ear. "*Oui*. It was handmade . . . an heirloom."

"Kinda swirly and silver?"

Babs nodded, shooting Berne a grin.

"Oh great mice of Marsden!"

Again, Berne looked at Babs who again shrugged. "Maybe it is a set saying?"

"She never takes the stupid thing off." Rebecca seemed to forget that they were hurtling Babs-style through the growing traffic. "She had it on the night he proposed. She really didn't want to swap fingers . . . *Merde!*"

"Now *that* I understood," Babs said with a smirk.

"She wore it until then?" What did it matter? It was not official. Doug's ring would replace it for good and then it would be nothing but a memory. A silly token from a past stranger.

"She *still* wears it now!"

The car screeched to a halt in mid-traffic. People beeped and swerved as Babs spun around.

Rebecca covered her face in her hands. "I need more whiskey to be in a car with you."

Babs pulled Rebecca's hands away as Berne looked on. Her heart hammered a pulsing march through her head.

"She wears the ring . . . now . . . still?"

"Yes, she only switches them when he's round." Rebecca took deep breaths, cringing as the traffic continued to hurl abuse at them. "Can we move already?"

Babs shook her head. "That means she must still love you."

"We know this already." Berne motioned to the wheel, trying

to calm her silly heart. "She told me she loves me. It changes nothing."

Roaring them into motion, Babs waved her hand in the air. "Oh no. It means we need to get her to that beach so we can make it official this time."

"You are forgetting Vivienne." Berne folded her arms as if that would settle the matter but Babs would ignore it, she always did. "You are forgetting that she wishes to be with him, that she left me to go back to her life." She wagged her finger in the air to stop Babs protest. "You forget that she has not explained this, only repeated the escape from him."

"You think she's a commitment phobe?" Rebecca chewed on her lip. "Maybe you're onto something there."

"*Alors*, it does not become a question of love then, *non?*" Berne's heart seemed to wilt with the reality. It still hurt, it still ached, nothing had changed. "It is more a question of who she loves enough to conquer this fear."

"Oh eggshells in Ealing, we'll be having DVD fests in a retirement home."

Berne frowned at her.

"I love Pip, I do. I adore her, but what happens if *I* fall in love?"

"Pepe talks of your wish for this never to happen." Berne raised her eyebrows, enjoying Rebecca's blush. "She says you like to be free."

"I do . . . but . . . well . . . things can change . . . can't they?"

Berne looked at Babs whose eyes twinkled with mischief. Pippa was right. No doubt this battle would be epic.

"Either way, if she comes to me, I cannot just break my promises to Vivienne. What if Pepe leaves once more?"

Babs slammed her fist onto her horn. Rebecca leapt up and smacked her head on the ceiling. "We need to find her heart, her courage. We need to draw her out and make her believe in love!"

Rebecca cheered in response. The pair were dangerous together.

"I will—*we* will—not do such a thing." Berne scowled at them both as Babs whizzed them into a parking space. "If Pippa wishes for more, she will need to explain much."

"*Merde*," Babs spat her way. "Pepe will simply need to flash those beautiful—"

Berne opened the door to escape, the station was busy and

humming. Pippa's train would be pulling in at any moment. Why, if she was so set on not caring, why was she rushing to her rescue?

Because they were friends?

Because they had once been more?

Berne glanced back and rolled her eyes as Babs squeezed her hands in a gesture that made Rebecca roar with laughter. They were trouble together that much was clear.

Looking up at the board, Berne tried to ignore the fact that she should be with Vivienne. She'd done exactly the same thing Pippa had done and left without an explanation. Would she be brave enough to tell the truth on her return?

Again, she was at Pippa's beck and call, again she was falling into that pattern of coming to the rescue. How could she not? Pippa was everything. Pippa was who she connected with. Pippa was—

Berne sighed and slowed to an amble as the train pulled in.

Pippa was on that train coming to her. Doug was in Paris. Pippa had run to *her.* Like always, she would be waiting, like always, with open arms.

Chapter Ten

THE NERVES SWIRLED around in my stomach as I caught sight of Berne standing on the platform. Although I'd seen her quite a few times since being back in France, my body seemed to hum, heightening in intensity with every glance. I groaned to myself, she was incredible. To call her simply beautiful wouldn't do her justice. She was one of those women who you could happily sit and stare at all day and still not tire of looking at.

She was forty-one and she had a line in the middle of her forehead. She had a longer face maybe but the years had added to her. I had no idea how to explain it but she looked even better than she had when I'd known her. I guess she was more herself now, more aware of who she was. Not that she'd ever been under-confident in any way but, well, she seemed stronger. I didn't miss her wince as she shifted between her feet however. So I wasn't the only one who was aching from digging after all.

As I got off the train, I couldn't keep the grin from my face as a pocket-sized bundle of French energy hurtled at me and nearly tackled me to the ground.

"Pepe!"

It had been years since I'd been Babs'd, but memory served me well enough to turn my cheek before she planted a smacker on my lips.

"*Ça va*, a million *bisous*, I cannot believe you are back here!"

I knew better than to attempt to smooth over my clothes and pretend that I hadn't suffered a full-frontal assault from the Flying Frenchwoman. No one in the station raised an eyebrow at the public show of affection. Nope, they were quite used to enthusiastic greetings clearly.

"And ah!" Babs pointed to my chest and I half-tensed ready for some smutty comment, only for her to tap my left breast. "This is familiar, *non*?"

She dragged me by the hand over to Rebecca and Berne. "I know this shirt, do I not?"

Feeling the cringe-worthy realisation of why she was making such a fuss, I glanced down at my French rugby top, or rather it had been Berne's top once. Hmmm . . . explain that, Saunders. Freudian slip much.

"*Alors,* how did she get this?"

Berne sighed as though she thought anyone would think she was tired of Babs teasing.

She wasn't.

They were a duo, they had always been.

I'd loved the fact that Babe, as I'd dubbed them, had been as close as Rebecca and I. It was one of the many things I adored about Berne.

"We should be escorting her to her thinking place, not digging up—"

"There's another story?" Rebecca's eyes glinted and my stomach wriggled with the embarrassment. "You *have* to spill it."

Babs grinned. "Oh, it will make you see her with new eyes."

Rebecca leaned in closer. "Please tell me it's something I can blackmail her with."

Babs tapped Rebecca on the nose with her nail. "Without one doubt."

I turned from the ping-pong conversation and glanced at Berne, who shrugged, seeming to read my thoughts. "You've been outnumbered for a good while, huh?"

"*Oui,* my mother combined with these two was . . . interesting."

I loved the way she talked. I turned to walk towards the steps and nudged her shoulder. "Do you have scars?"

Her gentle chuckle made the hairs on my arms ripple. It was a laugh that put visions in my head. Visions of long, hot summer days on a secluded stretch of sand with—

"Now, what do you whisper?" Babs yanked me by the hand and led me towards a very familiar red Clio.

"You still have her!" I ran over to the beaten up old beauty. "I have great memories of squeezing into the back of this baby."

"Did you seriously just call a car baby?" Rebecca raised her eyebrows. "Who are you and where is Pippa Saunders?"

"This is Pepe," Babs said. "She is the mischievous twin, *non?*"

I ignored the teasing and patted Clio on the bonnet. She seemed as well-loved as I'd remembered. How I'd missed this place. Every single part of it. Winston and Clio would be soul mates, this I was sure of.

"Where would you like to go?" Berne's voice held an edge of an untold question. I was confusing her. I was confusing myself. What right did I have to come crashing into her life after all these years and cause her chaos?

I swallowed back the ache that she probably wished she could be with Vivienne right now. Palpitations stuttered through my heart. Why *wasn't* she in Marseille or was Vivienne here? "I won't keep you. I just need to get to where we're staying so I can pack a few things."

"You leave?" Babs sounded irritated by my answer, she didn't look much happier either.

Wonderful, Saunders. Where were my manners?

"Well, not without catching up and letting you tease me mercilessly."

A smile burst onto her face and she bellowed her laugh out as she opened her door.

Rebecca started at the booming chuckle and blew out a long breath. "You know she's a lunatic on the road, right?"

"That's why I'll do the driving." I held my hand out and Babs happily threw me the keys.

"Hey, I didn't know that was an option." Rebecca looked more relieved than annoyed.

"You did not ask, my little English banana."

Her accent wrapping around banana gave it a joyful tone that made Rebecca's cheeks colour but only enough that I could see.

Rebecca waggled her eyebrows. "Well, my little French peanut, next time I most certainly will."

I looked at Berne and she wiggled her eyebrows in silent agreement. "I think they need to avoid beaches for a while . . ."

WE ARRIVED BACK at Ajoux-Sur-Rhône and Rebecca and Berne concocted a wonderful feast together as Babs cut some kind of business deal on her phone.

The woman was one of the most high-powered business women in the country. Her fortune made Doug's look small but she still lived in her tiny apartment and drove Clio. I loved her for that very, very much.

In fact I absolutely adored the three women with me in the little holiday cottage. Berne and Rebecca busy at work in a small, but functional bland kitchen. The brown tiles on the floor had been recovered from the eighties and the cupboards looked like something from the fifties.

The cooker and microwave looked modern enough though. Okay, cheap brands that meant they had to be newish. Nothing with those names on it lasted very long. Especially if there were oafs like me using them. Berne and Rebecca working together made it look more professional.

Berne always cooked with an apron around her waist. Why, I didn't know because she was always neat and tidy. Rebecca had her own habits, sleeves rolled up, jewellery off, and a baseball cap on backwards. I never understood why, because her hair was shorter than Doug's but yet she always did it. If she bore a faded green baseball cap, food was forthcoming.

I sat on the sofa because it was safer for all concerned if I stayed away from hot surfaces. Instead I curled up in the corner, tucked my feet underneath me, and enjoyed being in their presence. It felt good to be with them. I felt happier here.

Berne caught me looking and strolled over to sit beside me. "Where did you plan to go?"

Something I'd run over and over on the train. "Here's the thing . . ." I turned to look at her, hoping that if I looked, I'd not falter and end up causing chaos. Besides, with this angle, I could feel Rebecca buzzing about the kitchen and it would help me behave. "You know that I love you, right?"

Berne smiled in response and her eyes twinkled. I gripped the chair to stop from moving.

"Thing is . . . I need to know myself . . . I need to figure out who I am now." I wrapped my arms across my chest, it was better than launching myself into her arms. "I promised to marry Doug. When . . . if . . . I do, I want it to be truly me . . . to be right."

There was more. Much more I needed to explain but it was stuck and wouldn't budge. She needed to understand.

"That makes sense." Berne's dulled tones made my stomach ache.

"I love *you* though," I said, confusing her as much as myself, no doubt. "I mean . . . I need to know if . . . why . . . I need to understand if that's because we were young or if . . . well . . ."

Why wouldn't the truth come out? Why couldn't I explain to her why I'd left?

"How do you wish to do this?" Berne asked, her apron as spotless as when she put it on.

Wishing wasn't a wise subject with my heart in overload. No, better for the well-mannered approach. "Doug will be worried if I just head off into the country. He'll have the cavalry out before I can blink. I owe him an explanation for leaving."

"Then tell him that you want time to think." I didn't miss Berne averting her eyes. I owed her an explanation too.

I wanted to reach across and cuddle her, instead I hugged myself tighter. "It won't work. He won't listen. Besides, he thinks I'm pregnant for some absurd reason."

Berne frowned and I couldn't resist a quick squeeze of her hand.

"I'm not by the way. I need you, Babs, and Rebecca to cover me."

"Got your six, Saunders," Rebecca chimed from the kitchen.

"*Oui,*" Babs added, poking her head in from the porch.

"You aren't meant to be listening."

Both of them shrugged and went back to their tasks.

"Can you take a few days, I . . . well . . . can you?"

"Of course, my father will happily call in someone to finish the foundations." Berne smiled. "You wish to do the Ardèche once more?"

How did she know me that well? Why was she making this so easy for me? If I was her, I would have . . . well . . . no, I'd have done exactly the same. I would have done what she needed and pined away inside. I would be wearing that look she was now.

"Would that be okay?" I closed my eyes, hoping that she wouldn't tell me she needed to be with Vivienne.

"I will happily be your guide."

"Why are you so patient with me?" My mother's words about being less pedigree than her other offspring rubbed at my already raw senses. Especially my sister. She was so perfect.

"The same reason you suffer my presence," Berne said. "We fit well together."

I linked my fingers with hers. My breath quickened as she smiled. I needed to do something or I'd end up leaning forward, planting my lips to hers, sweet, slow—

"Food, ladies!" Rebecca threw the tea towel at my face. "You can dish out." She rapped my knuckles with a spoon as I reached for a taste. "And then you can tell me why Babs was so excited about your shirt."

"She's patriotic?"

Rebecca poked me in the ribs. "You owe me the truth, Saunders."

I owed a lot of people the truth. *Take a ticket and wait for your number to be called.* I sighed. It was the least I could do. It must have hurt to learn how different I'd been here in France. It must have been hard for her to realise how much had been buried.

There was much I needed to explain to everyone concerned but most of all, I needed to understand what I wanted to say. I needed to understand what I felt and what it meant.

However I found the answers inside me, I would still be hurting someone and perhaps, after my actions in recent weeks, I could end up alone.

I owed it to everyone, and I owed it to myself, to find out exactly where my heart lay even if that meant uncovering parts that I'd happily forgotten. There was a lot of pain I needed to face before I could get there. What hurt would I reawaken within my thudding heart?

DOUG WAS NOT in the best of moods when I called him later that evening. If he could have seen that I was lounging out on the sofa with my head on Rebecca's lap, he may have been even grumpier. It was the very reason I neglected to video-call him.

"Sweetheart, I know that you have some problems at the moment," he began with the tone that adults used with toddlers. "But running off like that makes everyone unhappy."

Everyone but me. I was perfectly happy. I had three people with me who made me feel like me.

"Doug, I need time to process everything." How could I say this without bottling out? "I need time to come to terms with how I feel."

"Your mother said you would be unreasonable at this time." His voice sounded more like my father's than a future spouse. "I suppose we will have to expect these little blips, won't we?"

The fact that Doug thought I was pregnant didn't take away

from his patronising. Okay, so I'd been a bit crazy but crazy did not mean stupid.

"I suppose you will," I snapped. "I'll call you when I'm ready to talk."

"Now, sweetheart. Why don't you let my guy come and pick you up? You don't need to be working now."

I looked down at the phone. I hadn't told him where I was. I looked up at Rebecca who shook her head. "How do you know where I am?"

"You told me."

He was lying.

"I did not. How do you know?"

While he tried to tell me that I had revealed my location, I got up and walked over to the window. Just as I'd thought. One of his drivers leaned against his bonnet, dosing in the sunshine. "I can see James."

"Oh, he is there to help you." Doug sounded distracted and distant. "Don't worry about him."

"That's creepy, Doug." I moved away from the window. "Don't turn into that weird guy."

"I won't . . . Look, I have to go . . . I'll talk to you later."

He hung up.

I stared down at the phone, frowning. He'd cut me off. Was he mad?

"That is pretty creepy," Rebecca said, peeking out the window. "He got some kind of mob ties or something?"

Even the thought made me giggle.

"Doug?" I raised my eyebrows until Rebecca laughed at her own dumb thought. He was about as mysterious as Clingfilm. Doug was what it said on the label.

"You wish to lose the tail?" Babs said with a grin. "I can arrange something to curtail your shadow, *oui*?"

"Is *she* in the mob?" Rebecca asked, thumbing in Babs's direction.

"Er, no . . . unless you count designer bathroom suites as illegal merchandise."

Rebecca looked thoughtful as she studied Babs. At five-foot-four, Babs was three inches or so shorter than Rebecca. Her hair was raven black with a white streak on the left temple. Like Berne, she exuded a sensuality that enraptured most who looked at her.

Babs was fiery, furious, passionate, and absolutely gorgeous. Her intense brown eyes, her Romanesque nose, her wide-lipped smile, and curvaceous contours made her catch most people's attention.

Rebecca, I could tell, was drawn like a moth to the flashlight. What I wasn't expecting was for Babs to be as drawn to her.

She was hiding it well enough but I knew better. I knew the flick of the eyes over Rebecca's . . . well . . . behind, when she turned away.

"You don't think Babs looks like a designer?" I asked, prodding the gawping Rebecca.

It was nice to get my own back. French women were enchanting. It was good to know I wasn't the only helpless admirer.

"What?" Rebecca smiled in a daze. "No . . ." She shook her head. "I mean yes . . . I mean, I was wondering why we hadn't dragged her into the design process."

"Trust me," I said. "Where Berne works, Babs will be . . . I think."

Babs nodded, eavesdropping again. "Always. It will be fun, *non*?" she shot at us before going back to her animated phone conversation.

I looked around for Berne. Where was she?

"Viper," Babs muttered. "Bebe was going to have to explain why she'd ditched her to play hero eventually."

"Viper?" I asked.

"Vivienne." Babs disconnected and nodded with complete seriousness. It made me feel a sense of pride that Babs disliked the woman.

"She's really as bad as that?"

"*Oui, oui*. She may think she is some gift to the women *mais*, she is nothing but a . . ." Babs "mmm'd" as she tried to think of the word in English.

"Bad influence?" I asked.

Babs shook her head.

"A drunk?"

Tutting, Babs shook her head again.

"A superficial twig?" Rebecca seemed to feel the need to join in and help too.

Babs roared with laughter then shook her head. "*Non*."

"A bitch?" Both of them turned to look at me and I shrugged. "What?"

"Who is a bitch?" Berne's voice behind me made me tense.

"Me," I said, plastering what I hoped looked like a confident smile on my face. "For . . . um—"

"Ditching your fiancé?" Rebecca said.

"Abandoning Berne?" Babs said.

"Not telling him you weren't pregnant?" Rebecca added.

"Hey!" I folded my arms and the two of them looked at each other. "Enough with the judgement. I suck, we know that I suck. This is confirmed, I heartily suck big time."

Both nodded and I turned to look at Berne.

She looked stressed, her eyes puffy.

"Did she upset you?" My anger shot through my veins with such force that I clenched my fists into balls. "How dare she yell at you."

All three looked at me with raised eyebrows.

"What?" I put my hands on my hips. "What?"

"Steady on, Pip." Rebecca's smug grin made me frown even deeper and my forehead ache.

"I will not take it easy." I looked at Berne. How did I explain that it drove me nuts to think of her going anywhere near some sultry, superficial twig, who was a drunken bad influence *and* a bitch? "I don't like her."

My words brought a smile to her lips and the light seemed to flow back into her. "I am very happy that you do not."

"Will you still be able to come with me? I don't want to cause trouble—" I held my hand up. "Actually, I *do* want to cause trouble but she is your priority."

Ouch, ouch, ouch that stung.

"*Oui.*" Berne blinked a few times. "I will guide you as promised."

Was the "*oui*" about coming with me or Vivienne being priority?

"Are you sure?" I tried to search Berne's eyes but she looked lost in her thoughts. "Berne, I have no right to ask you to do anything."

With a sigh, she wandered into the kitchen. The three of us watched as she snapped open a can of pop and wandered out onto the balcony. I looked at Babs, hating that I couldn't help to ease her mind in this situation. I was part of whatever problem she had, that much I knew.

"I will go. Perhaps you tell my delightful lemon slice about the rules of our favourite game, *non*?" Babs smiled. "She could do with some relaxation."

Helpless to do anything but nod, I watched Babs wander out after Berne and shut the door.

"This was why I didn't want to come back here." Running my hand through my hair, I strode to the table and pulled out a pack of cards. "This is my fault."

"Pip, why *did* you leave her?" Rebecca's voice held an edge of caution as though she expected me to explode like a firework.

I slumped down onto the sofa and pulled the cards from the pack. I hated feeling so unhinged and I hated making even the people closest to me tread on eggshells.

"It's a long story."

I felt her sit down beside me. "Pip, you told me that she was in the past but it's clear she's very present."

"Yes." I shuffled the cards, unable to meet Rebecca's eyes.

"Pip, you wear her ring all the time." Rebecca pulled me around to look at her. "You wear her ring not his. You still have a rugby shirt that we both know is hers too."

"Yes."

"When you're around her, you set off all kinds of vibes. I mean, where has this side been?" She laughed to herself. "I sound like my father now but I feel like I don't know you."

The nausea pulsed in my stomach. "I don't know myself anymore."

"I think you do." Rebecca held me by the shoulders. "I want you to know that I love you to pieces whatever you do . . . but, Pip . . ." She squeezed my shoulders. "If I'm gonna help you and support you through this, I need the truth."

"You're not mad at me?" I felt a trickle of warmth on my cheeks and rubbed at the tears. "I don't know why I have such a problem talking about things."

"Because you think I'll get mad at you and never talk to you again?"

I laughed through the sobs. "Something like that."

Rebecca looked up at the balcony. Berne and Babs were chatting away. Well, Babs was jabbering on while Berne stared out into the distance.

"Did you realise how you felt about her when you met?"

I shook my head and retrieved a tissue from my pocket. "I can tell you that she provoked so many emotions that I was completely overwhelmed."

I smiled. Berne had been playing that piano in the storm. When she'd turned to look at me, I had wanted to run away and towards her all at once. Such a collision of desperately wanting to know her and terrified to even look at her.

Berne was older, cooler, wiser, and effortlessly calm. She seemed to know what to say and what to do. She knew when to wait and when to charm me.

"I could barely speak when we met." My stomach wriggled at the memory. "She could speak English but just listening to her made every part of me ache."

"I am guessing she still has that knack?"

"Mmm." I tried not to stare too long at Berne and Babs, tried not to read Babs's lips in the hope of some enlightenment.

"Why did you leave her?" Rebecca was looking too. Babs held her attention though.

"Fear."

"Of?"

How could I explain how petty it all was? How silly it sounded all these years later.

"Losing her."

Rebecca looked at me but I nodded.

"Berne wanted to be in the gendarmerie, like her brother, but she wanted to be on the bikes."

"And?" Rebecca sat back, surveying me as though she had never met me before. I suppose it was the first time she'd seen me inside out.

"Walking home, I was so in love." I stared down at my hands. "I mean Berne meant so much to me that my whole life seemed to revolve around her."

"Kinda what happens, Pip."

"I know that, but it got too much maybe. I couldn't operate without her as part of my day." How could I explain the worry now? I couldn't understand it myself. How could I untangle the mess of emotions from that terrible day? "I passed a motorcycle accident on the way home . . . an officer . . . it was awful."

"Ah."

Confused by her tone, I met Rebecca's eyes, which filled with love. "You couldn't bear the thought of that ever happening to her." A smile drifted across her face. "You didn't want to stop her chasing her dream either—"

"So I did the only thing I could and walked away."

Not quite the full story but it was all I could manage. Rebecca pulled me into a cuddle. "Pip, you must have ripped out your heart and you went through it all alone."

"Trust me, you helped . . . you always do."

She rubbed a soothing hand on my back. "Actually, I do know you. Being so dumb and so sweet is exactly the girl I love."

"Look where it's gotten me. I'll have to walk away all over again and this time I'll have the searing pain of knowing some woman is sleeping beside her." The pain of that brought more tears to my eyes.

"Why don't you tell her?" Rebecca kissed the top of my head. "There's no reason for you to leave now is there?"

"I promised Doug to marry him. I can't ask Berne to give up Vivienne."

"Why?"

Again, it would be something that sounded ridiculous to most people. Why shouldn't I just be with the person I adored? Why shouldn't I have what I wanted? "Because, I don't want her to compromise who she is for me."

"I don't follow."

Sighing, I sat up and rested my elbows on my knees. "She always had to fix everything for me. Doug has to do the same. I always feel like a baby and I want to be a person." I stared out at Berne, searched for a sign that she was feeling better now. "I need to find who I am."

"And being in love won't give you that?"

I shook my head. "Not until I can stand up tall as an equal. Not until I stop being a coward. Be someone that whoever I am with looks to as much as I do them."

Rebecca smiled. "I get that."

Snuggling back into her, I let the relief ease through me. "I should have known you would. I'm sorry I kept it from you."

"Don't be," she said. "But sharing helps you get your thoughts straight, you know?"

"I know that I love you, how's that?"

Rebecca kissed me on the head once more. "Back at you, Pepe."

Chapter Eleven

MORNING WAS COOL but held the promise of a beautiful blue day. Berne clicked shut the tailgate of her truck. The equipment needed for their trip stowed safely, she leaned against the metal warmed by the gentle sun.

Her mind would not still. No matter how much she had tried to meditate this morning, her moments of inner quiet would not come.

The argument with Vivienne and the vision of Pippa took turns in tormenting her until she had rolled restless from her bed.

Even in times past, in times when she'd pined so deeply that her heart laboured with every beat, she'd always been able to meditate. That was the one thing that had seen her through that burning loss, that desperate despair.

If she could not meditate now, what would she do when Pippa walked back out of her life once more? What would she do when Pippa walked away with *him*?

"*Bonjour.*"

Berne turned and smiled at Rebecca as she strolled into the sunshine. She made the mental note to add more high-factor sun cream to the bags. For one so pale, Rebecca would not find the baking sun deep in the gorges forgiving.

"*Bonjour.*"

"You know as her best buddy, I am supposed to keep her confidence."

Berne nodded. She would expect no less. Babs and she were very much the same. A golden rule.

"But there are times when you know you got to do what is best, right?"

Not sure she wanted this conversation to continue, Berne shrugged. The last thing she wanted was to come between friends or be the cause of any rift at all.

"Pippa loves you and you know that." Rebecca wandered to

the truck and leaned against it next to Berne. "And you love her, which she knows."

"*Oui*." She loved both Babs and Rebecca for trying to help but the statement of feelings meant nothing. Pippa would marry Doug because it was better for her in the long run. Maybe because her mother would be happier or she wished to live a rich, happy life.

How could she compete with that? She could offer her no riches, no fancy holidays, or social status.

No matter how much Pippa said she loved her, she was still going to walk away.

"You need to show her you want more."

"Pardon?" Berne had seen Rebecca remind Pippa time and again of her obligations to Doug.

"Look," Rebecca glanced up to the house, "Pippa left you not because she was bored or ashamed or didn't love you anymore." She stared off into the distance. "I won't tell you exactly why because that's her job but it was for a reason that I know you'll understand and love her for."

As if Berne didn't feel that way already. "She never called."

"Berne, Pippa needed therapy when she came home. I mean years of it. Seriously, she really was hurting." Rebecca smiled. "I'd always been terrified of what happened to her here. It never once occurred to me that she might just be going through the same thing as me."

"You were heartbroken?"

Rebecca waved her hand about. "Yes and no . . . My father disowned me. He was all I had after . . . well . . . it was just the two of us."

Berne's heart pumped harder at the thought of her father doing such a thing. Every day she was thankful for her parents and their love. Blessed was too light a word for her upbringing.

"She helped me through the whole thing and never told me a word." Rebecca nodded as Berne looked at her. "Yeah, that's right. Pippa got me through the whole thing. She found us an apartment, we got jobs, she made sure that I knew I had her."

It didn't surprise her at all. "That sounds much like her."

"Problem is, Pippa doesn't see that she does as much for me as I do for her." Rebecca pushed off the truck and centred on Berne, her back to the house behind her. "Pippa thinks she's not your equal—that she can't be with you if she's not fifty-fifty with you."

Such a thought was illogical. Pippa was no less, Pippa meant everything to her.

"I know you don't see her that way and I know that she probably backs you up when you need her, right?"

"*Oui.* She helps just by being around." Berne swallowed the wriggle in her stomach. The argument with Vivienne re-surfacing. "Pippa is always present, always interested in me, deep inside."

"Then do everyone a favour and help us all show her that." Rebecca smiled. "I'm team Pippa all the way and since we've been here, I've seen her come alive. I want to see her shine like that. I know you want it too."

"More than I can express." There were no words, no sounds that could describe it. To be in her arms, to be in her heart, to be with her. It was sweet torture. "But she will marry him, either way, she will do this."

"Maybe." Rebecca looked over her shoulder. "But give her a reason not to. Fight for her. Berne, this is your chance to change her mind. Whether she's walking up that aisle or before, the truth will bring her back to you."

Berne turned to the truck, making a show of checking its road worthiness but all the while fighting the urge to slump into a heap on the ground. "Is it not better that I leave her to prince charming?" She kicked the driver's side tyre with venom. "Is it not better that she have the perfect life?"

"Doug is a great guy but I got my issues with him."

"You do?" Berne tried not to smile at the information. He seemed so perfect, a gentleman. It was hard to dislike his love for Pippa.

"Yes, he's possessive and controlling, in a nice way but still, Pippa is smothered when he is around." Rebecca looked up at the sun and pulled her baseball cap down further. "He'd look after her but she'd be what he wanted her to be. I don't want to lose her and right now she's terrified she's going to lose herself."

The sound of Babs and Pippa chatting filtered over the morning birdcalls and Rebecca looked once more at Berne. "If she does do the dumb thing and marry him . . . at least let's make sure she knows who she is."

How could Berne refuse? How could she turn around and say no, no, she wanted Pippa to love and be with her? She wanted

Pippa to save both their hearts and find the courage to walk away from Doug. Berne wanted more, she wanted Pippa to love her enough to come looking for her. She wanted not just a fleeting chance of something, she wanted a declaration of everything.

Was that not fair? Was that asking too much? Why couldn't Pippa have loved her enough to stay?

Berne kicked the wheel again with more force than she'd intended and bit back the sharp, shooting pain as her toe cracked. Rebecca was looking at her, expectant for an answer, so she did the only thing she could with the agony in both her toe and heart, she nodded.

I SHOULD HAVE known that Babs would be waiting for me in the morning. Rebecca had helped me to pack my things, only, I'd noticed that she stood back and gave pointers instead of taking charge.

Silly, but I was touched by the fact she'd listened and hadn't forgotten the moment the conversation had finished.

After breakfast, which was a silent, tense affair, I took a shower and changed, ready to go. Babs was there in the kitchen, texting someone, and I could hear faint sounds of Rebecca talking outside.

"You good to take a few days off?" I asked, knowing that Babs was waiting for me to start.

"*Oui.* The wonder of owning the company." She smiled at me with an expression that worried me. Babs was not one for hesitation.

"Is this your 'let her go' moment?"

"*Non.*" Babs pocketed her phone in her cargo shorts. "It is this. Why did you leave her heartbroken?"

Feeling the sudden urge to lock myself in the bedroom, I shoved my hands in my own short pockets. It was too complicated. If I started, she would want me to finish and unlike Rebecca, Babs wouldn't let me stop until she'd gotten the whole truth.

"Berne wanted . . . I couldn't lose her . . . Can you see how simple that is? I was scared of losing her." I really did not want to go through this again. Last night had been enough.

"You make no sense."

"I know that I don't . . . I . . . ." Tears welled up in my eyes. I *couldn't* go through this conversation again. "Please . . . It was for the best."

"You wear her ring. You gaze at her with longing. You are desperate to be with her. So why, why do you hide this?" Babs slapped the counter with her frustration. "I know that you adore her, that you have always done this. Why do you hurt yourself and her by being with this man?"

"She's better off without me." I headed towards the door, not willing to stay and face her interrogation.

Babs had every right to yell at me, it was only fair that she did. I'd have yelled at me too. In fact, I did yell at myself quite often in spite of the fact the counsellor had told me it wasn't a great tactic.

"*Non.*" Babs pulled me around by the hand. I half expected her to sock me one but instead, her eyes filled with patience. "Pepe, I love you like a sister. I will not let you run from this." She held tighter as I tried to pull away. "You love this man? You love him like her?"

"No."

"Then why is she better without you?" Babs wouldn't let go and I was stuck between yanking may arm away and bolting or standing and taking what I deserved.

"She has Vivienne. She found someone else, someone who cares." Someone who'd been with her for years, not the solitary one we'd spent together. That must have meant more.

"Vivienne does not care for her."

Stopping my struggle to escape, I scowled. "What?"

"Vivienne, she takes advantage of her. Berne is nothing to her but a secret . . . a mistress."

Well, if I disliked Vivi-vixen-viper before, now I wanted to . . . to . . . do something very unladylike.

"What?"

"*Oui.* You left her to be mistreated."

Ouch.

"Why . . . why would this *woman* do that?" I put my hands on my hips. I wanted to poke the wench. Yes, that's right. Poke her right in the eye. "Why would she mistreat her?"

"Why would you abandon her and never say a word?"

I opened my mouth to argue but then sighed. Good point. "Then I'm no better than this woman and she is better off without me."

"*Non*, without you, she is so lost." Babs took my hand. "She needs you to come alive again."

Odd images of me next to an operating table with lightning forking across the sky made me blink. Rebecca and I watched far too many films. "Berne doesn't need me or anyone else to be wonderful, she just is."

"And to be loved helps that to radiate from her. You are much the same." Babs wagged her finger as I opened my mouth to argue. "I hear enough to know that you pine for her too."

"Of course I do. That's not the point."

Conscious that Berne and Rebecca were waiting for us, I headed out of the door and locked it behind Babs.

"She cries much of the time because of that woman."

Ouch again.

"Why, what does Vivienne say?"

"It is subtle but I have watched it over the years. Piece by piece, she picks away at the confidence, she has Berne to think that it is okay to be shut away." Babs shrugged. "It is not that she means to consciously but her own fears drive so much."

"Vivienne is afraid?"

"*Oui*." Babs cocked her head. "You do not know why?"

"Of course I don't." Was I a mind reader? When would I have learned this information?

"Vivienne is an actress. On television, *oui*?" Babs shook her head as if astounded I didn't know. "You remember that Raquel work behind the scenes? *Alors*, they meet when Berne went to the set, *oui*?"

Raquel had been close to Berne and Babs back then. She was tall, leggy, blonde, with men following her everywhere. Another charming French woman who had intimidated me beyond measure. She'd been Berne's age. She and Berne could talk about things I didn't understand. Lucky for me she'd been straight or I would have seriously worr—

"They got together when Berne and Raquel split up."

I missed my footing and stumbled, Babs caught me before I face planted into the wall. "Berne went out with Raquel?"

"*Oui*."

I couldn't swallow. When did swallowing get so hard? I'd performed the action automatically enough times, surely you couldn't forget how to swallow.

"Pippa?" Rebecca's voice sounded somewhere nearby but I leaned over onto my knees, trying to breathe. Swallowing was simple, why couldn't I swallow?

"Pippa, you okay?"

I shook my head. My stomach swirled like it was ready to make a bid for freedom.

"What did you say?" Rebecca sounded irritated.

"I tell her of Vivienne." Babs sounded defiant. "And Raquel."

"Why?" Rebecca asked. "What good does that do anyone?"

Uh oh, Rebecca sounded mad. Swallow, you daft clot, why couldn't I swallow!

"Good?" Babs snapped. "Maybe she will see sense and stop this nonsense."

"Pip has the right to be insane if she wants."

Insane? Wow, thanks. I would have said something but every time I regained my breath, the name Raquel Rocher pulsed into my head. The way she'd smiled at me with such patience, like I amused her. Had she just been biding her time? Waiting for Berne to stop fooling around with me? Had Berne felt the same way?

"You admit that this is crazy?"

"Yeah, I do. They should be married and all domesticated. It's not my place to demand she stop messing around and get to it already."

Babs burst out with laughter. "I knew that I liked you."

Rebecca's incoherent mumbling reached my ears above the ringing racket of my own pulse.

Calm . . . calm . . .

"*Ça va?*" Berne's voice only made the inability to swallow rage into desperate sobbing breaths.

I covered my eyes to try and fend off the pulsing lights. Rebecca mumbled something about a paper bag and a second or two later one was stuck to my face.

"What did you say?" Berne's voice filled with angst.

It didn't matter. Even the sound of her voice now made everything worse. I wanted to explode into tears but couldn't. Instead I shuddered my breaths in and out, trying to hold the paper bag over my mouth and nose. It smelled of peppermint. I hated peppermint.

"She told her about Vivienne *and* Raquel." Rebecca sounded livid. "Now she's hyperventilating."

"You could not keep it secret from her." Babs was again defiant. "My little English melon here is passionate in her defence."

"That's because my little French pinball had all the tact of a bulldozer when she did it."

That was cue for them to start bickering. Were they seriously flirting? Now?

"Wait in the vehicle." Berne cut everyone to silence with her tone.

I heard them bicker some more as they trundled off to the truck. Berne sat down beside me. She waited until my breathing calmed enough for me to pull the bag away.

"It is something I do not wish to talk about with you."

"I'm not surprised." Ooh, I was mad. That was better, I could swallow when mad.

"You have no right to be angry with me."

"Well, suck it up because I am." I got to my feet, too quickly, and stars popped before my eyes. "I'm mad at you. In fact . . . stuff your flipping Ardèche."

I went to stomp off only for Berne to wrap her arms around me from behind. She buried her head in my shoulder. "You are marrying some rich man. You left me."

"I know I did . . . I don't care . . . Raquel Rocher . . . that's . . . that's worse than revenge . . . that's . . ." I flapped my arms about, unable to stomp off and unwilling to give in to the gentle custody of her arms. "You suck . . . you . . . I can't believe you—"

"I did. I do." Berne held on tighter. "You left."

"You said that you were just friends. You said you didn't feel a thing for her when I met her." Sudden thoughts of betrayal burst through my mind. "You used to stay at her place."

"I was never unfaithful to you." Berne turned me around so I could see the truth in her eyes. "You left me. She was there for me. There was no reason not to explore our feelings."

The visual of Berne being drooled over by Raquel made my entire body ache. Raquel was there to console her? Oh I bet she was.

"You swore you didn't feel anything for her. You swore it."

Oh crap. I felt like someone had ripped out the foundations from under me. There was Berne acting like she'd pined away. Hah. Raquel. If she'd left Raquel for Vivienne, what did Vivienne look like? What chance did a babbling idiot like me have against them? I was a fool. A fool to think she'd seen only me.

"Things changed. You left." Berne's irritated tone cut even deeper.

A clarity washed over me. Somehow the fact seemed to make a calmness settle inside.

"We're done."

I broke free of Berne's grasp and walked to the truck. "I'll find someone else to guide me."

"I will do as promised. I will."

"Pip, we'll never get another guide now." Rebecca looked like she wanted to plead for my forgiveness. She must have known what I was up against with Vivienne since they went to Marseille. Well, we were even on hiding secrets now.

Raquel Rocher.

I wanted to throw up.

"Fine. I'll take *you* in the kayak."

Berne said nothing. In fact no one dared utter a word to me as I snatched the keys off Berne and drove us to our starting point.

Of all the people in the world to sleep with, Berne found the one who could make the most impact on me. Logically, what reason did I have to be angry when I'd left her? What gave me the right to be livid about some friend from the past? Why wouldn't Berne fall for her?

I wasn't sure if I was angrier at Raquel for daring to touch Berne or Berne for being so calculated.

Then Babs's words popped into my head. She'd split up with Raquel. She was with Vivienne who took advantage of her. Vivienne who hurt her and made her cry. That sucked even more.

I wanted to run back to Doug and away from all the hurt. I wanted to run to him and make it clear just to hurt Berne back.

I was such a child.

"You taking the front or the back?"

Somehow we'd gotten to the river and I'd gotten my flotation vest on. I'd carried the kayak down to the river with Rebecca too. "Back."

Rebecca didn't argue. Berne and Babs got into the kayak in front and stowed the water and camping gear on board.

"You ready?" Babs was looking straight at me, all I could do was nod at her. She'd told me the moment she knew I hadn't been told.

The two women who *supposedly* loved me hadn't even bothered.

Well, I knew where I stood now and it felt pretty lonely.

MOST OF THE day passed by in silence. Babs and Berne were chatting quietly in their kayak but I centred myself on looking up at the green broccoli chunks of trees that hung over the craggy rocks. I adored the Ardèche and the sloshing of my paddle in the river. It was one of the most beautiful places I had ever been to. The cliffs on either side soared up into endless blue. Bird calls, insects, nature sang every second. In a little wooden or fibreglass boat it felt as though the stress of life was a million miles away. Out here it was as it always had been.

Life meandered on, bouncing and bubbling over the rocks, sweeping around bends and snaking around ancient pillars of stone. Up on the hills, little villages were somewhere beyond the trees, ancient structures and monasteries. There were prehistoric caves, Roman arches, forts, farms, people who lived in the same way generations before them had. Down here, on the winding river, I felt connected to it, rooted by it. I was one person passing through.

By evening we were at the first campsite. Our kayaks pulled up alongside. The beaches were pebbled and no one was allowed to camp on them unless they did something like sleep under the stars. Of course, sometimes the locals chose to ignore such things but Berne didn't. So we trudged up the slope in silence. Silence so thick it felt like a rain cloud or maybe I was the donkey from Winnie the Pooh. Tigger? No he was the bouncy tiger, Piglet was the pig in a jumper . . . Anyway, I felt like the gloomy one with a stick-on tail.

Berne, Babs, and Rebecca sat around the gas stove while I chose to erect my tent. It would take me much longer because I didn't have any idea how to do it but, boy, was I going to.

"You need to eat." It was Berne.

I nodded in her direction and carried on. I pulled out all the stuff from the pouch. Who knew you needed so many ropes. What were they even for? I put the ropes back and pulled out a few poles. Here went nothing.

"I have it here for you."

Stuff your food, is what I wanted to say. Instead, I nodded.

"It's going to get cold if you do not eat it."

Like I would care. I clicked another pole into place. My tent looked more like a wigwam. Hmmm . . .

"I forgave you." She placed the food down on a nearby rock. "All I ask is the same."

"Why? You're still going to sleep with Vivienne." Fury rumbled up from inside me. "You're still going to carry on . . ."

I snapped another pole into place. It was too numbing to put into words. My hands shook with the rage.

"You are still going to marry a man. A man who you sleep with?" Berne's voice pulsed with her own anger. "You have no right to judge me when you caused this. You did this to us both."

"Because you would have said no to Vivienne?" I shoved another pole in. Now it looked like I'd taken up cubism.

"I would have told her no everytime, always." Berne's voice was quiet but her words were clear. "Vivienne is not and will *never* be you." She looked up to the stars and huffed out a breath.

"Yet you let her treat you like you are nothing." The sheer force of my own rage shocked me. I was far angrier that Berne was being hurt by someone. I was angrier that Berne was hurting. How did that make sense? "You're better than someone's mistress."

"Am I?"

I looked at Berne, wondering if she'd gone loopy. "You think *I* treated you with such contempt?"

"*Oui*. When you leave and not tell me why. Why did you leave and return with a man's ring on your finger?"

I turned and glared at her. "I *don't* love him."

Said very loudly, the words echoed back off the rocks around us. A confirmation of something it had taken me to say, to realise. Oh *merde*. I didn't love him. At least I wasn't *in* love with him.

Berne glared back at me. "And I do not love her."

"So then why aren't you together yet?"

We both looked at Rebecca who threw her hands in the air.

"You're both going round and round. Get to the good stuff already."

"She has a point," Babs said, handing Rebecca a drink.

"This isn't a democracy. I made a promise, Berne made a promise."

I slotted in another pole. "I broke her heart and she'll never get over that."

Click, the pole fitted together. I swished it through the fabric opening.

"I'm marrying Doug, she's with Vivienne. We made promises to other people. Neither of us will go back on those promises no matter how much it hurts." I shook my head. "I trusted her with Raquel. I can't get over that."

Click, click, swish.

"We messed it up. Move on."

The pain in Berne's eyes was agonising to look at but she nodded. "Perhaps our chance faded long ago."

"Yes."

Rebecca looked like she wanted to cry and Babs was no better.

"We can finish the trip if you want to, then I'm going home." I shoved the pole through another piece of fabric.

Rebecca and Babs nodded, sloping off.

Berne stared long and hard into my eyes until finally adding her own nod. "Let us make it a good one, *oui*."

"You're the guide." I tried to smile but I felt too tired to lift the necessary muscles.

It was why the past needed to be left where it belonged. Why I needed to grow up and start acting like a sane adult instead of a love-struck teenager.

"Is there any way you can fix this stupid tent?"

Berne shook her head. "I cannot."

I frowned. "What do you mean?"

She walked past and tapped the tent with her hand, managing a small smile. "I cannot fix it because it is perfect."

I looked at my tent and could see that she was right. "Wow, that's . . . that's . . . lucky."

"Not luck. Just what is inside showing through." Berne turned and walked away, but I still caught her whispered words. "I will miss that."

Chapter Twelve

IT WAS A clear, calm night. The stars twinkled above and the wind was, for once, conspicuous in its absence. It was no surprise that many felt Van Gogh had cut off his ear not because of the argument but due to *le vent.*

The wind wasn't the only thing that seemed to drive people to madness. Berne stared up at the stars overhead, trying to fight back the tears.

This was cruel, so very cruel to suffer. Of course, it was Babs's plan to tell Pippa that she and Raquel had been more. It would give Pippa a chance to find herself while staying separated from Berne. It hurt that Pippa would think she would ever even consider it, that she bought the lies.

Raquel Rocher could have begged on her hands and knees, Berne could have loved her dearly but her loyalty to Pippa would still have made her say no. She swore to Pippa she had never felt that way and it had been the truth.

It was almost amusing to think that Pippa believed it at all. Raquel had been a close friend back then. She had been there for Berne. Now, she was married with three sons and their friendship had become more distant. Her husband was a sweet man. A handsome man. Berne liked him. It was a shame they were not as close as they'd once been. Raquel had been the first to warn her away from Vivienne but Berne had been too empty to listen.

"How are you holding up there?"

Berne offered Rebecca a smile but it was half hearted. Deceiving Pippa, even if it was in a bid to help her, went against every instinct that she had.

"She really socked it to you, huh?"

"Would you expect her to do any less?"

Rebecca shook her head and took a seat on a chair opposite. The campsite, just back from the river, was nothing but a clearing with a bench. "Did get her to put up her tent in some shape though."

She thumbed in the direction. "I didn't think pitching a tent so close to the stream was okay."

"It isn't." Berne poked the pot of boiling water. The stream was actually a small waterfall that slid down the rocks behind, over the rocks and pebbles and dropped off the edge into the Ardèche. "I will move it later."

"Maybe you shouldn't."

Berne met Rebecca's eyes. "Pardon?"

"Don't move it just tell her it's going to flood." Rebecca smiled. "You and Doug . . . even me, we all do it . . . we don't want to hurt her."

Rebecca was right. Pippa was such a sweet person, a kind person that often she made Berne want to protect her, to make everything perfect for her. Was there such a thing as being smothered by kindness?

Pippa was not useless or unable to cope or lacking in intelligence. No wonder it felt to her as though she didn't know herself. Who would when everyone treated her like a child?

Berne got up and walked over to Pippa, who sat in front of her tent organising her sleeping bag.

"Although the water is not reaching here, the ground underneath is wet."

Pippa looked from her to the tent and back. "I'll get soggy if I stay there?"

Berne nodded.

"Where is best?"

Gone was the anger from earlier in the night. Pippa looked as though she had decided that calm was far better than rage. That only made the feeling of separation worse. It was a risk to lie, a risk that could see Pippa fade into the distance.

"Berne?"

"*Oui.*" She stared at the bank behind, trailing over the available space, and tried not to let the wry smile show on her face.

"Next to mine." Babs had pitched hers and Rebecca's, leaving only enough space for Pippa to pitch next to her. They were co-conspirators in almost everything it seemed.

"Oh."

Berne didn't miss the quick intake of breath or Pippa's long neck flexing with her swallow.

"I can move them if you wish to be away from me."

Pippa's "don't be ridiculous" look made Berne smile inside. The affirmation that she was not hated threatened to break through. Pippa's eyes flicked to and fro until she sighed and got to her feet.

"I don't know how to move it."

Berne stopped herself from doing it for her. "You lift it up and carry it."

Pippa frowned. "Isn't that hard when it has pegs and—" She turned and groaned loudly. She picked up the bag still full of pegs. "That would have been clever."

"Perhaps you knew you would need to move, *oui*?" Berne picked up Pippa's rucksack and sleeping bag. She was trying to stand back but not helping at all was too hard.

"So, will it be wet now?" Pippa picked up her tent, jabbing herself in the shoulder with a pole and wincing. She was so adorable. "How do I dry it out?"

"It should not have been affected yet. You did not enter it?"

Pippa shook her head, colliding tent with the slope in front. She was *beyond* adorable. Berne caught herself smiling at the grumpy muttering, loving the sound of the soft English tones.

"You on the move there, Pip?" Rebecca, forever watchful, wandered over. "You'd make a terrible Ninja Turtle."

"Cowa-flipping-bunga," Pippa grunted as she tried to head up the slope. The tent poked her in the rib cage this time. "Is there a wall or what?"

"If you count a load of pebbles, then yeah. Try lifting it up, cloth-head."

Berne clamped her lips shut at Rebecca's taunt. That was one way to make Pippa pay attention.

"You wha—? Oh. Right."

Perhaps Pippa was insulted often because she seemed immune to being called such names. She followed Rebecca's advice and ascended the slope with ease, dropped her tent in place, and grinned.

"See, I got it."

Berne looked at Rebecca and shrugged.

"You want to crawl through the bushes?" Rebecca asked.

Pippa frowned. "No, why would I want to do that?"

Berne and Rebecca both looked at the tent, hoping that Pippa would realise.

"I don't get it . . . what?" Pippa looked from the tent to them and put her hands on her hips. "Why bushes?"

Rebecca walked to her and motioned to the tent dramatically. "Take a good look. What do you see?"

"Nothing." Pippa bit her lip. "I know I need pegs, right?"

"Well, yeah, but before you go there. What is missing here?" Rebecca once again motioned to what was obvious.

Babs, who had been working in her tent, poked her head out. "*Ça va?*"

"Rebecca and Pepe are in conference," Berne said.

Babs smiled and clambered out to watch as Rebecca and Pippa continued.

"Come on, Pip . . . seriously?"

Pippa waved her hands in the air. "I don't get it. It looks like it did down there. It was fine down there."

"What obvious thing isn't?" Rebecca was worked up by Pippa's lack of observation skills. It was funny, too funny. Berne clamped her lips shut and smiled at Babs as she stifled her laugh.

"I'm not an expert. I don't know." Pippa slunk onto one hip in a way that made Berne bite back the groan.

There was something about the way she did that. Something about the way she looked under the stars, her hair falling free from its band, her lip pulled to one side as she chewed on it.

Rebecca placed her hand on the top of the tent. "You don't need to be an expert. Why don't you test it out? Maybe it'll twig."

Pippa blinked a few times and then shrugged. She pulled her hair out of her face as she always did in preparation for some task. "Okay."

She knelt down and reached out to the fabric. She ran her fingers over it then hung her head. The chuckle rumbled through her shoulders.

"I mean there's dumb, then there's dumb," Rebecca shot at her, flashing a grin at Babs.

Pippa got up and rolled the upside down tent upright and then lifted it around so there was now a door. "How did they let me out?"

Her smile and laughter lit up her face. It lit up the air around her and lifted Berne's heart. Pippa's eyes twinkled as she beamed in Berne's direction. She blew the hair out of her face.

Berne brought over the sleeping bag and rucksack. Pippa looked invigorated and oh so alive.

"Survival one-oh-one. Make sure you don't pitch where you'll get soaked," Pippa said, tapping it out on her hand.

"*Oui.*"

"Second, make sure your tent is the *right* way up." Her slender, long fingers flicked out. She had the hands of an artist.

Berne tried and failed to suppress the chuckle. "It is important, *oui.*"

"Third, make sure said tent is facing the right way." Pippa grinned and reached out for her things. "See, this camping stuff is a doddle."

Pippa clambered into her tent to stow her things away. Berne knelt down beside the doorway. "There is one other thing I think you may find useful."

"There is?" Pippa clomped around until she was facing her, hair flopping into her face at will.

Berne fought the urge to brush it from her eyes. "*Oui.*"

"What?"

Berne lifted up her hand and rattled the bag full of pegs.

"Ah, foiled." Pippa reached out for the bag.

"*Oui.*" She held on as Pippa touched her hand. It was good just to feel her touch. Good just to be near, this near. Memories taunted her with how close she had been once.

"I don't suppose you'd show me what I'm doing with them?"

Relieved that Pippa was finally letting her help, Berne smiled. "With pleasure. Every adventurer needs a guide, *non?*"

She enjoyed the blush that elicited from Pippa. It was good to know that she wasn't the only one with those memories.

MORNING ECHOED WITH the sound of birdcalls. It would be a beautiful day. The scent of summer filled the air as Berne set out breakfast.

"Did you fix the problem?" Berne asked Babs as she wandered over in search of black coffee.

Babs had been very much distracted by something all evening, spending large amounts of time secluded in her tent.

"I think so but I am not sure if the client will approve."

"*Non?*" Berne handed her the coffee.

"He wants a little boy's room but I think he will find it more useful as a sauna. His space could be placed somewhere less . . . obtrusive."

"I think that he likes to be so." Berne looked up as Rebecca wandered over and threw her the sun cream. "*Bonjour.*"

"Thanks." Rebecca caught the cream. "What's up?"

"Babs wishes to move Doug's room to a more secluded place."

Rebecca laughed then stopped laughing when she realised Babs was serious. "Doug won't do that. Doug doesn't do compromise."

"I ask this once again," Babs said. "Why is she with him?"

Berne watched Rebecca put the sun cream on. She took her time, Berne guessed, to calculate an answer that would appease while staying loyal to Pippa.

"Well, we'd been in the firm for a couple of years when Doug's people hired us."

She lathered the cream on her arms. Her tattoos covered by the white goop. Berne noted Babs was riveted to the action.

"Doug was . . . and is . . . a cool guy. He was suave and he's a hunk. He pretty much made it clear that he wanted Pip."

"He pursued her?" Babs's lips parted as Rebecca splodged cream on her neck and shoulders.

Berne shook her head, concentrating on the food.

"Yeah, I mean Pip seemed to like him enough. I thought that was just her way. It wasn't until I saw her around Berne that I—" Rebecca smiled.

"*Ça va?*" Babs was leaning forward, avid in her concentration as Rebecca's hands stopped their motion.

"Well, it was then I saw how love became her."

"He does not see her true worth," Berne said, jabbing at the food. Still, she couldn't help but smile with the observation. It was good to know that even when Pippa was with this man, he had been far from her heart.

Rebecca "mmm'd" her agreement as she slapped the cream on her legs.

Berne took the tipping coffee cup out of Babs's hands as she drooled. "Why is she loyal if he is not so good to her?"

"He's a good guy." Rebecca ran her hands over her thighs, oblivious to Babs. "A dense guy, who doesn't know that Pip *isn't* playing hard to get. I have the impression that he thinks the moment they're married that she will melt into his arms."

The visual memories of Pippa doing just that in her own embrace made Berne's body pulse. Was it wrong to enjoy the fact that she had seen such a transformation and he hadn't?

"I know what you're thinking," Rebecca said.

Babs sat upright.

Berne shook free thoughts of Pippa from her mind.

"You do?" they said in unison.

"Yeah." Rebecca put cream on her face. "Surely he must have known, right? Surely we all must have noticed that Pippa was . . . well . . . gay."

Berne and Babs exchanged guilty glances.

"But you did not?" Berne asked, covering Babs who looked slightly warmer than could be accounted for this early.

"No," Rebecca said. "I mean, I never twigged but then she never looked at anyone like that . . . ever."

Again Berne smiled.

"I used to think the ring was an heirloom or something, that the French shirt was her favourite because it was comfy or something." Rebecca smiled at Berne. "Why *did* she get your rugby shirt?"

"You need cream on your back too, *non?*" Babs cut in to save Berne although it had nothing to do with loyalty and more to do with opportunity.

Fighting the urge to roll her eyes, Berne focused on making the rolls up and placing them into foil and boxes to be ready for the morning break.

The school trips and pleasure excursions were not in full swing as yet. The river would be quieter and there was no need to rush. Most tourists paddled down the river section in two days, starting at Vallon Pont D'Arc and finishing at Saint Martin. Berne intended for them to make a more leisurely trip. The schedule was dictated by Pippa. How long Berne could keep her on the water to give her the time to think was the important mission. They would take in some adventure activities along the way if need be—anything to give Pippa the chance to figure out her own desires.

Berne sighed.

Anything to help Pippa come back to her.

"I heard there's a nudist beach," Rebecca said. "Seriously?"

"*Oui,*" Berne said. "Not long after we go under Pont D'Arc."

"You will pass them on the way through. You wish to stop there?" Babs sounded far too hopeful for Berne's liking.

The only thing that would achieve was the poor woman getting sunburn in places that she doubted saw strong sunlight. Judging by how very white Rebecca's stomach was, Berne wouldn't like to take the risk either.

"You have a rash vest?"

Rebecca looked at Berne blankly.

It was not something Berne could think of the English for. Her mind ran through the alternative ways to explain in French. "It is a top you wear. It looks tight. It is worn by surfers." What was the English for it?

Again Rebecca looked lost.

"I have one. You are bigger than me but I like them to be loose," Babs said, taking over. "You can borrow it."

"Um . . . great?"

Before Berne could explain, a loud string of expletives filled the air. She looked at Pippa's tent in time to see the shape of her through the fabric. She laughed before she could stop herself.

"What is she doing now?" Rebecca went to go to her but Babs placed a hand on her arm.

"It is part of the camping experience to learn not to touch the canvas, *oui*?"

Rebecca nodded. "Yeah, condensation is a bitch."

Berne smiled. When she'd brought Pippa to the Ardèche all those years ago, Pippa had done the exact same thing. The memory of that howling and the fit of giggles her face had provoked seemed as vivid now as it had then.

"Oh she's going for the zip." Rebecca gripped hold of Babs's arm. "This could be brutal."

Much swearing and yanking made the tent rock violently from side to side as Pippa tried to negotiate the double zip.

"I locked myself in!"

Berne carried on with the lunches, anything not to run and help. Rebecca chose to hold onto Babs's offered hand.

"Hello?"

Babs shook her head and placed a finger to her lips.

"Anyone?"

More grunting, more tent rocking and the sound of a zip moving.

"Perhaps it is better you are not gawping when she releases herself, *non*?" Berne raised an eyebrow at them.

Babs and Rebecca nodded and hurried to Babs's tent in search of a rash vest.

Pippa's head popped out into the sunlight, hair wild as it always was in the morning. "You been there the whole time?"

Berne nodded. "I could not help you. I would burn the food, *non*?"

Pippa rubbed at her stomach. "I'm starving."

"I have your breakfast ready when you would like it." Pippa groaned in such a way that Berne's heart increased its heavy thudding beats. "I thought you would appreciate this."

Pippa went to walk out of the tent, not seeing that the zip didn't go all the way to the floor and promptly tripped over the remaining fabric. Berne was already there, waiting with her arms open, as Pippa tumbled at her.

"Guess I never learn." Pippa sighed. "You would think three stitches would have etched that part in my memory."

"If it helps," Berne said, trying to look anywhere but Pippa's captivating eyes. She looked so sensual in the morning, so wild, so untamed, and carefree. "*I* remembered it."

Pippa's cheeks coloured as she relaxed in Berne's arms. "I'm glad you did."

The warmth of Pippa's body made it hard not to feel how close she was. Close enough to smell the fruity scent of sun cream and shampoo. Close enough to brush the hair from her eyes, to trace her finger down the smooth cheek—

"I . . . we . . . breakfast," Pippa mumbled but she didn't move.

"*Oui*."

Closer, Pippa's eyes dropped to Berne's lips and she licked them in response. "Berne, I—"

"Hey there, bush woman, what are you doing?"

Berne sighed and relinquished her hold on Pippa and strode back to the breakfast. Rebecca was right to stop them but it still didn't make the interruption welcome.

She was surprised that Pippa was still so . . . responsive . . . even when she thought Berne had betrayed her.

"Falling flat on my face," Pippa shot back. "Lucky for me, my trusty French guide was at hand."

Berne bowed her head in acknowledgement, not daring to look

up and run her eyes over the pyjama shorts with faded hearts on them. Cute and sexy all at once.

"Yes, well, if you keep throwing yourself at women, I may pout." Rebecca poked out her bottom lip. "I never got so much as a lingering look."

Pippa poked out her tongue at Rebecca's teasing. Berne was glad to see that Rebecca now had on a tight rash vest.

Pippa noticed too and grinned. "Good idea. I don't know if I brought mine."

Berne would not stand back on this one. "I have one in my bag for you."

A quiet smile played across Pippa's lips. Berne's body responded to the look, memories swirled inside her mind. How she was going to stay distant from Pippa, she didn't know. Pippa finding herself seemed to make her even more attractive.

"As if it wasn't already hard enough," Berne muttered under her breath. Not being with Pippa was difficult enough when her own head kept betraying her.

When Pippa looked at her as she was now, with eyes full of hunger, it was almost impossible.

Chapter Thirteen

I WAS GLAD of the rash vest when we carried the kayaks down to the river. You could never be too careful with the sun, in my view. Okay, so I wasn't the snowdrop that Rebecca was but under the intense heat that wouldn't matter. I had a bit of an obsession with making sure I had enough cream on.

"Howzat!" I grinned at Rebecca as she smothered sunblock on her nose and cheeks. "Where's the wicket?"

"You may laugh at my war paint, Saunders, but white cheeks are better than pink stinging ones." She shrugged. "Besides, I'll come out in freckles anyhow."

"I like your freckles. They're cute."

Rebecca raised her eyebrows and put her hands on her hips. She was a picture with her long board shorts and white legs. Her vest was too small but her float-vest was a little too big, and all in bright colours. To top it off nicely, she had a lovely cherry red helmet on and all the sun block. "Are you flirting with me?"

Trying to suppress the giggles, I nodded. "Of course . . . who wouldn't . . . hot is not the word."

Rebecca narrowed her eyes. "I'll tell Berne. How quickly you turn when faced with my war paint."

"I know, it's terrible, isn't it," I said, getting into the back of the kayak. "But who could resist such a sight?"

Rebecca blew out a breath. Babs and Berne looked over from their boat. "Well, you'll have to try. You're not my type."

"Oh, really?"

"Really," Rebecca said as she stepped in.

"And there was me thinking that *female* was your type." I pushed off from the shore and swung us around. The sound of the strokes through the water calmed me. "Guess I should break the news to Babs, huh?"

Rebecca spun around, making the kayak wobble. "What?"

I grinned. "You heard . . . Oh, you need cream on your back too, *non*?"

Rebecca's blush shone through her block. "She was trying to help me, thank you very much. At least someone wanted to make sure I was protected."

"Nothing to do with lathering your back then."

Rebecca's mock expression of shock drew raised eyebrows from the others.

"There is a problem?" Berne's sly smile told me that she knew I was teasing.

"Yes. It seems that because Pippa is a floozy, she has labelled me . . ." Rebecca clutched her chest. "Me, such an innocent, with her loose morals."

"You should have taken drama, you know that?" I flicked water at her with my paddle.

"Berne, could you please tell this floozy that I'm as pure as the sunblock on my face."

Berne raised her eyebrows as Babs shot her a wicked smile. I didn't miss the second grin shot Rebecca's way. Hmm, Babs looked a wee bit smitten.

"I am afraid this may be so," Berne said to me. "Her English manners have her strung tightly, *non*?"

This time Rebecca's shock was genuine. "Did she just call me frigid?"

"In a polite French way, but yeah." Oh, I loved seeing her squirm.

Rebecca slammed her paddle onto her lap. "I demand a retrial!"

I flicked more water her way. The two boats bobbed side by side and I gave into the temptation. "Well, now, maybe I should call in an expert witness?"

"And who would that be?"

I smiled at Babs. "What do you think? Is Rebecca here tied up tighter than her float vest?"

Babs anchored their boat to ours as she made a show of examining Rebecca closely.

I smiled at Berne who nudged my shoulder with hers. She looked tense today, like she had a lot on her mind. What was going on behind her hazel eyes? Sometimes, I wished I had some kind of device so I could know.

Babs wriggled her fingers up Rebecca's side. Rebecca flinched and slapped Babs's hand.

"Hmmm . . . It seems Berne could be correct in her thoughts." Babs winked at me. She was enjoying herself, a lot.

Rebecca wagged her finger. "Uh huh, no way. That just means I'm ticklish."

All eyes turned to me and I shook my head and adopted the best forlorn and serious expression I could muster. "I dunno . . ."

"Try again." Rebecca took an exaggerated breath, rubbing her hands together like they did in Olympic gymnastics. "I'm ready for you."

Babs wiggled her eyebrows.

Berne smirked. She was enjoying the show as much as me. It was nice to see how much she liked Rebecca. Berne had always been incredibly protective over Babs, scaring most of those she deemed unsuitable. It was the way she carried herself. Even without intending to, she dominated the space around her. The way she walked oozed alpha female. From the outside, she could appear cold and arrogant but I knew better. Berne was shy, a deep thinker. Someone who said a lot without needing words *if* you could read her.

"Hey, cold hands, cold hands!"

Rebecca slapped at a giggling Babs, rocking the boats in the process.

"Steady, you'll tip us, *nitwit*."

"Less of the insults, *dreamy*."

Babs shook her head. "I think that is conclusive evide—"

Rebecca planted an enthusiastic kiss on her lips. "See, no prude would do that, my little French delight." She folded her arms as if that settled the whole thing.

I kept an eye on Berne but she seemed delighted.

Phew.

Babs sat in a daze, touching her fingers to her lips.

"I would say advantage England," I whispered to Berne.

"Don't count her out of the race yet, Pepe." Berne nodded towards Babs who dragged Rebecca into an enthusiastic response.

She pushed the stunned Rebecca back and nodded smugly. "If you are going to kiss, do it properly, my little English *belle*."

Rebecca blinked a few times, her blush a lovely colour against the white cream.

"First set to France, *oui*?" Berne whispered back.

"Undoubtedly."

Before the match could continue, we rounded the bend in the river and the gorgeous wonder of Pont D'Arc came into sight.

It looked like a giant had once had a doorway there. Its green-covered top gave it the look of a Roman ruin. A very tall Roman with the need for Rebecca's tanking method. It stretched over the river that flowed underneath it.

Rebecca saw it too, her eyes drifting over the natural arch. "Man, that's stunning."

"About sixty metres wide and fifty-four metres tall. It is a wonder of nature, *non*?" Berne's eyes lit up at the sight. I loved hearing her talk about the Ardèche.

"That's a lot of Babs piled on top of each other," Rebecca mumbled. "And you guys stick the Eiffel Tower on your postcards."

"*Oui*, there is nothing more pleasing than nature's work. Human hand does not compare." Berne tapped the boat. "There is a beach not far ahead. We shall stop for a break? It is a good spot to find inspiration."

I knew that she was addressing Babs who was the most incredible artist I had ever seen. Not that I would know a Matisse from a Chagall, I was surprised I even remembered the names.

"Inspiration?" Rebecca asked.

Why she was looking at me I didn't know. She'd *seen* me draw. Matchstick men were not art no matter how cute I made them look.

Berne nodded at Rebecca. "You will need it if you are to negotiate the rapids, *non*?"

Rebecca's eyes flew to mine. "You didn't say anything about rapids."

"Do not worry, Madame, I will be steering you." Babs flashed her a debonair grin.

"These two need their own court," I muttered. People would want tickets. It would be a sellout.

Berne landed her kayak and extended her hand to help me out of the boat. "I think you may be right about this, *mais*, it means I am with you in the rapids."

"Which means it's me getting soaked then."

I looked up at Rebecca. Should I tell her that the front was the raw deal? I watched Babs nudge her hip as they walked up the beach and thought better of it. Why spoil her fun?

FED, WATERED, AND back out on the river, Berne slowed
the kayaks. "Your helmets are all fastened?"

We all nodded.

"Your vests, they are secure?"

A few yanks and tugs and we nodded again.

"*Alors*, Babs and I know the route and so I wish you to enjoy
the journey, keep your arms inside the boat . . . and try not to fall
out, *oui?*"

We murmured agreement as Berne and Babs set off at a pace
and manoeuvred to the side of the river they needed to follow.

"We will go first. That way Pepe will be ready with the camera,
non?" Berne said.

Babs chuckled.

Rebecca gripped onto the front. "Why couldn't I be with
Berne again?" She leaned over towards me. "I've seen her *drive*,
remember."

"You are in erratic hands," I said, plonking her on the helmet.
"Enjoy it."

"Some friend you are."

I blew her a kiss as Berne set off. "See you in a minute!"

I pulled my paddle in and allowed Berne to take over. She'd
asked me on the beach if I wanted to be in charge and paddle us
through but I felt happier with her at the helm, or rear . . . Stern?
Could you have a stern on a kayak? No . . . port was left . . . or
was that right . . . Oh well, whatever the bit at the back was called.

"Do you remember the first time?" Berne asked as we entered
the rapids, the swirling water speeding us forward.

"I was terrified, I remember that much."

Berne's laughter echoed over the roaring white waters. We
swept past a rock. I held onto the front, glancing back at her. Her
strong arms were hard at work to manoeuvre us into the right
position.

Not a great time to start drooling.

"You were so glad that we made it through, *oui?*"

I had forgotten my very ardent response to making it through
the rapids and the recollection burst through my mind and every
single inch of me. Good thing we'd been alone that day.

"Now, is that why you're in my boat?" Was I flirting? What

was I doing? That was not concentrating on finding myself or being mad at her, was it? No, that was completely letting the side down.

"It was to protect Babs, *non*?"

I doubted Babs needed much protection. If Rebecca was the same as me, she would delight in the reward.

"So you *wouldn't* want me to thank you?" Flirty, Saunders. What was I doing now? I was supposed to be mad. Berne was mean . . . she sucked . . . I needed to focus. Mean Berne, mean, mean Berne.

Water crashed over me as the boat dipped down a level. I whooped with the tickle it shot through my stomach.

"That depends how relieved I can get you to feel, *non*?" The tone sent more tickly wriggles up and down my body.

Focus, woman . . . focus. Mean, mean . . .

"Oh, that's a big dro—"

Another wave of water crashed over us. I clung on, my bottom leaving the seat and clattering back down as we burst out through the water.

"Good thing I still have my own teeth, right?"

Berne's lively smile made my heart thud. Her mouth open, her arms pumping, her hair dripping, she was incredible. I turned back around, knowing I was sporting the same grin. It was just the rapids, just the fun of it all. It was a simple memory. I didn't really want to thank her, nope, not one bit. Uh, huh. Not focusing on very strong, very toned arms or the way the water dripped off—

"Nearly to the finish line, you wish to paddle?"

I grabbed my paddle and drove through the water at her command. Sun beat down on us, the water wild, the beauty of the sheer cliff faces on either side. I was giggling like a fool by the time we hit the chequered flag or more realistically, a load of branches stretching their knobby fingers across the water.

"That was not bad," Berne said, turning around to look upstream. "I think you may even have time to take a picture of her."

Without thinking, I leaned forward and brushed my lips against hers.

"*Merci beaucoup*." Before logic caught up with me and spoke sense into my giddy mind, I pulled out my camera.

"Do you think she's still on board?" I asked, trying to ignore the intensity of Berne's gaze.

"*Oui*, Babs is far better on the water." Her answer was quiet, her voice deeper. My legs felt wobbly at the hum of her tone. "There they are."

I put the camera to my eye, trying to calm my breathing. I needed some kind of aversion therapy. What was I doing kissing her in broad daylight on a river? What if someone Doug knew had seen?

I snapped a few pictures as Rebecca was dunked into the white foam and pulled the camera away.

Who did Doug know here?

As Rebecca was dunked once more, I leaned in but Berne was waiting for me. Before I could think, her mouth had reclaimed every forgotten sense. I had my hands in her hair as she reminded me exactly what I was missing.

Every second, so raw with emotion.

Berne broke free from me and nipped at my bottom lip before pulling away completely as Rebecca resurfaced.

"What was that for?" My voice was hoarse, my blood thumped a celebratory rhythm in my ears.

"I need a reason?"

No. Nope, not one. I placed the camera in the bag, did anything not to be recaptured by those eyes. Somewhere in the rapids, I seemed to have lost my sense of control.

"I . . . well . . . you are supposed to be with—"

Berne silenced me with another fleeting kiss. "This is *my* river, *oui*?"

My resistance was pathetic. "I guess it is."

"When you are on my river," Berne brushed her lips against mine once more, "you must pay the toll."

In that case, why argue? "Don't need to ask me twice—"

A load of water splashed over me. Rebecca and Babs sported matching wide grins.

"Oi, cut it out," Rebecca said. "I leave you for two minutes!"

"Did you enjoy the rapids?" I asked, ignoring the sudden urge to dive out of the boat and swim away from the heat rising in my cheeks. I was the worst fiancé in history. Stick me in a boat with a French woman and I was a floozy, just like Rebecca said, a brazen hussy!

"I gotta say, I *love* her driving this thing." Rebecca tapped the side of the boat. "She's like a mad thing."

"*Like* a mad thing?" I smiled at Babs who was eying me suspiciously. Yes, I know, I was an awful fiancé. I was meant to be mad with Berne, meant to be getting married, meant to be straight and loyal. "I would say there's no *like* in it, she *is* one."

"And proud of it no doubt." Rebecca's knuckles were still white on the boat. Berne was still waiting for me to look at her and Babs eyes felt like laser beams.

"Er . . . anyone fancy lunch. I'm starving."

Rebecca rubbed her stomach and nodded. "Sounds like a plan. You enjoy the rapids?" She smiled at me. "You look as dry as I feel."

"Berne likes to . . ." Every answer seemed open to innuendo. I didn't do innuendo. Was I really thinking along those lines? Oh wonderful. I was not only a floozy but turning into a teenage boy, like Rebecca. "It's an adventure," I managed.

"Certainly looked it," Rebecca said with a grin. "So much for mad and unforgiving, huh?"

"That *is* me mad and unforgiving."

Rebecca raised her eyebrows. "If that's you mad, what happens when she does something you like . . ."

Rebecca grinned at Berne who wiggled her eyebrows.

I stared pointedly at the cliffs to our right. "I don't know what you mean. Not one idea."

Chapter Fourteen

WE HAULED ONE boat on top of the other upside down and placed a blanket on top to create our lunch bar. Berne spread out the sandwiches and other goodies. She was magical with food. The woman made it impossible not to love her. Who could be angry with someone who turned a simple roll into something that should be served in Michelin star restaurants?

To attempt some kind of decorum, I went and sat by myself. It unnerved me how I'd given in so quickly. Yes, I had admitted to myself that I wasn't *in* love with Doug but did that really give me any right to go drooling over Berne? What did that say to her about me? I *couldn't* be with her and yet here I was acting like I'd never been away. My heart thumped as if it had woken up from a long doze. My palms were clammy, my body felt as though I'd been plugged in on high power and everything felt brighter.

Experts, like the ones I'd seen when I came back from France the first time, had told me it was simply the love drug. They reminded me that I was just a bunch of chemicals whizzing around driving me to procreate. That my entire existence was merely to breed. What a load of old codswallop. I had bought it as much as I bought the fact that men were just acting out of impulse to be cavemen when they were idiots.

If we were just here to breed then why did we like painting pretty patterns on walls? Plus, I'd never seen a monkey erect a shrine and try for spiritual awakening.

All that being said, science nor any kind of counselling could explain why, all these years later, it was still Berne who stirred every part of me. Why *only* she had ever done so. Honestly, I was akin to a eunuch . . . No, that wasn't quite right . . . Oh bother. I was just not full of hormones like Rebecca.

I sat chomping on my baguette, wondering how I'd got from food, to monkeys, to eunuchs in one thought process. Babs wandered over and I was sure that I was about to get lambasted.

I ripped off a chunk with my teeth so at least I wouldn't have to answer.

"If I did not know better, I would think that you came here with another reason than the one you say, *non?*"

Here it came.

I chewed, pointing to my mouth.

"What better way to earn back Berne's trust than to have her paddle you down your memories?"

That sounded very calculating and involved all sorts of forward planning. Babs must have thought I had changed my personality entirely. Cunning took focus and effort, and well, I couldn't even pack my suitcase.

"Do not look at me that way. I hear you say you cannot do these things, *mais*, I remember." She tapped her nose. "I remember how you helped me back then. I remember how easy it was for you."

I swallowed my chunk and frowned at Babs. "When was this?"

"I was in London, you met me, you took me around that weekend."

I grinned. That was an awesome weekend. Babs had been teaching at some posh arty college for the week and I wanted to show her all the treats of London that tourists wouldn't ever see. Babs and Berne had always made France so much fun, I wanted to do the same for her.

"You count showing you around a city help?"

"*Oui.* You knew who to talk to for tickets to the match, *non?*"

"That's because my dad is a member of the tennis club. It wasn't me. He was delighted I'd asked him." Not only that, we'd got the full five star treatment. It had been a great day on centre court, not that I knew what was going on but Babs did. I whooped when she did. The strawberries with cream over the top, I knew *exactly* what to do with.

"You were efficient beyond words. Anything I wanted, you got. Now you act like you cannot do a thing." Babs put her hands on her hips. Even in tiny red shorts, a blue tank top, and bright yellow floatation vest, she still looked fashionable. I wasn't sure how she did it.

"I was young then, fearless. I have obligations now."

She flapped her vest out of the way, looking like detectives stood on TV. "What fills you with fear so?"

It was a relief that she was more curious than angry. "Losing her . . . losing me . . . waking up years from now regretting everything."

I shoved more baguette into my mouth. Why had I gone and said that?

"What would you regret more, spending your life with the woman you adore?" She smiled at me, motioning over to Berne who sat soaking up the sun, head hung back exposing her long neck. "And do not tell me that you do not."

I cleared my throat. She had me there.

"Or," she leaned in, a frown wrinkling her perfect brow, "spending your life with a man you do not love?"

"Or," I said around my mouthful, "I could leave him, alienate everyone who loves me, move over here only for Berne to find out that I'm not such a wonderful person, and end up penniless, alone, and cleaning toilets on a campsite."

Sucking in the breath after my diatribe, I again wanted to take back my words. I'd said too much. I'd kept everything in when I was in London and now look at me? I was like one of those crazy women on chat shows.

Next thing Rebecca would storm over and tell me she was my mother's sister, or something along those lines. I watched far too much daytime television.

Babs cocked her head. "Your family would turn away from you?"

"Oh yeah." I shoved more bread in my mouth. Stop talking, woman, shut it.

"And if they loved her, how would your fears be then?"

They *wouldn't* love her ever. I knew that. She was a woman and she was a lesbian and she was not in any way part of a golf club. I doubted my mother would even like a man who wasn't part of the golf club. What was it with golf? "Babs, I love you, please know that, but Berne spent one year with me when I was a carefree teenager. She *thinks* she loves me but I'm not eighteen and I'm not carefree."

"*Non*," Babs said. "You are thirty-one and you are lost."

I had no idea why she was bothering to tell me that, I *knew* that already. "I have no redeemable features that make it worth her while." I put my hands over Babs's lips. "Listen to me. I adore her and that's unconditional." The truth of that sunk in with my words and stung. "Loving her like that means that I want what will make her life the happiest."

Babs nodded at me like I was a dense child. "Being with you."

I shook my head. "No, being with me means that she won't get to live the high life in Marseille with Vivienne or join the gendarmerie when her father sells the business." Not feeling quite as hungry now, I wrapped the baguette back up. "Being with me means that she'll spend her whole life trying to take care of me as I'm useless."

"Where has this loathing come from?" Babs's frown made my already churning stomach roll.

I turned to walk back towards the others who were chatting over the boat-bar. "I don't want to talk about it."

Babs touched my hand. "When you are ready, you know where to find me."

I offered her a smile. I doubted it showed in my eyes though, I felt miserable. I was up and down like an emotional yo-yo.

"So, you ready for the nuddies?" Rebecca asked, flashing a cocky grin my way. At least someone was having a whale of a time.

"We aren't joining them," I said. "Beached lobster is unbecoming."

"Ouch," Rebecca muttered. "Who sizzled your stew?"

I rolled my eyes.

"You did not worry before."

Everyone turned to Berne and her cheeky smile. Wonderful. I wondered how long it would take her to fill Rebecca in on that one.

"She's just being funny." I glared Berne's way. "Aren't you?"

Berne's smile slid up one side, her eyes twinkling. "You were the one who wanted to try it back then, *non*?"

"Nope." I tried to look for something to do.

Could I wade down a river the whole way? If I started now, I could make it to Saint Martin by the time the blush wore off.

"Pippa Saunders!" Rebecca's mouth hung open.

"Fine. It was part of the experience." I fiddled with the zip on my float-vest. "I was with Berne. It wasn't like she hadn't seen me naked before."

Even saying the word naked sounded wrong on my tongue.

"*Oui*, and someone had to protect you from the admirers, *non*?"

"More like the other way round."

Rebecca looked from me to Berne like she was watching a Wimbledon match. "There were admirers?"

"Not the naturists." I zipped and unzipped my vest for something to do. "The boys in the boats floating past."

"I'll say!" Rebecca looked at Babs who smiled. "You really did know another woman."

Berne lifted her chin as if she was proud of it. "She still lurks inside."

"Good luck finding her," I mumbled and felt the sudden sting of tears. I turned and walked down to the river's edge. How had I lost that life, that energy? Where had that young adventurer gone?

"I already see her," Berne whispered to me as she carried the boat back to the river. "She is more beautiful than her surroundings. Perhaps it is just knowing where to look."

My heart responded to her tone, her love, her gentle words of support. "What is it about me that makes you so blind, hmmm?"

Berne held out her hand to help me into the boat. "Not blind, *awake*."

THE AFTERNOON PASSED by with me deep in thought. Every moment since I had left Berne replayed in my mind. The reason why, the real reason, tormented me with a blow by blow account. Over and over I ran the pivotal moments in my life as though somehow it would resolve my issues, change my choices, make the howlers go away.

Why did a mind do that? Why did it dig out regrets, embarrassments, broken dreams? What was the point in torturing me with them now?

I'd not even paid attention to the naturist beach. Rebecca was quite disappointed that the only people there had been of pension age. What she'd been expecting, I had no idea. I'd just paddled, recriminated myself, paddled some more, brooded and . . . well . . . paddled.

"I think we will stop for the evening soon," Berne said to me. She had been observing my sullen mood in silence, letting me have peace to think. I had felt her watching me. "I would like to initiate Rebecca first though, *oui*?"

"Init—" I grinned, my mood lifted at the thought. "Oh, she'll love that!"

Berne nodded and banged her paddle on the side of the boat, alerting Babs. "We have a newcomer to the river, *non?*"

Babs face lit up and she paddled them over to us. "She will need to pass the test, *oui?*"

Rebecca screwed up her face. "What are you two *oui*-ing and *non*-ing about now?"

Feigning seriousness, I kept my voice deadpan. "You need to be introduced to the Chamonix family tradition."

"What does that mean?" Rebecca looked from Babs to Berne. "What are you going to do to me? If it involves traffic cones, I would like to warn you that I have form—"

"Calm, my little English éclair." Babs got to her feet, the boat wobbled ever so slightly. She launched into a raucous version of a camping song that Berne's forefathers had passed down.

"Karaoke?" Rebecca raised her eyebrows at me.

Berne got to her feet without causing the slightest movement and sang out, with gusto, the required response. Rebecca's face was a picture. In all fairness the song sounded more like a tribal challenge of some sort.

"You!" Berne said, pointing to me. "Do you love the Ardèche?"

I got to my feet, the boat wobbling until I remembered how to keep my balance. "*Oui, mon capitan!*"

"Do you love France?" Her voice bounced back off the cliff faces, drawing looks from a few kayakers paddling by.

"*Oui, mon capitan!*" I remembered that I had to salute.

"Prove it!"

I stood on the lip of the boat with my feet, remembering not to close my eyes. Keep my balance, core strength, focus on Berne.

With a grin, I bellowed out "La Marseillaise." At least the first verse and chorus that I knew. It didn't matter that I was singing about invaders and what the French army wanted to do to them.

As I got to the chorus, I gave it everything I had. It made me feel giddy and light, like I had back then, just turned nineteen and hopelessly in love. It was the same sensation of freedom.

I finished with gusto and got a hearty applause from the nearby paddlers. I saluted them with a wink.

"What do you think, Babs?" Berne said. She looked as

impressed as she had that day on the train. Her eyes hungry. "Does she pass?"

Babs grinned, clapping. I could have sworn she had a tear in her eye. "She could not fail with that one, *non?*"

Berne nodded solemnly. "Very well, you pass."

"*Merci, mon capitan!*" I carefully sat back down and looked at Rebecca's astonished expression.

"Wow, Pip. Where did that come from?"

Laughing, I leaned over and squeezed her shoulder. "Experience. You'll understand in a minute."

Berne and Babs, who were still standing, motioned at Rebecca. "Up . . . Up!"

Babs rocked the boat, making Rebecca grip on.

"Okay, okay already," she muttered, pulling herself to her feet.

"Do you love the Ardèche?"

Rebecca looked at me and I nodded in encouragement.

"Oh yeah!"

Bless her.

"*Pardon?*" Babs said, putting her hand to her ear.

I saluted to try and help her.

"Right," Rebecca said. "Oh yeah . . . er . . . *mon capitan?*"

Berne and Babs looked at each other.

Oh dear, poor Rebecca.

Babs dipped her leg. Rebecca lurched to the side.

Splash.

"What d'you do that for?" Rebecca spluttered out the river water as Babs gave her a hand back into the kayak.

"Perhaps you will do better with the next question, *oui?*"

Rebecca flicked water at Babs but I could see the twinkle in her eyes. The hint of challenge sparked between them.

"You betcha." Rebecca got to her feet once more, the boat wobbling.

"Do you love France?"

"*Oui, mon capitan!*"

Impressive, she sounded like a soldier. Babs looked impressed too. I made another saluting gesture, and Rebecca managed to get it in before the French court threw her overboard.

"Prove it."

"I don't know the anthem," Rebecca hissed at me.

"It's okay, you can sing anything."

"Right," Rebecca mumbled. "On the lip right?"

I nodded. *"Bonne chance."*

The boat wobbled and swayed as she tried to stay upright. Eventually she steadied herself. It had taken me a few tries when I'd done it first but Rebecca was more talented in sporty things.

"Okay, well, we had France. Now I got to do my own thing."

I laughed. Rebecca was a patriot through and through so out came "God Save Our Queen" at the top of her lungs. She didn't need encouraging, she sang it with such feeling that I had a lump in my throat. The woman had the St. George cross tattooed on her heart, I swore.

"What was that?" Babs asked, even though she had clearly enjoyed it as had Berne.

I looked at the paddlers who clapped in respect for Rebecca's verve.

Berne and Babs sighed heavily in unison.

"That does not prove that you love France," Babs said.

"Course it does," Rebecca shot back. "I love it enough to share my own heart with it."

Ooh, nicely played.

That stumped them. They looked at the audience.

"Dip or dry?" Babs asked.

The young boy in the front cheered for the dip while his father gave a reprieve. The mother in the second boat was with her son but the little girl was on Rebecca's side.

"It is a tie. What do you think, Bebe?" Babs asked.

It was a high tension moment. To dip or dry was a very important question.

Berne looked Rebecca up and down. "Well, she has a good voice, but her choice is awful. It is up to you."

Babs grinned. Rebecca grabbed for her. Pulled her over. The kayak tipped.

Splash.

Both of them were dunked.

It was so funny that I had to hold onto my aching sides. The family cheered as Rebecca surfaced.

"That'll teach you," she shot at Babs, splashing water at her.

Babs swam over and dunked her under. More cheers from the family.

"I think she is holding her own," Berne whispered to me.

"I think Babs is smitten."

Rebecca had a way about her that made women adore her. She was cheeky, cocky, confident but sweet. Babs was the kind of woman who could make women do almost anything for her. She was dashing, vivacious, curvaceous, and exuded confidence but right now, she looked a little doe-eyed.

"You are too quick to decide, Rebecca looks captivated herself, *non?*"

Rebecca was chuckling, her helmet on the wonk, her vest hanging open with sunblock dribbling down her nose. Her eyes were locked on Babs, eyes that glinted with joy. Berne was right, Rebecca looked smitten too.

"Good thing you saved the kayak tipping completely," I said. "Looks like someone lost their tent."

Berne looked at the bobbing cover and smiled. "Babs, I believe someone is sharing a tent tonight, *non?*"

Babs swam over to the tent.

Uh oh, I recognised that patch . . .

"It seems that Mademoiselle may need some shelter for the night." Babs nudged Rebecca who nodded. "She will need a roof over her head, *oui.*"

"Guess so, she'll probably sleep with m—"

"It is only right that *Berne* offers a place to stay, *non?*" Babs said, her hand clamped over Rebecca's mouth.

Rebecca went to shake her head but Babs dunked her. "Bebe, you are the guide, you are the one who helps."

Berne met my eyes. "*Oui.* We would not wish Rebecca to lose sleep."

"Oh, it's okay," I said. "I sleep with her all the time."

Rebecca, who had surfaced, shrugged at the two glaring French women. "She does . . . and before you both start, I had no clue she was gay." She shook her head. "I mean . . . glaringly obvious, right?"

"I am not." I folded my arms, hoping that the family, who were now paddling away, hadn't heard her. "I'm not."

"No offence, Pip," Rebecca said, clambering back into the boat. "But you sooo are."

"Am not!"

Babs and Berne started to row us over to the beach as I splashed water in Rebecca's direction. I wasn't gay. I didn't have a problem with her being gay or anyone else but *I* wasn't. I didn't run after gorgeous women, neither did I go to clubs or march in parades. They'd never let me in.

I was me, I was . . . sort of . . . with Doug. He was a man. I wouldn't feel anything for him if I was gay? Would I? Nope.

Rebecca was wrong.

Wrong, wrong, wrong.

"Pip," Rebecca said as we got to the beach. "Is that where this is coming from?"

"You lost me."

Berne let go of the boat and pulled the supplies and equipment out with Babs assisting.

"Is that why you're so worried?" Rebecca took the front end of the boat. We lifted it and carried it up the beach. "Because you haven't come to terms with it?"

"I don't need to come to terms with anything. I'm just not gay."

"Pip, you slept with a woman." Rebecca huffed as we placed the boat down. "You are in love, and I mean epically in love, with a woman." We trudged back down the beach to the other boat. "You want to be with another woman . . ." She pulled her helmet up as it fell over her eyes. "That's kinda gay."

I hoisted up the back end of the boat as Rebecca again took the front.

"It's Berne. That's all. I don't feel that way about any other women." We clomped the boat down. "The receptionist thought the same."

"Who?"

"The receptionist in Paris thought I was gay too."

Rebecca raised her eyebrows. "The receptionist? What kind of check-in service did they have there?"

I poked my tongue out and wandered over to my tent bag. We were in a makeshift campsite less than a minute's walk from the river. I checked around in case there were any more streams. Not that it mattered. There was no way I was using that again this trip. The patch had been to try and keep the cover as waterproof as possible but it had failed spectacularly. Served me right for not buying a new tent.

"I asked her if she thought I looked right with Doug and she pointed out that I'd asked her of all people."

I ignored Rebecca hovering next to my shoulder as I pulled out the sodden tent.

"And why was that important?"

I shrugged and laid the tent out over the ground. It wouldn't dry tonight in time but at least it would be dry in the morning. "She said something about being happy to have shown me had her girlfriend not been working."

"Hah," Rebecca said, and Babs wandered over to us. "Apparently she's picking up receptionists now. Every time she goes to France alone, she causes chaos I tell you."

"She has seduced someone else?" Babs folded her arms as if she really believed I could have managed anything of the sort.

There was no way they were dragging me into this teasing match. I wandered over to Berne and carried the little gas canister for her.

"You want this up and running?"

Berne nodded and I set about attaching it to the mini-stove.

"You don't get to walk away from that," Rebecca said. "Why was the receptionist hitting on you?"

Not missing Berne's suspicious glance, I focused on getting the flame going. "She was merely appreciating me. Either way she thought I didn't suit Doug because I'd asked her."

Happy with the flame, I placed the pan on top of it. "I asked her because she was the first person I saw. She was soooo wrong."

That wasn't technically right. There had been a few other members of staff but it was down to the fact the receptionist had talked to me. That was all. She was friendly.

"Is there something wrong with being gay in your eyes?"

My unimpressed face should have said enough but I knew that, after her father, Rebecca would need more. "You know it doesn't."

"Then why is it so hard for you to consider that you might be?"

Ooh, she had me there. I hadn't thought of that but still, I didn't need to *consider* anything. "This isn't about sexuality. We all know I love Berne. That's not the issue."

"But don't you wonder why Berne is so attractive to you?"

I shook my head and put olive oil in the pan like I'd watched Rebecca do a million times. "Not really. Berne is gorgeous. It's a fact."

That earned me a kiss on the cheek from the woman herself as she moved around me, adding ingredients.

"What did the receptionist look like?" Babs asked, putting out camp chairs for us all.

I'd make a rubbish witness, I could never remember details. "Dark hair, dark eyes, nice tan."

"She wear one of those slit skirts?"

I took the offered spatula from Berne and shovelled the food around the pan. "No, she was always in trousers, why?"

The three of them exchange glances.

"What?"

"What was that girl's name that you used to go to lunch with?" Rebecca clicked her fingers. "She was tall, athletic looking—"

"Heather?"

Rebecca nodded. "That's the one. You spent a load of time with her."

What did that have to do with anything? "She was interested in carpentry."

Again the three of them exchanged glances.

"Cut it out. I'm not gay so get over it."

The food smelled just like it did when Berne cooked it and I slid the mix of vegetables and stir-fry onto the large plastic serving plate. "It's not my fault Berne is beyond amazing. I didn't stand a chance."

A second kiss on my cheek, I leaned into it. Forgetting where I was and all other thoughts but the conversation.

I sat down and Rebecca pointed to her food. "For someone who doesn't cook, you make a mean stir-fry."

"I . . ." I looked at Berne who smiled. Hey, I'd made a meal, I'd done it. I hadn't burned it like my mother always told me I did. "It's edible?"

"Taste it," Berne said, offering a forkful of her food.

The delicious explosion of tastes on my tingling tongue made me smile. "It's not half bad, is it?"

"A woman of hidden talents," Rebecca said.

"A woman of *many* talents," Berne added.

Babs shrugged. "She's beautiful. I could not care if she was pathetic at everything as long as I could look at her."

"Hey!" I wasn't sure whether to be offended or slightly chuffed that she thought so much of my aesthetic qualities.

"It is the truth, Pepe. Berne is as handsome as you. This is why you look so good together."

Not daring to let that vision penetrate my mind, I scooped another forkful into my mouth. It tasted wonderful and what was even more amazing was that I cooked it and it was delicious. Yay me.

"You have always been good at cooking." Berne squeezed my knee and left her hand resting on top. "You used to make us dinner sometimes when I was training."

"No, I used to make you dinner when I was trying to keep you awake long enough for a conversation."

Rebecca looked up. "You *seriously* fell asleep on her?" She shook her head, disgust crinkling her mouth. "Even Doug keeps his eyes open for her."

"I was training full time for the gendarmerie. I was also helping my father at the weekend." Berne stared down at her food.

I hated to see her thinking of her lost dream. She'd always wanted to be an officer, always wanted to follow her brother's example.

"Couldn't you join again?" I asked.

Berne looked up. "In theory but I do not wish for that anymore."

That was something I was thankful for. "What do you want to do?"

"I want to take over my father's business and make it grow. When he became ill, I knew that to see his hard work be in vain, to let our traditions fade, it would be madness."

I took the hand resting on my knee and kissed it. "Are you happy with that choice?"

She nodded and kissed my hand back. "*Très content.* I find freedom in restoration."

The sun was setting gently over the hilltops and Berne's eyes glowed with the pinks and golds. Soft light bathed her sun-kissed cheeks as she licked her lips. I leaned in closer, just wanting to look more closely at her beauty.

"Whoa, Mrs. Fletcher-to-be." Rebecca's voice once again pulled me from the moment. "Kissing the locals is only permitted when you are single."

There was no missing the glance at Babs.

Subtle.

"I'm technically married to her," I shot back. "So I *am* allowed."

To prove my point, I kissed Berne on the tip of her nose. The small act of rebellion both revolted and excited me. One thing was abundantly clear, I was cheating on Doug and I needed to have a long conversation with him. No matter the outcome of the trip, I'd crashed over so many lines that I'd forgotten where they'd been drawn.

"If you're married to her, then it won't matter about you sleeping in her tent. Although, I think you owe her an explanation as to why you've been having an affair with a guy for eight years."

Rebecca needed to be a barrister or something. She was great at proving her point and even greater at reminding me of my duties. What must Berne think of me, kissing her when she had a girlfriend and was happy. How dare I barge in and make her cheat too.

Irritated by her uncanny and infuriating knack of knowing me too well, I scowled at Rebecca. "Eat your dinner and stop harping on, will you?"

She roared with hearty laughter as she held up her bottled water. "To Pip, growing a backbone at long last."

Berne and Babs joined in. "To Pepe!"

Chapter Fifteen

NIGHT FELL QUICKLY down in the gorge. Stars twinkled above as if they were winking down at me. The breeze had picked up a bit, and I'd snuggled into my jumper.

I looked at the tent and tried to suppress the sudden urge to giggle like an idiot. Berne had been watching me, ever silent, over dinner. Rebecca and Babs had rambled on about the induction and my rendition of the national anthem. Talk had then turned to the house and how Babs's plans would not make Doug happy, not a bit.

Through it all, I had been thinking of one thing only, the fact that I had to sleep in the same tent as Berne. Berne of the gorgeous voice and soft touch. Berne of the sensual lips and strong hands. Berne of the knowing looks and sweet, teasing kisses . . . Berne.

Merde.

Sighing, I ran my hand over the fabric, knowing that the woman in question loitered behind me. I could almost feel her without turning around, like her gaze could send heat waves up and down my spine at will.

"I need to tell you, to ask you something." My throat oddly dry, I tried to clear it, managing only a raspy cough.

"I am here." Her body heat rippled up and down me as she whispered in my ear.

A slow, gentle kiss on my shoulder.

"You and I are both with other people." Kisses trailed up my shoulder to my neck. Oh, she remembered . . . just there . . . oh yeah.

"*Oui.*" Berne's breathy mumble against my skin. Her hands snaking over my hips—

"We can't."

I spun around, catching my foot in the guide rope. A huge ripping noise made me forget the fact I was falling. Berne caught me, pulling me to her. Her arms held me steady. I shut my eyes and clung onto her, burying my head in her shoulder.

"Did I break it?"

Berne looked around me at the tent and nodded. "Unless you wish to see the stars?"

If the clouds weren't starting to creep over the sky, that would have been a great option. Unfortunately, I was beginning to smell rain in the air.

It was like a British superpower. Rain was my thing. The detection of it an art.

"*Alors*, I do not think we can fix it."

I turned around and saw the damage. "Oh no. Oh Berne, I'm so sorry . . . I—"

Firm, warm lips claimed mine and my trail of thought vanished.

Rebecca cleared her throat beside us. "Three things, ladies. One, I smell rain. We seriously camping in the rain?" She counted her points out on her fingertips. "Two, Pip, that means we're down to two tents. Guessing that means sharing is a group thing." The twinkle in her eye made me laugh. "Three, you are adults, shacked up with other people, if you want to smooch each other, do the right thing, will you?"

"And that is?" I asked. Was she seriously getting moral on me?

"Get a room."

Berne let out a hearty chuckle and I raised an eyebrow at her. There was a naughtiness in that sound that I'd never heard before but oh did I love it.

"There is a small campsite. They run tours. They may have room." Berne looked at Babs who was already stowing her tent away.

I looked up at the sky, to Rebecca, and smiled. Get a room. I could do that. "I never turn down a nice comfy bed."

TWENTY MINUTES LATER, we stood in a holiday village of sorts. Wooden chalets that looked like garden sheds dotted at angles around a concrete block. I assumed that said block housed the reception and a canteen but I couldn't make out much through the misted windows. It was belting down. Proper old-fashioned British-style rain.

The porch area was tiny so Rebecca, Babs, and I were huddled together to keep dry as Berne charmed the owners inside. The place looked busy and I didn't fancy trudging back down to the river campsite. For a start we would have to yank our kayaks back off the rack on the side and I *really* didn't want to be hauling that thing anywhere for a few hours. My back was more vocal about heavy lifting than it had been at nineteen. I'd be groaning when I stood up or sat down like my mother before long at this rate.

Berne emerged holding a key in her hand. "One room only. It has two beds."

"That's a little more sharing than I'd like." Rebecca folded her arms, glancing at me. "No offence, Pip."

Understanding exactly how she felt, I did not want to be within hearing distance of those two if Babs and Rebecca headed where Berne and I knew they would.

"None taken but it's chucking it down and I will take sharing a single bed with Berne here." More need to giggle. "But I think we should all make the decision to act like proper adults."

"Which means?" Babs asked, peering out at the rain.

"Behaving."

Babs looked like she wanted to protest but simply shrugged. "It is one night."

Berne's hearty laugh filled the air once more and she pulled out another key. "Perhaps if behaving is on your mind, I will take Babs."

The three of us folded our arms in unison.

"Sneaky, Chamonix," I muttered.

Berne smiled as Babs snatched the key off her. "Where?"

Berne led the way and pointed to two wooden summer-house-looking chalets side by side. Very cute.

"Time for bed, huh?" Rebecca squeezed my shoulder.

I stared at the door and bit my lip.

"Night, ladies." She grinned my way as Babs practically dragged her into the room.

"I'd say that they are stalemate at the moment," I muttered. "Both as bad as each other."

"Mmm," Berne purred close to my ear.

I turned around and frowned at her. "Now, I meant what I said . . . Berne, we're . . . we . . . can't."

She sauntered towards me like some kind of gunslinger.

"I mean it . . . Berne, what about—?"

My back hit the door. Berne slid the key in the lock beside me. Her eyes fiery and full of desire.

"I don't want . . . to belittle . . . what we have by—"

Berne clicked the lock open. I jumped as she slid her hand over my stomach to reach the door handle.

"I . . . I'll . . . I'll go sleep in the tent." My knees were shaking, my hands were shaking. I was officially a human jelly. "It's better that way."

Berne pushed open the door. I stumbled backwards into the darkened room.

"Now, Berne . . . don't look at me like that . . . I don't want—"

She grabbed hold of my waistband and kicked shut the door.

"Don't we need lights?" I could control myself. It was better for us both if we didn't do anything rash.

"*Non*," Berne whispered. She pulled me closer still. "I will work by feel, *oui*?"

"Oh."

Her hearty chuckle washed over me again. Wow, that was a glorious sound. I shivered. Uh oh. Calm, decorum, control. Resistance was futile. No, no, I could be controlled.

"Tell me to stop." Berne's lips found my neck once more. "Tell me that you do not love me."

Well that was just cheating. How was I supposed to fend that one off?

"I . . . we . . . you . . ."

More kisses, slowly, surely working their way down.

"No . . . fair . . ."

Berne ripped away my top. "All is fair in love and war, *non*?"

Her warm fingertips were impatient as they ran over my stomach.

"That's not . . . quite . . . what it's . . . supposed to mean." Breathe in. Calm. Focus. Control. What was control again?

Berne's lips claimed mine. I tried to shake free from the building moment.

I pulled back. "Are . . . we . . . at war?" If we were, I stood no chance. I couldn't even string a sentence together.

"*Non*." Berne guided me backwards. My legs hit the bed behind me. "We are both in agreement now."

"We are?" I murmured against her lips. "I remember obj—" Berne's kiss rocketed desire through me. Her mouth demanded. Her hands held me there, steady.

"If you are objecting, Pepe, your hands are not listening."

Aware of my hands with her words, I understood why she was pushing me back onto the bed.

Oops.

It would have probably been a good idea to stop running my hands over the nice toned flesh on her side. "Ah . . . I see your point."

"*Bonne*," Berne said, her voice hot and heavy in my ear. "Because tonight, you are mine."

NOT SURPRISINGLY, THE morning sunlight saw me wake with a large grin on my face. I turned over and saw Berne peacefully slumbering beside me. I just wanted to record the moment. Correction, I wanted to record the whole of the night too.

Moments like this transcended every emotion I could express. Moments when she dreamed, when the world was waking up and her gentle breathing purred through the silence. Moments when the outpouring of pent-up feeling had calmed and her body and mind were at rest.

Berne had always been the kind of woman who forever felt as though you needed to be a locksmith to unshackle what was going on inside her head. Behind deep, intense eyes that uttered words her mouth could not whisper.

"*Bonjour*." Her sleepy, husky tones sounded before the slow smile appeared across her lips. "I am told that you do not like the morning."

Cuddling my pillow, I laughed. "Yes, well, Rebecca doesn't quite have the same effect."

"*Non?*" Berne turned onto her side and I cleared my throat, pulling up her covers. "There is something you do not wish to see?"

"You *know* I do, but if you're chatting, I need to focus."

Berne's eyes twinkled. More of that playfulness I'd experienced last night.

"You are a lot more, *sure,* of what you want these days." It was a tantalising development, I loved it. Still, I was curious as to why.

"*Oui.*" Berne took my hand and kissed my fingertips. "I want that ring on your finger to be mine. I want you." Her eyes glinted with an intensity that sent a pulse of energy hurtling around my body. Oh wow. "I will not let you run again."

"What happened to me abandoning you and . . ." I fought the urge to spit the name. "*Her.*"

"We were never together," Berne whispered, brushing a strand of hair from my face. "Raquel and I, we have never been more."

I frowned. "What?"

Berne smiled. "You think I would do such a thing to you?"

I opened my mouth, then closed it. "You *lied*?"

She nodded. "We felt you needed your distance, to know what you feel inside without complication."

"We?" I raised my eyebrows. That kind of tall tale could only come from one person. "Let me guess . . . Babs?"

Berne smiled.

Enough said. Relief poured through me. They were just friends. I could deal with that. "But what about Vivienne?"

"You only have to say the word, Pepe. One word." Berne kissed my fingertips and I wondered if my heart telegraphed its soaring joy to her. One word. My heart seemed to clamber up into my mouth in a bid to scream it out, waving its arms in the air. *Yes . . . Yes . . . please!*

With it causing a commotion, thumping away through my ears, I couldn't make my mouth move to speak. Oh, how I wanted that, I wanted her.

But I couldn't.

Fear screamed in, smacking my heart off its perch and squeezing my stomach like it was trying to strangle it.

What if she changed her mind? I wasn't good enough for her? She would never be happy with just me. What if they found out? It would ruin her. I couldn't do that to her.

"What happened to you?" Her words were gentle, her fingers tracing my cheek. "I know that you would never go without good reason. I know this is more than the reason you say."

I shook my head, feeling the need to run, to flee from the bed but strong arms pinned me in place.

"No more running."

"I can't . . . please." I sounded like a frightened child even to my own ears. What must she think of me?

"*Non.* Tell me. Tell me what happened."

Although she was demanding, it was without aggression but more pleading.

"You wanted to be on the motorcycles. I didn't want to stop you."

Berne shook her head. "I know what you said to Rebecca *mais* I deserve the truth. No more lies."

Tears stung my eyes. The weight of her on top of me felt like a safety blanket. I was here, she was here, it was alright.

"Do you remember me telling you about my sister?" Not sure if I could continue, I buried my head in her shoulder.

"Catherine?"

Her name made my stomach crunch up even tighter. I clung onto Berne as she held me.

"What happened, she was hurt?"

"No," I shuddered out. "Nothing like that." Tears took over, clutching at my throat, robbing my words from me.

"I am here . . . Talk to me . . . *s'il te plaît*." Berne stroked away the hair from my forehead. "You were close growing up, *oui*?"

"Yes." Catherine was fifteen years older than me. I'd followed her around like a puppy. "She was my hero."

"Was?"

I took a few breaths to compose myself and looked up into Berne's eyes. She was here, she was surrounding me, her warm soft skin on mine. I could do this.

"I'd talked a lot about France, sent letters to her, postcards."

"*Oui*, we sent the one of the Notre Dame from Paris."

I smiled. Why it was a shock that Berne remembered that, I didn't know, but it filled my heart with some confidence.

"I told her all my secrets growing up. She was my champion. If I needed advice or help, she was there."

Berne said nothing but smiled to encourage me.

"Before I saw . . . the accident, I saw her." I took deep breaths, in . . . out . . . calm . . . calm . . . I could do this. "She turned up to surprise me. She saw me kiss you goodbye."

"Ah."

I murmured my agreement. At nineteen and besotted, I saw only Berne and so, quite often, our morning departures made for quite a show. So did our evening hellos but, thankfully, those were normally behind closed doors and not on the pavement.

"She didn't say a word about it at first. I was so delighted to see her that I didn't see the difference in her." I trailed my finger over Berne's strong shoulder. I felt safe enough to go back there mentally for the first time. "We got to the café and she told me about how disgusting she thought gay people were. How she'd seen a pair on the street while waiting for me and it had turned her stomach."

That café was so quiet and her voice hushed. I could still smell the strong black coffee in her cup and see every detail of her expression. The look of scorn and, for want of a better word, disgust. All the while, I kept quiet, not knowing she'd been talking about me.

"I told her that Rebecca was gay, that she was lovely . . . that people were just people." I closed my eyes. I felt as sick as I had then, the cold sweat pulsing from me. "Then she told me that she'd seen how nice I thought gay people were. How much I'd disgraced her, the family."

Berne held me, her sounds soft, her touches comforting. Her warmth anchoring me.

"I mean, she was my hero, my sister. As if that wasn't bad enough." Why did hurting make it so hard to breathe? Why did her venom still burn me up so?

"I am here, tell me."

I gripped onto Berne's shoulders and clung to the safety of her. "She threatened to tell my parents, who would have alienated me, but worse, she threatened to say that you'd *forced* me to be with you."

I didn't need to look into Berne's face. I could feel the anger tense her shoulders.

"She told me that even the complaint would see the contract cancelled. That my father's friend would see you bankrupt."

"You would have told the truth." Her complete confidence in me made the fact I'd run worse. Why hadn't I stayed? Why hadn't I told her?

"I was scared that even if I did, they may not listen. That even if they did, your name would be marked, that it would follow you."

Air seemed to burn my throat. I felt more tears sweep over my cheeks.

"I was a mess. I walked home to you and I saw the accident. I ran over to him and tried to help . . . there was so much blood . . . his eyes faded . . ."

The sirens, the chaos all around. I looked down into that poor man's eyes. I'd never even learned his name but I'd knelt there, clinging onto him, desperately pressing my hand to his neck.

He faded and I could do nothing. The ambulance crews came, the police, and I fled the scene. My thoughts of Catherine, of having to leave, mixed with the helplessness, the shock. I could stay and ruin Berne's life or I could run like a coward. If I bore the pain alone she could live her dream.

I never wanted that phone call or visit. Back then, there had been no rights, no marriage, no chance that I would be seen as important. If I left, I'd never know.

"I heard of the accident," Berne whispered. She sounded as affected by it as I felt. "I knew it was you who was with him." She pulled back to look at me. "You acted with love and courage." She scowled. "Your sister is a bitch."

"You think?"

"*Je connais,*" Berne said. "What happened when you went back to England?"

It was all so much of a deranged blur of recrimination, guilt, shock, and grief. Catherine had kept me under a watchful eye, the axe hanging overhead, looming high every time I thought of returning to France.

"For two years, I was a shell. I had counselling from a nice man about the accident but it didn't stop the pain. It didn't stop the ache from losing you. It didn't stop the guilt."

I couldn't understand how I'd survived that time. It was so gloomy, so grey, so lonely.

"Then one day Rebecca came to me. Her devastation shook me into life. Her dad kicking her out echoed everything I felt, you know?"

"*Oui,* she was living your fear?"

So, Rebecca had opened up to Berne, I was glad. Go girl. "Yes, he had her tutor fired and cut her off. It was brutal and she was drowning. I didn't want her to and so we got jobs in London, got out of there. We escaped together."

"What did Catherine say?"

Again the name, again the nausea. "She was livid but I told her that there was nothing going on. It was a phase, all that stuff. When Doug came along, it seemed like a way to get her off my back."

Oh great, that sounded cold, weak, and pathetic. "I mean, he was a nice guy. He isn't an ogre or anything and like my mum says, I'm lucky he puts up with me."

Berne's deep scowl made me tense. "He is lucky to have you look at him. You are beautiful. I will have no more of this. You are *incroyable*."

Now I knew I was blushing.

"Catherine loves Doug," I said, trying to keep to the topic. "She is no doubt the mastermind behind his sudden wish to get me pregnant and marry me."

"*Encore en fois*," Berne said. "Your sister is a bitch."

"I've spent my whole life hiding from the threat back then. It sucked the life from me." I shrugged. I was such a coward. "I'm not sure if there's any of me left."

"Pepe, you suffered from trying to help that officer." She took a breath as if it were painful for her. "You suffered at the hands of someone you trusted. You were only a young woman, you believed her words." She scowled again. "If my brother would dream of such things, I would ache for it too."

"You would?"

Berne smiled. "*Oui*. So what will you do?"

Being in her arms lit the places that had been long forgotten. I was no young woman now but a rather beaten and emotionally scarred adult. Twelve years of pain and emptiness. Years which I'd simply survived. I hadn't lived, I hadn't been awake even. This morning, I felt . . . *alive.*

"I need to break it off with Doug," I said, feeling the tension return. "I need to be an adult and tell him the truth."

Berne's gentle smile almost looked like she was proud of me.

"Then I want to win you back—" I placed my finger over Berne's lips. "If you're going to be with me instead of *her*, I want you to know you can count on me not to leave again." I kissed her sweet, soft lips. "I need to earn that trust back . . . please."

Berne nodded. "And your sister?"

"Can we just set Babs on her?"

Berne chuckled.

"In all seriousness, I don't know. She's kind of like that big ogre waiting with its club and I know I have to go through her to get to where I need to be."

"You could run through her legs, *non*?"

I pulled Berne downwards, my hands making my intentions abundantly clear. "Right now, I want to focus on what promises lie on the other side."

Berne smiled against my mouth. I loved that feeling. "Then, let's make this unforgettable, *oui*?" Her words brushed her lips against mine.

Safe, warm, and happy.

Lost in her touch, I briefly heard my mumbled agreement, which sounded very much like, "Oh, yeah."

Chapter Sixteen

BREAKFAST WAS SERVED in a little canteen-of-a-place in the middle of the campsite. The tables were all picnic benches with wooden garden chairs around them. The staff looked like they were a family, pottering around the tables, chatting to the stragglers who lingered over their *petit dejeuner*. Rebecca and Babs were already there when we strolled in.

"*Bonjour*," I said, trying not to grin at Berne.

Rebecca had a dopey expression on her face as she met my eyes. I guessed she had been inducted into the "I love France" club.

"Morning." She cocked her head. "I see you are the image of fidelity."

Tapping the ring on my finger, I smiled. "Actually, I am."

We sat down and I was glad that the place was next to empty this late in the morning.

Rebecca raised her eyebrows. "One night. Wow, that was some going."

Berne's hand rested on my knee and I listened to the cheery, if not tired, conversation. Sunlight bathed everything outside. Gentle tones of a radio filtered in the background. Smells of freshly made, warm bread filled my nostrils and with three people I absolutely adored the lights seemed to switch on in my head.

The world was no longer threatening, no longer a scary place of fears. For the first time in a who-knows-how-long it felt *welcoming*.

"She give you a lobotomy while you were there?" Rebecca nudged my shoulder. "Smiling inanely into space there, Pip."

"I'm leaving Doug."

Babs and Rebecca looked up from their plates. Rebecca's mouth showing her half-chewed roll. "Am I dreaming?"

Babs leaned into her. "Not unless we share the same head."

"Yes, very funny." I turned to Berne, expecting her to shake her head or perhaps roll her eyes but no, she was staring at me like I'd grown two heads as well.

"Um . . . you of all people should have seen that coming." I frowned. "You were listening this morning, right?"

She nodded, her expression blank.

"So you heard the bit about leaving him?"

Berne nodded again. "*Mais,* I thought you would change your mind." She shrugged in that adorable French way. "He his rich, handsome. I am an artisan."

Now it was my turn to stare at her like she'd grown an extra nose.

What? Had she been sleeping when I'd confessed everything to her?

"This is why I need to earn your trust again." I took her hand. "If you'll ever trust me."

"I do—"

"You have spent the night with me, the whole morning. I've told you everything and you still think I am going to go back to him." I kissed her hand. "Would you have thought that before I left?"

Berne shook her head. She was a woman of few words most of the time, now it was like prying barnacles off a boat. Oh wonderful, barnacles off a boat? Was I Rebecca now?

"Then when I come back, will you still give me the chance to earn it once again?"

"Pepe, I will do that now, I—"

"No," I said. "You're in a relationship. You can trust her not to leave, she's proven that."

Rebecca cleared her throat. "So, you're really doing this. I mean, really leaving him?"

"Yes, I *really* am."

She blinked a few times and a wide grin appeared on her sun-freckled face. "Wow, France does something to you, huh?"

I picked up another piece of bread and took a deep breath. Better out than in as someone said. "That, and I'm gay."

The coughing and spluttering from Rebecca was a wonderful reward. Berne's hand squeezing my knee was another. My cheeks felt like I could toast my bread on them but still, baby steps.

"Pip, look me in the eye and say that again," Rebecca said.

Another breath. "I'm gay."

A little easier. It sounded like I was confessing to a murder or being an alcoholic but still.

"Honey, I love you, you know that?" Rebecca pulled me up into a bear hug before I'd registered she moved. "You sure?"

"Fairly certain," I said. Wow, my cheeks were scorching and my ears were joining in. Could I have sun burned my own face?

A second later Babs launched herself at me. What was with all the hugging? Hadn't they seen me with Berne? It wasn't too much of a jump. Even the Parisian receptionist had guessed and she'd only known me a few days.

"Pepe, I knew you would re-emerge. Bravo." Babs sounded like I was going off to war.

My ears throbbed with the heat and my neck itched. No doubt I looked like a human lightbulb.

"Yes, well . . . thank you?"

Noticing that the staff were now staring at me, I went to sit back down and bury my head.

Berne however felt that she needed to add her thoughts. "*Tu es incroyable.*" She wrapped me up in her arms. Oh, did I love that feeling. "I truly adore you, you understand this?"

My poor neck itched with the heat, my face was on fire, my ears prickled away and all I seemed capable of doing was shrugging. What I must have looked like, I'll never know.

"I . . . well . . . you do?"

Uh oh, the daft grin burst into place. I was a bright red itchy lunatic with a shrugging problem.

"*Oui.* We should celebrate!"

Berne took hold of my hand and dragged me from the canteen, Babs and Rebecca in tow.

"Are you thinking the same as me?" Babs said, as we got to the boat rack.

Berne grinned. "*Oui*, it will be on tonight. It will be the perfect way."

"What will?" I asked, not liking the conspiring.

"I second that," Rebecca said and exchanged a worried glance with me.

"A celebration. Ajoux has its own tonight. My mother wished us to come, *mais*, I was not sure that you would feel happy there."

The list of panicked thoughts went as follows: Uh oh, Doug was going to be there. What if he saw me during the celebration?

What if Berne's mother caught me drooling over her daughter? What if Berne's father/brother/uncle/aunt caught me drooling over her? What should I wear?

"Tonight . . . in Ajoux-Sur-Rhône?" If I was red before, I was certain the blood had drained from my head, making me feel giddy.

"*Oui*. It is special to me."

Now there was a "suck it up, leave your fiancé, and stop messing me around" statement if ever I'd heard it. Was I backing down or going for my dream? Was I going to grow a backbone and stop running from the past . . . and, in all seriousness, what was I going to wear? What was appropriate? What kind of a celebration was it?

"Pip," Rebecca said. "You need to answer at some point."

Answer her, move lips, tongue, and speak. "Do I need dress heels, because I left them in Paris?"

Berne's lips claimed mine with such fervour, I was caught off balance and almost clattered into the boat stand. Wow, I guess she liked dress heels.

"Is that a yes?"

Rebecca folded her arms. "When do you think about heels, ever?"

Good point, I was about as fashion conscious as a tramp. "It's just I don't have them with me . . . What if we're in a—?" I stopped myself.

I didn't need to think about what people thought now. It wouldn't have a bearing on Berne's business or reputation if my skirt wasn't the right length. "Can I just wear jeans and a t-shirt?"

"You will be with friends," Berne said. "With me . . . and you would look perfect to me in anything."

"Or nothing," Babs added, earning a snigger from Rebecca.

"If you two are going to be this intolerable together . . . You are together, right?" I asked.

Both nodded.

"Good . . . where was I?"

"Intolerable," Rebecca said with a smirk.

"Right, yes. If you are going to be that way . . . yay!" I launched myself at Rebecca who did clatter into the boat rack.

"Hey, I got enough jumping from this one."

Too much information, not a great visual.

Think of Berne. Oh, there went my cheeks again. Maybe better to think of something else. Even if it was a really good—

"Pip," Rebecca said. "I know you're finding your feet with your sexuality but it's not polite to snuggle me in front of the ladies."

I snapped my hands from where they'd dropped to. I felt like I was burning up brighter than before.

"Sorry," I muttered, backing up. "Miles away."

Rebecca's lurid laugh deserved a slap on the arm, which was what I gave her, as Berne chatted away in rapid French on the phone.

"What's she saying?" Rebecca asked me.

"Pickles if I know, it's at light speed."

"She's making the arrangements," Babs translated. "You have me to help you now, my little English lemon slice."

I wasn't sure if it was me or was Babs getting more food orientated with the names.

"I like the sound of that, my little French merlot."

Did merlot go with lemon? I wasn't a wine connoisseur at any stretch but I was sure that wouldn't go at all.

"Can you just tell me if I need to dress up?" I asked. "I mean, is it a posh event or are we talking casual?"

Rebecca poked me in the ribs. "Pip, I don't think Berne minds what you wear."

"I want to look good for her, okay." That realisation was new but boy, I wanted Berne's jaw to drop when she saw me. I wanted her eyes to be riveted to me the entire evening.

"You already seduced the chilli peppers out of her, Pip. She's smitten, yours, signed up and ready to tango."

"Where did tango come into it?"

Rebecca shrugged. "It went with the chilli peppers."

While Berne chatted away, motioning for Babs to join her in her conversation, I turned to Rebecca. "I want to win her back."

Understanding why she would be a little confused, I didn't baulk too much at her "huh?"

"She's with . . ." I still couldn't even utter the name. "*Her* . . . and I need to prove to her and myself that I can do this."

"You slept with her, that's pretty conclusive."

I wished I had more time to tell Rebecca everything, to sit

down and talk it through with her. I made do with the shortened version. "I didn't just leave because of the crash—"

"Which I knew."

She did? Maybe I should steer away from crime as a future career as I was apparently so transparent. "Catherine caught me kissing her. She threatened me. I left to protect Berne and made us both miserable for over a decade."

Rebecca pulled me into a hug. "Babs thought it was something like that. She knew you wouldn't have gone without a fight."

When did Babs figure this all out and why hadn't she said anything? "She knew about Catherine?"

Rebecca pulled back to look at me. "No, she thought it was your mother. I have to say I went with her too. Catherine, really?"

"The one and only."

"What did she say?"

Not really wanting to go through the whole thing again, I leaned my head on Rebecca's shoulder. "She made a convincing threat. Can I say that for now? Enough to terrify me into going back with her."

"What a bitch." Rebecca growled to add impetus to her thoughts. "And to think, I was always nice to her." She shook her head. "She never said a thing to me, two-faced bitch."

"I concur. Either way, the second I tell Doug I'm leaving him for another woman, I'll have to face her."

Rebecca gave me a quick squeeze. "You'll have me, the French equivalent of a miniature tornado, and Biceps Bebe right behind you this time."

I chuckled at the description. The wave of love and comfort that washed over me threatened to make me crumple into tears all over again. Decorum, Saunders, attempt it at least.

"Speaking of Babs, how did it go?"

A rakish grin dimpled Rebecca's cheeks. "I think I see your point with French women."

There was something else I needed to know. "Who made the first move?"

Rebecca raised her eyebrow. "Why?"

Balls, she was onto me. "Simple question."

"Liar . . . why?"

This was the problem when she knew me so well. I sighed. "I

said she would break first." I hoped her competitive edge would surface. "England to win."

"You *bet* on us?" Rebecca put a hand over her heart. "I'm shocked . . . and so very, very proud."

"So?"

She wagged her finger in the air. "Who broke first for the story on the French shirt."

Balls again.

"Fine."

Rebecca folded her arms, that smug grin back in place. "Cough up."

With an exaggerated "urgh" to voice my disgust, I kept my eyes on Berne as I spoke. "The night we first . . . got together . . . I . . ." Here came the heat in my face again. People must think I had intermittent sunburn. "It was the six-nations rugby. Guy, who was one of the contractors, dared me that if the French beat us, I would run down to the beach at midnight forfeiting the loser's shirt."

Rebecca sucked in the air through her cheeks. "*Allez les Bleus* that year?"

Nodding, I kept staring at Berne who was now staring back with curiosity.

"It was so close. France scored in the seventy-ninth minute . . . and I had to do the forfeit."

Rebecca again sucked in the air. Me and nudity were not normally acquainted.

"Guy was, shall we say, interested in me and demanded I have a referee to prove I'd done it."

"Poor guy." Rebecca folded her tattooed arms.

"Yes, well . . . I said Berne."

I could still see her shocked expression. She had told me she was gay, I'd never said a word back. It was a split second decision which led to lingering looks. Just like she was now, back then Berne was trying to understand what was on my mind. I was trying to read what was on hers. Terrifying, exhilarating, and etched in my mind.

"So she walked me down to the beach front and told me that I didn't have to do it. She would stick up for me." Always the champion. "Instead of answering, I kissed her on the lips, pulled off my top, and ran like an idiot."

Rebecca chuckled. "I bet she loved that."

My laughter had filled the cold night air, soft sand under my trainers. Berne caught me, conveniently, next to a set of rocks. My shirt had dropped somewhere during my sprint. I had no idea where.

"I asked her if I could have her shirt. She had a vest on underneath and I was terrified I'd be locked in a French police cell."

"Yes?" Rebecca was now well and truly loving the story, eyes glinting. If I was honest, it felt good to share it.

"She told me that I could earn it if I kissed her again." Her husky voice, stars up above, that hunger in her eyes. She knew she had me defenceless. Nowhere to run and happy to give in.

"Oh, I like her more and more by the minute."

Turning to smile at Rebecca, I lowered my voice. "No way was I losing twice in one night." I wagged my finger. "Oh no. I wanted to win back some dignity for us."

"Atta girl," Rebecca said, leaning closer. We must have looked like we were in a scrum. "So, what did you do?"

"I made sure that *she* was asking me to take her top off . . . very sure." I shook my head at the memory, must have been the wine. "And . . . well . . . she gave it to me."

"The top or—"

"Both." I cleared my throat, ignoring Rebecca's open-mouthed expression. "I was nineteen and slightly tipsy. Now, so who kissed who?"

Rebecca closed her mouth, then opened it, then closed it again.

"You asked for it. Where Berne's concerned I'm without restraint." I sighed, seeing Berne saunter towards us, her hips swinging to and fro. She walked like a sprinter in the Olympics, which explained why I seemed quite drawn to the event. "So, who kissed who first?"

Rebecca shook her head. "One, stop gawping and two, wow. Where has this side been and why wasn't it in my bed?"

"Funny." I poked her in the arm. "Spill it."

"I kissed her." She grinned my way. "But not before she kissed me."

I hugged Rebecca like we'd won a match and gave her a big squeeze. "That's my floozy."

"Thanks, hussy. I take inspiration from you."

"Are you ready to leave?" Berne asked, hovering nearby. "I can wait if you wish to . . . er . . ."

I wandered to her and kissed her cheek. "It's okay. I was just telling Rebecca about my French shirt."

A large smile crossed Berne's lips which told me that I may have just earned that shirt after all.

Chapter Seventeen

THE GENTLE CHATTER of birds in the trees filled the barmy air. Le Vent was behaving for the morning as Berne watched her brother Erique pull into the campsite in her truck.

He'd been working overtime to earn his promotion and it felt like months since she'd seen him. He cocked his head as he came to a stop. She knew she must look different to him. She felt different. Terrified but hopeful. After Vivienne had told her she didn't need her, Berne had not felt the sting she'd expected. She felt free. Last night, this morning, Pippa's words all made her feel as though there was a true possibility now. Maybe.

"*Ça va?*" Erique pulled her into a hug, his strong arms squeezing her with such care. She relished it. "You look happy?"

Berne shrugged but she knew her eyes twinkled. She knew by the suspicion in his that he could tell.

"If I did not know better, I would say—ah." The answer to his questions wandered out with Babs and Rebecca. "So she returns!"

Berne smiled, following his gaze. Erique had always liked Pippa. It probably helped that she was incredibly attractive but then, who wouldn't be attracted to her. Pippa's dark tousled hair flopped into her eyes, her toned legs, and a—

"Cha-cha, who are you drooling at now, hmmm?" Babs said with a scowl.

Berne snapped her gaze up from where it had rested and met Pippa's eyes. Amusement filled her smile and Berne cleared her throat as she focused on Erique.

Erique grinned down at Babs as she launched herself into his arms. "Always you, you know this."

Babs kissed him on the cheeks and jumped back down. "Look who sailed down the river. Seems her heart paddled her back home, *non*?"

Erique flashed his best grin at Pippa. "*Oui, oui* . . . and she has grown some womanly wiles . . ." He wolf-whistled, earning a laugh from Berne. "*Bonjour*, Mademoiselle Saunders," he purred, bowing low.

Pippa giggled and gave a curtsey. "*Bonjour*, monsieur, you are looking as handsome as always."

Erique stood up straight and proud, then gripped her into a hug. "You are staying for a while?"

Berne saw a flicker of panic in Pippa's eyes. "I have to go back and talk to someone . . . but I hope so."

Erique smiled with true warmth at her. He wouldn't ask her too many questions. He seemed content that she was here. His gaze moved to Rebecca who loitered at the back.

"*Bonjour*," he said, holding out his hand.

"Hi, I'm Rebecca . . . Pippa's long-suffering friend."

She clasped his hand instead of offering a kiss and her French screamed Englishwoman. Erique's eyes twinkled as he gave her hand a squeeze.

"It is terrible to suffer such beauty," he said with his best charming grin.

Even Rebecca seemed won over by his words. Her laugh rumbled out of her lips and she kissed him on the cheek. "For that you get one." She held up a finger. "Only one or Babs will pout."

Babs nodded.

Erique shook his head at Babs and turned to Berne. "Maman wants you to help with the table. Most of the decorations are up already."

"Ah *oui*," Berne answered. "We go now?"

Erique motioned to his truck and Babs, Pippa, and Rebecca climbed inside. Berne helped him to stow the boats on the trailer. She knew he was watching her.

"So she returns?"

Berne smiled but kept silent.

"For you?"

Wasn't that the answer she would love to be sure of? "That remains to be seen . . . *mais* . . . she says so."

Erique cocked his head. "You do not believe her?"

Berne walked around to his side and lowered her voice. "She returned with a fiancé, a man. She tells me that she loves me still but there were many scars when she left." She sighed. "I have no doubt in her love. It is whether it will overcome her fears."

"What happened to her?" Erique frowned, his eyes filled with concern. "You were so happy."

"Her sister." She could hear the venom in her voice. "She made Pippa believe that a complaint would be made to the police about me. That the contract would be cancelled."

"They would not have believed it."

Berne yanked at the strap in her hands, the boat groaned under it. "*We* know that but a nineteen-year-old girl did not." Meeting his eyes, she blew out a breath. "And she confirmed that she was there . . . at the roadside."

"So it was her?" Erique looked up to the truck. His eyes filled with loss, with pain. "It . . . it . . . must have been hard for her to process."

"I do not think she has." She held onto his arm and squeezed it. "I think she has mixed it up with leaving me."

Erique rolled his large shoulders back. His usual way of trying to shake off emotion. "I can get a number, a good one. He helps many of the officers. He helped me."

Berne smiled at him. "If she stays for long enough, I would be thankful for the help."

They finished securing the straps and checked the boats over. Berne hesitated as she looked at the passenger side door. Fear rippled through her.

"*Ça va?*"

"What if she does not leave this man?" Berne shoved her hands in her shorts' pockets. "What if she goes back to him when we arrive in Ajoux."

"He is there?" Erique's eyebrows shot up.

She felt a swirl of excitement, nerves, worry, fear. "They bought the old cottage."

Erique slunk to one side, his hand rested on his hip. Normally it would be resting on his gun. Her main vision of him was in uniform. She'd wanted to be just like him. "You and Papa are working on that house?"

"*Oui.*"

He rubbed a hand over the back of his neck. "*Merde.* You know how to tangle the webs, *non*?"

Berne laughed and she hopped into the passenger side as Erique jumped in and started the engine.

"I am not a lunatic like Babs . . . *mais* . . . I will try not to be too boring for you," he said over his shoulder to Rebecca.

"I'll take safe and seat belts," Rebecca answered with a curt nod. "Safe, slow, with seat belts."

Babs's "*Non?*" made everyone laugh as they made their way through the gorgeous landscape.

Berne watched Erique drink in the scenery. He spent so much time in the city, working long, long hours, that it was a pleasure to see him come home. No matter where he was stationed, the Ardèche was in his heart just as it was hers.

"Oh, wow!"

Rebecca's awe energised them all as they pulled into the town. It was some event this year. There may have been only a handful of aging residents living in Ajoux but they knew how to put on a show. Every building in the square was decked with lights, flowers, and banners. Paper decorations hung from strings tacked between buildings. Tables were spread out, gazebos over for shade, and a large pile of firewood was stacked in the middle for the evening.

"How is work?" Berne whispered to Erique as they got out of the truck next to the house.

"I got the promotion." He smiled. "I have not told them yet. Leave it to dinner, *oui?*"

Berne squeezed him. "You deserve it. I had no doubt."

She knew that she said such things often to him, but the smile from him told her it never grew old. "*Merci,* it will be nice to move off the front line now."

An understatement, but nevertheless.

"Berne," he said before she went to join Pippa who leaned against the wall watching. "Does she know?"

Berne shook her head. Her hand ran over the small of her back. "I am not sure what to say."

Erique's unimpressed look made her flinch. "The truth, Bebe."

"Not even Babs knows." She glanced at Babs who gazed up into Rebecca's eyes as she waved her arms about with enthusiasm. "She thinks I travelled with Vivienne."

"Well, it is a time for celebration. Let them celebrate your triumph over the odds, *non?*"

Berne shrugged. He knew her far too well. She had managed to keep it from Pippa last night but should it . . . whatever it was between them . . . continue, the truth would come out. She'd hated the way Vivienne had recoiled from her the first time she saw it. It had reduced her to tears. It had shattered her confidence. She wasn't foolish. Pippa may have the same reaction. She tensed. She didn't think she could bear that same look in Pippa's eyes.

Berne found those bright, twinkling eyes on her. A smile on Pippa's lips. Pippa wasn't Vivienne. It would feel good to let it out. She rubbed her back again. At least she hoped.

I WATCHED ERIQUE stare after Berne as she rejoined us and caught a glimmer of sadness in his eyes. Wanting to ask him what had caused such a thought, I went to go to him only for him to shake his head and turn away.

"Is Erique okay?"

Berne must have been daydreaming as she offered a blank look and a smile.

"What is going on in that head?" I asked, brushing her hair away. "Is Erique alright?"

"Hmmm?" Berne focused on me, breaking from her thoughts. "*Oui*, he is well. He has gotten promoted. He wishes to surprise my parents."

"But?"

Berne squinted. Where was she off in her thoughts?

"Berne . . . is something wrong?" That familiar spike of fear panged through my stomach. "What's the matter?"

She led me away from Babs and Rebecca, who had been roped in by an elderly neighbour to hang his lights. She took my hand. "May I tell you something?"

"Of course. You can tell me anything . . . anything at all." I squeezed her hand, my words whooshing out.

We rounded the back of her house and Berne lifted up her shirt.

"Um . . . are we going for exhibitionism?"

Her chuckle lightened my panic but the solemn look in her eyes brought it straight back. She took my fingers and held them over her spine. I'd felt a ridged smooth section in the night but had been quickly distracted. It was a long ridge.

"At the beginning of the year, I work with my father on an old chateau," she said. "He was on a scaffold and he had . . . well . . . a moment."

"Another stroke?"

Berne shook her head. "No, the doctors said it was not so but he stumbled. I pulled him away from the ledge but my foot slipped." She met my eyes. "I fell. I was in hospital for a while."

Cold sweat soaked right through my t-shirt. "You fell? How far? How long were you in hospital?" More to the point, why had I been hiding in England and not with her? Why hadn't I been there?

"Three months."

Nearly choking on thin air, I fought to swallow. "Three months?" I needed to sit down, my legs were trembling like a violin string.

"I was . . . I was unconscious."

Now I did sit down, thank goodness for the patio chairs. "Are you alright?" Stupid question because she sat right in front of me and I was pretty sure I'd given her an intense physical examination. "Long term?"

"*Oui*, the scar was from the glass *mais* it missed everything . . . and I have had more scans . . . nothing permanent." She smiled, sitting next to me. "Only, I can't write or drive anymore."

"Why those two?"

Berne shrugged. "They think that it will come back in time. For now, I do not feel safe to be in charge of a vehicle."

I grabbed her and held her to me, wanting to fix it all for her somehow. Why hadn't she said something? "Is that why you wanted the lights off?"

Berne nodded.

"You think I would find any part of you unattractive?"

She flicked her eyes away.

I scowled. "But someone else said something . . . right?"

Her silence said more than enough.

"She's wrong. Whatever that poor-excuse-for-an-actress said, she's wrong." I felt the stress turn to irritation, more sweat stuck my t-shirt to me. "You're gorgeous, Berne Chamonix."

I made her turn around and lifted up her t-shirt. Oh wow, that was one big scar. How had I missed that?

It was still pinky-white like scars often are and stretched most of the way up her back, up her neck and into her hair.

It looked mean.

The thought of her landing on glass, lying there hurt made my heartbeat accelerate.

Flashes of the man on the road took over. His eyes locked on mine. The blood pulsing from his neck. His quiet, calm reaction to the fact he was lying there, dying. It terrified me. I'd kept talking to him. Stupid things in French, I talked about how much I loved the city, how much I loved Berne. Anything not to actually bring attention to the fact that I was pressing my shirt to his neck as he bled to death.

"It is in the past now," she whispered, bringing me back to her. "I am healthy now."

I took slow, deep breaths. This was about her hurt, not mine. Pull it together, Saunders. I wanted to ask if she'd hurt her head, if that was why she couldn't drive. I wanted to know why she was unconscious, how long for, and just what damage had been done. Oh, I felt sick now, sick and clammy and like I'd faint at any moment.

"Does Babs know?"

Berne shook her head.

"She will so kick your ass," I managed. Well done, Saunders, make her feel guilty about it, why don't you.

Berne nodded.

"I'll protect you." Because I was sooo scary.

She leaned in and kissed me. I slid my arms around her neck and caressed the scar. I wanted her to know I loved her, every inch. She moaned as I did it. Ooh, it was sensitive. I could work with that.

Her mother cleared her throat beside us.

I jumped.

The chair leg dropped off the stone patio. I lurched and ended up in a heap on the lawn.

"*Bonjour*, Pepe," Berne's mother said with a hint of laughter in her voice.

I pulled myself up from the grass and tried to regain some dignity. Why I was bothering, I wasn't sure. I had all the grace of a peanut.

"*Bonjour*, Madame Chamonix."

Her face, lined and ever smiling, was contorted with her attempt not to burst into laughter. The giveaway was her white puff of hair wobbling with the internal giggling. At seventy-five, she still had the spirit of a joyful teenager and was still quite the looker herself. Combined with her bubbly nature, Madame Chamonix was poles apart from my own mother.

"You are ever the suave seducer, Pepe." Her laugh rumbled through her words. "I can see why she finds it so hard to resist you." It didn't matter how many times I was teased by the woman, the inbuilt need to run and hide from a parental unit who had caught us pulsed through me.

Berne's mother was as laid-back as you could get with every facet of life. Nothing at all fazed her. She found my discomfort hilarious.

"Yes . . . well . . . it's all in the jumping technique."

With Berne sniggering and her mother breaking into laughter, I found myself grinning. How different it was here, with them. How much I loved it.

"I see that you come to experience the celebration." Berne's mother clapped her hands. "It will be the first of many, *non*?"

"Maman—"

Her mother tutted. "I see that she is here in heart. I also see that ring on her finger." She beamed at me. "I knew you would see sense."

At least someone had. "Thank you for the faith."

With a quick nod, she tapped Berne on the arm, ordering her into the kitchen.

Berne shot a nervous smile my way.

"I will be back later. I promise."

Her eyes lingered on mine for a few seconds and she disappeared into the house.

With grass stains on my knees, I wandered back onto the street. I waved to Rebecca, who dropped what she was doing to come to me. "You going to see him?"

"I am," I said, attempting to pick blades of green out of my knee cap. How did they get so stuck? "The sooner I leave that behind, the sooner I can start anew."

Mean, Saunders. That sounded cold, mean, and ungrateful.

"Er . . . It'll be better for him too."

"I'm coming with you," Rebecca said, taking off her rings. "I'll hang back outside but no way am I letting you do this alone, you got that?"

Apart from removing jewellery as though she were about to duff someone up, I was so relieved that I wanted to sing with it. "Yes, please."

"Settled." Rebecca motioned to Babs and gave her a thumbs up.

Babs nodded and yelled, "*Bonne chance*," at the top of her lungs.

"Wow, you speak your own language or something?"

Rebecca nudged me as we walked up the huge hill. "Nah, we were just talking about you. Babs is right behind you too."

Didn't that bring a lump to my throat? Ah, did I love these ladies. "I'll keep that in mind when I'm stammering like an idiot."

The hill was steep and I was unfit. Plus I was oddly tired for some reason. "So things seem to be going well?"

Rebecca bumped my hip as we walked. "This is about you, Pip. I'm really proud of you." She laughed and I glanced at her. "It's good to see you so . . . whole."

It was a good word, whole. Was that just down to Berne? "I get flashbacks sometimes, nightmares."

"From Catherine?"

"From everything. You know those dreams you get when something chases you?" I swore I was the only person whose issues could be represented in a nightmare by a giant sock. I spent my nights being pursued by knitted footwear. I really *did* need locking up.

"Yeah?" She didn't. Rebecca never remembered her dreams. She was one of those annoying people who, once her head hit the pillow, she was snoring for Gloucester.

"Liar."

She shrugged. "Bet you didn't get any last night?"

"That's because I didn't sleep—" I clamped my hands over my mouth. She chuckled at me, her loud bellow drawing the attention of two elderly men strolling on the other side of the road.

I waved at them, plastering a cheery grin on my face. "Yes, yes," I muttered at Rebecca, thumping her arm to stop her cackling. "I had sex, why is that so funny?"

"It's the fact it meant so much that your eyes glazed over when you said it." Rebecca wagged her finger at me. "You are completely gone on her." She grinned. "It feels great to see it."

I took her hand and kissed her on the cheek. "I love that you know me so well."

"Me too."

We rounded the corner to the cottage. My stomach seemed like it dropped out and made a sprint for it down the hill.

"Oh shit."

Rebecca gripped my elbow. "It's okay, I'm here. I'm not leaving your side."

I gripped hold of her, bending at the waist. I was winded. How could I be winded just by seeing them. Rebecca held on, grounding me.

"You can do this, Pip. You're not alone anymore."

Panic soared through me. My shirt felt like I'd dived into the Ardèche. Nope, I was going to pass out. It was official. I was the biggest wimp on the planet.

Rebecca rubbed my back. "You have to face them. Just think about how you felt this morning, yeah?" She pulled me up to look into her eyes. "Focus on how good you felt being yourself."

"Myself, right." I swallowed. My throat decided it had forgotten how to, again. Wonderful. I'd face them all with grass stuck to my knees, soaked through, stinky, and dribbling because I couldn't swallow. Suave, Saunders, really suave.

Rebecca held me by the shoulders. "You can do this."

I could. I could do this. It helped me get my feet moving and I stumbled towards the group waiting for me.

Doug, my parents . . . and Catherine.

Oh shit.

"Deep breaths. You're not alone. You love Berne right?"

I nodded. Why did the ability to swallow seem to be so intermittent these days?

"Do you love her, Pippa?" Rebecca turned me to look at her. "Do you?"

"Yes . . . Yes, I do."

Catherine was there. She looked mad. She looked livid. Oh boy. I couldn't face her.

"Tell me what you said this morning," Rebecca whispered. "Tell me out loud."

Panic seemed to have taken up residence in my soul, right alongside fear. Why were they all here? What were they doing here? Why were they waiting for me?

Oh shit, shit, shit.

"Pippa, tell me."

I focused on Rebecca's eyes and took a deep breath. "I'm gay. I love Berne. I want to be with Berne."

"Do you?" Now she sounded like she was recruiting me for the army. "Is that what you want?"

There was no doubt whatsoever. "Yes, I want that, I want to be with her."

Rebecca smiled. "Then, whatever they say, let it go. This is for you, not them, live for you."

"You'd make a great coach," I mumbled, in a half-hearted attempt at humour. My brain seemed wired to go on strike at any moment.

"Phillipa, why are you loitering there? Where are your manners?" My mother's voice ripped through my resolve until my knees wobbled.

Rebecca squeezed my elbow. "I got your six, Saunders. You can do this."

"Good morning, Mother." Strained, polite, terrified. What was I doing? I couldn't face them. I couldn't tell them.

Rebecca squeezed my shoulder as I dared meet my mother's eyes.

"Is it?" She tapped her watch. "It's two pm, young lady. *Where* have you been?"

Why did young lady make me want to run to the nearest bedroom and barricade myself in. Deep breath, slow breath. Calm. "With Babs, Rebecca and . . ." I rubbed at my throat. Say it. Be a grown-up. "Berne."

Catherine's eyes narrowed.

Rebecca gripped my elbow harder.

Doug and my father seemed oblivious to it all. They were too busy chatting to one of the workmen.

"Well, that's wonderful," my mother said. "Why haven't you called? I know that hen weekends are all the rage these days but really, in your condition."

I felt like I was walking into battle, striding into the hail of verbal bullets being fired off by an overwhelming enemy.

Rebecca held fast, not a word, only her physical presence.

"Hey, sweetheart," Doug said, walking towards me. "You look like crap."

Incoming at twelve o'clock. Verbal volley from the fiancé.

"You look fine, Pip," Rebecca whispered. "Berne loves you just the way you are."

She did. Berne loved me. She knew how much of a complete coward I was and she still loved me.

"I'm going in," I whispered back. "Cover me?"

Rebecca mock saluted, which made me giggle. It was a nervous "what am I doing, save me" giggle. Feeling slightly unhinged, I strode out to face foe number one. Doug deserved an explanation, a private one.

He ducked to kiss me. I turned so he found my cheek.

"We need to talk," I managed.

Ugh, I hated those words, they were never good.

"Alone."

He nodded, casting a glance at my mother. "Of course."

I led him towards the house, glancing over my shoulder. Rebecca ignored the glares from mother and Catherine, instead launching into a conversation with my father.

Her voice cocky and confident and every inch pouring love out towards me.

She believed in me.

I could do this.

"Look," Doug said as we got into the house. "I know what you must think. I wanted to tell you. It was a horrible mistake."

"It wasn't your fault. The way I acted, it would make anyone think that way." I felt for him, he'd obviously realised that I wasn't pregnant, thank goodness.

"No, I take full responsibility for this," he said, running a hand over his stubble. "I didn't realise that she'd contacted you."

Blinking a few times at him, I tried to figure out what that meant.

Did he mean my mother? "Who?"

Doug took my hand. "I knew something was wrong when you left that day in Paris. Then I got a call from her. I knew then. Pippa, I never meant to hurt you."

Did I walk through the door into another book or something? I wandered over to it and peeked outside. There was Rebecca, my parents, and Catherine. It all looked the same.

"Pippa?"

I turned back and frowned. "What did you do to hurt me?" Okay, so he'd been a bit of a patronising twit on the phone and there was the whole securing the heir stuff, but he hadn't been *that* bad.

Doug sighed and paced around the creaky floor. Why he was in a shirt and trousers in this weather I didn't know. "Fine, I deserve it. Make me say it."

Either he was crazy or I was. More likely me but completely confused, I managed a "huh?"

"Brandy," he said as though that revealed everything.

"It's a little early to drink, Doug."

He folded his arms, then dropped his chin to his chest. "Oh, you don't know, do you?"

Whether it was too early to drink? It was two o'clock in the afternoon.

"Are you telling me you're an alcoholic?" I'd seen no signs. How much did Doug drink when he was out of sight? Why hadn't I spotted it? He didn't seem like he had a problem.

"No," he grunted. "Brandy. The girl in my office."

Who called their child Brandy? I guessed someone rather fond of the beverage?

"What's the matter with her?"

His words, "mistake" and "I wanted to tell you" filtered in. I tried not to smirk. "You slept with a woman called Brandy?"

Doug burst into tears. He clutched me to him and sobbed into my shoulder like a little boy. "It was a mistake but she's pregnant. I have no choice, Pippa."

He was breaking up with me. "You're marrying her?"

Why was that funny? It was no laughing matter. Do not snigger, Saunders.

Doug sobbed harder, soaking my already sticky t-shirt. "I don't want to. She won't get rid of it. She's threatening to tell the papers, think of the scandal."

My, my, the golden heir of Fletcher enterprises knocking up a girl called Brandy. Golf club dinners would never be the same. Stop it, that's too funny. Nope, no laughing.

A gross thought chased away the mirth. "How long?"

Doug held on tighter.

"Doug?"

"Just after you resigned. You were crazy. She was there."

That made me feel better. We hadn't . . . well . . . since then. If I'd felt sympathy before, I definitely didn't now. Way to show support, numbskull.

"She the only one?"

He nodded into my shoulder. "Pippa, I adore you. I don't want to marry her. I promised you, I can't go back on that."

There was no way that Doug could survive cut off from his parents and no way that Fletcher enterprises would continue to thrive without him.

"Doug, I love you, even though you are a complete idiot." I stepped back from him, pulled his ring out of my pocket, and handed it back. "You are released."

His mouth opened and closed a few times but then he hugged me again. "You are trying to do what's best for me." He held onto me, confusing me once more. "You're such a good person."

"Er . . . thanks?"

Doug looked me in the eyes. "You can have this place. I know what it means to you . . ." He pulled a piece of paper from his pocket. "I just need you to sign this and I'll sign the deeds."

He'd certainly come prepared. The matter of me signing a gagging order and I got a house.

A gagging order?

"Doug, who am I going to tell?"

"You can't tell anyone," he said. His eyes wide. "My parents don't even know. I need . . . I need us to have split up . . . for a reason that . . . um . . ."

"Doesn't make you look bad?" I said, desperate to hold the grin back. He was so flustered it was cute. How was it that only now I realised he felt more like an annoying brother?

"You understand . . . thank goodness . . . will you?" He held out the gagging order again.

Thankfully, it was in plain English. I wasn't to go selling my story to the press about him or contacting him *ever* again. That bit hurt. I loved the daft clot. He'd been a part of my life for eight years.

"Pippa . . . I love you . . . please . . . please know that."

"Why don't you tell them I'm gay," I said, happily signing the form. "You could say that I left you for . . . say . . . Berne?"

Doug shook his head at first but then rubbed his chin in thought.

"That could work. I mean, you always dress so shabbily. You hang around with Rebecca . . ."

Nice touch there, Fletcher. Shabbily, wonderful. Thank heavens I wasn't breeding his rugby team. I waited until he handed me over the signed deeds to the house. He'd had them put into English for clear reading. One thing with him, he was fair in business.

"And, I *am* leaving you for Berne," I said, tucking the papers into my back pocket. "Doug, it'll work because I'm in love with her."

Now he was staring, then he laughed. "You almost had me convinced there."

"I should, it's the truth."

He scowled. "What?"

Before he could tear the deeds back off me, I held up my hand. "I signed your waiver, which I think you will see at the bottom, only counts if you leave me alone too and I get this place."

"I don't give a crap about the wreck. Why would you do that to me?" He put his hands on his hips. It looked more camp than threatening.

"Doug, you knocked up an office girl. Neither of us seems capable of fidelity."

He sighed and bowed his head. "How did it end up in such a mess?"

I nudged his shoulder. "We had eight years. I love you to pieces but maybe we just need different things now."

"In your case, a woman," he muttered.

"In your case, office girls."

He sighed. "I'm not sure what I'm going to do without you. I hate that we've ended up exchanging contracts." He stared up at the ceiling. "Who will I call when I need to talk?"

Did we talk that much? When had I become a valuable part of his life?

"You got me through fending off that merger, you made me believe in myself." He pinched the bridge of his nose, which I could see was to hold back more tears. "How will I cope without your voice to make me smile?"

Tears brimmed up in mine at his sweet words. "You don't have to tear me out of your life. You know where I'll be. You can always call." I stroked his arm, feeling strange that I was the one in control for the first time.

"What about the contract?"

I held his shoulders. "I'm about to go out there and tell my parents and Catherine that I'm in love with another woman. You really think I want to confess my life to some tabloid?"

He sucked in his breath.

"My thoughts exactly. You're a part of me." I straightened out his shirt and pulled out a hanky from my pocket for him. "I know when you're married to Brandy," oh what a name, "then you'll do your best to be honourable."

He blew his nose, loudly.

"If you don't love her, don't marry her."

He slumped down onto the stairs. "I have to, my father—"

"Will yell at you and then get over it. It's not like he hasn't done the same thing himself, remember?"

Doug scowled and then hung his head again. "I cheated on you and you're the one consoling me."

I sat next to him and leaned against his shoulder. "I cheated on you too."

He glanced at me. "Her?"

I nodded.

He squeezed my knee. "That why you didn't want to come back to France?"

I nodded again. "The only reason I left her was because Catherine threatened to ruin her life."

We both stared at the doorway. Eight years and we'd imploded like one of my mother's soufflés.

"Guess it's a good thing I'm not pregnant, huh?"

"Right. What kind of parents would we be?" He shook his head. "Can I really still call you?"

"If you understand that I'm with Berne and will always be . . . then yes."

He smiled and nudged into me. "You said that to me, remember?"

I tapped him on the nose with my finger. "That was before you knocked up Brandy."

Huffing out his breath, he stared down at the contract. Then proceeded to rip it up. "I don't want her. I do want to know the child though."

"You'll make a great dad." I got to my feet. "And you may want to leave before I launch my thunderbolt at them."

Doug didn't need telling twice, he kissed me on the cheek and fled like a gazelle from a lion.

I half wished I could flee too. The door looked pretty good closed, shutting them out.

I stared down at the deeds. I was a homeowner. Yay me. I tucked them in my back pocket and clung to the thought. With one last glance around the gutted shell, I pulled open the door. Hopefully I wouldn't resemble it after confronting my personal ogre.

I glanced up at Catherine.

Oh shit.

Chapter Eighteen

BERNE PULLED THE food out of the oven and flashed a smile at her hovering mother as she carried the delicious smelling pastries over to the counter.

"You have something on your mind, Maman?"

Her mother laughed that cheery laugh that filled Berne with memories of childhood. "What makes you think I have anything simmering?"

"Because you have been quiet since you saw Pippa kiss me."

It was nothing new, Berne had always brought her girlfriends home. Her parents had welcomed every one with open arms, but then they were like that, loving.

"She moves you so deeply that I worry." She passed Berne the melted chocolate and began work on her own half of the batch. "I have not seen you breathe so easily since she left you."

"She did so to protect me, Maman. I only wish she had talked of that time to me, written to me, anything."

Spreading the chocolate on, Berne tried to let go of those empty years. It didn't matter now. All that mattered was that Pippa may come to her and never leave again.

She would cling to that hope with every part of her, simply because the alternative to it was beyond unbearable.

"I know that she loves you," her mother said, touching a finger to Berne's cheek. "I know that to be away must have hurt her as much."

Berne shrugged. Her default reaction to anything she couldn't put into words.

"What will you do if she wishes to live in England?"

"I will commute. Maman, I love this place. I do not wish to leave."

Her mother smiled. It was clearly the answer she'd been looking for. Berne could see the relief shining through.

Although she would follow Pippa anywhere, Berne really hoped Pippa would want to stay here. Pippa belonged in the sun, she excelled in France. There was something about here that ignited a fire in her eyes. It was hard to imagine the dull grey clouds of London doing the same for her.

Babs burst in through the door. "Bebe, I know that we said we will stay out of it—"

"Where are they?" Berne strode to the door, her mother pulling her apron from her.

"At the cottage, the man has just left. Rebecca is there . . . *mais* . . . there are three of them."

Berne nodded as she walked through the doorway and strode up the roadway. Babs, whose legs were shorter, trotted alongside. "You think they will do something?"

"I do not know but I would prefer to be there . . . in case." It was silly to be so protective but she couldn't help it. She couldn't let her go this time.

Babs smiled. "And to give her a reason not to run, *oui*?"

Berne looked at Babs and let how she felt show. "If she loves me . . . I want her to run *to me* this time."

THE HEAT OF the sun tingled at my skin as I made the slow march towards the enemy. Doug had left nothing but a dust cloud and Rebecca was holding my father in conversation. I was sure that on TV shows and in books, women who faced their family found some kind of hero juice and presented their innermost feelings with complete and utter confidence.

I was anything but.

Okay, I loved Berne. I wanted to be with Berne. I had no real idea what that meant or why. Even acknowledging that I only wanted to be with her didn't seem to pump rainbow juice into my veins and make me want to ride a Harley.

Now, I was pretty sure that I was being slightly stereotypical but I could have really done with some kind of leather jacket "I don't give a monkeys, like me as I am or get stuffed" attitude. I could have also have done with the scary staring thing that Rebecca's ex had turned into a fine art.

Instead I felt like a toddler shoved in front of a pack of roaring lions. I also felt completely naked, which I wasn't, I checked, a lot. Naked, terrified, without confidence, and about to be devoured by lions. Yup, I was a wimp, a big wimp who wanted to run.

"Now look what you've done. I hope you didn't upset the boy because you can get right in that car and apologise." My mother launched a prize shot as I headed over to them.

What was it with that tone?

Mothers seemed to have this innate ability to rip the foundations from under your feet. I looked at Rebecca for help. She smiled, urging me on with her eyes.

"I . . . I . . ." Breathe. It helps not to pass out.

"I did upset him." Nice start, you birdbrain. "He and I have . . . we . . . called it a day."

A chorus of almost hostile "What?" filled the air.

My father looked like he may turn into a raisin with the purple colour he was sporting. "He will *not* abandon his child. I'll not stand for it!"

Oops, he thought I was pregnant. Quite moved that my father was leaping to my defence, it took a cough from Rebecca to hurry forward and stop him giving chase.

"Dad, I'm not pregnant."

He looked from me to my mother who threw her hands in the air.

"Daphne?"

"Don't tell me you *told* him that?" My mother's exasperation seethed through her words. "No wonder he left you. Why would he stay with you otherwise?"

Ouch. Sucker punch. I glanced at Rebecca. She nodded to me. She believed in me. I'm glad one of us did.

"I . . . I . . ."

"Yes, yes?" my mother snapped.

"I . . . left him." And silence. One way to stun the crowd, Saunders.

"Are you out of your mind?" My mother looked like she was about to storm over and shake me. She strangled her handbag instead. "Who will look at you now?"

"Daphne!" My father's shock echoed my own.

Ouch and then some. Was I *that* worthless in her eyes?

"Look at her," my mother shot at me. Her coiffed hair flopped about as she waved a hand at me. "She's on the shelf at her age." She wagged a finger at me. "Your biological clock is ticking. Soon she'll start to look like she dresses and then what?" She flapped the bag around. "Is she going to spend her life living with that?"

The "hey" from Rebecca made my jaw tense until my ears wiggled.

"Why flipping not?"

"Phillipa, language!" My mother placed her hand over her chest as though civilised society might just see her in this embarrassing situation.

"I told you." Catherine's half-smirk, half-pitying look stung. "She's sick."

Two words that at nineteen had brought me to my knees in a quivering mess. Two words that had robbed me of my confidence and instilled so much fear that I'd buckled. Two words that still rocketed agony through every pore. How could she think that of me? I hadn't hurt anyone. I had looked up to her and the disgust hit me as hard as it had back then.

"Sick?" Rebecca shot back at her. "You want to try that one with me, you uptight little bitch."

"Girls, enough!" my father boomed, stopping the impending fight. "Phillipa, what is going on?" His voice was soft. I'd never seen him so gentle.

"I . . ." Flashes of the motorcyclist on the ground. Cold English rain. Catherine's words, "you're sick," pounded through my head. "I . . ."

"Can't even say it, can you?" Catherine sneered. "Disgusted at yourself?"

"If you don't shut the—"

"I said quiet, Catherine. Not. One. More. Word." At his command she shrank back. My mother glared at me.

Rebecca nodded to me. "You can do this, Pip."

"I . . ."

What if they walked away? What if I lost them? What if they hated me? The motorcyclist, the rain, the taunts, over and over.

"I . . ."

"Phillipa, tell me the truth. What is going on?" My father positioned himself to block out the others. His warm hands over mine. He'd always been so distant, so busy with other things, would he hate me too?

"I left him because . . ."

Come on, Saunders . . . Come on. Will you run and hide forever?

"Because . . ."

Out of the corner of my eye, I saw Berne stride into view as though she was riding to the rescue. Every part of my body and soul got up and bounced around in joy. I *could* do this.

"I love her."

"Rebecca?" my father asked. No judgement in his voice, not even a bit.

"Well, yes, but no. I'm *in* love . . ." I pointed at Berne, Babs scurrying alongside. "I'm in love with her."

"Which one?" he asked, leaning into me.

"The short ass is mine, Mr. S," Rebecca chimed with such pride, I smiled.

My father looked me in the eyes, really looked at me. "You have known this for a long time?"

"Yes." I tried to keep my chin up, ignoring my mother's sobbing and Catherine's glares. "I met her when I studied here. We worked together. She's who Roger placed me with. She's . . . she's what makes me feel alive."

He frowned at me. I tensed ready for the abandonment. "Why did you go out with Doug, then?"

Well, I wasn't expecting that.

I glanced at Catherine. Her sneer was so venomous that I wondered just where that hero of mine had gone. How did someone get that mean and bitter?

"Ah, I see." My father straightened out his shirt and marched over to Berne who hadn't slowed at all. "Pleasure to meet you, I'm Phillipa's father."

Berne shook his hand warily. "*Bonjour*, I am Berne . . . Pippa's . . . friend?"

He nodded. "Yes, yes . . . Well, it's good to finally put a face to the name."

"*Pardon*, monsieur?"

"Doug. Has been talking about you and your father for months . . . poor chap." He shook his head. "Well . . . as you can see Daphne, Phillipa is happy and well. It's time we went home."

"Well?" Catherine snapped. "You just leave her to these . . . freaks?"

"Oh shut up," Rebecca snapped. "Like you're a picture of purity!"

"What would you know, you little tramp."

"Will you two desist?" My father motioned to my mother who was still sobbing. "What will they think of us, hmm?"

My mother stopped as did my sister.

"As I can see, these ladies have their emotions under control." He shot a fatherly smile at Rebecca. "This one has her own rules."

"You can't really be defending *that* against me," Catherine spat.

"Catherine, dear, if you don't wish to end up having a corrective nasal procedure, perhaps it's best *not* to taunt the redhead."

He pulled her by the arm and shoved her at the car. When she was in, he turned and glared at my mother. "If I find out that you knew about any of this, you'll be sorry."

My mother got into the car without a word. I was terrified for her. My father didn't do angry or raise his voice often but when he did, everyone took cover.

I ran over to him. "You don't hate me?" I felt all of eleven years old.

"Girl, what is there to hate?" He shook his head at the car. "Good old Roger has been the most amazing chap. Served together."

"I know, but what does Roger have to do with it?" I knew he'd recommended Berne as my tutor but huh?

"Fine man, *wonderful* golf swing."

Not sure if my father was about to drool, I touched his arm. "What does he have to do with it, Dad?"

"He's been living with a chap from Italy for years." He chuckled. "He has a terrible shot—the man couldn't hit a ball if his life depended on it."

I should have known that with my father everything came back to golf.

"His handicap would make your mother's look professional." He laughed at his own joke.

I dived at him and hugged him as the tears flowed down my cheeks. "He knew?"

"Wiley man, Roger. Wouldn't put it past him at all." He grinned at the thought, looking as if he needed braces to run his hands up and down. "You're the youngest. Not an easy place. Sibling rivalry is always a problem." He patted my back. "You know where I am if you need me."

He gave a quick clearing of his throat, a brief nod to the girls, strode around, and got in the car.

Stunned was too polite a word for such a feeling.

Of all the people I thought would be happy for me, it had been my father. Wonders never ceased.

"Wow," Rebecca said as they disappeared up the road. "I guess it pays to fix the guy's car."

"Definitely," I mumbled.

My hands were like I'd been on the sea in a storm, my knees and stomach weren't much better.

Berne nestled up behind me, wrapping her arms around my waist. "Bravo, Pepe."

I sighed. "Now I just have to win the girl—" I raised my hand to stop the argument. "We are not getting this wrong, Berne Chamonix. Deal with it."

Feeling her rumbling chuckle made me smile. I was still punch drunk and a little bit woozy.

Rebecca tapped me on the shoulder, one arm slung around Babs. "We also need to find a way to earn money."

I pulled the paper from my pocket and smiled. "At least we'll have a place to live . . . when we fix it up."

"*Pardon?*" Babs took the deeds and thumbed through them. "It is true. It is all yours!"

"*Ours.* The majority of the materials and contractors have been paid. It'll have more than enough room for us all." I squeezed Berne's hand. "When you're ready, there's a place for you too."

"*Mais—*"

"No buts. You need to trust me. That takes time . . . I'm not going anywhere."

The kiss on my neck was more reward than I could ask for but the sudden need to get it right surged into me.

"No more snuggling," I told her. "No kissing, no touching, nothing until I've earned your trust back."

Berne sighed. "Can I not say that you have already?"

"Were you storming down here to protect me or stop me leaving?"

She pulled a face.

"Exactly. Maybe we need to take it slowly. Make sure that, as adults, we actually like each other."

Berne looked at Babs who smiled at Rebecca. "I bet you fifty Euros that they will break this silly agreement by the weekend."

"You give them that long?" Rebecca said.

"Margins, my little English pit bull." Babs grinned. "You still have your courage?"

Narrowing her eyes, Rebecca held out her hand. "An extra fifty says that Berne breaks first, my little French whippet."

Berne shrugged at me as I turned to her. "They have great faith in our control, *non*?"

"We can prove them wrong," I said.

However, with the gentle twinkle in Berne's eyes and her sweet smile on her lips, I wasn't quite sure why I wanted to.

Chapter Nineteen

THE CELEBRATION SEEMED to begin the moment we arrived back at the Chamonix home. For some reason Berne's mother was delighted to see me. Quite perplexed by her glee, I was sure that she couldn't have missed me from the time I'd been dribbling over her daughter in the back garden until walking through her door.

Nevertheless, I was glad not to argue. I'd take the welcome, anything to wipe Catherine and my mother's faces from my mind. My stomach ached with their looks. How could people be so mean?

As the town gathered around in the square, tables were laid out with more food than would feed hundreds, let alone five families and a few over-fed dogs. Culinary delights were everywhere, any kind of French delicacy a mind could think of was on display.

Babs had enjoyed introducing Rebecca to many of her favourites and just as I had so long ago, Rebecca savoured every second of it.

France was officially wonderful.

As the sun set and the moon took prominence in the heavens above, everyone moved to sit around a large bonfire, chatting in family groups. Women popped across to gossip with other women while the men lounged on chairs, smoking cigars or cigarettes. I was quite sure that you weren't allowed to smoke in public places in France but the only police for miles was Erique and he sat chatting with a glass of wine in hand.

I closed my eyes, feeling the barmy summer night air caress my cheeks, and listened to the buzzing chatter, the crackling fire, and the giggling children playing nearby. So soothing.

Even in a foreign land, in a place where I knew only a few people, I felt happier and more centred than I had all my years back in England.

"You look like you are enjoying your freedom." I smiled up

at Rebecca who plonked down next to me. "I think I may end up fatter than that cockerel, you know."

"Try not to eat too much or you'll find it hard to move tomorrow." Two children dashed past us, giggling. "Remember that Berne and Babs are used to eating their own bodyweight."

"How are they so trim again?"

The children reached their mother who gathered them up into her arms. She squeezed them and murmured endearments at them.

"If you go running with Babs, you'll soon see."

It was so nice to watch the children be doted on. They looked secure, safe, happy.

"You're quiet," Rebecca said, tapping me on the knee. "You know I'm right here if you need to talk to me?"

"Yep, and I love you for it." I smiled at her and saw concern in her eyes. "It'll take a while for everything to sink in, for my head to catch up with what's happened."

The mother sat the children on her knee and bounced them as they giggled. My mother had never been like that. I'd been raised more by the nanny than her. Maybe that was why she was so alien to me. A nanny to a boarding school with Rebecca.

"Your dad was a trooper today. He's such a cool guy."

Yes he was. He had been a distant figure with a booming voice that had terrified me growing up. A man who I wanted desperately to impress yet could never seem to catch the attention of. That was his way. That was tradition. Men didn't get involved.

A man walked over to the mother and wrapped his arms around her. He kissed her on the lips and then cuddled their children.

I couldn't help but wonder how much my own father had missed out on. Children grew fast. There was no time to look away because they'd be grown, grown into people you could no longer influence. Grown into people that you may not even like.

"Pip . . . You having second thoughts?"

I shook my head. "I'm just thinking. Doug will be a dad soon. I really hope he takes the time to know the kid."

"Huh?"

Maybe it would have been helpful to fill her in on why I had the deeds to the house. "Seems like Doug was about as faithful as me."

How pathetic were we as a pair? How lucky an escape we'd both had.

"Some girl called Brandy."

"Bastard."

I smiled at Rebecca's anger. "It's okay. I think I got my own back."

The family started to sing songs together. The mother and father's lingering looks showed how complete they both felt. It was beautiful to watch.

"Still . . . he could have chosen someone with a more highbrow name." Bless her, Rebecca was always in my corner. A tad snobby but a champion. "I can see the headlines now. Doug Fletcher, lover of Brandy."

I snorted.

"Who is this Brandy?" Babs voice sounded strained as she wandered over to us.

Rebecca grinned up at her and pulled her into her lap. "Doug knocked up a woman called Brandy. That's why Pip has the house."

Relief made Babs eyes glimmer in the firelight. It was funny to see how two people that detested commitment in any way were so vulnerable now. It was about time, that was for certain.

"*Alors*," Babs said, snuggling in. "Are you really going to make Berne wait for you?"

When put that way, it sounded like I delighted in torturing the poor woman. "I want to make sure that I'm mentally ready and emotionally steady before I leap into happily ever after."

"Pip, that sounds like a line from a terrible song."

I poked my tongue out at Rebecca. Explaining why I was still holding off was as difficult as doing it. Berne was charming as always, helping her elderly neighbours, sparring with her brother, all while flashing her brilliant smile. Not for the first time, I found myself leaning on my fist to watch her.

"You could not resist her when you were with someone else," Babs said. "Why will now be different?"

"Because when she kisses me again, I want it to be the start of our lives together." I meant every word too. If that meant us both waiting, I would take it. What would a few weeks, months be, after years of pain?

"So how do we help you get the ball rolling, Pip?"

The pair of them were incorrigible. "I need to understand how I feel about today. I am not quite sure if that's it with my mother or what will happen."

Again, I was drawn to watching the family, mother and father side by side, their children snoozing on their laps.

"Good thing we have a house to fix up, right?"

"Right," Rebecca chimed. "I got to say, it's a definite upscale on our little dive."

That went without saying and I wouldn't miss climbing the damp stairs in the middle of winter. "I need to get Winston though."

"You think he'll make it this far?"

I smiled. "I am thinking he should get a free ride down here." There was no way my baby would make the journey but a Saunders never left a good motor behind.

Babs sat up straighter. "I know someone who can do this." She pulled out her mobile. "You need a . . . to move the belongings?"

Rebecca and I exchanged glances. Were we doing this?

"Yeah, that'd be handy. Maybe some help from a pair of Frenchies wouldn't go amiss too." Rebecca smiled up at Babs. "I would love to show you our London."

Babs smile oozed sultry. "Then consider me at your service."

More lingering looks. They leaned towards each other.

"Oh, get a room."

Rebecca had the good grace to blush which added to my feeling of ease and comfort. If I was going to uproot and relocate to France, the least I could do was have my best buddy beside me.

Babs hurried off to make her arrangements and I shot a grin at Rebecca. "Looking a little taken there."

She sighed. I'd never seen her do wistful but I liked it. "I think I'm in a bit of trouble there, Pip." Her eyes followed Babs as she wandered around chatting. "It's like getting hit by a wave. I can't even get it into my head why."

"She's gorgeous?"

Laughing, Rebecca nodded. "Well, there is that."

"She's successful, sassy, and sexy?"

Rebecca laughed louder. "That too."

"And she loves like she drives?"

Rebecca's mouth dropped open in shock. Her blush evident even in the dark.

"You forget, *my little English sugarplum,* that I knew Babs a long time ago."

Rebecca snorted at my attempted Babs impersonation. "Please

don't tell me you know from personal experience because that's just . . ." She shuddered.

I did too. "Oh no . . . Trust me, the moment I saw Berne Chamonix, I saw no one else."

Rebecca cuddled me, not just a quick cuddle but one of those ones where you wiggle the person about for good measure.

"I'm so happy that you're gay." She looked up and shook her head. "I mean . . . that you feel happy being . . ." She shook her head again. "I mean that you have found your inner gayness . . ." She sighed. "You know what I mean."

"You're glad I'm being true to myself?"

Rebecca squeezed me again. "I knew you'd get me."

I snuggled in, happy that she was happy that I was happy. "So Doug really gave you the house to keep quiet?"

"Yep. So I was thinking we might scrap the sauna and boys' room. What do you think?"

"Well, we could open it out so that we had an office space, maybe a workshop for you?" Rebecca sat back and pulled her foot onto her knee. "I thought that way, if we build a good reputation we could maybe sell some of those furniture designs you always had penned?"

Now, I was excited. "You think anyone would want them?"

Rebecca nodded. "If we can make a cool prototype, maybe Babs might find a niche to sell them. She does for Berne's statues and stuff." She smiled. "And you have me who's pretty adept at selling rain to the river."

"What about the architecture?" I loved the idea but Rebecca needed to have her dream too. I wanted her to have that.

"Dunno, it's a long road and it isn't cheap."

"If we do well with the business, will you do it then?" There had to be open university courses or something like that. "You love it so much."

"True, but I love sales too. I'm good at promotion and it gives me a kick." That cocky grin slid into place. "Gotta keep the charm oozing somehow if I get shacked up, right?"

"If?"

Rebecca sighed. "Yeah. That bit depends on the beauty swaying our way."

Babs's eyes were on Rebecca. A few of the younger men

watched her stroll past but all Babs was interested in was the cheeky sweetheart beside me.

"I don't think there's much *if* in it at all. I would say game, set, and match myself."

"Did you just throw in a tennis analogy?" Rebecca didn't take her eyes off Babs.

"I think I did. Dad would be so proud."

"Forget him," Rebecca said, pulling Babs onto her lap. "*I'm* proud of you. You even got it the right way around."

"Yes, well, just don't ask me to hit a ball and we'll be fine."

Babs raised her eyebrows to which Rebecca and I answered in perfect unison. "Hits like a girl."

Chapter Twenty

LONDON IN THE summer. It had gone from sunny to rainy in naught point six seconds. It had taken a mammoth effort to plan moving everything down to our house in Ajoux and more time to find opportunity to get to London and pack up our lives there.

It was too good an opportunity to miss when rain was forecast for the week and so Berne, Babs, Rebecca, and I had headed to London on the plane.

The removal team Babs had hired had made quick work of emptying a decade of adulthood and my father had already found someone to move in. It felt scary cutting ties with everything I knew but it was for happiness and the possibility of love.

There'd been no time to show Babs and Berne London as the removal took far longer than we had accounted for. It was funny how much stuff two people could collect and cram into a small space.

While I packed up the last of the boxes and taped it shut, I was aware that we could have built our own little fort from them. It was bittersweet leaving the place. We'd lived there for ten years together. We'd grown up in the tiny space.

I handed over the box to the moving people and turned to stare out of the window. Winston was getting his first class ride to his new home and the quiet street below looked odd without him.

"You are sad to leave?"

Berne's question wrapped around me like a warm hug. Having to make do with only her verbal comfort, I relished the sound of her.

"In a way. It's sort of like this place was our sanctuary, you know?" I turned and stared around at the bare walls. "We were lucky to find it, that my dad found it. So many people struggle here in the city."

"It is a vibrant place," Berne said. "So much history. It has been good to see where you spent your years away from me."

Liking the way she'd phrased that, I felt the urge to sink into her arms. I couldn't help gawp at her anyway. Her jeans were snug like they were sewn for her, cool brown boots that poked out the bottom. Her t-shirt showed off her slender collar bones, a suit jacket over the top. She looked like a film star.

Berne's eyes warmed and a slow smile spread across her lips. "*Friends* sometimes offer each other embraces, *non*?"

Friends? Why friends? Friends may embrace but they didn't do any of the things we'd done in the Ardèche. "If we cuddle each other, it won't stop there, *Friend.*" I hugged myself instead as Berne said nothing. "Besides, you can't do that to her . . . well . . . again anyway?"

Berne had said nothing more about Vivienne to me. I met her eyes in hope. Hope that she was going to take my hand and tell me that I was hers, that there was no one else. That Vivienne was history.

She didn't. Instead, she looked past me to the window.

"Right." Focus on the street, Saunders, or you'll make a scene. Friends and no statement on supposed ex. Not a great sign that she wanted something more.

Berne had been stoic since we had left France. She had been arguing with Babs in hushed whispers. Even today, Rebecca and Babs were arguing and had stopped as I walked into the room. I'd been too distracted before to notice but warning bells were clanging in my head now.

Maybe it was just my mood? I'd been fielding calls from my irate mother. My sister had been texting me to tell me just what she thought of me. To say I'd been withdrawn was an understatement. It had been a lot to process. Maybe they were just worried about me and giving me my space.

"Are you comfortable with me living in Ajoux?" I felt a sense of awkwardness. That horrible feeling when you knew you were doing something wrong but you didn't know what.

"Why would I not?" She motioned towards the door with a fed up sigh. "You are ready?"

Her nonchalant, bored expression didn't fool me. Something was going on. I wanted to ask her what it was. Had I messed up somewhere along the line? Why hadn't she come to find me, to hold me? Her body language was cold, cut off, disaffected. Yet I caught her looking at me. So did she want me or not? My head hurt. It was official. Women confused the toffee out of me.

"As I'll ever be."

I cast one last glance around the safe haven and followed Berne down the steps as the door swung closed behind us. The deluge was in full flow outside as if London was wishing me a wet farewell.

"Do you think we'll make the flight if we stop for dinner first?" I asked Rebecca, who was deep in conversation with Babs. They seemed to relish chatting about business almost as much as they relished something else they often snuck away for. Inseparable was too light a word.

"You thinking what I'm thinking?"

I smiled. "Gino will be wondering where we are."

Rebecca chatted to the cab driver and gave him instructions. I tried to ignore that, I not only sat next to Berne, but her thigh was pressed against mine.

"You going for the usual?" Rebecca asked.

"Of course." Silly question. It wasn't like I did anything adventurous, you know, apart from turning my entire life upside down.

"I peg you for a garlic mushroom girl," Rebecca said to Babs whose eyes twinkled in response.

"Perhaps. It depends who has cooked it."

Laughing, Rebecca waved her hands. "Well, Gino's is great. I mean they aren't Ajoux great but they still make a pretty tasty dish."

"I will take your word for this, *non*?"

Goodness, they were smushy. "Hey, doe eyes. We're in London now."

My words stopped her leaning in further and giving the cabbie heart failure.

"So, Berne," Rebecca said, covering her tracks as Babs folded her arms with a frown. "What is your dish?"

"Spinach tagliatelle," I answered without thinking.

"Ah ha!" Rebecca wagged her finger at me. "Got you!"

Feeling the blush spreading over my cheeks, I stared out at the rain-soaked city.

"There is something we miss?" Babs asked.

"Yeah," Rebecca answered. "See, before we came to France, Pip and I had to order food."

I hated that smug cocky grin. Traitor.

"This one didn't have a clue what Doug wanted after living in the guy's pockets for eight years." She grinned wider, I could see it in my peripheral vision as I continued to stare out. "But it seems she had a place for a certain person's favourite."

Babs murmured in agreement, the pair launching into teasing. Berne was looking at me, staring at me, I could feel it. Her thigh next to mine felt warm, familiar, oh how that night on the Ardèche flooded back into my thoughts.

"You remember well, Pepe," Berne whispered in my ear. From icy to red hot in one hushed sentence. "Do you remember the weekend we go to taste it in Italy?"

"Nope, not at all. Complete blank."

More laughter, more teasing, and the thoughts of Italy now pulsed into my mind. How many delicious memories could two people make in one year? More to the point, did she want more than just memories with me?

THE NIGHT IN Gino's was perfect. The food was phenomenal with Gino and his family pulling out the stops to wish us well. We had the best table in the house, which was next to a painted wall depicting a villa stretching out into olive groves. Babs looked quite perplexed by it, which made me chuckle. She probably visited the real thing often enough not to need to paint brick with an image.

Berne sat beside me during dinner as the conversation relied more and more on Rebecca and Babs. I found myself desperate to know what thoughts whirred behind the Berne's captivating eyes. She was hard to resist at the best of times but there was something extra special about her in a pensive mood. Something which beckoned to me, calling me to lean in, to whisper to her. Calling me to discover what lay deeper inside her. It was followed with a worrying undercurrent I may not *want* to know. What if it wasn't me in her thoughts?

Rebecca had dragged Babs off to show her some of the paintings Gino had composed and I leaned on my fist and enjoyed just being next to Berne. Her presence fired desire and contentment through me in equal measure. Even now, after all these years just looking at her provoked . . . need. A need for what I wasn't sure but it was still there, still connecting me to her.

"Do you remember the villas?" Berne whispered as if to

herself. Her gaze on the painting on the wall. "The Cypress trees flanked the country roads. We drove until we reached the shores of the lake."

It had been less than a week after we got together on the beach. I'd been a tangled mess of excitement, panic, and puppy love. Berne had been so patient with me. I had no real frame of reference as to how one should act with a woman they loved in public. This had led me to veer from acting as if I didn't know her to being attached like a limpet. I had a habit of retreating inside when I was trying to work things out and Berne was always the one to force me to talk, to let my feelings out.

She had wanted all of me, not just politeness. She wanted me free and open. It had been a battle but I'd been happier because of it then.

"Lake Garda. You took me on a boat tour." I smiled at the feeling of summer in my heart, cool breeze in my hair, and Berne's warm arms around me. She'd put up with me being cold until she spotted the boat tour. She'd dragged me aboard without letting me argue and held me the way she wanted to until I relaxed.

"You confessed to me that you were scared." Berne stared down at her hands, her long fingers linked together. "You say that it was like setting sail without knowing if you would ever reach safe harbour."

One of my more poetic moments. Berne had a tendency to inspire me. Although, I distinctly remember using the term armbands and not knowing the French for them. All of which had resulted in me flapping my arms around as if attempting to fly. Yes, a true poet.

After all, what was love without inflatable armbands?

"You told me that I would always be safe with you." Berne had said it through howling laughter at the time. Her belly chuckle had provoked a giggling fit from me. Goodness knows what the other passengers had thought. "We laughed a lot, didn't we?"

A smile drifted across her lips. "When you are young and in love there is much to be joyful for." She sighed. "It is not as easy as you change and grow. Things happen. Life happens. Laughter is not so easy to embrace, *non*?"

I felt dual twinges of jealousy and concern at her words. I had a feeling it had much to do with a woman in Marseille. "*She* doesn't make you laugh?"

Berne's gaze remained on her hands. She ran her thumb over her right middle finger. I had noticed a silver ring but now I was beginning to understand the meaning of it. A horrible cold squelchy feeling settled in my stomach. She was wearing her ring. I hadn't noticed it in the Ardèche but now it was back in place.

"Vivienne is not one for careless laughter. She is . . ."

An idiot? An ex that you left for me? Were my first thoughts but it was probably best I didn't share them. Don't make a scene, Saunders. "Intense?"

"*Oui.*" Berne grunted it so that it sounded more like "way" than "wee." A very French way of saying "yeah." The unimpressed flick of her eyebrows ignited hope in me. She'd told me she was loyal to Vivienne. I'd been sure she'd leave her for me. I thought she'd left her. Had I just presumed it? I racked my brain, trying to see if I'd missed something. Berne said she loved me. She'd been very thorough in showing me she did. The way she was talking about Vivienne now was very much in present tense.

I started fiddling with my napkin. I didn't know what to think now.

"I wish to tell her, Pepe. She should know." Berne met my gaze. "She will not take it well."

I didn't blame Viper-Vixen for that. I didn't know what lunacy it would have provoked from me. All I knew was somehow I was now consoling Berne about telling her as if I was a sordid affair. "About the Ardèche?"

"*Oui.*" Berne's eyes deepened.

My heart sped up. I felt so drawn to her that nothing else around me mattered. Confused and unable to do a thing about it, all I did know was that I was leaning in.

Berne placed her finger over my lips. "Pepe, I cannot—"

"Pip!"

I jumped. My hands shook from the realisation that I had forgotten my bearings. Had I really just gone to kiss her? I was in London. You didn't go smooching people in public. Berne's fingertip still pressed against my lips.

"You can't?" I pulled her finger away. Her eyes deepened in colour as I moved closer. London or not, I needed an answer.

"I—"

"Oi!"

Berne sighed and broke eye contact.

I turned to Rebecca, doing my best to avoid glaring at her. Not great timing. "What?"

"We gotta go. Taxi is outside." Rebecca waved at the door.

I glanced·down at my watch. Balls. We'd be lucky to get to the airport in time. I grabbed my coat off the chair. It caught my water glass. It clunked to the table, gushing liquid all over Gino's lovely white tablecloth.

"Gino, I–"

"It is nothing." He took hold of my shoulders with his puffy hands. "Catch your plane. If you come to London, you come here to eat." He gripped me in a rib-switching hug and gave me a smacker on both cheeks.

I nodded. Dumbstruck. Had Rebecca and I been such great customers? We did have a lot of takeaways . . .

"Pip!"

"Right." I offered Gino a smile as I followed Berne out into the belting rain.

Rebecca and Babs were already inside the taxi. Berne handed them their coats and I slumped down next to her and hauled the door shut.

"Good thing we booked a taxi. It's bucketing down." I glanced at Berne, wanting to be alone, wanting to hear what she'd wished to say. *Pepe, I cannot—*

Cannot what? What couldn't she do or say? It worried me. In fact, it terrified me. What if it was that she couldn't be with me? What if I'd got it all wrong? What if I'd imagined it? If the night on the Ardèche had just been a trip down memory lane? Oh no, hyperventilating was not a good idea. I gripped my knees, hoping no one would notice. Berne had said she loved me, right? Didn't she? She said she wanted it to be her ring on my finger?

"Didn't fancy missing the flight. Babs has to go to Marseille tomorrow." Rebecca poked out her bottom lip in a pout. Her tone said that she was hoping we'd miss the flight. If I wasn't panicking, I would have smiled. Go Whitely.

"I will be back after the party, *d'accord*?" Babs nuzzled the side of Rebecca's neck.

I glanced at Berne. Her eyes met mine. The rain peppered the windows, orange, white lights of the streetlamps, scent of damp, of her perfume. The flash of headlights bathed her face. There was a seriousness about her that unsteadied me. The way she was fiddling with that ring wasn't helping much either.

"What party?" I mumbled.

Her eyes locked on mine. She wet her lips. I was riveted to them as they glistened.

"Vivienne's birthday," Babs muttered. Her plaintive tone more likely for Rebecca than me.

My heart gave a heavy thud. Berne's eyes flickered with regret. My stomach crunched.

"Right." I tore my gaze from her and riveted it to the rainy London night outside. What had I expected? That she loved me enough to leave her? Did she only love me enough as fun, as a mistress of some sort? Is that what she'd been trying to say? I was good for her when she was young but now she was responsible. Vivienne was more in line with what she wanted. Why *would* she leave her?

Vivienne was a successful actress. She may have been a cradle-robbing-no-teeth-shallow-viper but Berne loved her, didn't she?

She was going to Vivienne's birthday. Even though Babs supposedly hated her, she was going too. She was happy to leave me behind.

Berne touched my knee. "Pepe—"

"You don't owe any explanation to me." My tone said she did and why had she gone and uprooted my life if she wasn't going to do the same?

A thought poked me, reminding me that I'd only just left Doug, that she'd endured seeing me with him. That I'd left her. Maybe it was payback?

I told the thought to go take a hike. I didn't care how silly or stupid I was. I'd assumed Berne would leave Vivienne the second I had left Doug and wait patiently, alone, until I was ready for her.

I expected her to . . . woo me. Was that even a real word? Who cared? I wanted that. I wanted romance. I wanted her to enrapture me. I wanted her to ignite that adventure in me. I wanted her to grip hold of me and demand I kiss her and stop her torment. Why was that too much to ask for, huh?

"I will be home after this," Berne said in a gentle tone. Because *that* would make me feel better wouldn't it. I glanced around, wondering if there was a paper bag. The thought of Berne with anyone else made me a wreck.

"Wish her a happy birthday from me, *friend*." My mood riddled my words.

Berne flinched.

"What time is the electrician coming tomorrow?" I focused on Rebecca. My voice crackled as I fought back angry tears.

Alarm flickered across Rebecca's eyes. Then they narrowed as she shot Berne a glare.

"Nine," she snapped as if wanting to smack Berne across the chops with her words.

"Julian is very good," Babs said, her gaze darting from Rebecca to me. "I use him a lot."

They started to chat about Julian and his ability as an electrician. Rebecca's tone rippled with her redheaded mood. Babs gentle tone showed she understood and was trying to calm her. Again the entire conversation was theirs. Berne said nothing. I said nothing.

I thought about getting out of the taxi. I wanted to run through the rain in some dramatic gesture of how betrayed I felt. Anything not to look at Berne. If she was going there for Vivi-Viper-Vixen then there'd be the expectation for romance. A party meant suitable attire. Berne would look as enticing as always. Viper would look stunning in some gown only actresses could pull off.

I shuddered. I felt sick.

"Pepe—"

"It's not like it matters anyway." I didn't mean a word of it. "I don't have time. We have to get it rewired."

Babs and Rebecca took over once more. Berne reached for my hand but I snapped it away and folded my arms. I was half-a-second away from throwing her ring at her. Something stopped me. Something that made me feel more pathetic than ever. I couldn't take the ring off. I didn't want to.

Berne's words that I'd always be safe with her seemed worthless right now. Safe? I didn't feel close to safe. I'd gone from contentment to lurching about in yet another storm. I felt abandoned. In fact, I felt like I'd been mutinied. She'd broadsided my nice quiet cruise with Doug, convinced me to make him walk the plank, and now she was getting back onto her own ship and leaving me to watch on.

I lay my head back and closed my eyes. The silence was heavier than the crushing feeling of helplessness. Berne was going back to Marseille, to her.

Chapter Twenty-one

ONE WEEK COULD feel like years. We'd brought back a summer storm with us which seemed to echo how I felt as Berne and Babs drove away. I'd avoided looking at them the entire flight. I felt lost. Logic stated that I had told Berne I wanted to earn back her trust but I hadn't been prepared to stand aside and watch Berne carry on with Viper.

Rebecca had kept her thoughts to herself but the irritation with Berne was evident. She wouldn't say so to me but it helped that she felt as confused by Berne leaving as I did. So she'd re-instated DVD nights, talked about nothing but the house, and chatted to me about Doug's latest text message.

Doug was a huge source of comfort. I loved him even more the way we were now than I had before. He did everything he could to make me laugh. He'd heard what my mother and Catherine had said and picked holes in them at every opportunity. The sweet clot thought I was down because of them. He'd defend me to the hilt, he'd make fun of Berne for me. I missed the numbskull, I really did.

I'd lay in bed at night, listening to the rain, feeling comforted by it. Rebecca and I knew rain. We understood rain and cold. They were our thing. If I closed my eyes and pretended, I could be back in London. This messy, confusing summer could just be a feverish dream. I could wake up and banish it and go back to safety, to Doug, to muddling along.

Only I was alone. Alienated from my family, in a foreign country, pining over a woman who could turn around and tell me she wanted more than I could give.

It didn't help that Babs had arrived within days of leaving but Berne had remained in Marseille. Neither had said a word. Babs couldn't meet my eyes. None of it inspired me with confidence.

I said nothing. I didn't ask. I didn't care. No, I'd managed to crawl up from the torment once before, I could do it again. Although I was a tune away from "I will survive," I'd taken control over my life and been truthful. Yes, I'd come out of my shell, faced Catherine, and ended up alone just as I'd feared. Well done, Saunders.

Still, I didn't care. Nope. I was too busy focusing on the house. Rebecca, the workmen, and I had made the downstairs liveable. I had learned how to wire things in French and I'd fixed the stairs.

A "Bonjour," echoed out somewhere behind me as I sat on the top step, grappling with the last section. If I wasn't careful, I'd mess up the screw head and then where would I be?

"Here," I mumbled, vaguely aware that I needed to talk for people to know I'd heard them.

I tightened the final bolts and sat back to admire my handiwork. My masterpiece looked fabulous. Go, Saunders.

"You work hard. It will be ready soon, for sure."

I registered that it was Berne speaking, and my heart cantered into a special happy rhythm then slunk into a pathetic heap. She'd been with *her*.

"It'll take months. We're moving into the ground floor next week." I didn't bother speaking French. It was a pathetic act of rebellion but it stopped me throwing things at her and, boy, did I want to throw things at her.

I'd followed the electrician, Julian, around during the week to the point where he'd offered to show me how to wire the rooms. I was eager to learn as much as I could. That way I could do a lot of the work myself.

Doug was subbing the house and the artisans but I wasn't letting him pay for the accommodation too. Rebecca had agreed. So in we would move. The ground floor was watertight so we'd make do.

Who needed traitorous French women anyway? Not me. No way.

"Rebecca feels it will be sooner?"

"Rebecca is a saleswoman. Don't believe a word of it." I examined the stairs. They looked great. The first floor still contained a host of gutted shells. Berne or her father would need to work on them before we could do more. I wasn't looking forward to it. I tried to block out that thought. Instead I stomped up and down the stairs to try them out. Solid.

"I missed you," Berne whispered as I reached the bottom. She was leaning against the wall. Funny to think I'd sat there with Doug not so long ago.

"I doubt that."

I threw my tools into my very industrial and professional looking toolbox. Why it needed yellow plastic compartments, I wasn't quite sure. Was an all black toolbox too drab for the discerning workman? Were workpeople fashion conscious enough to need yellow stripes on their screwdrivers? And why yellow or orange? What was wrong with a purple hammer? Or a beige drill? Of course, there were little green numbers you could pick up, not to mention the disgusting pink sets aimed at women. Because no one on site would know you were really a woman if you didn't have a pink hard hat? Were you any less female wearing the usual white or yellow?

"Why?" Berne took my hand as I turned to march back up the stairs. I tried to yank it free but she held firm. "Why are you so cold now?"

Me, cold? Me? I tried to pull my hand again. I was feeble. Ten year olds had more strength than me, I swore.

"Do you regret loving me?" She rubbed her thumb over my hand. "Pepe?"

Low blow. Purring my name was mean and sneaky. How dare she when she was wearing someone else's ring?

I tried to prise her off with my free hand but she caught that too and pulled me to her. "Do you love me no longer?"

Me? I wasn't the one gallivanting around with another woman, was I? I wasn't the one who had purred, "Tonight you are mine," when I'd been happily engaged to Doug. What did she want me to say when she'd gone from that to calling me a friend?

I glared at the wall beside her, aware that her warm body was against mine. That her breath tickled my cheek, my lips.

"Say it," Berne whispered. "Say what you feel."

I shook my head. I couldn't bear to think it let alone utter it out loud. Besides, I wasn't giving her the satisfaction. No. I was keeping quiet. Share. Hah. I wasn't giving her a peep.

"Open up to me. Scream at me. Shout at me. Let yourself feel." Her hand slid from my wrist to my cheek. I shivered as a trail of goose pimples followed her hand's journey along my arm, my shoulder, my neck. "Tell me what you want from me."

Anger pulsed up. "What *I* want? You give a shit what *I* feel now?" I made the mistake of glaring into her eyes. Hers intense. Her lips parted. Her hand slid into my hair. My voice seemed to echo in the silence.

I tried to push away. My legs wobbled. My resistance wobbled. "You're with her. You chose her."

"I did not touch her." Berne was far stronger than me. No matter how I braced myself, my hand on her shoulder, I couldn't break free from her. The longer I stayed, the less I wanted to leave. "I would not do this."

"You stayed. You stayed and Babs came back." I gave another push, hoping she'd just let go. My body was betraying me. I knew it. She knew it.

She slid her other hand to the small of my back. "She is suspicious. She demanded we go away for some time together. I could not hurt her on her birthday, Pepe."

I shut my eyes. Berne rubbed slow circles on my back. This was torture. "You're telling me that at no point did you so much as kiss her?"

Nausea rippled through me. I tried to wriggle free. Berne pulled me closer, closer, within inches of her lips.

"Look at me."

I shook my head, fixing my gaze to the wall behind her.

"Look at me." This time her husky tone oozed through me. It crept through every pore, rippling over my skin, through my heart. Sneaky, mean, underhand tactics. "I am sorry. Pepe, I had to go."

I clamped my eyes shut in protest. I was not getting suckered in. I could resist. I was angry. Really angry.

Berne leaned closer, her breath hot on my lips. "I say I was ill, that my back is bad. I make many excuses. I lied. I lied for you. I would do this always."

"You did?" Relief gushed through me. I was starting not to care if she was telling the truth. I didn't care if she was telling me what I *wanted* to hear. I felt like I was sprinting the way my heart was clattering about.

"Look at me."

I peeked open one eye. If I was only looking at her with one then I wouldn't give in. Nope.

"See it is the truth." Berne slid her hand over my cheek,

brushing over my closed eyelid, which opened on command. Traitor. "I love *you, je t'aime*, always."

The ability to speak disappeared the more she murmured, the closer she got, her eyes filled with desire. "Say that you want me. Say that you are ready. Ask me."

I clung onto her shoulder, trying to control myself. Futile was the operative word.

"Ask me," Berne whispered.

Her lips were close enough that I could sink into them. That I could let go. She felt so steady, so strong. Catherine, my mother, all that rolled through my thoughts. I squashed them back. Focused on Berne. "I—"

Her mobile cut through the silence. A cheesy love song. Real Europop. Berne backed away. I felt cold in her absence. She never paid much attention to her mobile normally.

"*Allo?*" Her gentle tone made my stomach crunch into a tight knot. The kind of tone reserved for a lover. "*Maintenant?*"

Her gaze flicked to the door. Panic and something close to guilt flashed through her eyes. Viper.

"*Oui*, of course, I am . . ." She met my eyes. "Helping a neighbour. I will meet you there."

I shoved my hands in my pockets. Nice, from friend to a neighbour. Viper was paying a visit. How wonderfully cosy.

"*Oui*, you know I do." She finished the call and pocketed her phone. "Pepe, I—"

I held my hand up. "Your *girlfriend* is entitled to come here. I'm just a neighbour."

Berne shook her head. Her eyes wide. "*Non*, you are everything to me. She has never been here. I do not know why she has come."

"She's fighting for you." I shrugged. I didn't blame Viper for that. "Least you can do is hear her out." It sounded far too rational, far too calm. What I wanted to say was tell the three-legged, toothless wonder to get lost.

Berne stared at the door. "I will tell her about us . . ."

"You had all week to do that." I folded my arms. "Spare me the 'there was never a good moment,' routine, okay?"

Berne's mobile rang again. Same ringtone. It provoked the same startled reaction.

"Well, don't keep the woman waiting." I turned, picked up

my toolbox, and marched into the room, which had once held a billiard table.

The door shut a few moments later and I slid down the nearest wall and buried my face in my hands. Vivienne could offer her far more than I ever could. The only reason they weren't more seemed to be Vivienne's reluctance to give Berne equal partnership. There was nothing like a bit of competition to realign a woman's wishes.

I didn't have anything to offer Berne. I didn't even have a job. Rebecca was buying food. If she thought I didn't know Doug was funding it, she was mistaken. Without my dear ex-fiancé, I was homeless, jobless, and about as useful as sun cream in a monsoon. Even though I loved her, I wasn't the greatest catch. I wore fluffy pyjamas. I bet Viper didn't. No, she was a suave actress. I bet hers was silk, lace, and minimal. I bet she didn't find crisp crumbs down her front.

I closed my eyes, wondering quite how I'd gotten into such a mess. A few months ago, I was engaged. I'd been in line to populate the English rugby team. I'd been trapped and unfulfilled but wasn't that better than this? Wasn't it better than being alone and knowing the woman I loved was off to see someone far better for her than me?

It was official. If Viper was fighting back then I was stuffed. Royally stuffed.

Chapter Twenty-two

BERNE TRIED TO ignore her mother's watchful gaze as she fixed Monsieur Coin's back door. His destructive golden retriever was actually an eight-month-old puppy. He'd decided to chew his way out to the garden and Monsieur Coin's backdoor was no match for the determined monster. It was a good thing he was so cute. She could hear him barking from her house most days.

"If she has come to visit you, is it not polite that you stay in the same place?"

Berne winced at her mother's tone and focused on the lock she was fitting. "Papa is showing her the area."

Berne felt her mother's gaze intensify on her cheek and sighed. She stopped her work to meet her unyielding eyes.

"You have not told her of Pippa."

Berne shook her head. "I thought it was over. When I called her, before the Ardèche, she was clear that she did not need me." She rubbed her hand over her forehead unsure how everything had become complicated again. "Now she acts as though this was nothing."

"You never speak of her." Her mother sat on one of the half-chewed stools and smiled as it wobbled under her. "The pup is hard working, *non*?"

Berne smiled back not sure how to explain herself. She felt so disloyal. "The first time I realise that she still thinks we are together is when I received an invitation." She went back to the lock, needing to do something to calm herself. "She never invited me before. She and Babs, they do not like each other."

"Yet she invited her too."

Berne nodded. "It was an important step for her. How could I not support her bravery?"

"Because your heart is with Pippa."

There was no point in arguing. It was the truth. It had always been the truth. "She has done nothing wrong, Maman."

"This isn't about right or wrong." Her mother shifted as the stool creaked. "You have no need to lie to her now. So why do you hesitate?"

The furry monster barked as Monsieur Coin opened the gate. A moment later, the elderly man was yanked through by a small lion.

Berne shook her head at the sight. "I am scared."

Berne heard her mother approach and turned to see her wave at Monsieur Coin. He lay flat on his front in the grass, lead still attached.

"What scares you so?" her mother asked.

"What if she leaves again? What if she walks away?" Berne felt the familiar surge of fear. "She will not even tell me that she wishes to be with me, Maman. She hides her wishes, her thoughts. How can we be together if she cannot even tell me she's angry?" Her screwdriver slipped off the head and gouged a chunk out of the wood. "She has a right to be so. She should be so. I know she is yet she hides it. She hides from me."

"Maybe this is just her way?" Her mother laughed as the puppy bounced around play bowing and barking at his flattened owner.

"I know her. It is not her. I cannot stand to spend my life battling for her to let me inside. I want more." She tested the lock, pleased that it worked. "I want all of her."

"And you think she is not able to give you this?" Her mother watched her for a moment.

Berne sighed under the scrutiny. "I think that if she cannot do it now. She will never do so. Someone else's thoughts, feelings will always dictate how she treats me." She tucked her hair behind her ear. "It is bad enough when Vivienne does this but when Pippa acts this way, it burns."

"You would risk losing her for this?"

Berne shrugged. Seeing the way Pippa had been with Doug . . . how little they knew of each other. How muted Pippa had been. It had been painful to see. She never wanted them to be the same. "Vivienne said she'll come out for me."

Her mother sucked in a deep breath. "And what did you say to that?"

Berne was startled by the vehemence of her mother's tone. "I did not know what to say."

"Bernadette, you do not love this woman. You love another. There is only one thing to say." Her mother put her hands on her hips. It was a gesture meant to scold but Berne found herself smiling. After seeing what Pippa had been through, she was blessed to have such a wonderful mother.

"I do not think you have called me this in a while, *non*?" Berne chuckled as her mother's eyes twinkled.

"You're not too old to be sent to bed without supper." She wagged a finger at her in mock fierceness. "Whatever your fears with Pippa, you must be honest."

Berne nodded. She knew that. She hated that she would now be reduced to unfaithful when she had been sure things with Vivienne were over. It was typical of Vivienne but it made her feel no less guilty. "So you do not think I should opt for security with a woman who has been loyal all this time?"

Her mother winced as the puppy pounced on Monsieur Coin, his trouser leg between his jaws. "Pippa has given up everything for you."

"I know." Giving wasn't Pippa's problem. Her courage to face her mother was incredible but she'd been forced into a corner. Would Pippa have done the same if her family hadn't arrived? Would she ever have told them?

Vivienne had made it clear she wanted her. In return, Berne had lied, distanced herself, and thought only of Pippa. She owed Vivienne an explanation at the least.

The puppy de-shoed his victim and bounded off with his prize. Vivienne appeared at the gate. She walked straight past the prone man to the door without so much as casting him a glance.

Her mother patted her on the arm. "I prefer Pippa."

Berne caught sight of the puppy bolting for the gate, which Vivienne had left open. She sprinted out into the sunshine after him.

"Berne?"

"Dog," she managed as she ran up the path.

It was a convenient excuse. She didn't know how to tell Vivienne. Perhaps it was much like Pippa facing her sister? She would rather appease and be miserable than face Vivienne in a mood.

Chapter Twenty-three

FOR SOMETHING TO do other than mope, I decided to take payment to Monsieur Chamonix. If I was honest, I was on a spying mission too. If Vivienne happened to be there and I happened to push her into a hedge or something then how could I help that?

So I packed up the teacakes that Rebecca had made for him and picked up his cheque. Doug had been good to his word and put the money into my account for me to pay the artisans. I noticed there was more than needed to pay everyone. I'd have to put it all back in his account. I could look after myself, sort of, a little, well . . . sometimes.

As I wandered up to the Chamonix household, I took a sharp breath. Perhaps Vivienne had offered her some kind of commitment at last? Perhaps she would be swanning around all the swanky places rubbing shoulders with the elite.

I ignored the deep throbbing that provoked. It hurt. How could thoughts physically hurt?

"Monsieur Chamonix?" I knocked on the door and pushed it open. Normally Madame Chamonix would be flitting around but she was clearly out somewhere. Maybe Viper had treated them to lunch somewhere. Three Michelin stars and food that looked like it belonged in a ration pack. I was going to make fish and chips tonight in protest. Real food. Real British food. Hah.

"*Allo?*" It was my best attempt at a French accent but it always made me sound slightly camp.

An odd gurgle came from the kitchen and I wandered in. "Oh shit . . . Are you . . . what's . . . where?"

Monsieur Chamonix was hunched over the table, gripping his chest. I went to him. He lifted his head. His eyes bulged, his face red. He spluttered for air.

"Heart?"

Flapping about a bit, I tried rubbing his back, hoping that it would do something to help. It didn't. He collapsed onto the table.

Did he have tablets? How did I get tablets into an unconscious man?

I ripped my phone out of my pocket. It flew out of my clammy hand and clattered to the floor.

"Monsieur Chamonix . . . please . . . I don't know what to do."

I scrabbled around on the floor, pieced my phone back together and punched in Rebecca's number. She'd know.

"Hello there—"

"Get Babs to call an ambulance. Berne's dad. Heart."

I hung up the phone and pressed my fingers to his neck. Oh shit, there was nothing.

"What do I do?"

Right. Think. CPR. He had a bad heart. It was bound to be his heart. I pulled him down onto the floor. I'd done first aid once for the office. What was it? ABC. Right A—Airway . . . okay, check his airway.

I rested his head back and stared down into his mouth. Apart from the fact he had dentures, I didn't have a clue. There was nothing I could see.

B—Breathing . . . He wasn't doing that. C—um . . . er . . . think. Comfort?

I placed my jacket underneath his head. "That's not going to help if his heart isn't beating, you idiot."

It seemed to help when I yelled out loud. C is for "Circulation!"

I blew out a breath. I'd done that.

"Then start CPR, numbskull."

I pulled his shirt open and traced my fingers down. Was it on the sternum, below it? The dummy hadn't had chest hair. Um . . . on it . . . I clamped my left over my right hand. Was it meant to be the other way?

"Who cares . . . pump!"

Like I'd done in first aid, way back when, I pumped as best I could. How many repetitions was it? Ten? I'd go for ten.

I needed to . . . to . . . "Breathe. Help him breathe."

Stopping the compressions, I went to his mouth and pinched his nose. Summoning as much breath as I could, I whooshed it out, looking downwards. His chest rose. Okay. Right. Start again.

Deciding on ten compressions to two breaths, I cycled back and fore.

Parts of my mind registered that, again someone was depending on me for survival. That again I was their only hope and again, I was making absolutely no difference at all.

"Keep going. Keep going," I called out to myself. "Come on, Monsieur Chamonix . . . stay with me . . . please."

REBECCA CLUNG TO the hand grip as Babs hurtled them up the road. An ambulance had whizzed past only moments ago. All they could do was pray that the old guy was okay.

"He has heart problems," Babs muttered more to herself than Rebecca. "Berne is always telling him he needs to retire."

"True, but what can you do, the old guy loves his job."

Shooting a scowl Rebecca's way, Babs lurched the car around a slower vehicle. "But the medical staff say he should not. And *where* is Bebe?"

Rebecca sighed. "Pippa texted me. Vivienne is in town."

"What?" Babs took her hands off the wheel. Rebecca lurched across to grab it.

"Yeah. Real nice from Berne. Really classy." She felt her anger bubble up. "She chased her enough. You'd think she'd be happy to get what she wanted."

Babs tutted. "Pepe said that she needed space. You know that Vivienne is sly. Bebe doesn't wish to hurt her. She said that she had not broken things off with her."

Rebecca folded her arms. "No offence but no matter who said it, I would never stay away from you."

"*Je t'aime,*" Babs whispered.

"Remind me of that when I'm smacking sense into Berne." Then the realisation of what Babs had said hit her. She turned, knowing she was grinning. "You do?"

"Of course." Babs shook her head. "I am about ready to do the same to them both. There is always an excuse, always a reason not to be together . . ." She snorted her disgust. "They have more drama than a football player on the ground."

Rebecca nodded. She was sick and tired of it too. None of it made sense and they should have been together years ago. Why were they overcomplicating everything? They were both unhappy, both pining, and both driving her nuts.

"I say we stage an intervention when he gets fixed up." Rebecca prayed that he *would* be fixed up. The old guy was awesome.

"This will be a good idea." Babs screeched them to a halt next to the ambulance and they hurried into the house.

"Pip?" Rebecca searched the rooms for them. "Pip?"

"In here."

They hurried into the kitchen and saw the ambulance crew firing conversation to and fro while placing a mask over Berne's father's face. Pippa had a bottle in her hands. She gave it to the men who nodded and wheeled the old guy past them, one working while the other pushed.

"Pip . . . you need to sit there, I'll make tea. Babs, will you call the family? You can articulate a lot better."

Babs saluted and hurried off with her mobile. Rebecca searched the cupboards finding an "allez les bleus" mug and settled the kettle to boil.

"You want to tell me?"

"He was gasping, he slumped over, and then he was quiet." Pippa rubbed her arms. "I did CPR the best I could. My arms feel like they are going to fall off."

"You know what the ambulance men said?"

Pippa shook her head, staring down at the table. Rebecca focused on the kettle, irritated that Pippa had been alone to deal with it.

Babs rushed into the kitchen. "I will take Berne, her mother, and Vivienne. They are in the village."

Rebecca glanced a smile at Babs, then caught her at the door. "I love you too. You know that, right?"

"I do now." Babs planted a lingering kiss on her lips and hurried out.

Rebecca touched her tingling lips, headed into the kitchen, and grabbed the bubbling kettle.

"Tea," she murmured at Pippa, placing it in front of her. "You need to wash up?"

Pippa nodded, blinking back tears. Rebecca helped her up and into the bathroom, flannelled off her tear-stained face and tried not to show how worried she was herself.

She led Pippa back into the kitchen, picked up the tea, and headed into the living room.

"Bound to have films, right?"

Pippa nodded and Rebecca sat her down, placed the cup in her hands, and rifled through the films on the shelf until she got to one that she knew would bring a smile to Pippa's face. It was all she could do but it was better than nothing.

THE LIGHTS OF the hospital were glaring. The sterile smell was nauseating and the feel of the place just made Berne feel woozy.

Her father had been in theatre for hours. There had been no word on how he was. Her mother had sat praying in the corner. Vivienne had attached herself to Berne's arm. The Vivienne she'd been with for so many years would not have even sat beside her. It felt strange but she shoved it to the back of her mind and was just thankful for the comfort. Erique had taken to wearing out the corridor. His boots squeaked on the floor.

The doctor finally joined them in the room, and Berne was sure it was some horrible dream.

"Madame Chamonix. Pierre is out of surgery now. He will be with you very soon." The doctor smiled. "I have had to fit a pacemaker but he is a strong one."

The relief of everyone in the room flushed out in one sweeping breath. Berne felt Vivienne squeeze her arm.

"No doubt someone was watching over him today, *non?*" the doctor said.

Berne had no doubt of the fact. Her father had suffered a stroke, had that funny turn up on the scaffold, and now, perhaps at last, there was a way to stop such things happening.

"He will pull through well?" Erique asked, his hands tucked into the belt of his uniform. "The nurse said he had stopped breathing."

The doctor nodded. "His heart had stopped completely. Like I said, he is very lucky."

Not sure that she understood, Berne looked at her mother and brother but they seemed to wear the same blank expression. "How did he survive if his heart stopped?"

"A woman gave him CPR until the ambulance crew arrived." The doctor smiled, bouncing from his heels to the balls of his feet. "You do not know of her deeds?"

"Woman?" Berne's mother had still been with Monsieur Coin and Vivienne. Berne had been chasing a rogue puppy.

She glanced at Erique who shrugged. "Who was it?"

The doctor shook his head. "I do not know. She found him and kept him alive. Perhaps you ask the ambulance team. They will know more."

Erique wasted no time. He strode out of the room. Berne untangled herself from Vivienne, went to her mother, and took her hand. "Will he be awake soon?"

"*Non*, it will take some time. He will be monitored. There is nothing much you can do for him at the moment. Go home, rest. He will be awake some time tomorrow."

Berne looked at her mother who emphatically shook her head. "Is there a bed, a room that my mother can sleep in?"

The doctor seemed prepared for the answer. "I will have the nurses bring one in." He smiled at her mother. "But please, rest. He is in safe hands now."

The doctor left and Erique strode back in. His face unreadable as if he was trying to keep it all together.

"What did you learn?"

He shook his head. He let out a few long breaths and met her eyes. "The ambulance crew have finished but they wanted to come, to see how he was getting on."

"That is sweet of them," her mother said, still thumbing over her rosary.

Erique nodded. "They said that when they got to the house, a woman was single-handedly performing CPR. She had been doing it for at least twenty minutes." He thumbed to the doorway. "They thought they might need to resuscitate her."

"Who was she?" Berne had a feeling it was probably Babs. No doubt she would have known what to do and been calm enough to execute it. She frowned. Surely Babs would have said. She'd gone in search of coffee an hour ago. Her thinly veiled irritation at Vivienne hadn't been helping.

"From the description . . ." He smiled at her. "Pippa."

Berne blinked a few times. She knew Vivienne was watching her. "*Pardon?*"

Erique smiled. "Wavy dark hair, attractive, was talking to herself and to Papa."

That certainly sounded like Pippa. Had she really saved Papa?

"Who is Pippa?" Vivienne asked. Her look told Berne that she had her suspicions.

"A neighbour." Berne ignored the tut from her mother.

Before Vivienne could ask anymore, her father was wheeled in by the medical staff. The methodical beep beep of his heart monitor filled the room.

Vivienne was still expecting answers. Berne couldn't help but think of how things would have been if . . . if . . . "Pippa . . . it was her?"

Erique nodded, tears in his eyes. "She didn't stop at all. Twice now she has been a hero."

Berne bit her lip and stared down at her father. Pippa had made sure her father had a fighting chance. She'd been through so much all those years ago that Berne didn't think it was possible. She smiled. Apparently it was.

"Berne," her mother said, making her look up. "Go to her, we will be here."

Vivienne got up from her seat. "Why don't I go with you?"

"It's not—"

Her mother cast a weary glance at Vivienne. "If today doesn't remind you of how important it is to treasure those you love and hold them close, what will?" Tired but wise, her mother's eyes filled with love. "Give her a million *bisous* from me."

Berne glanced at Erique, who nodded, and got to her feet. "I will. I'll do that." She kissed her father on the forehead, burst out through the door, and jogged down the corridor.

She needed to find Babs. She needed to get back to Pippa. She hurried down the stairs not listening to Vivienne's questions, to her demands. Pippa had saved him. She'd saved his life.

"*Merci*, Pepe . . . *merci*."

Chapter Twenty-four

REBECCA AND I had stared at French television for what felt like days. It was probably more like an hour and a half but it really did feel like a lot longer. What was it with time? How could hours feel so massively different in length?

Desperate to know how Monsieur Chamonix was and if he had made it, zoning out was the only thing I was truly capable of doing. My arms were so tired and achy that I could barely lift them to reach for my drink. When I did, they shook so much that I spilled half of it over myself.

A lot of it was shock.

"Vivienne went with them, didn't she?" I didn't know why it popped into my head or if it should really matter. It was surreal that I *hoped* she was with Berne. I didn't want her to be alone. I wanted her to have support. It didn't matter from whom.

Rebecca pulled out her mobile. "Yeah."

The television program was dreadful. This one actress was so poor that she kept doing a flickering look from side to side with her eyes. "Think she's forgotten her line again."

Rebecca sniggered. "Either that or someone has let off a stink."

"Oh look, she's after the CEO now." I snorted. "I mean what woman really puckers her lips out like that?"

Not normally one for picking holes in people, I put it down to the fact that I was worried. I wasn't mean and I never ever wanted to be like Catherine. My darling sister's parting e-mail had been so full of anger that I'd not bothered to read on after the third line.

Sad thing was, she and my mother seemed less of a problem now they were so far away. I had reached the point that I'd realised how much happier I was not having to pretend anymore. It made me feel like I'd released a dead weight.

In other words, good riddance.

The news flicked onto the screen and the reporter cycled through the events of the day. Apparently lots of drama had happened in a sport, I presumed football, and lots of suited men were being photographed leaving a court. It must have been relatively important because Rebecca muttered, "Terrible," at the set once or twice.

I didn't hear it. I was thinking about Monsieur Chamonix and hoping that he was okay. He loved football, he would have been shaking his head at the television too if he was here.

Rebecca went to stand then yelped and hopped about. She frantically rubbed at her calf.

"Come here." I patted the couch next to me and she plonked down. I rolled up her trouser leg and manipulated the muscle with my fingers as Rebecca studied my face. I broke out into a smile. "You haven't had this since you stopped training."

She sported a lovely blush. "Yeah, I know. Should have taken it more easy."

"You're training again?"

Rebecca had retired from triathlons when she had damaged her ligaments and had to have knee surgery. It had put her off and she'd never found anything she enjoyed as much to replace it.

"I know, I know. I only got the urge a couple of days ago. Babs went for a run and . . . I guess I got the urge to do something myself."

Working the muscle, I kissed her on the kneecap. "Well done. I'm glad you're doing something for you."

"You're not mad?"

I shook my head. "At least I'll have company if you compete this time." I tried and failed to keep the grin off my face. "You know, because you love her."

Rebecca groaned. "You weren't meant to hear that."

"Alas, your secret is out." I met her eyes. "She's good for you."

Rebecca grinned. "You really want a laugh?"

Anything not to have to think about waiting, about Monsieur Chamonix. I prayed he was okay, he had made it.

"Hit me."

Rebecca turned to the TV and searched until she found what she was looking for. On came the crazy TV show with the pouty-lipped woman.

I chuckled. "She's your new embarrassing crush or something?"

Rebecca flashed her grin at me. "Oh no. Pippa Saunders . . . meet your rival . . . Vivienne."

I turned to the screen and burst into laughter. What was Berne thinking? "Was she drunk?"

"Now, now . . . Miss Fish Lips is very charming when her face moves."

I'll bet. Why had Berne put up with her being nasty? "I can be mean to her on Berne's behalf, right?"

Mean fish-lips-viper who had hurt Berne so much. Viper who was with Berne now. Boo.

"Yeah, talk about being in love with yourself. The woman went on and on."

"Did Babs ever tell you why she caught Berne's eye?"

Rebecca nodded. "She's a legend, I guess. Pictures of her a few years ago showed that she was far hotter back then too. Maybe she ended up looking like she was inside."

"Poor Berne." I didn't like to think of her having to suffer the woman's wrath. "I don't think I can cope with her having to put up with it."

"Then do us all a favour and do something about it?"

I looked at her.

Rebecca shrugged. "Look, I love you, but stop with the drama already."

Consider myself told. "You and Babs both feel that way?"

Rebecca nodded. "Tell her, Pip. Tell her."

The woman, old fish face, on TV made me feel like I might just have a chance to win Berne back. I mean, the lady was probably saner, richer, and more well respected than me but I could build stairs and rewire stuff badly.

"Guess I should listen to you then, huh?"

ANY THOUGHTS OF reconciliation were put to one side as Berne came through the front door. I scoured her face for signs of hope that her father had pulled through but she said nothing until Babs . . . and Vivienne . . . hurried in behind her.

"Did you try to help him?" Berne asked, her voice hoarse, her exhaustion etched lines on her face.

I shoved my hands in my pockets unsure of her mood, bracing myself for the worst. *Please let him be okay, let him be alive.* "I tried to."

"They said you did this for over twenty minutes . . . alone?"

Had it been that long? It didn't matter. I would have done it until my arms had fallen off if it had given him a chance. "Is he . . . did they . . . ?"

The lump in my throat robbed me of my speech, so I gripped my own neck for support. I must have looked like I was trying to strangle myself.

"He has a pacemaker, they save him. The doctor says you made this possible." Berne searched my eyes. I could see Vivienne watching me like a hawk, watching her. Berne walked to me and wrapped me up in a hug. Her tears broke free as I held onto her.

"You saved him. *Merci. Merci.*" She sobbed the words into my shoulder, her body wracked with the tears.

Babs ushered a scowling Viper over to the drinks cabinet.

"Couch," I murmured to Rebecca, who nodded and helped guide me towards it. "Thanks."

I'd never seen Berne emotional. Never had her cling to me for support. I wanted to cuddle the worry from her. "Did you see him?"

"*Oui.* They say he will wake tomorrow." She sniffed and sobbed. I held on, rubbing her back, cuddling her close. "Maman wishes you to know her gratitude also."

"You don't have to thank me for anything. There was no way I was letting him go." I nodded up at Babs, who motioned to a whiskey bottle. Vivienne looked like she may throw her glass at me. "For a start, the Lyon game is coming up soon, isn't it?"

Berne chuckled. "No doubt he will be grateful for this."

"Let's hope they actually win then." I took the glass of whiskey from Babs and handed it to Berne.

Manners told me to let go and remove myself so that Vivienne could sit beside Berne. It took every ounce of dignity I had to do just that. I took a glass from Babs. I needed it. In fact, I needed the bottle.

"I'm not sure . . . er . . . Vivienne, isn't it?" I asked, pretending like I didn't know who she was.

"*Oui.*" Vivienne took her seat beside Berne, her hand on Berne's knee. A definite "back off," in her eyes.

"Berne told me you live in Marseille so . . . I guess you wouldn't be happy if Lyon won."

Vivienne had a way about her. Her scarf draped over her

shoulders, her styled hair dyed within an inch of its life. Her lips looked even more rubber in real life.

"I do not care for such things," Vivienne said, her eyes on Berne who knocked back her whiskey.

Babs poked her tongue out at Vivienne behind the couch. Rebecca stifled a chuckle.

Berne stared off into space. Vivienne glared at me. Rebecca and Babs glared at her. I stared up at the ceiling. This wasn't awkward, was it? Nope.

Whatever I was feeling, Berne needed us all to support her, whatever we felt about each other. I cleared my throat and turned to Berne. "No doubt your mother is going to be at the hospital the whole time, right?"

"*Oui*, they are giving her a bed." Berne sighed and stared down into the empty glass. "The last time she barely ate."

"I was thinking we can make up some food for her?" I looked up at Rebecca who gave me a thumbs up. "That way when your father is up and about, he can eat something he likes." Babs took Berne's empty glass. "Winston can make it there and back, so I'll shuttle you when Babs is in work."

Vivienne cleared her throat. "Why? When she could stay in Marseille?" She tucked a hair behind Berne's ear. "She prefers the city. She can be driven from there."

Apparently Berne couldn't speak for herself anymore. "I'm sure anyone would but Berne's father was working on the house. So I'm guessing Berne will be taking over?"

Take that, Viper.

"Ah so you are Rebecca's mistress?" She smiled the kind of sly smile that made me want to throw my whiskey at her. "Peggy, *non*?"

"Pippa." I squeezed the glass. Berne met my eyes. She needed me not to throw things. I downed the shot instead, then spluttered.

Babs raised her eyebrows at me.

"Not anymore," I said with as much confidence as I could. "She prefers shorter women."

Rebecca poked her tongue out at me. "I like French women." Her eyes lingered on Babs. Babs gave her a flirty wink.

"And what do you prefer?" Vivienne's voice held a threatening edge to it. She was oddly terrifying. Maybe it was the unnatural lips, I didn't know.

"It's not a preference." I put my glass down, feeling buzzed by the shot. Warm and fuzzy. "I *know* what I want."

Berne met my eyes. *You listening, you dumb clot.* I hoped she'd get the message.

"And this is?" Vivienne trailed a long finger over Berne's jaw. She leaned in and placed a kiss on Berne's lips. Her eyes twinkled with malice. "So, what is it that you want, Pippa?"

I was going to throw my glass at her. I didn't care. Rubber lips or not. What did I want? Oh, I'd tell her what I wanted.

Berne met my eyes once more. Her lost look stopped my temper short. She didn't need a catfight. "I really, really, really want a—"

"Pip, this is no time for the Spice Girls." Rebecca was doing her best to keep a straight face. I was quite sure she knew I wanted to slap fish lips across the chops with a wet haddock. "Pip and I will shuttle you to the hospital."

Berne looked relieved. "You have much work to do—"

"You got a problem with Winston?" I knew that Berne still hadn't gotten around to telling Babs about the accident. A lot of that was due to Babs using her as her chief artisan at times. Berne didn't want her worrying when she was up ladders. No one seemed to realise that Berne wasn't driving.

She bit her lip. Her eyes searched mine. "No, he is *très beau.* I do not wish to—"

"There is plenty of room for you at home." Vivienne met my eyes with a dangerous smile. "It will be easier for us to make the arrangements, *non?*"

What arrangements? I glanced at Rebecca and Babs who looked as lost as me.

"You have not told them?" Vivienne held out her hand. It was one vein-riddled claw. It also had a very shiny ring on it. "Berne asked me to marry her. I said yes, *naturellement, non?*"

My stomach lurched. Berne stared at Vivienne, startled . . . and not the kind of startled like she didn't want the secret out. Babs looked like she wanted to impale Vivienne on something. Rebecca caught me by the elbow as I clattered into the side table.

"Isn't that nice." My voice sounded maniacal again. Uh oh. "Very nice."

Berne sighed. "I am staying in Ajoux, I would like your help. If it is still offered?" She rubbed a hand over her face. Tears brimmed in her eyes. She needed support.

"Unconditional," I mumbled. "Anyway." I felt my hands trembling and shoved them in my back pockets. I wanted to cry. Even if they weren't true, Vivienne's words still hurt. "I'll leave you two alone. I need to . . . er . . . wash my hair."

What? Why? Where had that come from? Wash my hair? That was an excuse for not going on a date, not excusing yourself from a potential train wreck of a heartbreak.

"I'll help you." Rebecca shrugged as Vivienne raised her pencilled-on eyebrows. "She might need a towel?"

The pair of us were pathetic.

"I am going to stay with Bebe," Babs said, holding her hand up before Vivienne could argue. "This is Madame Chamonix's house. It would not do to have the happy couple share the same room, *non*?"

Vivienne blew out a breath. "I don't think that's necessary."

"I do. I will sleep here." Berne pulled away from her and went to the whiskey bottle.

I didn't want to leave her and I didn't know what I could do to help. It clearly wasn't my place to. The ring on Vivienne's finger was not something Berne would pick. Not only that, she couldn't afford a diamond corker like that.

Somewhere inside, underneath the shock and ripple of pain, I knew I wore the only ring she would give with her heart.

Steeling myself with that thought, I went to Berne and pulled her into a hug. "If you need me, you know where I am."

Berne held on. I knew she didn't want to let me go. I brushed my ring against her cheek.

"Just remember, you married me first, right?"

Berne nodded. Her eyes twinkled with tears. I kissed the ring on my finger out of sight of Viper who was being distracted by Rebecca dancing about. Cramp again.

"*Merci*." Her eyes filled with so much warmth that I knew she was saying she loved me.

"Unconditional," I repeated. I meant it. Where had all this strength come from?

Whiskey was good.

Vivienne muttered something at Babs as Rebecca continued to yelp. I squeezed Berne's hand and let go.

"Come on, Whitely. Let's get you a hot salty soak."

Again that provoked raised eyebrows.

"Seriously? You think washing hair and salt rubs are seduction?" I shook my head, whooshing out a breath. "And they say French women are romantics."

Rebecca sniggered through a yelp as I helped her to hobble out. I knew Babs was on my side. She'd keep the Viper at bay.

"You're kinda cheery considering you just got told they're getting married." Rebecca hopped down the road until her cramp calmed.

"Monsieur Chamonix is alive and well." I smiled. I'd helped that to happen, somehow. I said a silent thank you in prayer. "And . . . you know what? I think old Fish Lips feels threatened."

Rebecca laughed. "You think? I was waiting for her to p—"

I pressed my fingers to her lips. "Yuck."

She shrugged. "Proud of you, Pip."

I nudged her shoulder with mine, a smile filling me up. He was okay. I'd helped him. He was alive.

Chapter Twenty-five

MONSIEUR CHAMONIX WAS awake and in good spirits. Berne had taken on her role in helping me restore the house once more. We hadn't talked about Vivienne's announcement. The only thing I wanted to do was to help her take her mind off her father.

We worked in silence a few days later, late into the barmy summer afternoon. We were in one of the bedrooms upstairs. So far they were shells. Drafty shells with flapping sheet windows.

I wanted to be a part of Berne's day and Viper was everywhere. The only place she left Berne alone was here. Still, she was marrying her. It wasn't as if Berne had protested. She could have stopped me leaving, told Vivienne to go but she hadn't.

There were so many confusing emotions rocketing around me that I wasn't sure what to think anymore. Only a cryptic visit from Madame Chamonix had helped to steel me.

She'd brought bread, which we had. That was her reason for taking time out of her busy day to traipse down to the house. She'd talked about the decor and about how she and Monsieur Chamonix had been married over fifty years. Then she'd told me that he'd needed openness. He'd always been the same. He needed to understand her love was whole by her sharing her every day.

"He and Berne are much the same," she had said with a chuckle and left.

If that wasn't a hint, I didn't know what was. I felt quite chuffed that Madame Chamonix was on my side.

It wasn't helping me find the right words. At least none that didn't sound like I was in competition with Vivienne. No matter how I tried to place the right meaning, it wouldn't come. So I concentrated on trying to fix the floorboard I was working on. My thoughts kept going back to Berne and back to when we met. That summer, that storm. If "I love you" hadn't told her, if leaving Doug hadn't shown her, how else could I prove it?

"How long did you know you liked me before . . . ?" I heard

myself asking the question out loud. I was speaking *out loud*. Oh no.

Berne stopped her task of re-pointing the stone work. "*Pardon?*"

"You were older than me. You knew that you were . . . well . . . you know . . ." I scratched my head, getting dust in my eye. Ouch. I winked to try and get it out. Ow, ow. Suave, Saunders, really suave. That'll woo her, won't it.

"That I loved you?"

I sat down on the floor beside her. "Yes and well . . . that you were okay with that." I bit my lip. "And how did you know, about me?"

Berne swivelled around on her stool to face me. "This is what bothers you?"

"Yes . . . no . . ." I stared down at my dusty hands. "Will you humour me?"

"*Bien sur,*" Berne said with a smile. "It was not about if you were or were not attracted to other women." She chose her words, her careful tone full of the humming sound I adored. "I was only trying to understand if you feel this way about me."

"I did." I took her hand. I wanted to say *I still do. Pick me!* but couldn't find the courage.

Berne stroked my cheek with her thumb. "You were young and you were vulnerable. You look at me with such desire without realising. It was hard not to notice."

"I've always loved you." Hint, hint. As in always.

Her eyes twinkled but she didn't take the bait. "Then that is all that matters, *non?*"

I shook my head. Try again. Think of something else. Openness. "Vivienne makes you hide away." Great. State the obvious. Pick on Viper. That will win her confidence, won't it? I took hold of her hand once more and placed mine in it. "I mean . . . why doesn't she celebrate you . . . Why does she force you inside?"

"That takes us both to do this." She lifted my chin and captured me with gentle eyes.

Tell her, you numbskull. "You deserve better than the way she treats you."

Berne leaned in closer, her breath misted in the space between our lips. "You have a better way?"

I glanced down at her lips and up to her eyes. I could feel the heat radiating from her as I inched closer. "She never asks you how you feel, what you want."

Berne placed her finger over my lips. "Ask me, Pepe."

"You're marrying her." I felt her breath mingle with mine. "It's not polite for . . . me . . . to—"

Bang.

I jumped, ducked, and head-butted Berne's chin. She grunted as I clamped my hands over my head.

Ow, ow, ow.

Berne sighed and picked up the screwdriver that had clattered out of my pocket. I was too busy rubbing my head to care. She had a hard chin.

"You are right. It is unfair to act this way." She placed the screwdriver in my hand. "It is not fair on any of us."

"You didn't really ask her to marry you, did you?" I swallowed, trying to clear my throat. Time to face the truth.

"Even if I did not, why shouldn't I marry her?" Berne went back to her work. Her frown line prominent.

Ouch. I sucked in my breaths. "It's not fair."

Openness. Feeling. I could do this. Oh how did I say it? Berne lifted her eyes from her task.

"I mean . . . um . . . Does she know how talented you are?" I needed Rebecca to swoop in and speak for me. Why couldn't I say it? She could only say no and break my heart, which I doubted would ever heal. Where was the worry in that?

Berne raised her eyebrows at me. "*Moi?*"

"How you work the stone. I've always wondered how . . . what goes through your mind." I threw my screwdriver on the floor. I was useless at this. "I loved being taught by you. I loved listening to you."

All in past tense.

She held my gaze for a moment and her eyes softened. "It was mutual."

Again in past tense.

My eyes misted up. She could leave. She could marry the woman even though she knew I'd given up Doug. Even after all we'd been through. "I want you to teach me. You know, for when you leave."

She motioned for me to scoot over to her and handed me the pointed tool thingy that she always used. "When you re-point the stone, it is an art. You take the bare stone and strengthen it."

It sounded familiar. I felt like I'd been stripped back to the bare stone. Right now I felt like my whole heart was crumbling.

"Each stroke, each loving touch fills in another hole." She held my hand and moved the tool to the stone. "The more care you take not to rush, not to skim the surface, the more certain that the renovation will last, *oui*."

I loved the way she talked. "All it needs is a master craftsman to show you the way?" I leaned in and kissed her on the cheek.

Oops.

"I . . . um . . ."

Berne tutted and tapped the wall with the tool. "Would you kiss your teacher?" Her face was stern but her eyes twinkled. I knew full well she loved it when I did that.

"If she made it sound as romantic as you do, pretty much." I met her eyes. Pleading with her. *Don't marry her. Don't run off with Fish Lips.*

Berne smiled a sad smile and tapped the tool to the wall. "Concentrate."

"I can't." I kissed her cheek again.

She pulled my mouth to hers. Energy fired through me. She ran her fingers through my hair. The kiss grew. I had no idea how I'd ended up on the floor but I didn't care.

Berne murmured. Her hands roamed over my stomach, up my sides. I realised my hands were as busy as hers.

She pulled back. Her breath ragged against my mouth. "Pepe—"

I kissed her with every ounce of passion I felt. If I couldn't say it, I was going to show it. Berne groaned and her body responded. Her hands pulled at my top. I helped her.

"Berne?"

She froze. Her hands on my bra fastener. I peeked open an eye just to confirm it was Vivienne. Yup. One really livid rubber-lipped Viper.

Oops.

Vivienne spun on her heel.

"Vivienne . . ." Berne sighed and met my eyes. "I have to go after her."

I nodded. What could I say to that?

She put her hands in her hair as I pulled my top back down. "It is such a mess."

She shook the dust off her jeans and looked over her shoulder at me. Her eyes filled with desire, love, regret. I wasn't sure which of those was the strongest. Without another word she hurried off. I stared at her tools, groaned, and flopped back down with a thud.

What did I do now? I pulled out my mobile and tried to ring Rebecca but there was no answer. A cheery *bonjour* told me Julian had arrived. I got up, brushed myself off, and went to find him. Something, anything, not to think about the fact Berne had left me to go to her, again.

Chapter Twenty-six

REBECCA SPRINTED INTO the house sporting the kind of look that made me lift onto the balls of my feet. I'd spent twenty minutes attempting to wire the landing with Julian but so far all I'd done was make his job harder.

"Pip." She bent over at the waist, sucking the air in. "Berne . . . Viv . . . Shop . . ."

I hurried down the stairs, attempting to connect the dots. Berne and Vivienne shopping did not sound like sprint-worthy news. I'd be happy to forget I'd ever heard of either name.

"Breathe."

Rebecca shook her head. "Berne . . . Vivienne is . . . shop." She waved her hand over her head.

"Make sense." Water. Maybe water would help. I opened the fridge, realising that all we actually had was water. Where was the food?

"So?"

Rebecca stood up straight, cracked open the water, and downed it.

"Caught you?" Rebecca raised her eyebrows.

I shrugged. I had no restraint where Berne was involved. What was new?

"Vivienne is in the workshop with Berne. They are arguing. Vivienne wants her to leave to go back to Marseille. It's an ultimatum."

I frowned. "What are you doing, stalking her?"

"No, Babs and I were . . . well . . . out the back when they came in." Her blush said enough. Nice. "Hey don't look so judgemental. I heard what Vivienne saw."

Point taken. "Berne went after her if you haven't noticed. That's pretty conclusive."

"You need to tell her, shout it at her, whatever. Just don't let her walk away." Rebecca shoved me towards the door. "Don't let her get stuck with Fish Lips."

I sighed. "She is the one who has to make that choice, not me."

Rebecca gripped my shoulders. "Vivienne is demanding she go. You know. You remember that feeling?"

Flashes of Catherine filled my head. "It's not the same thing. Vivienne isn't Catherine."

"Berne is sweet and kind. Babs told you that she makes her cry."

I nodded. That made me want to throw things.

"You want her to cry when you can make her laugh?" Rebecca looked like she wanted to slap sense into me. "You want her to grow old with someone else?"

Urgency fired through me. "No."

"Then please, Pip, tell her."

I couldn't, I couldn't let Berne go. I spun around and sprinted up the hill. I was so unfit. My breaths sounded like Winston when he huffed along the road. My own rust bucket of a car was fitter than me.

I didn't want Berne to leave. I didn't want her to go. I wanted her to stay. I wanted her never to be treated like that again. I wanted to make her happy. I could make her happy.

The realisation rocketed through me. Openness. That's what she wanted. I could do that, badly, but I would. I'd do anything for her. I loved her. I loved her too much to let her go.

I found it harder running downhill than I did up. I'd need more than water when I got there, I'd need oxygen. Madame Chamonix poked her head out of her kitchen window as I huffed my way past her house.

"She is in the—"

"Workshop." I gasped in the air. "Got it."

"Show her your heart." Madame Chamonix's eyes filled with affection. "You can do it, Pepe."

What was I, Rocky? I stumbled through the boules game, mumbling apologies. Sweat dribbled off my nose. I would have been faster walking. Actually, Winston would have gotten me here faster even with a dodgy starter motor.

I could see Berne through the window of the workshop. Vivienne was pacing around like some kind of lawyer, or prison guard. I took a deep breath and shoved my way through the door.

"Pepe, *Ça va . . .* ?" Her argument with Vivienne stopped as she hurried over to me with water. "Did something happen . . . the house?"

I shook my head, desperate to catch my breath.

Vivienne folded her arms, slumped onto a chair, and crossed her legs. "Have you not done enough?" she spat at me.

Ignoring her, I turned to Berne. "You . . . can't . . . go." I gasped in between breaths. Now I knew how Rebecca had felt. That was some run.

Berne frowned, her concern more for me puffing than anything else. "*Pardon?*"

"You . . ." Openness. I glanced at Vivienne who had some kind of bespoke letter opener in her hand. She flicked it against her arm.

"Don't go." I met Berne's eyes. "Stay."

Berne cocked her head.

"You can find another artisan. There are plenty of them to go around." Vivienne clicked at the counter. "Berne, I am waiting."

I narrowed my eyes and stood up straight. She did not just click at Berne, did she?

"Berne is . . . unique." Catch your breath, Saunders. You can't verbally berate someone while keeling over. "There is no one as . . . talented . . . as special . . . as incredible as her."

"It's stone." Vivienne clicked again. "As for other services, she's no longer in business."

I saw Berne's look of utter disgust. Wow, Viper. Way to make your fiancé sound like a prostitute.

"She's everything to me."

Berne turned from Vivienne. I saw her shoulders rise as she took a breath. I knew that motion. I knew it when she was waiting. When she longed for something. I knew her.

"It doesn't matter. We're leaving. Now." Vivienne glared at Berne.

Berne flinched.

"Don't go. Stay. Please." I bit my lip. How else did I tell her? What did she need?

"What can you offer her?" Vivienne laughed.

I felt my teeth clench. She and my sister could be twins.

I turned to look at her. I didn't have a clue where the strength came from but I could see Babs loitering at the back and Rebecca creeping through the door. I needed a way to show her what she meant to me.

"Just to stand in the fierce heat reminds me of her." I took a breath. "When I was away, my heart was still with her. I'd stand in the sun. If only for a fleeting moment, a secret, unthinking moment, I could close my eyes and feel the touch of her."

"Pepe?" Berne's eyes softened. "You don't have to—"

"I *need* to." I took her hands in mine. "Your warm fingertips, light, teasing, trailing their way up my bare back."

Vivienne went to move but Rebecca blocked her way.

"Your soft laughter in my ear. Its sound seeped into every breath I've taken since." I felt tears well up and didn't hold them back. "You're the thudding of my heart, the wriggle in my stomach, the hammering of the pulse in my ear. You're everything. You're my safe harbour."

"Pathetic." Vivienne stood up.

I gazed at Berne. Her tears trickled down her cheeks.

"I can't stop you leaving but if you do, let it be because you want it. Not because someone tells you too." I sighed. "I speak from bitter experience."

Berne took my hands in hers.

Vivienne pushed past Rebecca. "You are cunning. I give you this."

"I'm sorry that what you saw hurt you," I told her. I could see the shock in her eyes. "I'm sorry Berne is in this position but I'm not sorry I kissed her." I met Berne's eyes once more. "The only thing I ever regret was leaving."

Before I burst into tears, started begging or throwing things at the Viper, I walked out. Madame Chamonix clapped at me from her front door.

Whether Berne would run after me, I didn't know. I wasn't sure if it was enough but it was all I had.

Chapter Twenty-seven

THE SUMMER AIR was filled with the scent of hope. Well, some kind of weird flower that set off her sinuses as Rebecca ducked behind the wall. Vivienne had stormed out after Pippa had left the shop. Berne had stayed in there, alone, all night. Pippa had sat in the house watching DVDs until she fell asleep.

She didn't know what Berne had decided. Quite honestly, if she'd been Berne, she would have proposed to Pippa on the spot. Okay, so they'd all been a bit dumbstruck with Pippa's heart-soaring words. Even Babs had had a tear.

Rebecca and Babs had decided to intervene. No way were they giving up without a fight. Three cheers for next day delivery.

Rebecca placed a finger over Babs's lips. She was giggling like a naughty school girl. "She'll hear us."

Babs nodded, eyes wide with mischief. "You think it'll work?"

"It has to, that's what started them off, remember?" Rebecca peeked around the corner. The excitement made her shudder.

"Need some warmth?"

Rebecca slapped at the cold hands snaking their way inside her top and smiled. The woman was insatiable, just how she liked it.

"Focus, my little French marshmallow. Do you want them to get together or not."

Babs sighed. "*Oui.*"

Rebecca chuckled at her bored tone and raised eyebrow. "Quit making me laugh. Right, the package is being delivered."

She gripped hold of Babs's hand. Babs ducked underneath her arm to see.

Up came the postie, special delivery for Mademoiselle Saunders. Rebecca knew that Berne was getting a very similar package in the mail. Hiding around the corner was the only way they'd know that Pippa would definitely answer the door. It was the only thing that dragged her out of her workshop during office hours. Plus she was brooding.

Berne, of course, *always* dragged her out but Berne was

brooding too. She didn't know much about the Frenchie but if Pippa sanded any more wood, she'd have no hands left.

The postie knocked on the door a second time and Rebecca prepared herself to rugby tackle him for it if he decided to leave.

"Come on, Pippa, you dozy clot."

Rebecca shrank back as the door opened and Pippa poked her head out. As always, she was covered from head to toe in paint, sawdust, and other crap. After a brief conversation, she signed for the parcel, squinted down at it, and cocked her head.

"We need to get closer," Babs whispered.

The postie headed back up the road and they dashed across the yard like very badly trained secret agents.

"You see anything?" Babs asked as Rebecca peered in through a window above her.

"Yeah, she's reading the note."

Babs gripped hold of her arm in acknowledgement as Rebecca gave her the running commentary. "She's smiling . . . and shaking her head . . . all good so far."

Pippa pulled at the package but couldn't rip it. Rebecca ducked as Pippa scanned the worktop next to the window.

"*Ça va?*"

"We got incoming."

Babs sniggered and dragged a crouching Rebecca from underneath the sill. They trampled over the weeds sprouting up before stopping at the side window. Babs thumbed at the glass. Rebecca nodded and slid upwards until she spotted Pippa.

"Okay, she's found the scissors." Rebecca sighed. "Those won't work, they're paper scissors . . . use your Stanley knife, you ditz."

Considering she was so clever, she was a bird brain. Rebecca watched her struggle until Babs burst into another fit of giggles.

"You would make the worst spy ever."

Babs nodded, clamping both hands over her mouth.

"Oh . . . wait . . . she's twigged they aren't useful." Rebecca shook her head as Pippa walked over to the knife block and pulled out the butcher's cleaver. "Whoa, Pip, it's just a plastic fastener . . ." She clamped her hands over her eyes and peered through splayed fingers. "She's going to cut off her arm or something. I should go in."

Babs yanked her downwards and shook her head. "*Non*, this is interference. We do not know of this, *non*?"

Rebecca sighed. "I know but if she cuts off her thumb—"

Thwack.

Rebecca popped up. Pippa wasn't on the floor, no blood, no screaming. The box had been felled well and truly though. "She's murdered the packaging."

Babs giggled again.

"Shhh . . . she'll hear you."

Pippa frowned and glanced in their direction. Rebecca dropped down. The laughter from Babs filled with intermittent snorting.

"Will you zip it?" Rebecca could hear herself sniggering. She dragged Babs with her as they ran around to the back.

Pip opened the side door. "Rebecca?"

Why her own name sounded funny she didn't know. Tears squeezed out of her eyes as she clamped them shut.

"Rebecca?"

Babs had her hands over her mouth to block the sound of her own laughter.

"Must be the birds." Pippa shut the door and Rebecca blew out a breath and looked through the back window.

"Opening the package now . . . here she goes . . ."

Pippa's laughter rang out through the air.

Rebecca high-fived Babs. "Stage one is complete."

Chapter Twenty-eight

FOLLOWING THE INSTRUCTIONS on the note, I made my way down to the living room "in the uniform provided." On entering, I shook my head at the two innocents sitting on the sofa with a bowl of crisps between them.

"I'm guessing this will be a new tradition?"

Rebecca flashed a smile and turned to the TV.

"I'll get my own crisps then?"

Both were fixated on the screen.

There was a knock at the door and I wandered towards it. I had a nagging feeling who would be on the other side because the two criminal masterminds in the living room burst into giggles again. Still it didn't settle my nerves. Berne had texted me late in the night to tell me she needed to think. At least I'd made her think. It was something to cling onto.

"*Bonjour*," Berne said as she came in, shaking the rain from her coat. "Sorry I am late. The Coins had a leak in their roof."

I took a breath. Small talk. I could do small talk. "Please don't tell me you were up there in this weather?"

Berne shrugged and I took her coat from her. She was daft and kind. I adored her for it.

"Did you manage alright?" I watched her take off her shoes as I held her coat like a life raft.

"A few moments where I became more religious than usual but . . . not bad."

She turned around and I groaned at her top. "Let me guess, you got a mysterious package too?"

"And a note. I have no idea who could have sent it." She flicked her gaze at the hysterics from the other room.

I hung her coat up, trying not to stare. "Game on, I guess."

We wandered into the living room and I poured crisps into a bowl. Berne sat beside me as the anthems blared out. It was only a friendly. France versus England. Which meant friendly in an ironic sense. This one was in Twickenham. A rugby match that could go either way.

"Nice top, Pip." Rebecca was grinning inanely. "I take it, you both accept the terms?"

Berne was still here, in Ajoux. That had to mean something. I hoped it meant something.

"From the giggling gorillas?" I asked, smiling at Berne. "Why not."

Berne's eyes twinkled. "*Vive La France.*"

"Swing low, sweet chariot," I whispered back.

The match began in brutal fashion. As always with the two nations, the history pulsed onto the pitch and men clattered into each other with deafening crunches, blood splattering, and mud spraying everywhere. A torrential downpour added to the madness with the French slipping and sliding through tackles to score, only for the English to come back through metronome penalty kicking.

Eighty minutes, the game was hanging in the balance, the scores level. The ball was fed out from the scrum to the English fly-half. He took aim, drew his leg back.

Smack.

The French number nine drove him backwards to the ground. The ball rolled over the sideline. The whistle blew. All square.

"Well, that wasn't in the script." Rebecca threw a pillow at the TV for good measure.

Berne and I burst into laughter. They tried so hard, bless them. The entire match, I'd felt Berne's thigh next to mine. She was here, she had worn the shirt. Was she staying?

"You didn't leave with her?"

Berne smiled. "*Non.*"

My heart burst into a sprint. "Are you staying for . . . well . . . me?"

Her eyes twinkled. "Perhaps."

Why I giggled, I didn't know but an idea washed over me.

"I tell you what," I said to Rebecca. "How bout we *both* do the forfeit?"

Rebecca and Babs perked up at that.

Berne's eyebrows shot up as I turned to her. She looked something else in a French shirt. *Vive La France* indeed.

"You too scared to run in the rain, Chamonix?" I got to my

feet. My voice sounded like I knew exactly what I was doing and that I had clearly done this kind of thing before. "Think you can't cope?"

Berne was up and marching to the front door. "I have no problem with the rain." She opened it. "*Après toi.*"

I looked out at the crashing torrent and wobbled. "Couldn't we wait for it to pass a bit?"

"You afraid of a little water, Pepe?" Her eyebrow arched. Hunger pulsed through her eyes at me. My stomach wiggled and I was quite sure that I may have fanned myself.

I tore my eyes from hers to spot Rebecca and Babs in the doorway. They gripped hold of each other, not making a sound. They looked like they were still watching the rugby match.

Rebecca gave me a curt nod and I tapped the rose on my chest. "Never. No proud Englishwoman would be scared of such drizzle."

Drizzle? It looked like something you'd see in a hurricane.

"I only worry that *you* won't be able to keep up." I launched forward, planted my lips on Berne's, ripped off my rugby shirt, and sprinted into the freezing cold rain.

I howled with laughter, the sensation of the water washing away my cares. I felt free. I felt . . . flipping freezing.

My flip-flops flew off as I giggled. I held my face up to the sky as the rain poured down onto my skin. I felt whole.

Two warm, strong hands caught me as we got to the bridge. "You owe me a kiss, *non*?"

I turned. Berne's eyes were intense, filled with desire, and twinkling. I stared into them. Stared up at the face I'd spent my life dreaming of. I felt blessed beyond any words I could find. The heartbeat in my ears sounded like it was launching into a mad victory parade.

Still, I had to fight a bit. "Do I?"

The smile slid across her lips. Oh, how I had longed to feel them again.

"*Oui*, you kiss me. It is only fair."

She made a good argument. I let Berne pull me until only inches separated our parted lips. I felt that finally I was well and truly alive. I could give in now. I was ready to give in. I'd earned back her trust. I felt like I made an impact now. I had fixed up a house, been with Monsieur Chamonix until help arrived. I'd taken on my past, taken on Fish Lips, and you know what, I'd survived it.

I got scared, I made mistakes, and I messed up, and you know what, I was okay with that. I didn't have to be perfect anymore. I could be something better. Me.

"There is something else in that too," I whispered. "Paying back the kiss, I mean." I closed my eyes, enjoying the feel of her skin against mine.

"*Oui?*" Berne purred. Her hands ran up and over my back. "It is important?"

"Yeah, it is." I brushed away her hair, hoisted myself up, and wrapped my legs around her waist.

If I was doing this. I was doing it in style. I sank into the kiss, letting every single want, need, desire, and hope pulse through me into it. I could hear her groan against me, then whimper as I pulled back and jumped down.

"Now we're equal."

She strolled towards me and I smiled, holding her bra in my hand. She narrowed her eyes, that mischief shining through.

I giggled and turned to run, howling like a madwoman as I splashed through the puddles towards the house.

I grinned at Rebecca who looked prouder than I'd ever seen her. "I'd say advantage England!"

Babs poked her. "Pepe kissed her first, that is France win, *non?*"

Berne caught me, hauled me upwards, carried me inside and up the stairs that I'd fixed.

"What do you think, Pepe?" she asked, the rain dribbling over her strong, sexy shoulders.

"It's pretty decisive," I murmured against her lips. "Game, set, and match . . . to love."

About the Author

Jody Klaire is an author and a massive tennis fan. At the grand old age of thirty-two, she has been everything from a serving police officer, to recording artist/composer and musician until finding her home in writing. She lives in sunny South Wales in the UK with a lively golden retriever called Fergus and other furry friends. Oh, and she has a slight affection for cake . . .

Website: http://jodyklaire.wordpress.com
Facebook: http://www.facebook.com/jodyklaireauthor
Twitter: @jodyklaire